Once Upon a Gulf Coast Summer

Once Upon a Gulf Coast Summer

A NOVEL

SUSAN OLIVER

BROADMAN & HOLMAN PUBLISHERS

NASHVILLE, TENNESSEE

0-8054-2777-5

Published by Broadman & Holman Publishers,

Nashville, Tennessee

Dewey Decimal Classification: F

Subject Heading: MOTHERS AND DAUGHTERS—

FICTION \ FAITH—FICTION

Scripture quotations are from the Holy Bible, New International
Version, © 1973, 1978, 1984 by International Bible Society.

2 3 4 5 6 7 8 9 10 08 07 06 05 04

For Jackie, Nancy, and Betsy

Chapter 1 ❧

Katy

Before September, I'd never seen a real person die. I grew up on an urban homestead with concrete pastures and silos made of glass-fronted skyscrapers with spinning restaurants on top. In the city we don't generally tolerate death in broad daylight. We even take our fading pets to discreet staging areas where death can be administered in a civilized manner, properly out of sight. At sixty-one, then, I'd rarely ever even seen a mammal die.

Once, as I walked through my neighborhood early enough on a weekday morning to get home and showered before work, I spotted a bright-colored heap lying along the curb about three blocks from our house. As I neared, the outline of a husky man took shape. I knew it instantly as an "it" rather than a "he" because of the way it was positioned in the street—the face straight down, nose first, without any concern for bones or ligaments or breathing. The corpse's orange-and-royal-blue nylon running suit contained a wallet that identified its owner as seventy-three-year-old Nathan Grossman, who'd lived two streets over. After a few shaky misdials on my cell phone, I managed to summon all sorts of flashing vehicles to the scene of my gruesome discovery. Still, I hadn't actually seen Nathan Grossman die.

So when my mother's nurse told me that it was time to take her to the hospital to get her the help she needed to "pass," I had no idea what to expect. I didn't doubt the outcome; Mother had made it quite clear that she did not mean to dally here any longer. But I couldn't imagine how she would pull it off. Mother had never been a very courageous person. And when I saw how she sauntered right up to this hardest feat in all of life, I wondered, *Who does she suddenly think she is? Shouldn't dying require some minimal level of competence, some threshold of bravery or goodness or badness—something?*

What followed silenced me. It surely wasn't a common thing—what I saw happen to my mother.

If it were, human history might have a very different shape.

In a crisis, my mother typically withdrew to the periphery and let clearer heads and stronger hands respond. As she receded, she would ooze superiority, as if to say, "I need not be capable in such things, for they are below my station in life." Preferably, one of the strong-handed people would first take the time to escort her to the sidelines, safely out of danger, before joining the fray. She was like a queen sequestered in an impenetrable underground fortress or flown from one undisclosed location to another during times of national insecurity. And the rest of us generally played right along.

But on Mother's last afternoon, when I tiptoed into her room after talking with the nurse, she pulled herself up slightly and nodded at me very deliberately, the way a fifth-grade teacher might nod at the class clown hoping to discourage his antics before they began. I, of course, trotted up to her bed and sat down anyway.

"Mother, Nurse Simpson says you need to go to the hospital. Do you really think you're ready for that? I mean, we've already brought in all this stuff to help you do your business." I waved my hand toward the portable toilet, railing, and oxygen tank that were lined up against the far wall, ready for action. "There's absolutely no reason to go before you're ready," I managed to add, my firm tone breaking up and fading to a plea somewhere between "go" and "before."

Mother didn't so much as cut her eyes in the direction of the expensive medical equipment that I had ordered on the morning ten days earlier when Dr. Lawless had disclosed what Mother apparently already knew but hadn't yet bothered to share with me: the cancer was back—back and busily gnawing away at every conceivable healthy cell in her body. Things would move along quickly now, the doctor had said, perhaps as quickly as four or five months.

I had done what any other helpless daughter would do in similar circumstances. I'd arranged for Mother's last months to be as comfortable as possible. I would ensure that her dying was not too unpleasant. She'd have everything she could possibly need to peter out slowly while I somehow warmed to the prospect of a world without her.

But Mother had rebelled from the start. What a time for her to tap in to her belligerent streak. She always did know her own mind, even when she chose to disregard it. This time she knew she had no interest whatsoever in moving from bed to toilet and back for the next five months. Or four months. Or three. Or even two weeks. What queen would?

As I sat there on the edge of her bed waiting for some reply, Mother only gazed at me. It seemed that she was struggling to hold on to something. I reached out and put my hand over one of her gnarled, arthritic claws, her fingers jutting out diagonally from swollen knots of knuckles the way palm fronds flatten landward during Gulf Coast hurricanes. Her transparent, poreless skin felt so delicate against my own straight, pink fingers. I wondered how much longer it could cover those knuckles without tearing and letting the unruly bones fall right out.

"We don't have to go before you're ready," I repeated, willing her not to be.

But she nodded again—the nod I'd never seen before today.

Then she waited. She even closed her eyes for a minute, as if to give me some privacy. Or perhaps it was all part of her holding on. When she opened them again, her yellow-red lower lids that had begun to hang lazily off her eyes the last few days were stretched full of tears. I felt responsible. Was I really going to require this of her before I would stand down and allow her to attend to her real business?

I kissed the face. I tasted the salt that slipped generously down her saggy cheek. And as I laid her head gently back on the pillow, she loosened. Her eyes let me go and refocused somewhere beyond me. She had quit holding on.

I told Nurse Simpson to call the EMS, and my husband Eliot and I followed the ambulance to Houston's Magdalene Memorial Hospital. Along the way I called my brother Clay and my daughter Samantha. They agreed to pass the word along and get everyone to the hospital as soon as possible. As we pulled into the "Emergency" driveway, raindrops were beginning to clutter our windshield.

It was a terrible storm—so terrible that my grandson Patrick couldn't get a flight in from Austin where he was a freshman at the University of Texas. He wanted to try driving down instead, but by the time he realized that all the flights would be canceled, it was eleven o'clock and we didn't think Mother would last another three or four hours while he sped exhausted and grieving through the dark rain. He might as well come the next morning.

The rest of us huddled all night long round Mother's bed: Eliot and me; Clay and his wife Lillian; my daughter Samantha; my son Seth, his wife Gretchen, and their two teenagers; and Clay's sons Jonathan and Max, who had flown in together from Dallas before the airports had closed. We had never met for such an occasion as this, and no one seemed to know quite how to act.

I should have realized sooner that it would not be up to me to smooth it all out. When the driver of Mother's ambulance had pulled her gurney from the back and was asked by a young ER attendant why she was there, Mother had assessed her own condition for them in the simplest of terms. "I'm here to meet the Lord," she'd said. Not knowing just what to do with that answer, the young man just nodded and wheeled her inside.

The emergency room doctors looked her over and confirmed her self-diagnosis. With very little fanfare, they admitted her and assigned us a small private room at the far end of the cancer floor. The room was homey and lamp-lit, devoid of medical stuff, as if not much healing was expected to happen there. Even the bed seemed misplaced in a room where a doctor might walk in any minute to peek at a chart or administer a drug. For one thing, it was wide enough for a person to sit comfortably on each side of the patient. Dark green sheets and a paisley bedspread further set it apart from the narrow, white-sheeted beds we had glimpsed through the open doorways on the way down the hall. This bed had no wheels on it. Only its tiltable top half hinted that it lived in a hospital. We were in the Dying Room.

But I don't think Mother even noticed. This had all been staged for the rest of us, and I for one was grateful. An orderly lifted my shrunken mother off her transport gurney and laid her on the deathbed as effortlessly as he might have lifted a child. Then he left and took everything else that was stark white with him.

5

Rain hammered the one small window in the room. Pulling back the drape, I looked out at the vague, yellow streetlights that dripped like liquid down the outside of the pane. Swearing under my breath, I thought, *She won't even get a last clear look at the city where she spent her whole eighty-five years!*

"Oh, Mom, I don't think Gammy will care. She isn't worried about out there," Samantha said softly from a few feet behind me. Apparently I had spoken out loud.

I turned on her. "How do you know what she's worried about?"

"I don't. But whatever it is, it isn't out there."

"Oh? So, how do you know so much about what runs through people's minds before they die?"

"Please, Mom, I wasn't contradicting you. I was just trying to help. Don't take this out on me. I'm scared, too, you know."

It was just then that Mother first lurched off the sheets and contorted her wasted little body in a way that I thought would have killed her instantly. For hours after that she twisted and strained toward something that only she could see, flopping back now and then to rest before heaving forward again like a woman caught up by contractions. These life-ending contractions seemed to utterly enthrall Mother. She labored to admit them, refusing to be distracted even by her children and grandchildren who attended her throughout the night. If she was fighting a battle, it was not against death. I'm sure she was trying to leave us. But that's not even quite it. I think it truer to say she was moving on.

Or maybe she was simply being ravished.

Every year, millions of cicada nymphs burrow up from subterranean Houston where they've incubated for thirteen years around the roots of the pine trees. Almost en masse they shed their old, dried-up skins in the dead of night and leave them cleaving to

6

doorframes and perched on sidewalks all over the city. No one ever sees what torture they must endure to win their new lives as fat, winged grasshoppers, but we hear their cries all through the spring. If we judged only by what they left behind, we would think them sad creatures indeed.

At about three in the morning another line of severe thunderstorms moved into our part of Houston—no doubt a bright red patch on the Doppler radar. Gretchen had long since taken the kids home to bed, and the men had all claimed couches and chairs in the lobby down the hall where they sprawled snoring and sputtering uncomfortably. Lillian, Sam, and I stood guard at Mother's bed, finally getting used to her pitching back and forth. A tremendous clap of thunder that reverberated through the building and shook the windowpanes woke my brother Clay, and he stumbled back down to the room. Seeing Mother still laboring, Clay wrapped himself around her as if to siphon off all her fight and absorb it into his own body.

In a last flash of coherence, Mother whispered into his rumpled gray hair, "I've never died before."

He rested her on the pillow and whispered back, "It's OK, Mother. You can do it."

After a moment she had returned her gaze to the invisible place and tried to pull herself up again, but she was wearing out. That's when I went for help.

The nurse I dragged back with me managed to listen to Mother's breathing while I cooed in her ear to keep her quiet. Then the nurse straightened up and looked intently at each of us.

"Would you like me to make her more comfortable?" she asked.

"Just like that?" I said, wondering where she had been all night.

"Yes, of course."

7

"It will make her sleep," she warned vaguely as she pulled a vial and syringe from her pocket. Clay held Mother, and the nurse gave her the injection.

About twenty minutes later, Mother settled down and closed her eyes. She tugged a few times on her blue cotton nightgown as if she didn't need it anymore, and then forgot that struggle too. From my perch on the side of her bed, I watched her inhale, exhale, inhale, exhale. Her breathing grew softer and more jagged. At 6:15, Mother failed to take another breath.

I laid her ravaged hands, one atop the other, on her still chest. They were loose, like knots about to come untied. Mother had won—finally she was free of them.

Outside, the remnants of the storm still pattered against the windowsill, in no hurry to desist, and the streetlights were snapping off in the dawn.

She'd done it. Whatever death was, my mother had done it.

Later, when I finally got around to cleaning out the bedroom where Mother had slept for the last few weeks of her life, I found a large, leather book in the top dresser drawer. On the first page, in a hand so shaky that I couldn't have deciphered it without my sixty-year acquaintance, she had scrawled, "My Unraveling." On the subsequent pages were journal entries written in steadier days dating from the previous October. I believe they reveal why Mother rent herself away from us on the night she died.

This is her story. And so, by necessity, it must be my story too.

CHAPTER 2

Jo

<u>October 13, 2000</u>

I snatch these few minutes while Lenny is strapped to his beating pad to record a dream that has haunted me all morning. Usually, of course, dreams slip through my conscious mind like water through a spillway, but this one woke me with its loud pounding reverberating throughout my childhood home, and still it seems to play in the background. I had lost my father in the dream and went to search the house for him, but I found every doorway blocked by a shabby brown piano that was stained and dented except on the keys. As I tried to enter each room by crawling under or climbing over the pianos, they expanded into every inch of space like something in Alice's Wonderland. One by one, the bloated pianos began to play Beethoven's sugarcoated Minuet in G. Soon I could not make my screams for Daddy heard over the din. Nor could I escape the house, hemmed in as I was by the music.

Just when I thought I couldn't bear it any longer, the pianos quit their playing, ending abruptly on the same note, midbar, and disappeared. In the void, I heard a soft, mechanical ticking, with a slight accent on every other stroke. A single instrument—the shiny, black Steinway I grew up with—materialized in the corner and stood silent, waiting for me to mount it and play along with the beat. I had to find that pulse and make it stop.

As I ran from room to room, our old house on Front Street mutated liquidly, the way places do in dreams. One minute the kitchen was attached to the dining room, and the next it was boxed in by nothing but bathrooms or exterior doors. I tried not to be distracted by this. Daddy forgotten, I focused on the sound.

Finally I blundered into my mother's room, where she sat straight-backed on the side of her bed hemming a white piece of linen that I took to be a napkin. She looked up when I appeared in the doorway, and her vague, gray sewing eyes momentarily narrowed into nasty red slits. But she didn't speak. Her tongue extended into a long metal needle that jutted straight up from her lower lip and moved rhythmically back and forth across her face. With each jerk of the needle, I heard the tick.

Then I woke up.

October 14, 2000

Back again, still needing to write. After nineteen years of abstinence, I find that I'm suddenly willing to risk exciting my husband with such private scribblings as these. He'll surely come snooping the moment I'm in the shower or go off to the grocery, and that danger used to control me. But it's not enough now.

I believe Lenny knows something is terribly wrong. This morning he brought hot tea to my bedside three times before I was ready to wake up. "Josephine, hon," he wheedled into my deep fog each time. "Don't you want to get up now? I've brought you some chamomile, just as you like."

"I've never liked chamomile, you old goat!" sniped my sleeping self to a white-haired servant who was bent over my bed trying to reach his teapot under my covers.

To the real man I mumbled with my eyes clamped shut, "I'm asleep, Lenny. Go away!"

Yet back he came until finally I slapped off the sheets, pulled myself up, and plucked the pretty pink cup off the tray he held out to me. I'd already begun to sip when I noticed the steam rolling up from under my nose, and my tongue began to sizzle. Apparently, he'd been toting the cup back and forth between my bed and the microwave the whole time. Yes, he's definitely worse than usual.

I'd like to keep Lenny calm until I decide what to do with him, but his radar is so perfectly calibrated to my moods and movements that even his dementia gives me little breathing room. And so I write because I have to now, and I have nothing to lose.

October 15, 2000

This morning Katy and I met with an oncologist at M.D. Anderson. Katy thought we were there to interview a potential surgeon, but I really just wanted a second opinion. I wasn't convinced that it's necessary for me to give up part of my lungs, but the specialists assured me that it is. They say my tumor is stage-two cancer, possibly stage three. My best hope is to let them hack it out, they said.

"Well," I replied, once they signaled that I'd used up my time for this news to sink in, "I'll think it over and let you know."

Katy scoffed audibly from the guest chair of the examination room. Even before she could scold me, the surgeon warned, "Mrs. Van Zandt, we recommend that you have the surgery as soon as possible. This week would be preferable. Your tumor is quite large already."

11

But I wasn't ready to commit.

Katy barely spoke to me as she barreled her Explorer through the wet backstreets that threaded between Houston's Medical Center and my house on Lear Drive. She has always known how to make a silent statement. And when she came inside to help me move the porch plants to the greenhouse for the winter, she only grunted at Lenny's clamoring to know what we'd bought at the dress shop.

"Katy got a few things, but they're out in her trunk," I tried to dismiss him.

"Oh, Mother!" she said.

"Just hush," I replied. "Everybody hush. I need some peace and quiet!" And I walked out and busied myself getting a glass of water in the kitchen. But when Katy made no move to leave, I finally came back in and said, "Lenny, why don't you go get the mail."

He furrowed his thick, wild-haired eyebrows, titled his head forward, and peered through the long-range portion of his giant, horn-rimmed trifocals from me, to Katy, and back to me. Then he crossed his arms and announced, "The mail's not here yet."

"Why it most certainly is!" I said. "We saw the mailman walking down our street as we drove up. Now go get the mail."

The hot prospect of all those envelopes sitting in our box awaiting his touch soon overshadowed Lenny's suspicions, and he hobbled off to get the mail.

"You need to have the surgery this week," Katy hissed as soon as Lenny had cleared the doorway.

"Well, dear, I couldn't possibly be ready that fast, even if I had decided to do it."

"Mother, this isn't like deciding when you want to go to a movie. If you don't do it soon, you may not be able to at all. We had the chance to schedule something today, but you let it go. Who knows when you'll be able to get their attention again? You know, people from all over the world hope to get their cancer treated at Anderson."

"Yes, well, I'll consider all that."

Katy just glared at me.

"You know, Katy, I didn't particularly like the atmosphere there. Everyone seemed so somber. Maybe I'll try somewhere else."

"If you wait, you may be choosing to die," she assured me.

Had Lenny come in one second sooner, he might have heard the word die, and my day would have been even worse than it's already been. As it was, Katy snatched up her purse at the sight of him and stomped out of the house. Somehow I convinced Lenny that Katy was just angry about an insensitive comment I'd made to her at the store.

He's in there now, caressing every piece of junk mail that has his own precious name on it. And I sit here wondering, Do I want to die?

October 16, 2000

I remember how hard it was to see Daddy grow old, even though it seemed to be happening from the moment I knew him. The first time I heard it said out loud, I was about twelve and he was fifty-seven. Daddy was in his garden on a Saturday afternoon in February, kneeling in the dirt in his grubbiest suit. He was putting in spring flowers he had grown from seed in his greenhouse. After thirty-five work years crouched over a sewing machine, Daddy had stiffened in a permanent hunch, but he looked quite natural crawling around a flowerbed.

I'd been inside practicing the piano—the foreboding baby grand that, in my childhood memory, dominated our whole living room. The moment my three hours were up, I snapped off the metronome and rushed out onto the front porch to see what Daddy was doing.

He heard the porch door slam and started to turn toward me. It literally happened in slow motion. His head came up, and he began to straighten and turn at the same time. But somewhere between the flowers and me, he got stuck. His smile twisted into a grimace as he grabbed his back and fell over sideways across a row of freshly planted snapdragons.

I got to him almost before his face touched the dirt. "Daddy, Daddy, what's wrong?" I begged. But he couldn't manage a coherent response.

I believe it was my screams rather than his that eventually brought other adults who got Daddy inside and called the doctor. After giving Daddy a shot to ease the pain, old Doc Kramer patted Mother's hand on his way out and said, "Not to worry, Irene. Joseph probably has a slipped disk, but nothing life threatening. These things just happen as we get older. He'll need to lie flat for several days, and then we'll see how his back is."

But Mother clutched Doc's sleeve and pulled him around to face her. "Will he be able to work again?"

"Why, I can't say yet, Irene. You know better than anyone how physical his work is. You might have to take up the slack for awhile," he answered, edging toward the front door.

"I already do his finishing work for several hours a day!"

She ended on such a shrill high note that Doc Kramer cringed, but didn't pull away.

"Uh-huh. Well, let's just wait and see what happens before we worry too much. He might be back to normal in a very few days."

Mother met this assurance with stone silence, and Doc Kramer finally wandered on out the front door and left us alone. I darted from where I'd been hiding behind Daddy's easy chair and ran to his bed, trying to nestle myself into his side as he slept.

"What are you doing?" Mother cried. "Are you trying to finish him off? Get away from him and go clean the kitchen. We all have to work harder now."

After that, Daddy was always old to me. But somehow this just made me love him more.

October 17, 2000

I've been hiding all day long in my upstairs sewing room where Lenny can't get to me because of his bad knees. He regularly tells people that his injuries date back to his high school football days, but in truth he's just such an awkward cluck that he's ruined his knees tripping over sidewalk cracks. I sometimes doubt that Lenny ever played football at all. I wonder if there's any chance he might have tripped over himself and fallen on his peanut butter knife downstairs? Or perhaps he's wandered out the front door and forgotten where he lives.

While in hiding, I cleaned out the storage closet, stopping to reminisce often enough to keep from totally wearing myself out. At the very back I found a dress box I probably haven't opened in forty years. Inside were my baby clothes. Not my children's baby clothes, which would have been bad enough, but mine—all of them embroidered batiste. Holding my breath, I traced my fingers over Mother's exacting needlework and the crisp, paper-edged folds of cloth. Eighty-something years and still not a wrinkle.

Imagine the energy and attention that went into such garments. And for a baby! A baby that I know would rather have been hugged even a fraction of the time that it took to hand-embroider a dress she would just spit up on. Or maybe I wasn't allowed to spit up on them. Maybe I wasn't dressed in them at all.

I shoved a towel under the upstairs bathroom door and burned the little gowns in the bathtub.

October 18, 2000

Ginger has really been dragging me down lately, moping around the house sad-eyed—pouting and disdainful, demanding that I snap out of my gloom and go back to entertaining her. Until now, my dogs have always been a comfort to me, but I suddenly feel all this guilt associated with her. I'm just not up to meeting expectations, even those of a dog. How pathetic is that? Maybe I'll have her put down. After all, how good can her quality of life be at fifteen years old, and blind, with the sword of Damocles poised over one owner and the other unable at times even to potty himself? We should never have gotten her.

Of course, I know why I did. Her namesake was the dog of my heart. The real Ginger first pattered up our porch steps in the summer of 1925—a "present" from a neighbor with a whole litter to dispose of. To my delight, she immediately baptized my white stockings with her slobber, and then swaggered sideways across the porch trying to keep from falling over. By the time she scrunched down to pee in Daddy's deck shoes, she'd won my full devotion.

Thereafter, I entrusted Ginger alone with all my secrets and was amazed to find that she felt the same way about me. She wanted to be wherever I was; to her, at least, no one else would do. And when the house was still in the sultry summer afternoons—in the after-practice hours before it was time to go meet Daddy midway between home and his shop, and the only sound was the repetitious tug of thread through the lining of a buttonhole—Ginger kept me company in the worst possible way. She made me hope. Because of her playful, doting presence there, in that house, in those moments, I dared to hope that something, someday, might satisfy my longing.

October 19, 2000

I feel blue this morning. A pleasant memory might serve me well right now—might get me through the day. The only thing that comes to mind is something that happened the first time I visited a hospital. I was about eight, and I'd had an emergency appendectomy a couple of days before. In 1924, they kept you in the hospital until you actually healed a little, so my stay lasted several days. On this particular afternoon, my favorite nurse—a young, orange-haired pixie with a contagious laugh—popped in and asked me what I wanted for lunch.

At first I just fidgeted and looked away, waiting for her to notice that none of my decision-makers were in the room and to take back her offer. But, without a glance in another direction, she winked at me and crooned, "Come on, Jo-Jo, what will it be? Surely you're hungry. Don't turn shy on me."

Now understand—she didn't just give me a choice between two or three things, which would have shocked me quite enough. She was letting me choose from the whole universe of foods that I could conceive of as "lunch." Blushing, I asked her if I didn't need to wait for an adult visitor to answer her question.

"No, missy," said she. "You can tell me right now."

I thought about exploring the boundaries of this freedom a bit further, but something told me to seize the moment. She wanted to know what I wanted—me.

Even from a distance of seventy-five years I remember just what I ordered—every detail: a ham sandwich on white bread with mayonnaise and lettuce. I believe I threw in the lettuce just to test them. Did I really have such power—so much more here, in the hospital of all places, than I'd ever had anywhere before?

She returned with a sandwich perfectly fitting the description I'd given her. I ate it slowly, savoring it despite the risk that I'd get caught and be made to pay for my presumption. But no one came to stop me, and as far as I know, I was never found out. Nothing has ever tasted so good.

October 20, 2000

Writing about Ginger has made me long to see her picture, though I'm not sure that we ever took any of her. All I could find from those years was a handful of family portraits stuffed into a tattered old copy of Oliver Twist. Three or four were of me, ranging from about six to eleven years old, standing around in the big yard outside our Front Street house. They all show a plump little girl with a fresh-cut pageboy, always in a white dress, white shoes, and white knee-high stockings—always alone. She ever looked studiously away from the camera, with her hands clasped firmly behind her back, and endured the picture taking without opening her mouth, even to smile.

But one picture was different. In it, I was about fifteen, a little thinner, and wore stockings that extended well above my chubby knees. I let my arms dangle at my sides; my hands were fisted. The girl in this picture looked directly at the camera and dared to smile ever so slightly. She had a secret.

Most every day at school she ate her lunch very quickly and then allowed herself to be enticed under the gymnasium bleachers by one of the upper-class boys. She necked with him there for ten or fifteen minutes until the bell rang for class, and emerged feeling only slightly less powerful than when she'd gone under.

Home is where this really made the difference. At home—as she pounded out concertos for hours a day, while she scoured pots and tubs and floors, and every single time she chose a plain, white, homemade dress from her wardrobe full of them— she reveled in the secret life she led under the bleachers. And this gave her the courage to smile.

October 21, 2000

I called this morning and scheduled my surgery for the twenty-fifth. Katy gushed her relief when I told her. They want me at the hospital by 6:00 A.M. to be prepped for a nine o'clock ordeal. That gives me four days to dispense with Lenny and get myself ready for a "complication," should one occur. I just hope the girl in those pictures proves worth it.

19

Chapter 3

Katy

At 4:30 A.M. on October 25, I swallowed a dry bagel and coffee the way a stalwart old Buick submits to the gas pump—with no higher purpose than getting down the road. Already, on this disagreeable day, I felt guilty.

I had slept soundly right up to the alarm and drowsed on through a rare, idyllic weather forecast that KVVF trumpeted as if the radio station itself had invented clear, dry, and sixty-five degrees. I nestled deeper into my pillow and floated off into a clear, sixty-five-degree field of California poppies. The dense, orange-red blooms—all supple and spotless—took no more notice of me strolling among them than the ocean takes of lovers wading through its surf. At first I was enchanted.

But a confused breeze soon sent the tide of poppies swaying out-of-sync. As the flowers nearest me leaned eastward, those fifteen or twenty feet out tilted to the west, then south, then back to the west. I'd already begun feeling sickly when the winds picked up. Then the whole crop flopped this way and that until the delicate poppy cups began to fly off their stems and swirl above the field in a blazing, fire-colored funnel reaching up to a now sooty sky. The funnel danced just above the tops of the headless stems and finally touched down, charring the ground where it struck. I heard a loud swish. Something silver and sharp fell out of the grayness, shot through the funnel, and drove into the burned place. The poppies sailed off like ashes. In their wake, a huge, gleaming scalpel jutted out of the sore.

I knew the day at last. Today they would cut Mother's cancer out.

Ye gods, I thought, punishing myself with another unsweetened sip of coffee. *You don't care enough to suffer a moment's insomnia the night before your mother may die. No wonder she didn't want to have this surgery. She probably only agreed in the end because she thinks she won't live through it. And it would serve you right.*

A car pulling into the driveway interrupted my silent recriminations. A minute later I heard a soft knock on the back door, and I let Sam in. She had the decency to appear puffy-eyed and pale, as a good granddaughter should on such an occasion. Neither of us spoke until she'd poured herself some coffee and stood to face me.

"What about Dad?" she asked.

"It's been a bad couple of weeks. He won't be going."

She nodded. "And Seth?"

"He'll meet us at the hospital later. But we're picking up Lillian and Clay. We'd better hurry. We have to be at Gammy's by five."

♊

When we pulled up to my brother's house in the darkness fifteen minutes later, he slipped out the front door before Sam could make a move to go get them. Lillian emerged several minutes later wearing a tight, low-cut sweater and a peasant skirt. She carried a thick paperback in one hand and a soft-sided cooler in the other.

I kissed Clay, who slid in beside me, and grunted slightly as Lillian crawled into the back with Sam. Somehow I drove the ten or so miles to Mother's without asking Lillian if she'd packed any caviar to go with her wine and cheese. About halfway there, Clay turned on the radio, and we listened to another station promise a glorious day.

♊

The four of us huddled outside Mother's back door at 5:15, shivering in the fall pre-dawn. No one reached out a hand to knock until

Lillian finally pushed through the rest of us and made a jab at the door. Mother opened it at once and stood gazing out. Backlit and facing the dark, she was the ageless woman I'd seen similarly framed in that doorway thousands of times over the past forty years. But when she stepped back into the light to let us file past, I saw her a diseased old lady bound firmly to the present day.

Inside, she had straightened everything—not a magazine, not a napkin nor a pencil was out of place. On the kitchen table, two economy-sized, ziplocked baggies bulged with pill bottles, foil-backed sheets of individually partitioned tablets, paper prescriptions, and detailed instruction sheets. A thick strip of masking tape across the outside of one bag read "Lenny Van Zandt," and an identical strip across the other was labeled "Josephine Greene Van Zandt."

The once snazzy, baby blue overnight case that Mother used to carry on trips overseas with my father waited along the breakfast room wall. The sight of it, willing to be dispatched on this grim new mission, paralyzed me. It seemed that any move toward the bag, any complicity in actually picking it up and taking it away, would be the most savage act of violence. I wished to be anywhere but here.

Then I saw the other suitcase—an oversized husband to the first. This one loomed in the den shadows, and behind it Lenny was folded up in my father's rocking chair, his head drooping such that I could only make out his bald scalp in the darkness. For once he took no interest in us, did not flail like a drunk grasshopper to his long-legged feet and hover about trying to contain us in a corner or around a table.

Clay went over and patted Lenny's back a time or two. "Len, how ya doin'?"

After several seconds, Lenny hauled himself upright. "It's the worst day of my life," he announced, his head bobbing like a marionette's, ever threatening to flop back down.

He might as well have ripped open his own torso and offered us all a peek. Clay pulled his hand back and fumbled with his collar.

"Where's Ginger?" I asked Mother.

"She's at the vet. I paid them for ten days. If for any reason it's longer, will you go get her, Katy?" Her voice quivered slightly despite her definitive tone. She slipped a crisp sheet of notepaper from her jacket pocket into my own. "Here's all the information."

Catching her eye, I inclined my head toward the den. And where was Lenny going with his big suitcase and his drugs?

"Lenny's sister, Charlotte, will be here in a few hours to pick him up," Mother said, loudly enough for him to hear. "He's going to spend a couple of weeks in San Antonio with her and his other sisters. He'll have a nice time."

"I won't have a nice time," Lenny whined from the dark. "I don't want to go there. And I don't want you to go to the hospital. Can't you do it later, Josephine? Can't I have just a little longer?"

Mother sighed with her whole body, all five feet of her. I thought she might not give him any other answer, but she finally said, "Lenny, I explained this to you last night. It has to be now. You want me to get better, don't you?"

Unfolding to his full six feet two inches, Lenny hobbled into the breakfast room and grabbed at Mother's hands. "Josephine, tell me again. Tell me again what's wrong with you."

"No!" She jerked free. "We're not starting this over again. I've told you ten times already. Now, you stay right here and wait for Charlotte. Don't go anywhere. Don't cook anything. Don't try to shower; you're clean enough. Just sit here and wait for Charlotte. She'll be by in an hour or two. Do you understand?" As she spoke, Mother waved us toward the door. "It'll be OK, Lenny. Trust me. It'll be OK."

Without hesitation now, I snatched the blue suitcase and the baggie with my mother's name on it and charged out behind Lillian and Samantha. My last glimpse of Lenny was so characteristic—him clutching at Mother while she tried to edge him away from the door. Clay finally had to intercede, backing Lenny into the den and forcing him down by both shoulders into the rocker.

With the rest of us safely out on the driveway, Mother locked Lenny inside, then hid the key in the barbecue grill. We loaded her into the car and sped away Butch Cassidy-like, entering the freeway just as the stars faded into the glow seeping from behind Houston's downtown.

Within an hour or two, Mother had been assigned one of the pre-operating rooms reserved for cancer patients, and we were allowed in to wait with her. By that time, Seth and Gretchen had arrived, and a female minister from Mother and Lenny's church had also stopped by on her infirmary rounds. When we walked in, Mother was propped upright on the bed with the covers tucked in around her. Her thin, auburn hair—recently dyed and set—stood out vividly against the white sheets and loose-fitting pastel hospital gown that swallowed her.

She struck a Joan of Arc pose—folding her hands complacently in her lap while the rest of us circled her, taking turns touching a sleeve or an arm or a cheek one last time before the lighting of the fire. There again was the familiar overnight case, hoping to see action in the days ahead. My stomach churned.

"Why don't we pray for Josephine's operation," the minister suggested then.

This was an idea none of the rest of us would have thought of. Even Mother squirmed. Finally, I asked, "You mean out loud?"

"Well, maybe I could do it out loud and you all could pray with me silently. Would it be OK if we held hands though?" she asked, holding hers out to me.

When you're cornered, you're cornered. I took the hand she'd offered and extended my other to Seth with a look that said, "If you don't help me out here, see if I ever babysit again." Sam even brought Mother into our strange little circle.

"Our Father," Reverend Sykes said, and my head bowed, "who art in heaven, hallowed be thy name. Thy kingdom come, thy will be done, on earth as it is in heaven. Give us this day our daily bread. And forgive us our trespasses, as we forgive those who trespass against us. Do not lead us into temptation, but deliver us from evil. For thine is the kingdom and the power and the glory forever. Amen." By the end, we were all repeating the only prayer we knew.

But it rattled me. What if God's will, with which we had just so clearly aligned ourselves, was not for Mother to live beyond today? Why hadn't Reverend Sykes just asked him to fix Mother, plain and simple?

While I was preoccupied with these thoughts, the surgeon breezed in to see if Mother had any last-minute questions. It was 8:30, and Dr. Petzel had probably extracted two or three malignancies already that morning. I wondered if it would be inappropriate to ask how his previous patients were doing.

"Will I be medicated before I get to the operating room?" Mother asked him, "or will it all happen there?"

"You'll get a little something in a few minutes, but the anesthesia is strictly for the operating room. Anything else?"

Mother shook her head. I, however, had quite a few questions. "Could I speak with you outside, Dr. Petzel?" I began, motioning toward the hall.

"I'd rather not," he surprised me. "I believe that Mrs. Van Zandt has a right to hear anything I might tell you. What would you like to know, Mrs., ah, ah . . ."

"Ardelean."

"Mrs. Ardelean."

"I guess I want to know . . ." How could I put this delicately? "Are there any decent alternatives to surgery? I mean, considering whatever the risks are."

"Katy, it's too late for that," Mother interrupted. "It's what we've decided."

"I know. I know. But I'm afraid I pushed you into this surgery. And if some less drastic treatment has a chance of helping, maybe it would be a better way to go."

"I told you, it's too late," she repeated.

"Actually, it's not too late," Dr. Petzel said. "It's never too late to make that decision until we begin the operation. Unfortunately, your cancer is a type and size that needs to be surgically removed as soon as possible. We have to consider your age, of course, Mrs. Van Zandt. You're at a much greater risk in the operating room than a younger patient would be, but the same would be true for chemotherapy or other treatments we might try. And the chances of eliminating the cancer with those alone are minimal. We might want to talk about some moderate chemotherapy as a follow-up to surgery, but let's cross that bridge when we get to it."

"There, Katy, you see. This is the right thing to do," Mother said, apparently undaunted by his tactful warnings.

"I just don't want to force you, Mother. You changed your mind about this so abruptly that I was afraid you were only appeasing me. You don't have to do anything if you don't want to, you know."

"Oh, I want to. Now, Doctor, where's that 'little something'?"

By four o'clock we knew the surgery had been a success. As soon as we got the news, Lillian shut her novel and announced that she was starving. Since the doctor assured us that Mother would not wake up for several hours, we all agreed to meet at an Italian restaurant a couple of miles from the hospital for an early dinner. Walking through the breezy afternoon sunshine to my car, I thought I might treat the whole family.

Once we'd been loaded up with quart-sized teas and were busy on our breadsticks, I decided it would be OK to waste a little energy on the subject of Lenny. "Do you suppose we ought to call Charlotte and let Lenny know that Mother is OK?" I asked the table at large.

When Seth asked what Charlotte had to do with it, I quickly brought him and Gretchen up to speed on our early morning escape.

"Well," he said, "it sounds like he might not catch on even if we call and tell him."

"Yes, he really was pitiful this morning. I've never seen him quite like that," I said.

"And how about Gammy?" Samantha asked. "Have you ever known her to stand up to him that way? Usually she'll do anything to pacify him, but this morning she was a fortress."

"There was no talking her out of that surgery either," Gretchen noted. "Funny that she was so wishy-washy about it a few days ago, and today it was set in stone. She seemed fearless."

"Maybe she figured she'd at least be free of Lenny if she died on the operating table," Lillian offered.

Sam spared us the silence that often threatened to hang about following Lillian's comments. "Yes, well, if we call Lenny, what do we say if he wants to know when he can come home?"

"Yeah, that raises a good point," Clay said. "I don't see how those two can live there alone any longer. Lenny's too big for Mother to handle when he's being belligerent. And who knows how long she'll need to recover from this surgery. Maybe we should think about hiring somebody."

"You mean to live with them full-time?" I asked.

"Either that or try to talk them into an assisted living home of some sort," he said. Clay opted not to voice the obvious third option, possible only in theory—Mother and Lenny coming to live with one of us.

"Hey, why don't we just wait and see how your mother comes along," Lillian interjected. "We might not have any decision to make after all."

Now there was a cheery thought.

I have visited my mother in numerous recovery rooms. I've seen her in casts after knee replacements, coaxed her to the bathroom after bladder realignments, and given her pep talks as doctors unwrapped her swollen, butchered face after two plastic surgeries. But I was ill prepared for what confronted me hours after they removed half of Mother's eighty-four-year-old lungs.

The male nurse who showed us into Intensive Care said we could go in two by two and sit with Mother after scrubbing our hands with special soap and a hard-bristle brush. Clay and I stepped forward while the rest of the family paired off. We followed the nurse through the heavy, windowless metal door that looked like it should open to a prison cell rather than a hospital room. On the way in, the nurse instructed us to try waking Mother up.

After we washed, we passed a dozen beds loaded with such

Frankensteinish lumps of humanity that I kept my eyes flitting so as not to take it in too deeply. But I could not so easily flit from the sight of our Mother. The nurse escorted us to the last bed on the row and introduced us to its occupant with a wave of his hand. "This one is yours," his gesture assured us, but I wasn't convinced he had gotten it right. Little here was familiar to me.

The woman's eyes were closed, and it seemed impossible that they would ever open again of their own volition. Her whole body was misshapen, like the mold had been set too near the burner and had melted in several spots just before she was poured. I recoiled, but Clay took my hand and coaxed me closer. As if to prove this really was our mother, he reached over the railing with his other hand and caressed the veiny, arthritic fingers that she so despised. Her eyes peeped open. Clay tightened his grip on my hand.

After a second or two, however, Mother closed her eyes very deliberately. It seemed she had other business to attend to; I suspected it was breathing. *What have we done to her?* I screamed to myself. *How will she get by on what she's got left?* As my panic rose, I gulped air into my own constricting lungs and became light-headed. I longed to run away.

But Clay held me tight as he got down in Mother's face. "Mother," he called softly. "Mother, wake up." His white goatee grazed her doughy, yellow-purple cheek as he spoke. "You need to wake up now, darling."

She frowned slightly and clamped her eyes shut a little tighter but did not otherwise respond. Clay took it up a notch. "Mother," more firmly, "wake up. You can do it. Please wake up." Nothing.

Mesmerized by this standoff, my breathing evened out and I was able to join Clay's team. "Mother, Fran has been calling from Milwaukee to see how you're doing. She seems a bit frantic. What should I tell her?"

Although Fran was Mother's oldest and closest friend, she scowled at the question. "How . . . should I . . . know?" she whispered in a halting, ethereal voice that defied her harsh words. "Ask . . . the doctor."

Well, at least she was awake. And because she'd hurt my feelings with that answer, I pushed harder. "All right. And what about Lenny? Do you want me to call and tell him you're OK, that he'll be back in no time, and this really wasn't the worst day of his life after all?"

At that, Mother opened her eyes wide and glared at me so severely that I worried over the consequences to her insides. She took several short little breaths, storing up enough air to fill the sails of her venomous reply. Squeezing both hands into fists, she hissed, "Lenny . . . is never . . . coming . . . home."

CHAPTER 4

Jo

November 8, 2000

Charlotte called this morning, and before I could tell her I wasn't up to it, she put Lenny on the phone.

"Josephine? Josephine? Is that you, Josephine?" I pulled the receiver away from my ear and listened to him squeak my name another time or two. There he was, trapped in the telephone like Genie in her bottle. From there he couldn't grab at me, bring me things I didn't want, or hover over me, ever trying to bar my escape. It seemed that I could simply cork him and drop him back into the sea from whence he'd come.

On the other hand, from this safe distance I could afford to be magnanimous. I put the receiver back up to my ear. "Yes, Lenny, it's me. But I can't talk long. I'm not breathing so well yet."

"I miss you, Josephine. I was afraid I wouldn't see you again. I'm ready to come home."

"Lenny, I'm not ready to take care of you, dear. I can barely walk."

"Oh." Silence. Then, "Charlotte won't let me watch Wheel of Fortune. She says the news is more important. I think she should let me watch Wheel of Fortune."

"Well, maybe Charlotte will get you a little TV of your own to watch."

"Do you think she would do that just so I could watch for a few days?"

"I'll make sure she does."

31

"Then, when can she bring me home?"

"I'll call when I feel well enough, Lenny. But it may be awhile. The surgery was much worse than I thought it would be."

"Maybe I can help you. I'll make your meals and bathe you. Or, or I won't touch you if you don't want me to. Just let me come home and I'll do whatever you say."

Where was that cork? "Lenny, I have to go now. I'll call you when I feel better. Good-bye."

As the receiver dropped into the cradle, I heard his tiny, far-off cry. "Joooosephi—" Click.

November 9, 2000

The human body really is a remarkable piece of handiwork. After eighty-four years—servicing husbands and children and self—my old bones can still weather this great a loss. Someone certainly knew what he was doing when he puffed up the dust and erected man. Dr. Petzel was so confident of my enduring that he discharged me six days ago to figure out on my own how to breathe again. Sure enough, it's coming back to me. But I'm weary.

I suppose I should have been more grateful all along for my, my . . . let's see . . . how would Adele have put it? Tent, yes. But the truth is, this particular tent has always displeased me. When I was young, it was fat and indifferent to sex. When I was middle-aged, it was prone to addictions. And now that I'm old, it reacts badly to everything from clothing labels to vegetables. Just to get it this far, I've had to shore up or replace almost every conceivable part. All to arrive at my present condition—torn asunder, and grateful for it.

But I hereby pledge to refuse chemotherapy even though

they'll try to talk me into it. I'll finally show this venerable old tent some mercy and let it be. When the cancer has eaten too much of me to keep the rain out, I'll fold up. Katy may not like it, but I'm weary.

God, please just give me cover enough to retrace my steps.

November 13, 2000

I met my first husband—Victor Franklin Greene—at the drugstore down the street from Daddy's shop. It was 1933 and I was seventeen. Vic was bulky and red-necked in his starched white dress shirt, bow tie, and tired gray fedora. He had a coarse, spread-out appearance that made him seem almost middle-aged at barely twenty-one. Without any introductions, he spoke to me in words swift and suggestive. He was going to be an important man, he had all sorts of plans for how to get there, and to accomplish them he needed the right wife. I was sure I'd heard him say that he wanted me. This strong, danger-ous stranger wanted me.

When he asked me to marry him so soon after we'd met, I didn't hesitate. I told myself he was the one who would teach me how to live. Vic was ages older than me in the one way that mattered then—he was independent. He had left his large, fatherless family in rural, southern Louisiana a few months before graduating from high school in 1929, and had come alone to Houston to make his fortune in the frenzied econ-omy. Filled with huge, untested expectations, Vic took the same face kick as the rest of the country when it all fell apart a few months later. I didn't waste time wondering what he'd been doing for the last four years, or, for that matter, what his specific plans were for the future. He put a diamond ring on my finger fat in the middle of the Depression. What more could a plump, naive tailor's daughter hope for?

I also didn't wonder why Vic wanted me. It was enough to sashay into our parlor on his arm—fourteen days after we had met—and listen while he announced that he meant to marry me the next week. The effect of his words took my breath away. There was stunned silence at first, followed by Daddy's angry questioning and pleading—the only part I regret. But into the fresh chasm that I saw open between the piano and me, there surged an indignation that I'd waited seventeen years to cause. It had shape and substance and a ferocious power that lashed across the breach but couldn't touch me. It couldn't touch me so long as I clung to this man's arm. And I even found the gall to laugh at its throbbing impotence.

It was my moment. A million moments were answered for in that one.

November 16, 2000

The afterglow might have lasted longer with another man. But then, another man would not have afforded me such a satisfying retribution. When I finally turned to face real life with my deliverer, I discovered that my happiness was not Vic's primary concern. He had uses, as he had said, that he planned to make of me. I resolved to pay off the enormous debt I owed him for my triumph in the parlor. That, I gathered, must have been all the glory I was due.

November 17, 2000

My initial payments to Vic were physical. In those days, a girl like me usually came to the marriage bed with little education and no practical experience; most boys were hardly better off. But Vic had long been unbridled and knew how he meant for things to go. My forays under the bleachers had given me just enough skill to surprise and arouse him. After that was used up, it seemed that I was losing. He didn't even hold my hand, except to hold me down.

The one thing I always managed to offer Vic sexually—my presence—seemed to be all that he ever required, especially as time went by and his demands were less frequent. I still marvel that he never once complained to me about this aspect of our marriage. How could the same, God-given act so diminish one participant and yet gratify the other?

But I well understood the need to be gratified. I did not begrudge him this.

November 19, 2000

Harmony with Vic was harder to achieve during daylight hours. Though he was normally generous and quick with a compliment, I soon discovered that Vic fell to brooding whenever his ego was insufficiently buoyed. Early on, then, I taught myself a trick that went a long way toward soothing him for our whole forty-six-year marriage.

I stumbled across the strategy not long after we moved into our first house—a modest, frame one-story on a little half street called the Byway. On this particular occasion, Vic was pretty nervous about a dinner we were to attend with the heavyweights at the insurance company where Daddy had gotten him a job. Even Tommy Dawson, the owner and founder, would be there. I was more than a little nervous about it myself, mostly because Vic was so edgy.

He had told me it was to be semiformal, so I dutifully asked around to find out what proper women wear on such occasions. Then I did a little sewing, a little dyeing, a little borrowing, and in the end managed to put together a presentable ensemble consisting of a brilliant blue, tea-length taffeta dress with matching handbag and heels. I was very pleased with myself.

When I waltzed into the living room to show off my ingenuity on the big night, Vic just hovered in the corner growling over a scotch. Something was very wrong.

"Vic, don't you like it?" I tried, knowing that for some reason he didn't.

He let that question lie for several seconds. Then, slow and measured, "I can't have my wife calling all over town telling everyone we've ever met that she doesn't know how to dress herself. How do you think that will make me look?"

For just a second I thought I'd misunderstood his words, but everything about his look confirmed them. And then the old familiar shame crept up my chest and throat into my face, and I fought the urge to run because that's part of it. Bearing it without being allowed to run away was always an important part of it, from the time I had first thought to run.

I couldn't speak, so he spoke for me, sneering. "I suppose you'll say you would have asked me if you'd had any idea I knew about such things."

And that's when I saw it—my gift from Fate, who had no doubt grown weary of watching me replay the same pathetic scene. "Yes," I agreed, hoping the relief I gushed would sound something like sincerity to his hungry ears. "I just didn't know, Vic. I need your help."

I watched his face go soft as I said that. It filled with air, went from red to pink. The change was so conspicuous, the reason so transparent. I quickly ran the calculation in my head, and it appeared at the time that this was the lesser shame.

Beginning that night, I made an art of helplessness. I could appear cheerfully dependent without a hint of contempt. I'm not sure whom I'd have aimed that contempt at anyway. And as far as Vic ever knew, he was the only one who could steer me onto safe ground.

November 21, 2000

So, the little mantra I'd used to coax myself to marry Vic proved largely true. He did teach me how to live; he wouldn't have had it any other way. And, beholden as I was, I warmed to this imposed discipleship without any of the angst that another woman might have suffered. I didn't complain about it to my girlfriends or seek advice from more seasoned married women. I simply considered it the natural order of things. As my reward, perhaps, Vic turned out to be both adventurous and as shrewd a businessman as he had boasted. Otherwise, things might have gone very differently for us.

The economy that haunted the first few years of our marriage brought many lesser and greater men than Vic to their knees. I've not forgotten the mile-long soup kitchen lines or the wild-eyed fathers in ragged suits who glutted the sidewalks of Houston's downtown holding "Will Work for Food" signs that their wives had scrawled on the insides of long-empty cereal boxes. It seemed to last a lifetime—just when you thought that people could bear it no longer, news went round that augured more bad times to come.

But somehow Tommy Dawson did not lose his company to the Depression, and Vic did not lose his job there. I've never known which of them this says more about. I do know that by the late thirties, Tommy had already begun to rely on Vic to help run Dawson Insurance. But I've always suspected that in 1934 and '35, as we began to fathom just how deep and wide the despair was going to be, Tommy's continued provision of a $100-a-month job to my young husband was more paternal than anything else. So we got through it.

This was all the more miraculous because Clay came along less than a year after we married. To say that Clay was an "accident" belies how ill equipped we were emotionally and financially to receive him. Why, we were still virtual strangers to each other and not at all sure at that point that we really wanted to be more. Not only had we not discussed having children, we had not even discussed having been children, or why we had married, or what we thought marriage was about.

But Clay didn't care about any of that. He arrived character- istically early and clinched his spot in the continual lineup of life-changing events that seemed to begin the moment Vic first sidled up next to me in the drugstore on Main Street, and didn't end till I watched his casket lowered into the ground at Jefferson Cemetery. Somehow, like most everything else, we took Clay in stride.

And while I'm not sure that either of us ever wanted or intended to be parents at all, I was determined not to mother an only child. So, after a few years of careful maneuvering, I was rewarded one night when Vic announced that he thought it was time for us to have another baby. This made Katy, born a year later, the child we both wanted.

November 22, 2000

As I read back over yesterday's entry, it sounds a bit shameful that Vic and I experienced so little relative suffering during the Depression. But truly, at the time it felt like we were barely hanging on. And there were always plenty of stories—of someone's brother or uncle or best friend who had stopped hanging on—to make us ever fearful that our demise was just around the corner. This anticipation, I think, made it almost as awful for those of us who got through it as for those who didn't.

But the war that followed was a different story. And across these fifty-nine years, the steps we took to keep Vic out of it ring unpatriotic indeed. But again, that's not how it was to live it.

Clay was five and Katy was a newborn when the war first broke out in Poland. We were as concerned about it as the next guy, but, like the next guy, we were mostly wondering how Hitler's actions might affect us. We believed Roosevelt's promises to keep the United States out of it. So we went on with our lives, strongly supporting all legislation vowing American neutrality, and we only occasionally looked over our shoulders at the strides the Mussolinis and Stalins were making in the rest of the world.

The things that really mattered to us were so much more mundane. Clay was still wetting the bed some nights, Katy was doing all the things that one-year-olds do, and we were busy enclosing the porch of our two-bedroom house so that Clay could have some rest from his baby sister. A few months before, my father had had a heart attack, and I helped care for him several afternoons a week.

Professionally, Vic was poised to deliver on all he owed to Tommy Dawson. Over the past eight years, Tommy had not only kept Vic employed, but he had somehow transferred to Vic much of his cunning and business acumen. To these skills, Vic had contributed his own considerable raw talent and charm. By 1941, Tommy was sixty-two and ready to work and worry a little less. Vic was senior vice president in name but already shouldering the duties of president. And he had big plans for Dawson Insurance. The distant war was playing right into them.

But life never seems to follow the expected path, and wars are certainly no exception.

In any given lifetime, there are a handful of events that leave heavy marks on the same square of every calendar—events so sudden and far-reaching that ten out of ten men on the street who were alive then can tell you just where they were and what they were doing the moment they heard, no matter how many years have intervened. Pearl Harbor was such an event.

On Sunday afternoon, December 7, 1941, Vic and I were getting ready to go to dinner with some friends at our country club. The kids were in the living room listening to the Jack Benny Show while they waited for the babysitter, and I was following along with the program as I put on my face. Fresh out of the shower, Vic was drying off in our bedroom. His towel was powder blue. On the radio, Jack paused in exasperation with something Rochester had said. "Well!" Jack finally retorted, and the audience roared. But their delight was cut short for a special news bulletin from Washington: the Japanese had severed diplomatic relations with the United States in the most offensive way possible—with a surprise attack on some huge chunk of our navy and air force sitting ducklike in Hawaii's Pearl Harbor. No one knew yet how many had been killed, how many ships had been sunk, or how many planes shot down. Only one thing seemed certain: we were finally in the war.

The next day President Roosevelt made it official. He declared war against Japan, and more such declarations followed in the coming months. The United States hunkered down and got serious about its draft. Men headed off to training camps in droves.

At almost thirty, Vic was not among the first to be drafted, but he would be called up soon enough. Our children were seven and two, and Daddy was still not doing very well. I had never worked, except as a part-time store clerk during our first year of marriage, and we really had no other relatives who could have pitched in and helped us out. So when Tommy offered to tell the local draft board that he couldn't run his business without Vic, that neither our country nor our family could afford to lose Vic to the war, it just wasn't a hard decision to make.

We did it and never looked back.

November 23, 2000

This morning I called Lenny and eventually made my voice heard over his pleas to come home.

The moment he took the receiver, he swooped down. "Are you feeling good now, Josephine? Are you well enough for me to come back?"

"Lenny, I need to talk to you about that. I don't think I can do it."

"Oh, I'll get Charlotte to do it. She can bring me this afternoon."

41

"No, no, Lenny. That's not it. I mean I don't think I can let you come back."

"Are you dying? Is it because you're dying and you won't tell me?"

"No, no. I'm not dying. At least, if I am I don't know it. I just need to live alone now, Lenny."

"But you're my wife."

"Well, I'll still be your wife."

"How can you be my wife if you don't let me live with you? Who'll take care of me?"

"Charlotte and I will figure something out. Maybe you can stay there with her, or live with Jeanette or Olivia. One of them will have room for you."

"But, Josephine, my things are there. It's my home."

"Look, Lenny, you know this is my home and always has been. Vic and I built it and lived here for twenty years before you came along. Now I want to live here alone. I have to. Please, just don't argue with me over this."

"Why? Why don't you want me to come back? You must not know how much I need you."

"Yes, I do! That's exactly why you can't come back. I can't meet your needs, and I can't stand your demands. Lenny, I'm not strong anymore. I don't have enough energy to let you drain so much off of me."

"I don't know what you mean, sugar. Why can't I come home?"

"I'll never let you back in this house. That's all you need to know."

November 24, 2000

Katy came by this morning with some groceries—all the bland white stuff she seems intent on starving me with for the rest of my half-lunged life. I'm sick to death of oatmeal and cottage cheese day in, day out. Katy can keep bringing it by, but I'm just going to throw it in the trash. I guess this is in keeping with my new resolve not to let anything live in my house that I don't want here.

Speaking of Lenny, Katy asked about him several times: whether I miss him, how he's doing in San Antonio, how often I talk to him. Her sudden concern for our relationship is a bit suspicious. I'd have expected her to be whispering in my ear, "You're better off without him, Mother. Why bring him back? Isn't it pleasant to have free run of the place, without him around to dog you and everyone else who comes in? He's probably better off with Charlotte anyway."

But she hasn't whispered any of those things. You'd almost think she knows it isn't necessary, that I have no intention of letting Lenny live with me again. But even if she has somehow read my mind about Lenny, why would it worry her? Those two have become such staunch rivals over the years that I can't imagine her feeling sorry for him now. I recall the moment I first had to choose between them. It was Christmas Day 1993.

It had long been our tradition for all the out-of-town children, grandchildren, and spouses to spend Christmas Eve at my house, and the in-town family to join us the next morning for breakfast and "Santa" before I began the laborious ritual of preparing Christmas dinner. Of course, all the gals helped me in the kitchen while the men and boys snoozed through two or three football games interrupted by occasional live wrestling matches on the den floor.

As one of his earliest acts of overprotection, Lenny presumed to upset this tradition by scolding Katy and Lillian for leaving the bulk of the work to me. He told them that the job of cleaning, grocery shopping, pre–Christmas Day cooking, and Christmas-Day oversight was far too much for a woman my age. At the time I still found such sentiments gallant, so I didn't contradict him. I suspect Lenny secretly hoped they would abandon me and take their celebration somewhere else, letting him lay the last brick in the wall behind which he hoped to seal me in. But, of course, no one considered that an option.

Instead, beginning the next year, the girls simply decided on their own what to have for Christmas dinner and brought most of it to my house already fixed. As soon as they arrived in the morning, they shoved the turkey into the oven and shooed me out of the kitchen to sit amongst the comatose men with nothing to do but nurse a holiday bottle of wine.

The great irony of this resolution was the hardship it proved for Lenny himself, who didn't like to watch football anymore than he liked to travel or socialize or have his home invaded by my relatives. Unlike his captive wife, the girls would not tolerate his hanging about in the kitchen, importantly disclosing the locations of ingredients and utensils they'd been using for twenty-five years. They nudged him, too, out of their way—politely at first but with a firm elbow by 1993.

That year, as usual, in came Katy and Lillian at about 10:00 A.M. hauling breadcrumbs, fruit pies, Jell-O salads, vegetable casseroles, and a turkey-in-a-bag. Lenny greeted them at the back door with an elaborate, rehearsed Christmas jingle that he might have memorized off a cereal box prize back in 1965. He threw it out at them as if he deserved some great reward for his clever performance. But they brushed him aside with a grunt, as was by this time their custom, and rushed in to say hello to the rest of us. I could see Lenny—left holding the open door, butler-like—shifting mentally into "see, I tried, but they won't be civil so I'll act however I darn well please" mode, when the truth was that he had purposefully provoked them with some asinine, insincere expression that he knew they wouldn't bother to respond to.

For the rest of the morning and afternoon, Lenny willfully misunderstood much of what was said to him. When these imaginary insults were heaped upon the palpable indifference with which many of my family navigated around him and the intentional belittlements aimed directly at him by others, Lenny's ego was understandably in tatters by the time we arrived at what had become the tensest moment of every Christmas Day for the past several years—cutting the turkey.

Now the girls considered the turkey to be part of what had been so rudely delegated to them. They bought it, brought it, cooked it, and had every intention of designating its carver—a privilege each of them meant to bestow upon her own man if possible. Lenny, on the other hand, had somehow come to view the turkey carving as a right vested solely in the man of the house, and since our ungrateful throng insisted on celebrating Christmas in his house, that meant him. Never mind that he carved a turkey in the same way he did most everything—art-lessly and in slow motion. But the girls seized on this, his incompetence, as reason enough to refuse Lenny the small distinction on which he suddenly determined to stake his honor.

At around four o'clock, with the natives in front of the television clamoring for us to "serve the blasted food already," I slipped into our bedroom where Lenny had been brooding for the past half hour because someone had told him he was setting up the card tables too early. I said that dinner would begin shortly and that I expected him to pull himself together and be an obedient host by the time it got underway. He nodded complacently for a change. This mission accomplished, I rejoined the family, but I was still uneasy about Lenny.

Five minutes later, he followed me out looking more chipper than he had all day. He headed for the kitchen, stopping in the doorway just long enough to survey the status of things. He watched nonchalantly as Katy drew the turkey out of the oven and placed it on the counter to cool. Then, without a word to anyone, Lenny slipped into the kitchen and got himself a glass of water. While he drank it, he moved toward the pantry. This put him mostly out of the girls' way and very near the knife drawer. The four of them—Katy, Lillian, Samantha, and Gretchen—bustled all around him as if he weren't there, and he made no detectable moves to interfere with their final preparations.

Lenny waited until the girls had shifted their energy to setting tables in the living room, and for a moment the kitchen was empty. Then, from my perch at the breakfast table, I watched him quietly open the drawer and extract the largest, dullest knife in it. He walked right up to the turkey, seized the nearest fork on the countertop, and went to carving with an exaggerated, hostile air of ownership, quivering as he cut.

Before I could react, Katy discovered Lenny hunched over her beautiful turkey, tearing it into crosscut shreds. At first she just glared at his back in stunned silence. Seconds later, the other three scampered into the kitchen on Katy's heels and nearly smashed into her seething frame. Lenny's line in the sand came into focus for us all at the same horrible moment.

When Katy suddenly turned and stalked out of the kitchen, the others knew to follow, and they quickly fell to huddling in the living room. I stayed on and eyeballed Lenny like a mother who had lost control of her toddler. Why couldn't he have minded me just this once? Lenny threw me one slightly sheepish look, and then resumed his defiant hacking. The thing had been set in motion.

Presently, Clay swaggered into the kitchen from the den and approached Lenny. Katy and Lillian were poised just within earshot to make sure he followed their orders.

"Len, old boy, I do believe you've gotten stuck with my job," he began. "I drew the short straw last year, and I mean to carry out my duty no matter how unpleasant. So you're relieved of this mess. I bet you're glad for that!"

If they were going to execute Lenny, I thought it at least generous to let him pretend they were doing him a favor. But Lenny had staked too much on this battle to surrender so easily. He didn't even waste energy responding to Clay, except to cut faster and shake more visibly.

Clay glanced back into the den, where Katy and Lillian nodded their vigorous encouragement. There would be no last-minute pardon. He turned back to Lenny and moved a little closer. "Lenny, I have to insist," he said, meaner than I thought him capable. And then he stood back to let his words take effect.

The whole house fell silent, except for a jabbering announcer somewhere in Buffalo, assuring us that the Bills would be no match for Dallas in the Super Bowl even if they somehow made it through the play-offs. In the kitchen, Lenny's carving arm froze, and he stood there sweating over the mutilated turkey, obviously weighing how high a price he could pay for his self-respect. Finally, with his whole ungraceful, juice-splattered self, he turned to face me.

In a relationship, as in a life, turning points slip up on us when we least expect them and present themselves incognito. They catch us aiming only at our comfort over the next few minutes rather than at the next ten thousand hours that we'll dictate by the choice we make right then. I perceived Lenny's pale little plea for support with nothing but my five senses, which told me in five different ways that Lenny was ruining my family's Christmas—the one happy day each year when all my little chicks came to visit me. I was actually relieved that he had called upon me to end this nasty scene and put things back to normal.

"Lenny, pleeease put the knife down," I said, then turned my back on him and went to pulling festive red-and-green napkins from the drawer next to the pantry. Presently I heard the massive knife clatter into the sink, and I glanced around to watch Lenny shuffle out of the kitchen, dripping grease and turkey skin from his dangling fingers.

Thereafter, Lenny only made halfhearted bids to carve our Christmas turkeys. More and more, I looked forward to the rare moments when my little chicks chucked around me and I could forget where I lived the rest of the time—behind a wall with every brick now firmly in place.

November 25, 2000

This afternoon, it was Charlotte who called me. She said she needed to talk to me about Lenny. I mentally marshaled my arguments and prepared to defend myself to a rational opponent.

"Charlotte, I hate to leave Lenny in your hands, but you of all people know how he's gotten," I began.

"Yes, but it's not important now——"

"What do you mean, 'not important'? That, along with my illness, is the whole point. Otherwise, Lenny and I could have gone on as before. I don't think that Lenny understood what I was saying about that."

"No, I don't think he understood."

"You know, a few weeks ago he tried to convince me that he needed to clean out the swimming pool even though no one has used it for over a year. He kept saying his great-nieces and nephews might be coming for a visit and he wanted it ready. In October! I couldn't stop him, so I stood by the telephone ready to call 911 while he teetered along the edge of the pool for two hours scooping up waterlogged leaves. What if he had fallen in? Do you think I could have done anything? Especially in the condition I'm in now?"

"Josephine, Lenny took my car this morning. . . . He took the keys out of my purse while I was in the shower."

"Oh, my God. Charlotte, is he lost? Did he wreck your car?"

"Yes. He made it several miles before I guess he ran a red light. A truck hit him. Broadsided him . . . on the driver's side. I just came from identifying him. Josephine, he's dead."

After many horrified moments, a lone question rose defiantly above all the rest in my mind. It was like an old wound screaming to bleed freely. "Charlotte," I half-chirped, half-whispered, "do you know . . . where he was going?"

I was granted the guilt I sought. "He left a note saying he was going home."

Chapter 5 ✑

Katy

I learned of Lenny's accident on the morning after, just as every other Houstonian did—by scanning the obituary columns of the *Houston Post*. Like the burglary victim who comes home and discovers a big hole where the high-dollar stereo used to sit, my mind at first refused to comprehend the words on the page.

"Leonard Jean Van Zandt, 86, passed into the presence of our Lord on November 25, 2000 . . . ," the item began.

Isn't that funny, I thought, still firmly anchored in a world where a mother would tell a daughter such a thing. *That man has the same name as Lenny! And he's roughly the same age too.*

" . . . when he was killed in a car accident in San Antonio, Texas," the sentence concluded. That got my attention. Now I was staring at the hole, sans the stereo, thinking, *Is this a joke? Who would pay to run an obituary for a living person? Doesn't a newspaper have some duty to confirm these things?*

"He is survived by his wife of 19 years, Josephine Greene Van Zandt . . . ," it went on.

I fumed and hurled the newspaper aside. *Mother isn't up to this sort of prank right now*, I thought, and grabbed the phone.

She didn't pick up for eight or nine rings. When she did, she mumbled, "What? Eh, hel-, hello?"

"Mother, were you asleep? This is Katy."

"Uh, no. I, I don't think so. I'm not feeling too well, Katy. I can't talk," she said, with hang-up finality.

"Mother, wait! In what way are you feeling bad?" I couldn't blurt something like this out to her if she was experiencing a real health crisis. "Are you having worse trouble breathing?"

A few trial breaths later, she said, "No, I don't think so."

"Is it your stitches? Does it hurt where they cut you?"

"No more than usual."

"Mother, have you taken all the medicines you're supposed to?"

"I don't know, Katy. What difference does it make?"

"What do you mean? Is it something else? Are you having pains in your chest? What is it?" I practically screeched this portion of my interrogation. Clearly I would not have made a good nurse. But then, my mother didn't make a very cooperative patient.

"Katy, I can't talk anymore. Maybe I'll call you back later."

"Wait! Don't you dare hang up unless you're passing out. Should I call the EMS to come over there? I demand that you tell me what's wrong!"

"All right," she screamed half-lunged, "Lenny is dead! There! Are you satisfied?"

With that, I spied the broken window and the half-emptied china cabinet. Finally I grabbed hold of the thick, slippery conclusion: "A stranger has been in my house."

Out loud, I announced in bewildered monotone: "Lenny was killed yesterday and you didn't tell me."

"Yes," she said. "I killed him."

As it turns out, Charlotte had fired off Lenny's obituary to the *Post* while Mother sat alone that first night thrashing herself. By the end of those seventeen hours, she had assumed the blame for so much bad—everything from Lenny's death to Texas's three-year drought—

that I couldn't stay angry with her for letting me dumbly read about him in the paper. To hear her tell it, she had all but buckled Lenny into that car with the keys in his hand and pointed him toward the offending intersection. I'd already pretty much come to the same conclusion, but there was no need confirming this to her.

Lenny's siblings were more charitable than we. They rejected any suggestion that Mother's cool emancipation had brought about Lenny's ending and credited her instead with all the years she had let Lenny hang around. Mother's suicidal conscience finally had to make do with details of Lenny's crushed torso and the extra hours that the embalmer had spent rendering him presentable for the leave-taking line at the funeral.

As her guilty *coup de grâce*, however, Mother informed us on the morning of Lenny's service that she did not even feel entitled to make an appearance there. I snapped. Like an overwrought Rhett Butler, I stuffed Mother into her drabbest black dress and dragged her off to the church where she somehow found the courage to cry out loud while the rusty old widows from her and Lenny's Sunday school class sat in the front row opposite, clucking about "the duties that a wife owes her man."

Once all this was over, I'd hoped that Mother might actually feel a little bit relieved about Lenny. After all, she no longer had to do the dance—ever trying to keep him fed without becoming the meal. Never again would she have to "handle Lenny."

But by mid-December, Mother was still spending about twenty hours a day in bed. She began complaining about her legs swelling—swelling so much that it was hard for her to walk. Afraid this might be a sign that the cancer was back, I whisked her off to the oncologist. But his tests showed that her leftover lungs were still clear. He recommended an orthopedist, who recommended an endocrinologist, who recommended a cardiologist, none of whom could figure out why the ankles of a 103-pound woman were as thick as railroad ties. On a hunch that was never adequately explained to me, one of them finally tried her on steroids, and this inexplicably reduced her ankles to at least a bendable size.

Still, Mother ebbed. Soon I'd had all I could take of people slouched in dark bedrooms, uninterested even in food and clean clothes. Eliot—so often bedroomed away in my own house—had beat me up for the past forty years with his recurring self-hatred, and I wasn't up for another assignment along those lines.

One morning I slid a big packing box marked "XMAS" up to Mother's bedside and thumped the top. She pulled the covers down just far enough to look out. "What's that?"

"Time to decorate," I answered, camp-counselor peppy but firm.

"I don't want to decorate. I don't care about that."

"Oh, but maybe you didn't notice which box I brought. These are your Santas. How many do you suppose you have now—close to a hundred?" As I chatted, I popped the flaps and started hauling out Santa Clauses of every conceivable make and size. I lined them up all around her on the bed with the verve of a schoolgirl displaying a pilfered stash of her mother's makeup. "I bet you've collected about three per year on average, don't you think?"

I thought I saw a flicker of her old yuletide spark when I produced the two Santas that Clay and I had made for her when we were children—his, carved tall and haggard out of a narrow strip of balsa wood, and mine, a fat collage of bright felts and glitter. Mother reached out and caught a silver sequin that drooped precariously from the rim of my Santa's hat. Perhaps she was thinking that she should get some thread and shore it up as she had so many times before. But the next moment the spark extinguished and she pulled her hand back, letting the sequin flop down into Santa's bedraggled, cotton-ball beard. Lenny was dead. She'd killed him, her indifference reminded us both.

"I'm not doing Christmas this year," she said, rolling over on a delicate, porcelain Saint Nicholas that my father had bought for her on a trip to Switzerland in 1952. Fixing her wet stare on the wall opposite me, Mother didn't check to see if she'd broken the figurine. She didn't even slide over to find herself a Santa-less slab of the bed to occupy.

For the second time in two months, I felt myself slip below the surface, frantically holding my breath amidst the unfriendly waters of my mother's dying. I saw that no amount of steroids would magically erase her present pain.

Or would it? One more trick wiggled down my sleeve.

Fran McClendon had been online since about 1994—long before I'd distinguished between the World Wide Web and some pernicious, brain-devouring virus called "Internet" that Stephen King might have dreamt up for one of his horror stories. Fran was a technological whiz by this time, surfing for hours each day researching the genealogies of various friends and relatives. She had already backed the family lines of her own father and mother out of the United States and deep into Ireland and Denmark, respectively.

I knew all this about Fran because I was on her e-mail forwarding A-list. I got every sappy story, every warning of toxins lurking in substances I consumed twenty times a day, and every well-traveled joke, clean or crass. Occasionally, I even received some intimate tidbit about Fran herself, always sent to the same eighty-seven people.

So I knew how to find her. And after I packed up all of Mother's Santas, I went right home and shot Fran the following note:

Dear Fran,

Good to hear from you the other day. I will cease immediately all microwaving in plastic or paper containers. I hate to think how long I've put my life at risk with such reckless behavior!

Seriously, I need a favor. Mother is convinced that her resistance to letting Lenny come home after her surgery is what pushed him to do the stupid thing he did. She won't let it go. She's even skipping Christmas this year. I haven't seen her this bad off since Adele died.

Any chance you could come for a short visit? Something tells me you might be able to give her some fresh insight.

Katy

When I checked my e-mail before bed that evening, I found the following response sitting in my in-box:

Dearest Katy,

I arrive tomorrow at 2:45 on Delta Flight 23. We'll talk then.

Fran

ॐ

I could not have picked the woman who approached me the next day in the Delta terminal out of a lineup, not if you'd paid me fifty dollars.

True, I hadn't seen Fran in more than a decade. Back in 1989—

after her husband Silver got sick and during one of her and Mother's periodic estrangements—the McClendons had moved to Milwaukee to live near one of their sons. Still, the change in Fran over those ten years was remarkable.

This Fran was four sizes smaller and what seemed like two decades older, which is saying a lot for someone who had started out size twenty at seventy-three. She'd surrendered to her whitening hair but won the weight war, and she'd emerged looking a good deal tamer than the Fran I remembered. I fretted that surprising Mother with such an unfamiliar best friend might just send her further down her hole.

Then Fran opened her mouth. "OK, baby doll. Let me have it. Nothing you said in your e-mail sounded one bit like Josey Greene to me. Why in the heck isn't she grateful? After all, she's finally rid of that lunk without even having to shoot him."

There, now. That's the perspective I was after.

It took just under half an hour for Mother to accept that Fran really was sitting right there in her own living room, in person. No, the medications weren't playing tricks on her. No, Fran wasn't there to help break anymore bad news. The notion that Fran would have come all that way just to surprise her sent Mother's self-esteem soaring well above the zero mark.

Still, she had to test the ground. "You know, Fran, Lenny pretty much begged me to let him come home," she confessed for starters.

"Yeah, I'm sure he did."

"I'd already decided not to. I would never have let him come back, no matter how well I got. Never."

"There's no way you could have, Josey."

"You mean because he was getting so obstinate and forgetful."

"No, honey. I mean because he was *always* such a pain in the rear, sucking the life out of you from that very first night when you put up with his droning old war stories until two in the morning. He knew Vic had just died. When Lenny pointed his weakness detector at you, it went haywire, so he plied you with those revolting, awe-shucks love letters and all kinds of lies about how much you two had in common. As I said then, he latched onto you like a vampire at a blood drive."

"Yes," Mother murmured, her guilty fret lines smoothing out some.

"Are you gonna give him the last drop you've got, Jo?"

"Hmm." Well, apparently there was one last thing. Mother told it as if she were confessing that she'd been the Second Gunman. "Fran, I only agreed to the surgery as an excuse to get rid of him."

Had I heard that right?

"I know, Josey. I know." Fran hugged and absolved her. Then she scrambled around in her bags and pulled out a bottle of expensive California Chardonnay. "Now, how about a little cocktail, girls?"

That's when Mother remembered I was there, off in a corner, eavesdropping on the priest dispensing her easy grace and the gleeful sinner drinking it in. Mother glanced over at me, the worry lines back and deeper than ever. Her face was one big question mark.

I made myself go along, walking over and kissing my mother's cowardly cheek. "I have to pick up some documents first," I said. "You two go ahead without me."

I got held up at the court reporter's office and didn't make it back to Mother's until nearly eight o'clock. When I walked in, Mother was doubled over on the sofa, and Fran was gasping for air on the floor near her feet. After assuring myself that neither of them had been shot or was ill, I waited for them to calm down and notice me.

Fran straightened up first, but only long enough to point at the living room wall and shriek before melting over on her side and going back to gasping like a tuna on the deck of a fishing boat. "Ahck," gasp, "ahck," gasp, "ahck," gasp. I suppose a tuna wouldn't have made the noises between the gasps. They sounded more like a duckling learning to quack for the first time.

Mother didn't make any noises, but her body sort of heaved up and down, and I could imagine the merry tears that were peppering her lap.

I cleared my throat. "Just what's going on here?" I asked, mock principal.

My charges looked up, anything but chastened. Fran pointed again at a painting hanging over the couch and snickered. "Your mother has just been showing off some of her recent masterpieces, including that one of her great-granddaughter, . . . Miss Piggy!" she squealed and toppled over once more.

"Fran thinks the one of Seth in the hallway looks . . . like . . . Kermit!" Mother blared. "And she wants to know if that new landscape I was working on before I got sick is supposed to be a backdrop for a puppet show!" With that, she went back to heaving and crying into her lap.

Fran pulled herself together enough to slap Mother upside the head with a compliment of sorts. "Josey, you've never painted a realistic, three-dimensional face in your whole life. I don't even know why you attempt portraits. But I thought you could do better on a landscape!"

"Just because you were blessed with God-given talent doesn't mean the rest of us don't have to struggle, Fran. There are things I naturally do better than you," my tipsy mother retorted, "like . . . like . . ."

"Yes, like what?"

"Like, play the piano," Mother said. I thought she had Fran there, but Fran wasn't giving up.

"Oh? I bet you haven't played since Adele's funeral. Have you, Josey? You sure you still can?"

Adele was our family's heartbeat for more than twenty-five years. She was also our housekeeper, teacher, and confidante. Mother had agreed to play a favorite old Negro spiritual at her funeral only after Adele's husband Isaiah had begged her. Nothing else could have enticed her back onto that bench, and nothing had since. I was sure of it.

"Well, I think I did OK that day," Mother said. Truly, she had played beautifully, like she thought Adele might be lingering there and take it as "good-bye."

Mother and Fran paused then and inclined their heads the way people do when they pay their respects—what Adele would have called a "selah."

"Yes, Josey," Fran conceded. "You certainly outdid yourself that day."

CHAPTER 6

Jo

December 27, 2000

I suppose I shouldn't have been so surprised that Fran would insist on making a panful of caramel apples when we put her in charge of dessert for our Christmas dinner. Of course, she couldn't be talked out of it, even when I warned her that the two of us would likely lose all our teeth if we tried to eat them.

She just winked at me and said, "It's for the youngsters. Do you really think they care two hoots about pumpkin pie? Or rhubarb?" She pronounced this last word with such exaggeration that a disdainful thread of spittle spewed out of her mouth with one of the b's and affixed itself to her chin. This might have embarrassed a more genteel old lady but not my Fran. She sucked it back in and went right on.

"You can make that cheesy Jell-O mold for whoever's not young enough to appreciate a caramel apple, Jo. And I'll give you a hundred dollars if you have any takers."

So much for tradition. What had promised to be my worst Christmas ever became the most relaxed and unconventional holiday I've had in many years. Somehow, Fran gave me permission to enjoy myself. Despite everything.

Only one thing marred my relief at being alive and Lennyless and surrounded by those I love: Lillian's increasingly shameless attempts to manipulate Clay. It's times like these that I'm a teensy bit grateful for my son's impenetrable emotional armor. He apparently didn't notice that his wife sat off in a corner most of the day speaking only to her sons, or that she took several potshots at him as the family sat around the dining room table sucking on caramel apples (while my Jell-O salad melted on the counter). Nor was he perturbed early on when he was handed a gift that failed to identify its giver, and in front of us all he unwrapped a book entitled, *From the Fairway to Foreplay: How to Put the Woman in Your Life First for a Change*. I saw Lillian gasp ever so slightly and look away, but she hadn't fooled me. Or Clay either. He laughed like it was some great joke, and then simply dropped the book into the nearby trash bag with all the torn wrapping paper on his way to the kitchen to pour himself another cup of coffee.

I've long wondered what my son ever did to deserve life with Lillian at his throat. In the whole thirty years of their marriage, it seems to me that she has never tired of digging in her nails. But then, Clay still refuses to acknowledge what a pain Lillian has turned out to be. Thank goodness he married late; at least that gave him a few years of peace.

I know I shouldn't talk this way about my daughter-in-law. And I wouldn't anywhere except here, where I sort of feel entitled to say all the things I shouldn't and haven't said for the past eighty years. Maybe if I'd been more honest about my feelings and opinions all along, some of these things would never have happened, or gone on as they did. Am I deluding myself to think I could ever have been so powerful? Well, who knows what greater influence an honest Josephine might have had.

But I couldn't be that person. Look at me. I can't even tell my diary the truth without apologizing!

No. I'm determined to try harder here. So, what do I really think happened to Clay?

I was so relieved when Clay turned out to be a boy. I thought that would make it OK with Vic that this child we weren't ready for was nevertheless on our doorstep. I remember the moment I realized that Clay's maleness didn't endear him to his father one bit.

It was soon after we left the hospital. Until then, it had just been the two of us—Clay and me—entwined in this mother-baby cycle of basic life functions that made me feel frighteningly, wonderfully, like an animal. It was all so wet, so smelly, and so necessary. It completely took me by surprise that I could feel that alive.

Then we came home.

On our first full day there, Vic got in late from work and seemed preoccupied. I fluttered about, still high on my new assignment as life-giver and sustainer. But I felt a certain urgency about bringing Vic into the symbiosis I had found myself in with my baby. I sensed that the sooner this was accomplished, the better.

"Vic," I ventured, "would you like to help me give Clay a bath?"

"A bath? How dirty could he be after one day?"

"Well, honey, he dirties himself constantly, for one thing. For another, I don't want to forget how they taught me to do it. And besides, I thought it would be special." I ended whiny because Vic's look told me that he was unconvinced by my first two arguments. Why did I have to persuade this man to bathe his newborn son anyway?

"Never mind," I muttered and stomped off to the nursery with the baby.

By the time I had drawn a little water and stripped Clay down, however, Vic was standing at the threshold, propped stiffly against the doorframe, and he watched me lift Clay out of his bassinet and dangle him over the water. What I would have given for Vic to actually experience this with me, or even to really care if his son was clean or whether I was about to unwittingly drown him. So I brought out my trump card.

"Honey, I can't tell if the water is too hot. Will you pleeeease test it and see what you think?"

Vic cocked his head and squinted at me hard. It was one of the only times I think he suspected my duplicity. Then he dismissed me and stared at Clay. I saw ten different emotions play across his face. We waited so long that the baby finally got cold waving naked in the air, and he started whimpering. Vic just kept staring. So Clay began to wail, and I instinctively drew him inside my housecoat to my body and warmed him.

Then I heard Vic shift his weight to both feet. I looked up as he seemed to start forward into the room. But it was really a turn. And when he had shown us his back and started down the hall, he finally answered.

"That's your deal," he said.

December 30, 2000

Over the next few years, Vic always remained an arm's length away from his son. This was a familiar scene: me in the kitchen making supper or cleaning up after it, Vic in his easy chair reading through reams of actuary tables, and Clay playing on the floor by himself, stealing glances at his father in hopes of catching him looking his way.

After awhile, Clay would make some specific demand or just start crying in general. If he didn't scream for me at this point, Vic always did because they did not interact with each other. I once walked into the living room and found Clay rooted a few feet in front of Vic, mesmerized by the backs of the papers that shielded the father from the son.

And I hated Vic for this. But the more inadequate he was at these aspects of fatherhood, the better he got at providing for us, especially considering the times in which we were living. I felt so lucky in that respect. And, for the most part, our family fit the common pattern of the day. It was the deal we all made. Still, I knew there was something more going on with us.

I tried to channel my anger into making up for Vic's indifference, but I don't think a mother can ever soften that particular pain. It's like a boy's name—so much a part of the person he feels inside and presents to the world. He wants to say, "Hello, my name is Clay Greene, and my father is proud of me." But without his father's affirmation, it seems that a boy is never really able to make friends with the world. And that, I think, is what happened to my little Clay.

January 2, 2001

One thing I could never say about Vic is that I knew what to expect from him. Oh, I thought I knew at times, but he constantly surprised me. One such surprise was his sudden conviction that we should have a second child. Of course, I'd been angling a few years for this, but it still shocked me when he actually gave the order.

My thinking was that Clay deserved some company besides just me—someone to help offset the disappointment that Vic continually generated. So I was hoping for another son. When I told Vic that I wanted a boy again this time, he simply said, "Be careful what you ask for, Jo. It won't be a boy."

Just like that, he'd decided who we were going to have! Somehow he was right too. I think that out of sheer force of his will he withheld all his Y sperm from my egg and sent in only Xs to conceive his second child. And I would soon find out why.

Katy's arrival was like day to Clay's night. For weeks afterward, Vic came home early almost every day. Usually, each evening, he would make a big production out of contributing in some way to Katy's care—helping to feed her, changing a wet diaper, or even holding her when she cried. It was such a drastic contrast to his treatment of Clay that I wondered if they'd accidentally switched husbands on me in the hospital.

One night Vic suggested giving Katy a bath and took the lead in accomplishing it. As I watched him tenderly dip her into the water he'd taken such care to cool, the incongruity became too stark for me to keep to myself.

"What is it, Vic? Why are you doing this? Why are you so interested in Katy? Why not Clay?" I demanded, making no effort to choose the right words.

Blindsided by my sudden interrogation, Vic barely managed to keep Katy's head above water. Finally he lifted her out of the sink and snarled, "So, you don't want me to be interested in Katy?"

"You know that's not what I'm saying." What I wanted was the bottom of this thing.

Vic hung his head slightly and sighed in a hurt-paw sort of way that I'd never seen before. After a long pause, "I want . . . to do better this time." I had to strain toward him to hear this whispered confession. And then I surprised myself and just kept on moving forward and instinctively pulled him into my body and warmed him against my breast.

"Why don't you start with Clay?" I whispered, still holding him, our baby mashed gently between us.

"I don't know. I can't." And he dripped his regret all over our daughter.

Vic was the first to see Clay in the doorway, watching us. I saw my son reflected to me in the fear that crawled across Vic's wet face. I turned, and there he stood with his five-year-old wounds hanging open for all to behold. Here we were, and there he was, with no good reason for why it had to be this way.

Vic was terrified of fathering a son.

January 4, 2001

Sure enough, Katy turned out to be a great companion for her brother. She has always loved him in a full, unflagging way that . . . that "covered over a multitude of sins," as Adele would have said. And now, at sixty-six and sixty-one, they are still fiercely loyal to each other.

One might consider this a tribute to Clay, who had every reason to resent the little sister who got all the paternal affection that he once so craved. But I can tell my diary that it's not a tribute at all. For somewhere along the way, Clay just went dead to his father and everything having to do with him. In fact, he sort of went dead in general, at least to a vibrant, emotional existence that most people would call living.

So I think Clay saw Katy simply as the little sister who adored him. He accepted this at face value in the same way he came to accept Vic's repulsion and everything else about life—calmly, with neither angst nor exhilaration. He's one of the most plodding people I've ever known. That is surely what has made it possible for him to stay with someone like Lillian without ever seeming to be swayed one bit by her juvenile attempts to get more of his attention.

OK, I see the chicken/egg problem in that conclusion. If I'm going to be totally honest with my diary, I guess I must admit that thirty some-odd years with Clay probably hasn't been too easy for Lillian either. In her shoes, I might also have tried anything to yank my husband's heart out of the deep freeze. There, I've said it.

January 7, 2001

An important postscript on Clay before I go on: he wasn't without any paternal influence or affection. On some gut level, my own father discerned the problem while Clay was still in grade school, and he did all he could to fill the gaping hole in his grandson's childhood. It seemed that compensating for others' shortcomings was to be Daddy's main calling in life.

Though in his mid-to-late seventies by this time, and bent too far over to help Clay with sports even if he'd enjoyed better health, Daddy talked to him—and listened. In the summers, he invited Clay out to the house for weeks at a time and took him for meandering hikes along the same tangle of city sidewalks that he'd taught me as a girl. When my son came home from those visits, full of familiar stories about Daddy's immigrant parents and the small town in Germany named for our ancestors, I noticed a marked increase in his sense of himself. This, too, I remembered receiving from Daddy.

January 10, 2001

It was 1942 when Adele first came to us. We had just received confirmation that Vic would not be drafted, and Tommy had taken that opportunity to name Vic president of his company. Heady with his good fortune, Vic came home early one Friday afternoon and unplugged my vacuum while I strained to reach a rat-sized dustball under the china cabinet.

I cursed and bumped my head on the cabinet door as I yanked the attachment out from under the furniture to see what was the matter. Then I saw Vic standing behind me, jingling his pocket change with one hand and twirling the plug in the other. He looked poised to start whistling some show tune at any moment. I glared at him, a little tipsy from my head-down chore and the bang on my scalp.

Vic wasn't fazed. He held the cord up to my red face and asked, "Dawlin', how'd you like to forget all this?"

"What are you talking about, Vic? Have you figured out how to immunize the house from dirt? Don't tell me you're volunteering your own services?" I snapped, fretting over the rat ball that remained at large while I answered silly questions.

"In a way, I suppose," he said mysteriously, dropping the cord and starting to saunter out of the living room. I knew I was supposed to follow and sweet-talk this out of him.

"OK, OK," I started after him. "What is it, Vic? What are you up to?"

He slipped into the kitchen before I caught up. When I rounded the corner, I nearly tripped over a large woman who was busy examining the inside of my oven with a critical eye. She wore a spotless white dress that made her skin look like high-polished mahogany. Withdrawing from the oven on my sudden approach, she extended to her full height, towering over both me and my stout, five-foot-nine-inch husband. I judged her to be about forty-five or fifty at the time but found out later that she was a hard-lived thirty-eight.

Vic straightened his double-breasted suit with a delicate tug on his lapels, waved broadly, and announced, "Jo, this is Adele Smith, our maid!"

The woman in my kitchen smiled at this one-sided introduction, made as if she were a zoo animal or a new building Vic was dedicating. The knowing glint in her eye clashed curiously with the hole she flashed on one side of her rickety smile—an unexpected, tooth-framed window to the pink of her tongue.

"Howdy-do, Mrs. Greene," she said, when I failed to respond in any way.

Only vaguely did I wonder what had possessed Vic to bring me a maid. Mostly I was smitten by the presence before me—something about this woman struck me as fearless and gentle all at the same time. Was it her great height that gave her an advantage?

I gawked, still mute, and Adele Smith bowed to me slightly, encouraging me without presuming to offer her hand. I finally held mine out to her and was pleased when she took it in both of hers and shook it in the robust, fortifying way a grown-up might shake hands with a small child.

Vic apparently took my dullness for gratitude. "It's time we started living according to our means, Jo," he explained. "We can afford to pay someone else to do the hard stuff. Having Adele will free you for more important things than chasing dust-balls and changing diapers all the time. She'll be coming three days a week to start with."

Once again, Adele helped me out. When she saw I didn't know how to respond to my husband's grand proclamation, she jumped right in. "Mrs. Greene," she said, "where are your little ones? I'd sure like to see 'em."

"It's Jo, Miss Smith," I corrected her quickly.

Vic frowned at me hard. Here I'd relinquished my higher status at our very first meeting! It surely was not the way he'd meant for things to go. But I just couldn't let this woman—so clearly my elder—grovel to me in any way.

Once Adele saw I wasn't revoking my offer, she said, "Well, I'm a Mrs., not a Miss, myself. I have me a husband, Isaiah, and seven children. But you'll have to call me Adele, Miss Jo."

I rarely defied a single order Adele ever gave me, beginning with this one. We had settled it between us in a way that was at least halfway acceptable to Vic. I led her off to see my napping toddler while he soothed himself with a cocktail.

Our lives were never the same after that.

January 12, 2001

At the Greene household, Adele was saddled with two, full-grown religious illiterates. Having her around eventually made us both acutely aware of this. It came into focus for me the first

Wednesday morning that I handed over all of our current sugar and coffee rations so that Adele could buy our groceries for the week.

"Adele, do you think this'll get us enough sugar for Clay's birthday cake as well as everything else we need it for?"

"Oh, we can stretch it out somehow," she answered, stuffing the coupons into her plastic handbag and heading toward the back door. "Man don't live by bread alone, you know." And out she went.

This last comment gnawed at me for the next thirty minutes. Adele was always throwing out little ditties that I'd heard before but could never quite place. I was pretty sure that she didn't memorize Bartlett's Familiar Quotations in her off hours, so something else had to account for it. I determined to track down this particular saying.

I was by now in the habit of taking all my questions to Vic. Any hesitation I had about bothering him at work with something so trivial was offset by the points I thought I would make for needing his help on such a thing. I rang his number.

"Yes, Jo, I've certainly heard that adage before, but I can't place its source just now either. Maybe it'll come to me later on," he said. "I'll call you back if it does."

"Well, could you ask Miss Perkins? I want to figure this out before Adele gets back from the store."

"No, I won't ask Miss Perkins!" he bellowed so loudly that I was certain it had carried to Miss Perkins's desk just outside his office. "What if she did know? Wouldn't I look stupid then, shown up by my secretary? You'll just have to ask Adele, and don't tell her you asked me first!" Click. It rarely paid to need Vic for anything he wasn't good at.

Well, what about old Bartlett? Maybe he could help. I rummaged through all our bookshelves until I found the copy someone had given us for a wedding gift, and I looked up bread in the four-hundred-page index. Two-thirds of the way down the long bread column, I found "man doth not live by only." That had to be it. And on page 1099, I learned that this quote came from Deuteronomy, VIII, 3, which the top of the page identified as part of "The Bible—Old Testament."

Of course! Adele had been discreetly quoting Bible verses to us for weeks, and we'd been too obtuse to realize it. Feeling like a fool, I determined to confront her on it the moment she got home.

When she arrived, Adele deposited two boxes of sugar in front of me rather than the one we'd had rations for, and winked. "Looks like you don't need to worry 'bout tomorrow. It has plenty of worry of its own," she chirped, flashing me her big, porous smile.

"There!" I pounced. "You're doing it again! Is that the Bible you're quoting at me, Adele? Did you think I wouldn't notice? Are you ridiculing me?"

I heard the kitchen clock tick off several seconds as the merriment drained from Adele's huge brown eyes to make room for grief and worry. "Oh, my Lord, child. I didn't even know I was doin' it. I wouldn't never, ever make fun of no one with God's Word. It's just my wont to resemble the truths that's carried me through life, that's all. I sure don't mean to hurt you, honey."

Ashamed, and fully assured, I vowed to embrace this unusual penchant in our humble housekeeper. Eventually, I didn't even notice she was doing it. I just always assumed that

73

the wisest things Adele said came straight from the Bible. Over the years, I got quite an education.

It was late that afternoon before I suddenly recalled the "thud" of that second box of sugar. Just where had it come from? By this time Adele had been gone for more than an hour, and the Smiths had no telephone, so I couldn't call and ask her. The possibilities, as I could imagine them, were two: some sort of theft or some sort of gift. Recalling all that I knew about Adele thus far, I quickly discounted the former. Who, then, might have gifted us with an extra box of sugar? Probably not the grocer, who barely knew us, and besides would be held accountable for enough ration coupons to cover his missing stock. Might Adele have chanced upon a stray sugar ration dropped in the baking aisle by the last housewife who had passed that way? Perhaps. But I strongly suspected that Adele wouldn't have rested until she'd tracked that woman down. Only one explanation made sense: Adele's huge brood would go without sugar for a week so that my son could have a birthday cake. Which Bible verse, I wondered, expressed what that taught me?

<u>January 15, 2001</u>

Once he was savvy to her quirk, Vic privately took to calling Adele "our Bible savant." It was his derisive way of excusing his own inadequacy in this regard.

Worse, about a month after my little altercation with her, Vic woke me early one weekend morning to inform me it was Sunday. Unimpressed with this intelligence, I rolled over and went back to sleep. Not five minutes later, he shook me again and ordered me to get dressed for church.

Now Vic had grown up Southern Baptist back in Louisiana, but I'd never seen him set foot in a church the whole nine years I'd known him, including the day he'd opted to have a justice of the peace marry us. My own father had once been a loyal Lutheran, but he'd spurned the church after seeing a deacon take money out of the offering plate. It seemed Daddy had attributed that man's actions to God. The point is, my parents were devoutly opposed to such "hypocrisy" as church. And, married from such a young age to an apparent apostate, I'd never developed any curiosity of my own.

But on this Sunday morning, as per Vic's inexplicable instructions, I put on what I thought a woman ought to wear to church and then went in to help dress our two children; Vic had roused them from bed with the same cryptic command he'd given me. At three, Katy didn't need any explanation, but my eight-year-old son was mightily confused. When I found him in nothing but his boxers, staring into a dresser drawer and pawing at the cowlick that always spoiled a neat part of his otherwise sedate brown hair, I sat him down on the bed and went to pick out a pair of trousers and his nicest shirt from the closet.

"Mother, what is church like?" he asked, still twirling his hair.

In my mind's eye, I pictured the plain little Methodist church that I passed on the way to Clay's school each morning, with its dark slits of stained glass and deserted parking lot. But I couldn't get close enough to see inside, so I tried a different tack.

"Well, you remember when we went to see How Green Was My Valley a few months ago?" I asked, and he nodded. "That nice man who helped the little boy learn to walk again after he got sick was a minister. At church you listen to ministers like him give sermons. Oh, and you sing hymns too."

Clay mulled that over while he pulled on his pants. "OK, but what's a sermon?" he persisted.

"It's a bunch of stories about how God helps us to be good," I answered cleanly. Who knew? This seemed as plausible as anything, and, again, it fit my recollection of what I'd heard movie ministers say.

"So, what's a hymn then?" Clay asked.

"It's a song about God."

He thought on that while I licked my fingers and tried to mash down his prickly part. "I think we sing hymns at school sometimes after we say the Pledge of Allegiance," he said. "You know—about how God blesses America."

Hmm. "Well, most hymns are more about God than about America, I think. But that's the general idea."

Clay took this all in and was satisfied, trusting me in the bland way only Clay could. With this groundwork laid, he was ready enough to face the next few hours without angst. Not so his mother.

Vic informed me on the way out to the car that we weren't going to any meager little neighborhood church; we were going to the massive new Baptist church downtown—First Central Baptist Church. Now that word Baptist scared me quite enough, and the fact that this was in some manner the first or the center of them did little to ease my qualms. The only thing Daddy had been more skeptical of than church itself was the Baptist church—"everyman's placebo" he'd called it. Somehow, the same prejudice had seeped into me.

But the beast itself turned out to be harmless in most

respects. Although the sermon was pretty loud and ominous, I dismissed this as theatrics contrived for the benefit of those in the audience who were obviously of a low order. I only suffered any real discomfort at the very end of the service when Pastor Jeb Cash demanded that those of us "without Jesus in our hearts" invite him in by marching up the aisle to the front of the velvety blue sanctuary and praying out loud. I was puzzling over the conceivable meanings of these phrases when I noticed people popping out of their pews all over the auditorium. One by one, they streamed up into "Brother Jeb's" welcoming arms while he paced the stage, seductively rebroadcasting little snippets of his invitation between hugs.

Before long, my own son—ever literal and obedient—tried to squeeze past me to reach the aisle, his blue eyes wide and watery and far away. But when I grabbed his arm and whispered for him to "Stay put!", he turned back to his place, close to me again and clearly relieved.

That afternoon Vic caught me in the backyard folding sheets off the laundry line. "I guess you can't take the tailor's daughter out of the executive's wife," he couldn't help jibing me.

"Something you need?" I asked.

"Yeah. Why'd you stop him?"

"Stop who?" I still hadn't gotten completely accustomed to the Spartan way that Vic often conversed with me.

"Clay. Why didn't you let him go down?"

The absurdity of this question completely nonplussed me. Vic might as well have asked why I hadn't sold my son into slavery or flung him into the middle of a bank robbery. I'd taken it for granted that Vic saw this in the same definite way I did—so definite that it was not even worth talking about. Now I just stammered and tried to imagine what he could possibly be thinking. "Why would I have let him?" I asked finally. "He's old enough to make his own decision."

Once again, I wasn't sure what language Vic was speaking. "What do you mean, 'decision'? He wasn't deciding anything. He was hypnotized! He was just going along with what some big foghorn told him to do. I should think you'd be more worried that he even considered 'going down'?"

"I did it when I was only seven," Vic said, jutting his jaw out and narrowing his eyes.

I sighed deeply and stared at the sudden stranger inhabiting Vic's body. How could I argue about such a riddle? Still, this was Clay we were talking about, and I felt his only line of defense. Crossing my arms and planting both feet, I asked as calmly as I could, "'It' what, Vic? What is the 'it' you're talking about? I don't understand."

He seemed befuddled by this frontal attack on his terms. I watched him grapple with various responses. Apparently, none of those he could articulate were immune from some similar challenge. I thought for a moment that I'd stopped Vic cold and protected Clay from this vague monster, whatever "it" was. But then Vic's grimace smoothed out, and his face set in childlike disregard. "We're going back until Clay walks the aisle," he said. Then he walked back inside.

<u>January 16, 2001</u>

For the next few days I was beside myself. I could hardly let Clay out of my sight or bear Vic in it. Nothing I'd experienced in life to date helped me to embrace or even comprehend what

Vic wanted Clay to do, and I didn't dare ask for help or clarification from anyone who Vic knew for fear it would get back to him.

It's not that I thought Vic's aisle-walking would harm Clay exactly, for Vic himself didn't seem to have been harmed by it. In fact—as I mulled the matter over in the tub, in the car, cooking dinner, and chasing after Katy—I realized it could not amount to too much if in nine years I'd never noticed any mark it had left on Vic. But then perhaps that's what so bothered me. Vic seemed intent on Clay's publicly declaring the naked emperor fully clothed. I worried that such highly sanctioned fraud would wreck a steadfast little soul like Clay's, which had already weathered a very hard truth and yet bravely anchored itself to the real world. Yes, I thought Vic had done quite enough to wreck Clay's soul already.

My great fear was that Vic would pressure Clay, and my son might perceive it as one last chance to penetrate his father's stony indifference. That's why I watched them both so closely, anxious that they should never be alone.

On Friday of that week, Vic came home early from work just about the time Clay usually got in from school. Adele was still there, having volunteered to stay late and teach me how to make a new casserole she'd discovered at a potluck dinner the week before. Vic ducked into the kitchen and asked if Clay was home.

"He should be in shortly," I answered, feeling like I was tipping off the spider to the arrival of the fly.

Vic watched but didn't say anything for five minutes or so while Adele and I chopped onions and fried some sausage. Just as we were about to pour all the ingredients in together, Vic declared, "We attended First Central Baptist last Sunday, Adele." This pronouncement, smacking as it did of a challenge, so unnerved me that I let a glass measuring cup full of cream slip out of my hand and crash to the kitchen floor.

Just then we heard the front door open, and Clay clattered in shouting, "Mother, I'm home!" Vic brushed a spot of cream off his suit pants and headed toward Clay's voice, leaving Adele and me to wipe up the mess that bound me to the kitchen, out of earshot of whatever they might say. My hand shook as I picked glass out of the ivory goop that Adele slopped up with a hand towel.

"It's OK, missy. We'll get it cleaned up. Mr. Greene weren't mad at you for a-droppin' it."

"It's not that, Adele." I felt a little silly, being so overwrought about this thing, but I so fiercely wanted to protect Clay just then that I couldn't calm down. I grabbed at a piece of broken glass, and when the ragged edge dug deep into my thumb, I jumped backward and lost my balance. I landed on my bottom about a foot north of the cream, the shard protruding from my thumb a good half inch. I yanked it out and started crying.

"What . . . has . . . got . . . in . . . to . . . you?" Adele demanded. She stood up, dropped her soggy towel in the sink, and stared at me as she wiped her hands on her apron.

I couldn't hold it in any longer. For five days I'd longed to tell Adele about last Sunday. If anyone could help me figure out what "it" was, Adele could. "I'm worried about Vic in there with Clay," I confessed. "I'm afraid he's telling Clay that he needs to walk down the aisle at the end of the church service on Sunday and pray with that . . . that . . . Brother Jeb!"

"You mean to accept Christ? This Sunday? Does little Clay know anything about Jesus, Miss Jo?"

"Not that I know of."

"Does Mr. Greene know anything about Jesus?"

"I don't know. He told me that he did that aisle-walking thing when he was seven, but I've never heard him say a word about Jesus."

"Has you and Mr. Vic ever been to church before Sunday, child?"

"Never, Adele. And I'll be frank with you. I'm not sure I ever want to go again."

"Well," she said, untying her apron and laying it on the counter, "that's just crazy talk. You don't have no idea what church is yet if you don't know nothin' about Jesus. But we can talk about that later. I'm goin' in there and settin' him straight."

"Oh, no, Adele! You can't say anything to Vic. He'll be furious if he knows I told you about this."

"Right now we have to think about little Clay, Miss Jo. That boy don't need to be herded down no rabbit trails by his confused daddy. Just give me a crack at Mr. Greene. And it won't hurt none for you to be a-prayin' while I talk to him."

Sure enough, Vic had cornered Clay in his bedroom—the back porch we'd enclosed off the den. Adele and I crept up to the open door and I heard Clay ask, "You really want me to?"

"Yes, son, I think you should. I did when I was about your same age." Vic said this in a tender, paternal tone that I doubt Clay had heard from him before.

"Well, what does it mean for me to do it?"

"Uh, . . . well, . . . it means you'll go to heaven when you die," Vic managed.

Had I not lived through last Sunday, I would not have believed that my otherwise rational husband could utter such foolish words. Would he next have me wearing a garlic necklace to ward off evil spirits? Outraged, I was about to step around Adele and risk charging in when she wrapped her long, firm fingers around my elbow and rooted me there.

"Why does it mean that?" Clay asked. This calmed me considerably. I thought it showed a healthy, grown-up suspicion hinting that Vic's fatherly massaging might be backfiring.

"Because . . . because it's in the Bible that we have to accept these things if we want to go to heaven," Vic said.

"But what things?"

"All that the pastor talked about on Sunday, Clay. Weren't you listening? Why did you try to go to the front if you weren't listening?"

"I don't know. Cause . . . he was yelling . . . and all those other people were doing what he said . . . I don't know," Clay stammered.

"Well, he was right! You do need to do it. You need to go down there and get this taken care of. OK?"

"Wait!" Clay cried, "I remember what he said now. He talked about Jesus and said we have to accept him into our hearts. But I guess I don't really know what that means."

Adele tightened her grip on me. She leaned forward not to miss a word of Vic's answer, and I saw her lips moving in silent conversation.

"Right. Jesus. Let's see . . . eh . . . you ask him into your heart when you go pray with the pastor," Vic said, repeating the recipe as if this clarified everything.

"I don't understand," Clay said for the umpteenth time.

"Well, dang it, Clay, if you're that dense—"

It was then Adele pounced, silent and sure as any jungle cat. One second she stood next to me, digging her powerful fingers into my forearm, and the next she was smack in the middle of Clay's bedroom, blocking my boy from his father's inadequacies.

"I really need to tidy up this room before I run off, Mr. Greene. It's Friday, you know, and if I let it go till Monday, it'll be twice the work. I trust I'm not interrupting nothin' that can't wait." Though this sailed right out of Adele, I noted that she hadn't told a single lie.

Inspired by her ingenuity, I plunged in right after her. Vic almost fell off the bed in surprise. I couldn't tell whether he gaped at us with anger or relief. "Yes," I said, "why don't you do this room and Katy's before you go, Adele. Just attend to what shows."

Clay and Vic seemed frozen on the bed. I simply sat down between them, and the three of us watched Adele put away Clay's clutter. While she worked, she chattered as if she were entertaining us around a campfire. "You know, Mr. Greene, it's funny you should have mentioned to me that you went to First Central last week," she began, slapping third-grade readers onto a bookshelf, one by one. "Have I ever told you that my husband Isaiah is a pastor at the little Baptist church in our part of town? Of course, he don't make enough to do just that. He also has a little mechanic shop down the street. Anyway, I've heard him say that the pastor over there at First Central is a fine man and a good preacher . . . most of the time. Isaiah says the only problem with him is he sometimes don't explain the gospel too well, and lots of people go outta there thinking they've done something to make their salvation sure when they really don't know much at all about Jesus' sacrifice of hisself for their sins."

Vic actually blushed when Adele said this, but she took pains not to notice, dropping down to her knees and sticking her head under the bed to retrieve Clay's toys and dirty clothes.

"Isaiah says it ain't their fault," she went on, slightly muffled, from under the bed. "These folks just go to church a-trustin' in God's man; but he's still just a man, and all men make mistakes. Sometimes seems that the bigger the opportunity to get things right, the worse we trip up, don't you think? Anyway, a man can make heaps o' huge blunders with thousands of people a-listenin' and relyin' on him to lead 'em to God."

Adele then shifted to the closet and began moving things indiscriminately from shelf to shelf. Vic, Clay, and I sat lined up along the bed, captivated. "Isaiah says that Pastor Jeb is usually vague about the sin part, which as you know, Mr. Greene, is the whole reason we need a savior like Jesus to start out with! How can you understand why it's such an amazin' thing that the Son of God would come to earth and let hisself be crucified for us, unless you first understand that we're all sinful and beyond hope without this grace? We all turn our backs on God—over and over—and have to be forgiven and fixed if we hope to spend eternity with our maker. Jesus suffered on the cross to pay the penalty for our sins so's we can come to God free and clear of our proud guilt. Did Pastor Jeb say that part when y'all went?"

Getting no intelligible answer, Adele flitted around looking for something else to do. She snatched up an old T-shirt of Clay's and started dusting the furniture with it. "Isaiah says that tiptoein' over the punch line is common at some of those big churches that has what he calls 'hefty reputations' to think about. He doesn't mean no disrespect, though, cause he says they also do lots of good. You just have to be careful, wherever you go. The Bible is the only place the whole truth is said with nothin' that's heavy left out or deformed."

With that, Adele seemed satisfied, though none of us, still, had said a word in reply. "Well, I guess that's all I can do here," she chirped, tossing the T-shirt into Clay's dirty-clothes basket. "I just thought I ought to tell you what Isaiah's told me, Mr. Greene. I wouldn't a-felt right keepin' it from you. But if you want to know anymore than that, you'll have to ask him."

How could there possibly have been more? I held my breath, waiting for Vic to say something and hoping it wouldn't be cruel.

Finally, finally, he said, "Thank you, Adele. That's helpful information. Maybe I would like to talk to Isaiah sometime about the good and bad of organized religion. Have a nice weekend." He stood then and walked out, leaving me to fill my lungs with the first really satisfying breath I'd taken in the past half hour.

Adele walked over and mussed Clay's hair. "You can talk to Isaiah, too, if you want, Clay. And you can talk to me anytime, you hear? Now I'll go and touch up Katy's room. You think she's ready to get up from her nap, Miss Jo?"

"Oh, Adele, I'll do Katy's room. You go on home to your own family," I answered. "And, Adele, be sure and thank Isaiah for me. OK?"

January 20, 2001

Yesterday, I think I nearly died. I woke up at around seven feeling cold and nauseous, sure I was going to vomit. So I tried to get myself to the toilet. Instead, I flew straight out of the bed onto the floor, and I lay there unable to move for almost an hour while I got colder and colder. I remember staring at the ceiling and wondering if dying felt like freezing. I thought that it wasn't as bad as I'd expected. If this was dying, then maybe I could do it after all. Maybe, if I was already halfway there, in fact, I should just give myself over to it. But I couldn't commit.

Eventually I turned my head and the phone on my night-stand came into view. The cord was within my reach, and after a time I managed to tug hard enough to pull the whole contrap-tion crashing down on the floor next to me. Then I saved up enough energy to call Clay's house. Lillian answered the phone, and she adopted her usual wary tone when she recognized my voice. I rather enjoyed informing her that I was lying on my bedroom floor unable to get up. It forced her to soften a bit, and she finally offered to call the EMS and meet them here. Saved by Lillian. Imagine!

Chapter 7

Katy

On the morning of Mother's fall, I took a cup of coffee into my office and settled down with it in front of the computer. As I flipped the On switch and waited for it to boot up, I listened to the ragged snoring that pulsated from the adjoining bedroom in which Eliot had been burrowed since mid-October, refusing to take his medications. The wall that we shared seemed to close in on me with his turbulent, full-bodied inhales, and expand back out during the intervening calm stretches. I focused on the "whir" of my processor and tried to forget he was even in the house.

For the next several hours, I researched cases interpreting the word *endanger* as used in Texas's worker health and safety regulations. My findings largely cut against the position I'd been told to argue by the law firm that had contracted me to write a trial brief. Still, I had a few leads on favorable Arkansas and Missouri decisions interpreting similar laws, and I hoped I might be able to patch together some reasonably reputable argument out of those.

When I shut my computer down at around noon for lunch, the wall that separated me from my husband and his latest funk had become but a wall again—silent and inert. Hungry, I wandered to the kitchen thinking that I might catch Eliot there in the act of caring for himself. But all I found were three Popsicle sticks stuck to the counter like the slashes of a Z left by the mysterious sword of Zorro. This was Eliot's disturbed way of telling me that he was still interested in eating but wasn't yet ready to come out of his room. I'd just pried the sticks off the counter when the phone rang.

"Mom, it's Sam. Listen, everything seems to be all right now, but Gammy has been at the hospital all morning. She had a problem with her blood pressure that they think was caused by the way her various medications were interacting. Her heart was beating so slow that she couldn't even get up off the floor. They've got it under control now, though."

"When did all this happen?"

"Gosh, several hours ago. We've been trying to call you, but your phone's been busy. We figured you were online. I was even on my way over to tell you, but they needed me to go by Gammy's house and pick up her pills so the ER doctors could better evaluate her condition."

"Yes, I've been working since about eight. I suppose I'll have to figure out some way to afford a second phone line if this keeps up. So, where is Gammy now, Sam?"

"She's still in Cesar Chavez Memorial Hospital. Room 515. They want to keep her overnight to be sure she's OK."

"Well, I'd better get over there."

"Yeah. Uncle Clay's out of town, and you were tied up, so only Lillian and I have been with her all morning."

"Lillian?"

"Yes. Lillian is the first one Gammy got through to. She sent the EMS over and met them at Gammy's. Then she called my office from the hospital when she couldn't reach you."

"Well, I'm sure your grandmother appreciated that! It's probably time to find some safer living situation for her. Too much can happen with her living alone in the condition she's in. And being at Lillian's mercy just isn't good enough."

"Actually, Lillian was very good to Gammy today. She even took Ginger home with her. But as a general principle, you might be right."

"Well, we can talk more about that later. Right now I'd better leave for the hospital. Thank you, dear."

I'd heard the telltale click on the line just a few seconds after I'd answered the phone. By eavesdropping, you see, a hermit can monitor life outside the hermitage without ever sacrificing his cover. It's like reverse wiretapping—listening out instead of listening in. Usually, for Eliot, listening was enough.

❦

When I got home from the hospital at around seven that evening, I went into my office and worked uninterrupted on my brief until midnight. Then I phoned the hospital to make sure no one had tried to call while I'd been online. Everything was fine; Mother was asleep.

I was ready for sleep myself, so I got a snack and headed toward my bedroom. Halfway there, something deafening stopped me—the silence from Eliot's room. No snoring, not even any rustling, in the whole five hours I'd been home. I decided to check his door, though he always kept it locked. It wasn't this time. And Eliot wasn't there.

❦

Three days later, the Houston police called to report that they'd finally located my husband in Louisiana, where he'd spent each night on a riverboat that catered to Texas gamblers willing to ease over the state line to indulge in a little blackjack or roulette. Since we only had the one car, which I'd taken to the hospital, Eliot had taxied to our bank, then to the bus station, and had ridden a Greyhound to Lake Charles. There he'd lost the whole $9,200 he'd withdrawn from our account—everything I had in savings—plus the $7,000 cash advance he'd finagled out of Visa.

Texas is a community property state. That means that any spouse, merely by "borrowing" a credit card from his wife's wallet or nail polish drawer, is free to spend all that she's managed to eke out as the only steady contributor to the family's upkeep. That startling legal principle ought to make Texans squeamish about marrying recklessly, but it hadn't held true in my case.

And now I had to go and get him. Much as I was tempted to leave Eliot out in the marshes with the alligators, I couldn't trust him for an extra five minutes by himself in a state that boasts attractions such as floating blackjack. I flew across the border, wondering for the thousandth time in my life how I could afford to stay married to him for even one more day.

Not until I neared Lake Charles did a ray of empathy threaten to penetrate my thinking. I battled this softness. I told myself I didn't care if Eliot's spree had mostly been the desperate act of a very sick man. Empathy had never helped with Eliot. I'd tried that first—for nine long years—and all I'd gotten for it was bankruptcy and the broken rib I'd had to hide from my father. Mother, as I recall, had insisted on that.

When I drove up to the Waffle House where I'd agreed to pick him up, Eliot ventured out with his head hung so low that I could see only his cleft chin. Somewhere along the way he'd apparently rented himself a room with a shower, and he wore a relatively nice sports jacket that was only a size or two too small. When he was actually seated next to me, I took one good long look at him and tried not to register the tears that drizzled down his cheeks onto his lapels. "Nine long years . . . bankruptcy . . . a broken rib," I chanted the mute miles away. One had to be cold sometimes—stony—if one hoped to survive. Above all, I reminded myself, "Empathy never helps."

About ten miles from home, he spoke to me, and I could do nothing about that either. "Katy," he said, like a person with some right to use my name though he'd stolen my money. "Katy, I just wanted to make a contribution to . . . to . . . I wanted to show you that I'm not completely contemptible."

"Don't you dare try to blame this on me," I shot back.

"If I could just have made us some money—at least enough to pay for a second phone line for your computer—I thought you might care as much about my condition as you do your mother's. I just couldn't think of any other way to earn it. Not quick enough."

Where would I begin to respond to that? And what would have been the point? I reached across the physical distance between us and gave his hand one very brief pat. It required every ounce of self-will I still commanded. But it did nothing to bridge the vast emotional and mental universes that separated us. I had long ago lost any desire to reach across those.

As we pulled into the driveway, I pondered the hours I'd have to spend on the computer over the next few months to make restitution for Eliot's newest indiscretions. I saw that a second phone line would be a necessity now, and the irony of that almost started me laughing. How else was I to stay sane?

CHAPTER 8

Jo

January 27, 2001

I worry these days that Katy is trying to do more saving than a mortal is capable of. First Eliot; now me. What a tenacious woman my daughter is! Where in the world did she get that? In her shoes, I'd have sloughed Eliot off long ago. I say that even though I endured Lenny for nineteen years. But my reasons were less respectable. Katy believes it her fate to absorb all of Eliot's wreckage and so spare the world. I just didn't want to be alone. She has embraced the terribleness of her commitment, while I pretended mine wasn't terrible at all. Her strategy is surely superior, but I fear that some situations are just too malignant to be lifted up, no matter what spin we put on them. It warrants some investigation.

January 29, 2001

As she grew up, Katy naturally folded the rest of us into discrete orbits around her—each one attracted by a different intensity of her magnetic pull. I guess mine was a tight, circular orbit. Clay circled loosely, lumbering along at a grateful distance. And Vic rocketed around Katy on an incorrigible ellipse that nearly singed her as he came in close and then flung far off into space.

With Katy, Vic put aside his prickly manner and let her in where no one else was welcome. In the evenings she demanded his lap, nudging his actuarial tables out of her way until he hoisted her up in lieu of his work. He'd toss it all on the floor and set about arranging her blonde hair into braids. Or he'd ask her about her day, commiserating with her concerns over this or that playmate who'd refused to share her dolls or who wouldn't take her turn as the evil witch in their after-school reenactments of various fairy tales. He'd let her tell him the entire plots of such stories, showing the appropriate emotions even when she forgot critical details that explained the action. These were the times I could imagine that Vic himself had been a child.

Once when Katy was in first grade, Vic left a business meeting to drive over to her school and accept the kiss she'd refused him that morning for not letting her wear her tutu and ballet slippers to school. It seems she'd started grieving her cold heart almost the moment Vic had left for work, and she was inconsolable by the time she got to her classroom. Nothing but Daddy's cheek could set things right.

Two years later, Vic cheered Katy's performance in the third-grade Christmas play as if she were Ethel Merman on Broadway in Annie Get Your Gun. Katy played a second-tier angel—one of five girls in the angel chorus who were to flutter gloriously among the shepherds in the field. Even the barn animals had bigger parts. Still, Vic waved and whistled so obnoxiously while Katy was on stage that I was relieved when her appearance lasted only a few seconds.

But their favorite moments together were at bedtime, when Vic tucked Katy in and serenaded her with Cajun love songs until she somehow fell asleep. He sang loud and without regard for the tunes, intent on mocking what didn't come naturally to him. As a little girl, Katy giggled at all Vic's squeaky high notes and the yodels that resulted whenever he deigned to scout out an actual melody.

Through it all, Katy mostly did just what we wanted and expected, though always in a thoughtful way that made it seem like her own idea. She was the child we had planned, loved, nurtured, and shared. Adele, who had early on sensed the terrible disconnect between Vic and Clay, said that God had given us a reprieve with Katy, that she was a beam of light to help draw us out of our darkness. When I asked her what darkness she was talking about, she didn't miss a beat. "Why, the darkness we're all born into, Miss Jo, 'cause Adam and Eve turned on the Lord. It's the shadow of death that now covers us like a blanket and keeps us from seein' God." She flailed her huge black arms skyward when she said this, and then smiled at me comfortingly.

"Why would God want us to be in darkness, Adele?" I couldn't resist.

"He don't want it, Miss Jo. He allows it 'cause he gave us a choice to love him or not. We chose not to, so he sent us out of the light. He condemned us to die, and now we live in death's shadow where we can't help but do evil."

"OK . . . and so how is Katy a light?"

"Well, God is fixed on getting his children back into the light with him. Jesus came to open up the way out of the darkness. And from the start to the finish of our lives, God is busy sending other, littler lights to draw us along through the dark to his Son. They're like beautiful lanterns that we want to touch and admire and put in our houses 'cause they come from another world. We keep lookin' for more of 'em 'cause they seem to promise to take us there. And then one day, if we look back, we can make out a path behind us, just as plain as the nose on this here face. It's lit entirely by these otherworldly lanterns, and then it dawns on us that we've traveled down it. There we are, 'bout to step out o' the shadows and into pure light."

My daughter—a lantern!

February 2, 2001

There came a time—around her eleventh birthday—when Katy quit asking Vic to tuck her in. It seemed a perfectly natural transition to me, just as she had abruptly stopped seeking my breast as an infant, and at two-and-one-quarter had determined ever after to sit on a toilet rather than prolong her carefree diaper life. I kidded Vic that he couldn't expect Katy to pretend to be tone deaf forever, but he insisted on labeling this baby step toward independence a "problem" and brooded that it might be symptomatic of a simmering prepubescent rebellion that would thwart us in the coming years. It was so unlike him to think the worst of his daughter in this way that I knew he was deeply hurt. He'd been flung off into the outward-bound portion of his long, flat orbit.

Perhaps it had to be. Katy was an attractive teenager—as tall as her father, with long shapely legs and a blonde ponytail that captivated the opposite sex. Once she entered high school, there were always boys underfoot around our house. Even Clay's friends, four or five years older than Katy, seemed to stop over more often after they got a glimpse of her. It was all Adele and I could do to keep her supplied with party dresses for the many dances she got invited to as soon as we convinced Vic to let her date. I still have a banging bag full of them stowed away upstairs, and that's just the remnant after years of donations.

I remember wondering if Vic's exile to the outer reaches during Katy's adolescence was her way of giving her boyfriends a break. It was not so much that Vic would have bad-mouthed them if Katy had asked for his intimate, trusted opinion. Rather, I think Katy worried that her own barometer for measuring the value of a man was too likely to be prejudiced by Vic's always being near at hand. That, at least, was how I chose to view it at the time.

February 3, 2002

Too soon, Eliot came into our lives. Katy started talking about him sometime during her junior year of high school. I discovered her crush in the way I discovered many things about my children over the years—by eavesdropping on their conversations with Adele. I say eavesdropping, but really there were only so many places to be in our little Byway house, and you could overhear what was said in most of them from anyone of the others.

This Wednesday afternoon, Katy was home early because her pep squad had been excused from their last two classes to decorate the gym for a football rally the next day. As the head Pep-ette, Katy had herded them through ahead of schedule and then gotten a ride home with one of the ballplayers they'd be idolizing the next day. This boy, named Eddie Blunt, was "nice but bor-ing," Katy confided, as she held the colander for Adele to dump in the spaghetti she'd been boiling for our dinner. "He's just like all the others. None of them ever wants to talk. Practically the only time they say anything is to try to get me into the backseat with them. Adele, I'm so tired of it."

Adele ran cold water over the pasta for a long time, probably stalling to keep herself from screeching her outrage about the backseat part. From the den, where I'd found some clean towels handy to fold while I listened, I'd boned in on the same inadvertent disclosure.

"You haven't met anybody who's not like that?" Adele asked finally. "I know for a fact that some men like to talk, 'cause I got one of 'em. You just need to be patient, sugar. . . . Oh, and stay out of backseats." I couldn't have said it better myself.

"I would not dream of giving one of them the satisfaction!" Katy squealed. "Surely you don't think I'd roll over just because they flex their muscles at me and offer me rides? The man I give myself to will have to deserve me. I want to be charmed, Adele, not beat over the head with a club and dragged off to a cave."

That sturdy, uncluttered declaration flung me back to my own high school days and the steamy underside of our gymnasium bleachers. There, watching as I crawled out from under adjusting my dress and smirking at the caveman I'd let tousle me, was my incredible, self-respecting daughter. Accusing me. Her statements scorched me from the inside out like I'd spontaneously combusted. I was ashamed and proud all at the same time. But mostly ashamed. How grateful I was to be on the invisible outskirts of this conversation.

Katy must have stepped in closer to reveal the next part, or maybe it was the breathy way she suddenly spoke that made it so hard for me to make her out.

"There is one boy I've noticed," she cooed. The cagey, helpless way she'd said "one boy" was so unlike the crisp manner in which she said most things that I dropped the washcloth I was holding and inched closer to the kitchen pass-through.

"What's he like?" Adele asked.

"Well, he's intelligent. And I don't just mean he makes good grades. I mean that he says intelligent, interesting things. And he's very funny . . . clever you might say."

"Has he noticed you?" Adele voiced my next question.

"I think he may have noticed me. But, you know, he has a girlfriend right now. They're very tight, and he seems loyal to her. I like that about him."

"So, it's clearly best not to put any eggs in that basket," Adele counseled. "You don't want to be the bustin'-up sort of girl. And I promise you, sugar, he's not the only one. Don't get in no hurry. You're only sixteen and time is what you got."

"Hmm, right. . . Adele, did I tell you his name? Eliot Ardelean. It's pronounced AR-DEH-LEH-AHN. It's Romanian. You know, one of those poor Eastern European countries being bullied by the Soviet Union. Isn't that romantic?"

February 6, 2001

When it turned out that Eliot Ardelean had in fact developed quite a keen interest in Katy, and that his loyalty to his girlfriend was not nearly so firm as Katy had surmised, her estimation of him did not diminish one whit. We met him on the night that he escorted her to his senior prom.

Although Vic had not been privy to the spaghetti-straining conversation in the kitchen, and I had studiously avoided relaying it to him, I could see that he was on high alert the night Eliot first called on our daughter. A circling father senses these things, even from the cold end of his orbit. So, while I helped Katy curl her hair, lent her a few choice pieces of my jewelry, and ironed whatever needed to be ironed, Vic silently helped himself to two highballs rather than the one that he usually indulged in before dinner. Katy flitted about the house, oblivious of Vic's deteriorating mood or any damage she might be doing to the calm, poised image her parents had of her. She kept checking herself in the mirror to ensure that the last additions to her coiffure were still in place, and giggled at the slightest provocation, as when she overshot her cheek and rained down powder on the mustached snout of our schnauzer, Isabel. At precisely the moment when I'd gauged Vic was about to start yelling, the doorbell rang.

He was nearest the door and lurched for it. The boy outside—in black tuxedo pants and bow tie, a yellow cummerbund, and a white dinner jacket—at first smiled expectantly into Vic's rough stare. Under one arm he carried a clear plastic corsage box through which I could see baby's breath surrounding three yellow roses, each in a different phase of bloom. It would set off dramatically against the cream bodice and butter-colored skirt of Katy's ball dress. I let myself form a first impression: "This boy is smooth."

Eliot Ardelean stepped inside before Vic actually invited him. He even looked a bit miffed that Vic had been so tardy in moving aside. In response, Vic somehow assumed a more hostile stance and pushed the door closed from several feet away. It smacked shut, barely missing Eliot on its flight.

The boy jumped back as if to save himself, and then turned on Vic with his fists clenched. This was the precarious situation—achieved in under two minutes with nary a word—that Katy floated into. She reached for her father's arm first.

"Daddy, let me present my date, Eliot Ardelean," she purred, just as warm and easy as if she'd interrupted a joke or a neighborly handshake. Then, standing by her father's side, Katy lustily took stock of the young man opposite her.

"Oh, Eliot, you look so handsome! I think we match perfectly, just as you said we would. This is my father and mother, Mr. and Mrs. Greene."

Katy's shimmering compliment and introduction seemed more in keeping with Eliot's script of this meeting, and he graciously opted to respond in kind. "How do you do, Mr. Greene, Mrs. Greene. Katy, you look gorgeous," he said, daring to kiss her cheek in front of her still mute, rigid father. "This is for you. May I pin it on?"

The two of them really took no further notice of us. I dutifully snapped a picture or two, and a few minutes later they were gone.

Over dinner that night, Vic repeatedly harrumphed but said little else. His most articulate utterance came during dessert, when he dragged his tired eyes from the cake plate upon which they'd been fixed for several minutes and observed ominously, "That boy is smooth."

February 8, 2001

A year later, on the night of Katy's graduation, we had a fancy family dinner for her at home before the ceremony. We were all wedged around the table in our tiny Byway dining room—Vic, me, Clay (in his first year of the MBA program at the University of Houston), Madelyn (Clay's fiancée de jour), Katy, and Eliot, whom Vic had allowed there only because Katy had begged him for this, her special occasion. I suspected that Eliot, too, had needed a good deal of coaxing, as he was none too fond of Vic's usual contemptuous treatment of him.

Since his own graduation a year earlier, Eliot had done little but try to prove to Katy what a promising fellow he was. In the credit column: Eliot was intelligent, funny, and Katy adored him. She also claimed he'd been gifted with many other talents to which he would one day apply himself and thereby make a real contribution to the world. All Vic and I saw was an unemployed kid who expected the applause first, and to contribute only after that.

I remember that I felt light-headed all through that dinner. I couldn't quite catch a breath, not a big enough one. I tried to disguise this by bustling—running off to the kitchen more times than was necessary, ever forgetting two of the three things I went in for.

As the dinner progressed, the room became increasingly pregnant with things not being said. I didn't want them to be said. Vic didn't want them to be said. And without a word between us, we somehow collaborated and managed to fend them off all the way through dessert.

I had just refilled coffee cups and thought we were safe. The ceremony would start in an hour, and we had to leave for it in ten minutes. That's when Eliot somehow had the nerve to stand up at our dinner table as if to address Vic and me. Everything about him was trembling, so much so that if I hadn't been as furiously fixed on what he was about to say, I might have wanted to prop him up. Though no such urge overtook me, it did Katy.

She grabbed his hand on one of its violent passes by her face and pulled herself up to stand next to him. Suddenly it was them, instead of him. She had chosen a side. Something about this felt vaguely familiar, but I couldn't bother with that then.

"Mr. Greene," Eliot began, "Mrs. Greene." He stopped, gulped. Apparently, he could not go on.

I saw Katy squeeze his hand, but to no avail. It seemed that the tremendous hostility with which we had responded just to his standing up at our table had paralyzed him. Finally Katy got exasperated and took over. "Mother, Daddy," she said, "Eliot and I are getting married. We'd give anything for you to be happy about it, but it's OK if you're not. We're doing it anyway."

Now, it was Vic's habit to meet the most important moments of life with silence, and this was no exception. We all knew what his silence meant. The truth is, Vic's face was so expressive that he didn't have to translate it into words.

Katy turned to face him squarely. "We're doing it tonight," she said.

Once this registered, Vic, too, stood up. Still looking at Katy, he said, "Eliot, I want you to leave now. We'll be along shortly." For once his face was blank, like an iron mask had slammed down over it.

Eliot lurched from the table. Tugging his hand free of Katy's, he glared once at an oblivious Vic and rushed from the room.

All hell broke loose then. Vic found his voice with a vengeance. He let fly with every shortcoming we'd ever noticed in Eliot, and then some. He promised her that life with him would be tepid at best, more likely a nightmare. "That boy will never, ever be good enough for you, honey," he concluded—I thought on a very strong note.

But, as I said, Katy was always thoughtful and self-possessed, and she hadn't made this decision without holding it up to the light and examining all the angles. The thing is, some of the shadows had eluded her. We talked her out of eloping that night but not out of the marriage.

Occasionally, living longer really does give us more wisdom. How I wish it hadn't been so in this case. Her dad and I had foreseen what she discovered the hard way, through years of working long hours while Eliot struggled to "find himself," and then being left with the whole burden of child rearing and bill paying and making their home seem normal to two children who wondered why their father frequently sat alone in a dark room, refusing to go out.

Seth and Samantha have definitely been Katy's bright spots. She made them what they are almost entirely despite Eliot. And that is saying a great deal, both for who they grew up to be, and for what it cost Katy to deposit them into adulthood so whole and well.

Perhaps she is a lantern from another world.

February 12, 2001

Maybe I'll take all that "lantern" stuff back. For three weeks now, Katy has been tormenting me about my blood pressure. She refers to my crisis last month as the "idiot doctor incident" and asks me about it every chance she gets. "Do you feel OK, Mother?" "What are you going to do if something like that idiot doctor incident happens again?" "Are you weak today?" "Well, what about last time? Did you have any clue before the idiot doctor incident that such a thing might be about to happen?" "Have you felt that way again at anytime since the idiot doctor incident?" Thanks to her, the aftermath has proved almost worse than the "incident" itself!

Didn't someone famous once say that every person's greatest strength is also her greatest weakness when it's not corralled and put toward a good cause? Maybe that was one of Adele's proverbs. At any rate, my bossy daughter could be its poster child. Where, I wonder, is she going with this?

Chapter 9 ❧

Katy

Considering how blithely Mother sidestepped responsibility for her own health, you might have thought she'd grown up in a small town attended by a country doctor who could faithfully recite the medical histories of each and every person under his care. Generationally, economically, and certainly temperamentally, she was among those who still expect that their doctors will gather and convey whatever information is necessary to make precise, comprehensive diagnoses and achieve quick, full cures. These folks never seem to notice that their doctors are preoccupied with shortening appointments and minimizing patient chitchat, hoping to compensate for the fees that the insurance companies routinely deny them.

Mother had long flaunted her commitment to this delusion. She acted as if her willful reverence in and of itself raised her doctors above the fray and engendered their handling of her case, at least, with bygone fidelity and care. Typically, when I talked with her after this or that doctor's appointment, she was unable to answer the most rudimentary questions about her condition and how she was to deal with it. Then, anticipating my annoyance, she'd jangle her big gold bracelets, throw her nose up, and retort, "I don't have to know everything. I trust my doctor. He knows." For years I resisted asking such obvious next questions as: "And how does it help you one bit for him alone to know how many times a day you should exercise your new knee?"

All this was well and fine when we were talking about arthritis, bladder infections, or even replacement joints. It was altogether something else when the concern was strokes or heart attacks or fist-sized tumors gobbling up Mother's major organs. I had hoped that the hours she'd spent on her bedroom floor wondering if she could muster the strength to call for help might have forced her to reassess her Pollyanna approach to her own health. And, in fact, I did begin to notice a change in Mother after I brought her home from the hospital late in January.

But she only seemed changed toward me.

❧

My daughter Samantha is one of the best listeners I know. Even as a child, Sam usually didn't speak until she'd carefully observed and appraised a person, group, or situation. Combined with a relentless curiosity and a forthright, Abe Lincoln manner, this trait has won her many confidences and helped her to become a successful investigative journalist for the highly acclaimed *Lone Star* magazine. I've always appreciated and admired her interviewing skills, particularly when they are aimed at other people. So, given Mother's increasing reticence to talk to me about her health, I set out to garner Sam's help in obtaining the information I was after.

I drove up to her condo at about nine o'clock on a Saturday morning in February and dialed her phone number from the front seat of my car.

"Hello?" She queried in the slightly wary tone in which she always answered the phone.

"Hi. It's me."

"Hi, Mom."

"Sam, I need to talk to you about Gammy. Do you mind if I come over?"

"Why? Is something wrong with her? Something else, that is?"

"Not necessarily. That's what I want to talk to you about. . . . That's OK, isn't it? For me to stop by?"

"Actually, Mom, I'm really tied up today. I have to finish two articles and get ready for a party this evening. It's work related. What if I call you tomorrow night?"

This is precisely the response I'd expected. "I'm out front," I informed her.

"Then why did you bother asking?"

"Well, I know how testy you get when I come over without calling first."

"Uh huh. So, you're calling from out front? Oh, OK. Come on in."

On my way up to Sam's front door, the neglected little flower garden that ran along her sidewalk seemed to cry out to me. "Waaatter. Waaaatterrr," it whimpered. One scraggly pansy that had laid its gasping purple face on the white concrete where I'd be sure to see it was so pathetic that I'm sure I felt it grab at my ankle as I stepped over. I was around the side turning on the faucet when Sam stuck her head out the front door and called, "Mother? Are you there?"

"I'm on a mission of mercy, dear," I chirped, rounding the corner with the hose running. I directed the flow to the roots of that plucky little pansy first. "Your plants are all dying, Samantha. If it doesn't rain, you know, you have to water. Even in the winter."

At that, Sam let the door fall completely open and gave the whole neighborhood a gander of the pea green flannel bathrobe I'd seen her knocking around in for about ten years. Her venerable old tomcat, Gumbo, was tucked under one arm, and she carried a huge Gauguin coffee mug painted with dancing Polynesians in the other. Her cheeks, usually pink and vibrant, looked pale except for purplish smears under her eyes. I chose not to say anything about that; I had no need to know what she might have been doing the night before.

"Hey, when you finish there, why don't you take that hose around to my back porch?" she said, forcing a smile.

"Honestly, Sam, if you haven't figured these things out by the time you're thirty-five, I don't know when you will. Why do you bother with winter flowers if you don't mean to pay any attention to them?"

"Well, as I recall, you kept telling me that I needed to plant flowers there, and I finally gave in to you. Is that not how you remember it?"

"Never mind." I flitted around the side to turn off the water and then joined Sam on the front landing. "We have more important things to discuss," I said, waving her backward into the entry hall and shutting the door behind me. "How about a cup of coffee?"

"OK, but I'll have to brew some. I only made enough for myself." She dropped Gumbo onto the tile and scooted into her tiny kitchen to haul the coffeemaker out of the pantry. While she set it up, I wandered around, concerned for what else she might be letting die.

There were her article notes, spread across the den floor. Next to one stack were two or three pictures of a horrendous car accident and several others of a person whose face and hands had apparently been burned off in the resulting fire. Next to the other stacks were photographs of the elderly Bushes outside the Bush presidential library in College Station, and one especially dramatic picture of our brand-new president standing calm and tall with his wife under a lonely, embattled umbrella on inauguration day. "What's your story about?" I called, puffing up at the prospect of my daughter actually interviewing a president, even if it was just George W., the hometown boy.

"I assume you're talking about the Bush story?" she answered from the kitchen. "My angle is how the father's struggles and experiences in office may have helped the son to keep believing in himself even when the whole world was doubting his intellect and questioning his right to the presidency."

"What if the father's experiences didn't help the son? What if the son somehow came to that place all by himself?" I tossed back, surprising myself.

"Or maybe he got it from somewhere or someone else," Sam added mysteriously, joining me in the den.

"Well?"

"Well, I see it as all three, frankly. But a great deal of it can be traced back to George Senior, in both positive and negative ways."

"What do you mean, negative?"

"I mean that in some ways the son is strong despite the father. Isn't that always the way?"

I found myself hesitant to agree with that proposal, suddenly unsure whom we were talking about. "I guess I'll wait and read your finished story to find out exactly what you mean. Now, can we chat about Gammy?"

"OK." Sam handed me a cup and plopped heavily onto her Queen Anne couch opposite the chair I'd already taken. "What's the problem?"

"Well, you remember the day Gammy went into the hospital because of her blood pressure, and you and I talked about how dangerous it obviously is for her to be living alone at her age and with her health problems?"

"Yes, I remember you saying something to that effect."

"Well, I haven't forgotten. I worry about it quite a bit, and I feel guilty every day for doing nothing to remedy the situation."

"Have you talked to her about it?"

"That's the problem. I've tried to talk to her repeatedly, but each time I bring it up she gets snippy with me and says she feels fine in regard to her blood pressure, so quit asking her about it already. Even when I try a different tack and simply ask if she feels safe living there alone, she gets her hackles up and just says something nonresponsive like, 'Good gracious, Katy, I've lived here over forty years!' Then she changes the subject."

"She must be suspicious about why you're asking. Why don't you just tell her outright that you're worried about her living alone and want her to think about some other arrangement?"

"I don't know. I guess I sense that she already knows why I'm asking and she's refusing to cooperate."

"If she doesn't want to leave, Mom, what can you do about it? Besides, what alternative would you propose to her living in her own house?"

"That's a good question. It's the real crux of the matter in my mind. If there were an obvious place for her to go, I'd already be pressing my case against her. I could never live with myself if something else happens to her over there and she can't get through to anyone for help."

"Gosh, I'm afraid I don't have any suggestions on that score. She'd be welcome here, but of course both of my bedrooms are upstairs and she couldn't easily get to them. I don't know what else I can do to help."

"I know of something."

"Yes?"

"You can go over and talk to her about it. I think she'd be more likely to tell you what we need to know. For some reason she seems to feel threatened by me."

"So you want me to spy for you?"

"No. I want you to help me help Gammy."

"What if I disagree with you that she needs to move out?"

"Do you?"

"I don't know. I'd have to talk to her about it first."

"OK. Isn't that what I'm asking?"

"Yes, well, even if I were to talk to her, I don't promise to tell you what she says. I can't pretend to personally care about her situation when really I'm just stooling for you. She'd never buy it. And besides, once she found out that I'd repeated everything to you, she wouldn't tell me another thing. Then there's the fact that I do care personally."

"I don't see how caring about Gammy rules out telling me what she says. That's really insulting to me, Samantha."

"I'm not saying it rules it out. I'm just saying that I can't promise in advance that it won't. And I also can't approach her on any sort of false pretenses."

"Oh, for crying out loud, Sam, why do you have to make everything so difficult? You should have been a lawyer the way you dissect things from every angle. How often do I ask you to do anything for me? Why can't you just help me out this once?"

"I will help you out. I promise I'll go talk to her. But what I can't promise is to tell you everything she says to me."

"And just what good will it do me if you decide you can't tell?"

"I would hope you'd consider it a good thing for someone who loves Gammy to be in communication with her on this issue, and that you might trust me to do whatever I think is best based on what Gammy says. Is that possible?"

"I suppose it'll have to be."

๑

For several days after that unsatisfying exchange, I managed not to badger Sam about whether she'd talked to her grandmother yet. Finally, about a week later, she invited herself over for dinner.

"Would you like to bring a guest?" I had asked, intending by that to extend an invitation to her current boyfriend, Paul the dentist.

"No, thanks," she'd answered, thereby signaling that Paul the dentist was now out of the picture.

When Sam was in college, she once asked me what it felt like to be in love. I cleared my throat quite a few times trying to assess whether I had any answer. Had I ever been in love? I certainly thought I was at one time, but the man I thought I loved turned out to be an apparition, a wish as illusive as the lover from Brigadoon who appears for one day every hundred years. In no time at all he had vanished and left behind a feeble impostor whose insecurities had mocked and smothered my feelings for him. This was not what I wanted for my daughter. "Don't ask me such questions," I'd said.

After that, Samantha and I didn't communicate overtly about romance. I trusted that she'd inform me of a pending marriage when and if she was sure one was going to transpire, and she trusted me not to question her choices on such matters. In the meantime, we occasionally entertained her young men, and now and then I even alerted her to well-employed bachelors when I heard about them. Frankly, I envied Sam's freedom and individuality. I wanted her to have all the wonderful things that life has to offer, including a good marriage, but I was glad at least that she didn't have to endure my misery.

On the night that she came to dinner, Eliot was out and about in anticipation of Sam's visit. He had a great soft spot for his daughter and was typically at his most social when she was around. Tonight he was clean-shaven and wore a dapper, hunter-green button-down and black slacks. When he volunteered to grill the steaks for our dinner, I couldn't resist a rare evening of normalcy. I handed over the three gorgeous rib eyes, and went to work on my salad.

Sam arrived late and out of sorts. Though it was freezing outside, she wore no coat and only a thin cotton jumper. She'd swept her long brown hair into a hasty bun that camouflaged how badly I suspected it needed washing. Throughout dinner she seemed preoccupied, repeatedly letting the conversation die when it was her turn to contribute. Unusual as all this was, I was sure it had to do with Mother.

I knew I'd burst if I didn't hear soon, but I could never get alone with Sam to ask her about it. When the dishes had been done, instead of withdrawing to himself as I'd expected, Eliot asked if we wanted to play rummy. I immediately said no; Sam immediately said yes. Convinced at that point that we wouldn't shake him for the whole evening, I recklessly broached the subject right in front of him.

"Have you talked to your grandmother lately?" I queried.

"Yes," Sam answered, "but she didn't have much to say." Then she turned back to the table and laid down a four-card run, clearly meaning to leave me no entrée for a follow-up. But this created too much ambiguity for my taste. And I had this much to work with: Sam would never lie.

"Did she say anything about her blood pressure situation?" I tested.

"Yes," she answered over her shoulder.

"Do you think she's going to need any further help with that?"

"Not anytime soon. I think she's got it under control for now."

"Do you think that's wishful thinking on her part?"

Sam turned from her game and faced me straight on. Very deliberately, she warned, "I can't say, Mom. I choose to accept what she tells me."

"What if she's wrong, and something happens because of it?"

I knew right away that I'd pushed her too far. I could see it reflected in Samantha's worried brown eyes that suddenly glowered back at me. "What if Gammy moved off to a nursing home where they protected her from every conceivable sickness or accident?" she demanded. "That way she could be preserved indefinitely in a safe state of despair."

Eliot chose that moment to offer his inflammatory perspective. "Your mother can't live forever, Kate. Even you can't arrange for that."

"I guess you'd both be in favor of euthanasia then?" I blasted. "Why don't we just call Dr. Kevorkian in to help take her off our hands? She'd apparently be in favor of that. You two wouldn't be so apathetic if it were your own mothers we were talking about!" And then I looked right at my stunned daughter and lashed out in the worst way yet. "Or should I just get used to the fact that you apparently would?"

The problem with saying things out loud is that you can never retrieve them once they're loose. In a sense, a spoken sentiment has come to life. It begins to breathe and grow and affect its surroundings. That's why certain slanderous or unreasonably prejudicial things, once said in the hearing of a jury, can only be remedied by declaring a mistrial and starting over. Of course, you can't declare a mistrial with the people you love, but that fact had never yet been enough to tame my white-hot tongue.

Sam slowly stood up from the table and dropped her rummy hand faceup. She bent down to kiss Eliot's cheek, whispered, "Bye Daddy," and then walked past me out the front door.

Eliot shook his head as he collected the playing cards. "Katy," he said, "what were you thinking?"

114

CHAPTER 10

Jo

February 15, 2001

Yesterday was only the second Valentines in my entire life that I've had no man to dote on me. My granddaughter got me through the day by escorting me to dinner at an intimate bistro down the street from my house.

Since Samantha assured me that this place had no steaks on its menu, I wasn't worried that Lenny might ever have taken me there and so spoil the evening with any bad memories. Still, once we sat down at our little corner table, I couldn't shake a nagging sense of familiarity. And when I surveyed the tiny dining room's twelve or fourteen tables, each lit with its own dim sconce poised on the wall above, I caught a flash of those same tables filled with earlier diners, generally older and better dressed. The table-cloths in the phantom dining room were red rather than white, the walls papered, not painted, but the sconces were the same. And though I could find neither my dinner companion nor myself at any of the past-tense tables, I knew I was there; I could sense it, as when you're certain that you've met someone before though his face stirs only the vaguest sense of like or dislike. I fancied that I'd liked my prior visit here—liked it very much— and assumed that it had probably been with Vic.

Samantha, in the overprotective mode that most of my fam-ily has fallen into with me since well before my surgery, practi-cally carried me to my seat in the restaurant. I've come to enjoy this sort of fawning on the most part, but for some reason with

Samantha I don't. After the waiter handed us menus and went away, I admitted to her that I don't actually need to lean on anyone to get from the car to the table, that in fact I'm feeling pretty well all things considered. Having come clean with her, then, I settled back and ordered my favorite dish—broiled Atlantic salmon. Pierre's, as it turned out, served it with grilled asparagus and a rich, smoky sauce. All the way around, the dining was superb. I'm afraid the conversation will take me much longer to process.

We were still waiting for our appetizers when Samantha launched on an uncharacteristic diatribe about her mother. "I'm glad to hear you're feeling so well, Gammy, because Mom seems really worried about it. You know how she can be about things once she starts obsessing over them." Her emphasis on the last sentence seemed both warning and indictment; I was not sure which, and she gave me no opportunity to ask. "Really I think it's best not to present her with any information that might conceivably serve as grist for her worry mill. You know what I mean? Take that deal a few weeks ago with your blood pressure. Once that sort of thing goes in, she grinds it and grinds it until it produces fears totally out of proportion to any probable dangers. It's kind of scary to think of sharing any real worries with her."

I chewed on that until they brought my escargot. Finally I admitted to Samantha that I really didn't know what she was talking about. "Are you trying to tell me she can't let go of the 'idiot doctor incident'? If so, I've already noticed, but I don't know what she can do about it. At some point she'll have to accept that it happened and now it's over." I popped a snail into my mouth and savored it while Samantha fidgeted with her salad.

"Well, let me ask you this, Gammy. Have you given any

thought to moving out of your house so you won't be alone all the time . . . in case something else were to happen, or you got lonely or something?"

I felt my back stiffen at the question. I couldn't deny that I occasionally dwelt on the things that might happen to me—things that maybe I couldn't get out of on my own. As useless as Lenny had been, he at least knew how to dial a telephone, and he was always attuned to my needs. It had been pretty strange these last several weeks living with such a conspicuous void all around me. And I was also surprised by how lonely I'd been since Fran's Christmas visit. It had never occurred to me that loneliness might overshadow the thrill of my newfound liberation. But one stark fact brought all of these others into submission: I had nowhere else to go.

"No," I answered. "I've lived there for over forty years, and I plan to live there for as many as I have left."

"And you feel safe there alone?" Samantha asked it like she was building a case for me.

"Safe enough."

"Would you feel better if we got you a cell phone and a security system?"

"Yes, probably. I've been thinking about such precautions myself."

"Even so," Samantha continued, "what if something else happened and you still couldn't get help?"

I gave the answer that anyone gives when they've no other options. "Everybody has to go sometime, Samantha. Why would this way be worse than any other?"

"But it might come later if you were living with people who could keep an eye on you."

I drew upon all my wisdom and dignity for a response.

"First of all, I'm ready now . . . almost. Second, you can't say what would happen under different circumstances. I might go live with a bunch of old people and catch some fatal virus from one of them, or be beaten up by a teenage attendant who's sick and tired of emptying bedpans. You never know."

"You're absolutely sure you don't want to be talked into moving somewhere else?"

"I'm absolutely sure," I insisted. For, as I said, I have nowhere else to go.

"Then you probably should be careful what you tell Mom," Samantha counseled. "That's all I'm saying."

"Samantha, I've never known you to talk this way about your mother before. What's brought all this on? Has she said something to you?"

"You know how she is, Gammy. Just be discreet. We all need to be discreet. Maybe you and I can just tell each other whatever needs to be told." She scowled and looked away as she said this, mumbling the last sentence as if she meant it only for her swordfish entrée. But I'd caught it, and I held on.

"What sort of things, Samantha? What sort of things might you need to tell me?"

"Oh, whatever comes up. Little things that shouldn't be made too much of."

"Has anything like that come up already, honey?" She piddled with her fish. Finally, "Yes."

"What is it?"

"You won't say anything to Mom before I decide to myself?"

"Not if you don't want me to."

"I know exactly how I'm going to handle this, Gammy."

"OK. What is it?"

"It's that I'm pregnant. I'm pregnant, and I plan to have and keep the baby. That's all there is to it."

I've lately begun to see that mine is a family of rash decision makers. We're very conservative about things like jobs and investments, how we dress and behave in public. But when it comes to the big stuff, we're prone to jump headfirst into boiling cauldrons with nary a glance at the steam rolling up the sides. Do we have some genetic defect? Do we teach it to each other? Of all of us, I had dared hope that Sam had somehow escaped this curse, for I'd never known her to do anything reckless. She's even sidestepped some of the ordinary risks that most everyone takes. So this seemed like a complete turnabout.

"You call this a 'little thing' that shouldn't be made too much of?" was all I could think to say.

"Anything can be made too much of, Gammy. And Mom is usually the one to do it. I know this must sound harebrained to you. And I didn't exactly try to make it happen. But I didn't try to keep it from happening either. Now that it has, I realize it's what I want. Maybe I did seek it out."

"Well, when did it happen, Samantha, and more importantly, who's the father?" I asked. "I didn't even know you were dating anyone that seriously."

"OK," she said. "Here's the thing. I'm two months pregnant, which means I'm still in plenty of danger of having a miscarriage, especially since I'm old and this is my first pregnancy. As for the father, that's not important. I don't intend to marry him. I don't even intend to tell him, necessarily. And that's all I really want to say about it right now, Gammy."

"Hmm. Of course, you'll have to tell your mother soon. How long do you think it'll be before she notices on her own? That wouldn't be the best way for her to find out, not for either of you."

"Actually, I think I might sneak by for quite awhile without her noticing. She's pretty preoccupied with other things right now, and . . . well, she and I are sort of on the outs anyway."

"Don't let it go too long, Samantha, or I'm afraid you'll discover just how much your mother really can make of something."

February 17, 2001

After Samantha's confession to me a few days ago, I read back through all my diary entries since I started keeping this thing back in October. Why, I wonder, are these the things I need to rehash? I believe it has something to do with confession for me also.

But I'm tired of confessions at the moment. As I told Samantha, I've been feeling pretty good for a few weeks, and I'd like to celebrate by writing about some happy times. There were plenty of those.

Some of the best were the after-war years when the people around us were no longer starving or dying or grieving as a general rule. During this time, Vic was going gangbusters at Dawson Insurance, which kept him happy. And because the firm was doing so well, he was not at home much, which kept Clay happy.

Katy was just entering puberty but doing it with infinitely more grace than I remember being capable of in my own youth.

And Adele was supervising my home in her devoted, loving way. On top of all this, I made my first friend.

What initially caught my attention about Fran McClendon was how exceptionally she painted portraits. I, on the other hand, could not make a few globs of red, yellow, and blue resemble a realistic human face to save my life. In that respect I did not stand out from my classmates in the intermediate oil-painting course in which I enrolled in the spring of 1946. Franny stood out.

I eventually came to find that Fran had no more training or experience than the rest of us; her superiority was all in her gift. She had the vision, the touch, and the all-important connection between them that allows a true artist to reassemble the world onto a piece of canvas in a way that makes people prefer the painted world. I admired and envied her talent from across the art studio for several months without ever actually speaking to her.

One afternoon when I left class, I hurried over to the new department store down the street to do reconnaissance for Katy's birthday. She was striving to look grown-up these days, and I had agreed to let her pick out a few new dresses toward that end. But I wanted to know what we were in for first. As it turned out, I found a couple of inoffensive sale dresses that I thought might fit the bill, and I decided to risk surprising her. I was at the register with them when the clerk turned her attention to me.

I probably wouldn't give this little gal a second thought today. But in 1946 most salesclerks were either buxom, gray-haired old women whom you were tempted to call Aunt Gladys, or they were smart, sophisticated younger women who looked as if their real job titles might be "buyer" or "fashion specialist." This one defied all stereotypes. Her mass of stringy brown hair was unrestrained except by her own periodic jerking to untangle it from the pen she was using to write up my sales ticket. When she finally did drag the greasy strands out of her face for a moment, I saw that she was just a child, her chin still splattered with pimples. Eventually she managed to work out my bill, and stood to look at me.

"Thwent fee, thitty thee," she said, clamping a large blob of bubble gum between her front teeth.

I could not bring myself to decipher the figure she had quoted me. Much louder than necessary, I finally responded, "Pardon me?"

She straightened slightly in response to my reprimanding tone and said more soberly this time, "Thwent fee, thitty thee." The gum, green and wet, now dangled out the front of her teeth and over her bottom lip. She sucked a little then, perhaps extracting the sugar, and waited round-eyed for me to pay her. "What is the problem?" her look suggested.

That's when I heard a snort, followed immediately by a fit of uncongested coughing. I turned to find Fran McClendon standing just behind me, apparently in the throes of some spontaneous illness. The salesgirl leaned over the counter and around me, gawking at Fran in alarm. And I felt my annoyance evaporate and my grip on self-control slipping fast away.

Above all, I knew I must not speak to her. As deliberately as I have ever done anything, I turned my back on Fran and handed the clerk thirty dollars, hoping that would cover whatever amount I owed.

Behind me, Fran finally settled down. And once she could walk, she mumbled something about water and then peeled away from the vicinity of the cash register, much to my relief. Before long, however, I saw her peering out from behind a rack of blouses about thirty feet behind the clerk—right in front of me.

From this safe distance, Fran bore her teeth at me gleefully, an imaginary wad of gum clenched between them. Then she doubled over once again in a seizure of hysterics.

I looked away, stabbing my fingernails into the palms of my hands. The salesgirl struggled to get the register open, and then began the monumental task of making change. I determined to think of a song and sing it in my head until I was free to go, but not a one came to mind. By now Fran had disappeared, but I fully expected her to pop out again at any moment, closer than I could ignore. I was slipping, slipping.

When she did resurface, about fifteen feet away at the ten o'clock position, Fran was feigning great interest in a purse. A whole pack of Wrigley's Spearmint Gum stuck out of her mouth like a cigar. The oblivious salesgirl emerged from the register and tentatively handed me a few one-dollar bills and some coins. I didn't care how much. It was now a matter of great personal honor for me to somehow keep this girl's elusive dignity intact. I grabbed the money and my bag, thanked her majestically, and ran.

I was almost to the main lobby when I spied Fran waiting for me in cosmetics, somehow having outrun me. She grabbed my arm without a word and joined me in my sprint for the front door. Once we had cleared it, we laughed until neither of us could make any noise. We were a sight—two middle-aged *mothers flopping all over the sidewalk, laughing and crying, crying and laughing. We abandoned ourselves to it like children. And, despite everything, that's pretty much how it's always been with Fran.*

Last week I got this letter from her:

Dear Jo,

I hope this finds you feeling well and still enjoying your new life as a fox, sans the hound. On the other hand, I'd be the first to admit that being alone can be pretty tough. You know, I think I'm only just now getting a little bit used to life without Silver. He was an old fart, to be sure, but he was my old fart, and somehow I still adored him even after fifty-four years of putting up with his infinite quirks. I was shocked to realize a few days ago that it's been over six years since his death.

Hey, I have a great idea: Let's be roommates in some ritzy old folks' home! Do you think such a thing exists? We could be the founding residents, and then only allow fun people in to spend our last days with. You let me know if you're interested, OK?

In the meantime, I can report that my children still insist on treating me like some sort of national treasure. My only complaint is that I can't see well enough to drive anymore, so I'm at their mercy. You know how much I love to be dependent on people!

So, write back when you can. With much love to you,

Fran

February 18, 2001

Despite the humor, Fran and I found that the road between the department store and our shared widowhood was in much disrepair, filled with bumps and potholes, almost ruined in places. We were prone to wrecks, and I was sure we wouldn't recover from some of them. After all, friendship isn't like marriage—you don't commit to it forever in front of God and everybody. At many junctures we were tempted to walk away while we could still walk, mostly, I think, because Fran and I were about as different as two white, middle-class, Houstonian housewives could be.

She was lighthearted and charismatic, always gliding across the surface of life finding the things she could delight in and stepping right over or around the rest. That's not to say she was naïve or easily satisfied. Rather, she was intuitive, hilarious, utterly shameless, and often able to bring forth like qualities in others. Just as often, however, she was the sun, her bright light blinding, washing out all the lesser lights around her. In a crowd, once she got going, Fran seemed to use up all the air in the room. The rest of us could only stand by and enjoy her. It was either that, or die of jealousy.

When I met her, she had already succeeded in attracting the man—maybe the only man—who could keep up with her: Sylvester McClendon. Here's how she first described him to me not long before I met the real person: "Jo, he's the only man I've ever known who it hasn't flattened out with. The others all bored me after awhile, but Silver is new every day. He's not normal. I want him all the time."

With such a buildup, I expected to be swept away, enchanted. So I couldn't have been more surprised to find that

Silver was, quite frankly, a big windbag. His objective in life seemed to be indulging himself, and he did so in almost every way imaginable. Over the years that I knew him, he devoted himself and a good deal of their income to a string of elaborate and useless fetishes that Fran charitably referred to as "hobbies." First there was bridge, in which he lost interest the moment he became a Grand Duke, or some other such silly title. Then there was antique collecting—one of his most expensive obsessions. After that he took up gourmet Cajun cooking, became a colonel in the local Civil War Reenactment Brotherhood, and ultimately won the venerable title of West Houston Senior Ping Pong Champion.

Physically, I watched Silver grow into his personality, sprouting a second chin some time in the 1960s and the third by around 1980. He also chain-smoked until he was an old man. His amazing longevity despite all this surely points up how remedial our "advanced" understanding of the human body really is.

Not surprisingly, Silver was also a trivia whiz. Between sales of his property listings, he apparently studied the encyclopedia. Or maybe he picked up his random knowledge from radio and television shows. Who knows? He would have liked us all to believe that he was born knowing the vast scramble of odd facts that he so effectively wooed people with at cocktail parties. He was smitten with his own talents in this regard, especially the affected humility with which he usually dropped these useless tidbits into conversations. It was this delivery that disgusted me most, and it drove Vic mad. We were never the small-talk types anyway.

I wish I could say that I liked my best friend's husband. But that would be against my diary rule. So I guess I'm back to confessing. My saving grace is the fact that at some point Silver and I made a truce. If we were both going to love Fran, we couldn't openly hate each other. And so my clash with her husband receded into the background of our friendship. But an even bigger wedge soon threatened to sever it.

February 20, 2001

I've been brooding over this part for days now, and that seems to make it mandatory for me to relive it by writing it down. So here goes.

It seems a truism that for every takeoff, there is a landing. That's what makes life so bittersweet. In the late 1940s, Vic and I were taking off while Daddy was beginning his descent. His was to be a blind landing, though not quite a crash. It was the type that must somehow occur in the midst of a thick shroud of thunderclouds, with zero visibility, entirely by instruments. It was a harrowing ride.

We first suspected that something was really wrong with Daddy when he started coming in from his greenhouse frustrated and angry, complaining vaguely that his seedlings "just wouldn't go in right" and that "nothing could grow anymore." At about seventy-eight, Daddy had spent close to sixty years nurturing plants, routinely coaxing them to do the most amazing things. They had always been his best friends, and this new enmity between them was a worrisome mystery to us all.

By this time, though, there had been many dimmer signs of trouble that no one had pieced together into a coherent story. Once he walked straight into a single-paned, full-length window that he mistook for a doorway. More generally, he had become discontent, short-tempered and sarcastic, even vulgar at times. This from the gentlest man I've ever known. One night he declared furiously that the house was simply too hot for him any longer, and he set up a cot on the porch where he slept alone for several months. Baffled by this, I asked him repeatedly if he felt bad, but he just kept hollering about how "seventy some-odd summers in Houston is enough to kill any man!"

We'd been begging him to see a doctor for some time when he had a mishap that effectively took away his choice in the matter. It was early in 1950, and Daddy had inexplicably been collecting discarded electronics for the better part of a year. He went out to the landfill almost every morning after breakfast and enticed the gatekeepers to search the periphery for broken radios, clocks, lamps, and telephones—anything with wires hanging out. They had affectionately dubbed him "The Wire Man," playing on his appearance as well as his compulsion. And when he was not up to this errand, he often dropped by a neighbor's house instead. He'd chat them up about whatever happened to enter his head but would almost always come around to the point of his visit eventually: Did they have any gadgets or old appliances they were looking to get rid of?

One Sunday he sneaked off to the landfill and found the gate locked. With no one nearby to rant at about this, his rage got the better of him, and he decided to break in. He apparently tried to jimmy the lock but couldn't manage it. And so he started to climb. I can hardly bear to picture it—my frail, foggy, eighty-year-old father crawling up an eight-foot, chain-link fence. I don't know how he got as far as he did. Thankfully he didn't clear the top, or he probably would have impaled himself on the wires jutting out of it. Instead, several feet off the ground, he lost his footing and tumbled onto that trick back of his, by now contorted in a manner that would be too difficult to describe. A patrol officer found him a few hours later and opted to take him to the hospital instead of the jail. After that incident, he spent the rest of his life mostly in bed. The insightful doctors who treated him explained to us that Daddy was "old and had a bad back."

February 21, 2001

While Daddy's body and mind languished, Vic and I seemed to find our stride. It was about this time that one of Vic's more tenuous investments unexpectedly came to fruition. He was a silent partner in a tiny exploration company whose very first well hit oil. Lots and lots and lots of oil.

It's more telling than I'd like to admit that Vic never asked me what I'd like to do with the royalties that now began flowing in. I can't even say specifically what he did with them. Vic never really bought into the community property aspect of our state's law. And for that matter, neither did I. He earned the money, and it seemed fair that he orchestrated our spending it. To his credit, the first thing he did with this particular windfall was the one thing I would have wanted anyway—he created college trust funds for Katy and Clay. With what was left, we had fun.

After all the sacrifice and sorrow of the thirties and early forties, we felt entitled to treat ourselves to a few luxuries at this point in our lives. Daddy's debilitation served as an odd blessing on these choices. "Look what will happen to you one day," seemed his sober portent. "Live while you can!"

So when Vic mischievously passed me a blank white envelope one night after dinner, and inside I found two airplane tickets to Paris, I was beside myself. From Paris, three weeks later, we drove to Geneva, then to Rome, Florence, Venice, Vienna, Munich, Heidelberg, Antwerp, and Brussels, and finally we crossed the English Channel on the ferry and ended our odyssey in London.

The flavor and import of this trip were captured early one morning as we drove through the Swiss countryside, the Alps soaring up before us, purple and a hazy blue. With no explanation, Vic pulled the car off the road and got out. He stopped at the trunk on his way around to open my door, then took my hand and led me off into a field where he spread a blanket and sat me down in the middle of it. Not far off, several young men harvested hay with sickles, and we could smell the fresh cuts from where we sat watching the sun roll westward through the mountains, highlighting first one peak, then another, and another. Vic unveiled a basket and produced both a bottle of wine and a thermos of coffee, ready to satisfy my every desire. When I'd chosen the coffee and was warming my hands around the cap cup, enthralled by it all, he did something that made it even better, if that were possible. He drew a flat, rectangular box out of the bottom of the basket and placed it tenderly in my lap. He had bought me a gold collar and a pendant made entirely of diamonds, amethysts, and opals—my three favorite stones. When he put it on me, I couldn't not cry.

A moment that idyllic is the saddest of all things because you know that it will end.

February 22, 2001

The next two years were relatively uneventful. Most of the money from the wells went back (I think) into more wells, which eventually pumped slower and slower until they stopped altogether. The reservoir hadn't dried up, but there was some geologic problem that made it too expensive for them to extract what was left using available technology. We were glad we'd spent our share on such good causes while we'd had it.

But now it was time to do what people did in the 1950s—work hard, buy ugly cars that didn't stand out, paint our houses white, and hide our spare change in coffee cans in the cupboard. We got a television set, putting it in the place of honor where our dependable old radio had long stood challenging us to see for ourselves. In no time, it seemed, the new box had so captivated us that we were inspired to give it the best part of every evening. At least we were still eating dinner at the table; I don't think anything so depraved as TV trays had yet been devised.

It was on such an evening that I got the call. Daddy was gone, just like that.

How could death have toyed with him for so long—at least six years that I know of—and then leveled its final blow with no warning at all? I've never been so angry in all my life. Over the past twenty-four months, I'd read him all the major works of Dickens, Steinbeck, James, and Hemingway while he lay, day after day, more completely in a stupor. I had changed his diapers, mashed his food into a form that wouldn't choke him when he refused to swallow, and sat by his bed praying that he would come to the forefront one last time before he left me forever. And then somehow I'd missed it. How does one distinguish between your basic vegetative state and the commencement of death itself?

I remember hanging up the phone in the kitchen and walking back into the living room to tell Vic and Katy. They were lounging in their evening spots—Vic in his ragged old easy chair now permanently contoured to his unique shape, and Katy propped against the couch doing her homework in front of the TV. The scene was so comfortable and mundane. I found it unbearably arrogant, and I had to disrupt it.

"Daddy's dead," I said flatly.

The two of them gazed back wide-eyed. See, it had shocked them too! How! How? How were we to know?

"What's the matter?" I snapped. "Didn't you know he was going to die?"

My fearless daughter stepped back up to the plate first. Sweetly, "Mother, of course we knew he was going to die eventually, but he's been bad for so long."

"That's exactly why you have no right to be surprised, isn't it?" I slashed back, barely waiting for her to finish her sentence. What does a sixteen-year-old know anyway? I brought her up to speed. "We should have been expecting it at any moment. Ye gods, he's been trying to die for months! We have no excuse; we should have been there."

"Jo," Vic took a turn, "honey, this is the best thing. You know it is. We should be grateful that he's finally free of whatever this was. You said so yourself—he's been trying to die. In fact, I'm not at all sure that your father didn't die a long time ago. But if he was still in there, at least he's free now."

"That is not the point!" I screamed. "The point is that if he was there, I let him die without me!"

My hysterical admission fell like a cannonball into the middle of the room. It couldn't be argued with, and neither of them was foolish enough to try. Then Vic said one of the most sensible things I think he ever did.

"I'll call Adele."

February 23, 2001

I wanted the darkness, so I retreated into my bedroom and left Vic and Katy to find Adele and bring her to me. It didn't take any of them very long. Before an hour had passed, she and Isaiah were ringing our bell.

Vic let them in, and through the bedroom door I heard a muffled man-hug punctuated by a grunt and lots of back-slapping. Isaiah and Vic had met several times over the past thirteen years, and Vic had often commented to me afterward how impressed he was by the firm, effective way Isaiah had raised his seven children and provided for his family. Of course, Adele had pitched in by working at our house in the mornings. But most days she'd tried to get home before her kids did from school. Though all of them were grown now, she was just as busy in the afternoons with her eighteen young grandchildren.

She waited a respectful moment after the men had separated, and then asked, "Where is she, Mr. Vic?"

"She's in her bedroom," he answered gravely. Adele's look must have probed further; after a few seconds, he added, "She's pretty angry at herself for not being there."

"May the Lord have mercy on us," was all she said. And the next thing I heard was her knock on my door.

She didn't wait for an invitation. In she came, flipping on the light and wearing a no-nonsense look that was somehow neither defensive nor accusing. In a foggier moment, I might have been tamed by that look. I might not have seen behind it. But tonight I did. Tonight everything was clear to me, and what I so clearly saw lurking there behind her look was a tidal wave of compassion poised to strike the shoreline just where I stood. I couldn't tolerate that.

"Don't you dare tell me it wasn't my fault," I said, without a syllable of thanks for her rushing over. We were here to do war. Adele was the pure young shepherd they'd sent in instead of the men. And I, I was the nine-foot giant.

"I wasn't a-gonna' say that," she said, stopping to load a small pebble into her sling, and calmly she began to rock it back and forth a few inches above the ground.

"Saturday was the last day I was there," I said. "Five days ago. I thought he looked worse than I'd ever seen him. I didn't go back because I didn't want to see him that way." My crescendo throughout this confession didn't seem to faze her.

"Uh-huh." The pebble had reached a height on each swing that called for a decision. She slowed it down so that it didn't circle over.

Me, shrieking, "You see, I knew. I knew!"

Now she completed one revolution . . . two . . . three.

"Yes, I see." As she said this, she brought the spinning sling up over her head and jerked it faster.

"I could have been there," I whispered.

Faster, faster.

"Yes, but that wouldn't a-changed the fact that he's gone, and you don't have him no more." She had released her pebble and watched it hit its mark.

Adele opened her arms then, and I fell into them, broken

and raw. That big old wall of compassion crashed square into me, but somehow I could bear it now. She wrapped herself so tightly around me that she finally squished the grief right out. I might have drowned in it if Adele hadn't been there to absorb some into herself.

February 24, 2001

As I've noted, we weren't a churchgoing family, so between us we mustered only one proposal for who should conduct Daddy's funeral. It seemed perfectly appropriate to us, but I'm sure there were plenty of Daddy's friends and associates who might have come if the service hadn't been in Isaiah's little church, presided over by a black man. Enough came to fill up the pews anyway, and none of the guests seemed so uncomfortable that we ended up feeling bad about it. I'm not sure I would have cared if they had.

The service had already begun when I saw Fran and Silver slip in the side door and take a seat at the very back. In the three days since Daddy's death, I'd only spoken to her once—to tell her that he'd passed. She hadn't offered to come by or help out in any way, and for some reason that didn't strike me as unusual at the time. But still, I remember being relieved when I finally saw them come into the church.

Isaiah said some beautiful things, I'm sure. As numb as I was, even I could tell that he was eloquent, and almost everyone who came up to me afterward said how well he had captured Daddy, considering that he'd never even met him. We were still receiving such condolences when I finally saw Fran marching resolutely toward me as if there were an invisible gun to her head.

In her defense, I admit that I was a fright. Insomnia had never looked good on me, and the bout of it I'd suffered since Daddy's death had been brutal. She eyed me apprehensively as she got closer.

"Oh, Jo, I am so very sorry for your loss," she began as soon as she was within earshot. She read this script with all the proper emotion. "I know you must be miserable. Is there anything I can do?" Her fearful look told me that this was a rhetorical question of the social grace variety. I wasn't sure if I could play along.

"No, thank you," I muttered.

It's never pleasant being relegated to small talk with someone whom you think you know almost as well as yourself—the person you call first when you most want to be understood. This is especially true when what you really need from them at that moment is resuscitation. What was this all about?

"I want you to know that it was really a lovely, lovely service," Fran continued. Then, having apparently used up her last sympathy line, she closed. "Ahhh . . . well . . . I guess I better go see what trouble Silver's gotten into. He was eyeing the choir's purple robes last time I saw him." And with that, she reached across the foot or so that separated us and patted my hand once before flying away.

I didn't hear from her for the next several weeks. We no longer had any mutual art classes that brought us together artificially; we had to go out of our way to accomplish it. And as time passed, it seemed to me that I didn't want to make the effort anymore. Maybe it was best to let our difficult, if long-standing, friendship die a natural death.

February 25, 2001

Holding grudges had always come pretty easily to me, but this time was an exception. Usually, when I felt injured badly enough, I could just turn off of someone like a light switch. I guess this was a ruthless practice, especially since it never seemed to cost me much anguish once the decision had been made. But letting go of Fran was a different story.

The problem was that I missed her so much. I tried and tried to convince myself that she was just a selfish, arrogant monster who had left me in the lurch when I'd needed her most, and would do it again. It would have been hard to come to any other conclusion, quite frankly. But all the demonizing in the world didn't make me miss her any less. As selfish as she may have been, we understood each other. And besides that, no one else could make me laugh the way she could.

Maybe if I hadn't been missing Daddy at the same time, Fran's absence wouldn't have overwhelmed me as it did. His death—the loss of the one person who had always been devoted to me no matter what—made me feel totally exposed. What about my hideous scars, my self-indulgences, my hatreds, and the ugly, childish fears that still thrived in my shadows after thirty-nine years? Who else could ever look square on such things and love me anyway? I was frantic to push away anyone who might be wise to me, and for this reason I think I welcomed the rift with Fran and maybe even helped to create it. But, just as badly, I needed a living person to accept my flaws, and I guess I'd sort of hoped that Fran would fill that role when the time came. This was the terrible ambivalence I struggled with as the spring of 1955 melted into a savagely hot summer, atypical even for Houston.

Vic offered me sympathy for awhile, but he had no tolerance for "endless female analyses" that he said took a great deal of energy and inevitably missed the point. The point, in his estimation, was for me to bounce back already and resume the full-time business of being his wife. Normally, I would have answered this complaint by thanking him for all the comfort and attention he'd lavished on me thus far, and promptly ceding his rightful place as the focal point of our family. Such was the power of my old friend panic. But my wounds were too fresh and the summer too hot, and panic just didn't seem all that awful against the backdrop of depression, grief, and self-doubt that already plagued me. So I didn't bother thanking Vic or puffing him up one bit. Instead, I said something to him that a wife should never say to her husband because no matter how you mean it he thinks you're questioning his manhood. I told him that I didn't feel fulfilled by my life. And he told me I was free to go and find another one if I wanted to.

A hurting person is repelling. I know that well enough from personal experience. Somehow, as June seared by, I managed to repel almost everyone still speaking to me. And so I was wary when Adele approached me one morning and said she wanted to talk.

"Is it something about Katy?" I tested.

"No, Miss Jo, it's not about Katy."

"Is it the vacuuming? If you can't get to that, I understand, Adele. It doesn't have to be done today."

"It's not the vacuuming, neither. It's you. I want to know what's wrong with you." She said this like she was entitled to such information. And of course, she was. But as much as I owed her an honest answer and needed her help, I couldn't risk another rejection just then.

"Adele, I'm happy to talk to you, but, really, I think I'm doing OK, probably as well as can be expected. It's like you said—it'll just take awhile to heal, that's all."

"Honey, I haven't heard you say nothin' about Miss Fran lately. What's happened between you two?"

How she could cut right to it.

"Absolutely nothing, Adele. I haven't heard one word from her in five and a half weeks, since she greeted me at Daddy's funeral as if I were just some stranger she'd once met on a streetcar."

"Have you called her?"

"Come on, Adele. Surely you see that I can't do that. She's abandoned me! I just can't be the one to do it. It would be humiliating. Most of the time I feel like I couldn't talk to her even if she called and begged me to forgive her. Please tell me that you see this. I'm not crazy, am I?"

Adele sighed loudly and took my hand. I awaited her verdict while she closed her eyes for almost a full minute. Finally she squinted at me and said, "No, you're not crazy. But you are askin' for untold grief. It just ain't that black and white."

"What? What ain't that black and white?" I demanded.

"Almost nothin' is!" she cried. "Where'd you get the idea that good and evil stay all nice and sweet in their separate corners? That ain't this world! Here they're all mixed up together in every one of us. God made us in his image, and then we fell. So we all have the good and the bad in us—both of 'em. You got it, I got it, and Miss Fran's got it. The trick is, lovin' anyhow. That's how Jesus—up there on that cross a-payin' for all our wickedness—loved us."

"Adele, I don't understand most of that. Are you saying I should keep being her friend even though she has disappeared on me, even though she isn't even asking for me to keep being her friend? Why would I want such a friend? How can I accept that?"

"Maybe you could start by remembering how long she's looked over the fact that you won't take to her husband," she answered, sounding like she'd waited years for the chance to say it. My God, did Adele know everything?

Yes, that's just the way it happened. I can't believe it. I haven't remembered it that way for forty-five years. But this is precisely how I came to make my peace with Silver McClendon. Life is such a mystery while you're living it.

February 26, 2001

I held on to Adele's correction long enough to get back on track with both Fran and Vic. Neither of them had been cursed with a memory like mine—prone to register and record every disrespectful look or gesture, every careless word, every evidence that another person has acted against my interests. As different as the two of them were in other respects, they were both content to keep their backs to the past. And so, once I extended my hand, they were as quick to lay down their respective resentments against me as they had been to take them up.

Maybe this was another of Adele's lanterns.

February 27, 2001

Last night I lay awake until two or three in the morning yearning for Daddy. Writing about him as I have the past few days has made me feel like I've just lost him all over again. Neither is Fran around to regale me, nor Vic to boss or romance me, nor even Lenny to drive me mad.

While I wept, I reached out and stroked Ginger—my only bedmate since October. I felt a number of large lumps beneath her skin, all in places they shouldn't have been like the meaty portion of her hind leg, beneath her shoulder blade on one side, and on the other side all along her rib cage. Her vet tells me these are probably just age tumors, full of fat. Some of them may be full of cancer, but I'd pay a fortune to find out which. Despite these strange mutations, Ginger melted under my touch, flopping onto her back and offering her tummy like a pup, moaning in pleasure all the while.

I, too, still feel like a child in my heart.

Katy

I saw that I couldn't count on my daughter or husband to join in my campaign to move Mother to a safer place. I had only two other prospective allies who might assist my cause—my brother and my son. Clay would surely have the most influence with Mother, but I wanted to approach him with a well-researched, well-reasoned case. And so I set about building one.

The obvious weakness in my position was the matter of where Mother would live once she moved out of her house. If I asked her to come and live with me, I couldn't predict how Eliot might perceive and respond to the arrangement. It was a colossal struggle for him to surrender attention that he felt rightfully belonged to him. When such was demanded—no matter how obviously an act of God—Eliot was prone to retaliate in some reckless manner that he must have hoped would regain him the ground he'd lost. His gambling spree the month before was just the last illustration of this troubled *modus operandi*. And, despite all our years of marriage, I was about as effective as a carnival fortune-teller at anticipating Eliot's erratic twists and turns.

One incident especially stands out. Back in 1977, when I added up our savings and realized that we wouldn't be able to send either one of our children to a good college on what I'd scratched together being a legal secretary, I took a wild gamble and enrolled myself in law school at the University of Houston. I'd already obtained my undergraduate degree taking night classes at the community college and slipping in an occasional day class at the university. Now, if everything went along as I planned, I figured I could graduate and land a law firm job earning an extra thirty or forty thousand annually by the time Seth started his freshman year. What I hadn't planned on was Eliot's creative reaction to my arduous new schedule. He decided he would take a few classes of his own from the Homer Emerson Zuck International Correspondence School of Marketing. For a few hundred dollars, Mr. Zuck promised to transform his students into highly effective, positive-thinking salesmen in only eight weeks. He made his real money, and ostensibly also helped his graduates along on the sure path to success and riches, by setting them up as distributors of his marketing books and tapes, the first shipment of which arrived at our house the same week I was scheduled to take my all-important, first-year contract and constitutional law finals.

I was suspicious from the moment the doorbell rang and Eliot leapt from the kitchen table and ran to answer it. Then, when he stepped outside, shut the door behind him, and didn't return, the small knot that had sprouted in my stomach began to send out tentacles that wrapped around my other vital organs. But I told myself I was being paranoid—weakened by the stress of my pending exams—and I didn't budge from the couch where I was curled around my constitutional law outline hoping to memorize it before 9:00 A.M. the next day. Thirty minutes soon passed without Eliot rematerializing. "No, no, no," I told myself. "He wouldn't do anything to sabotage you. These are his children you're doing this for, after all. Just relax." I concentrated on the privacy rights snuck into the fourteenth amendment and reviewed the facts and holdings of *Roe v. Wade* and its progeny. Still no Eliot.

About forty-five minutes after the doorbell had rung, Eliot appeared at the back door looking very inflated. He sat back down at the kitchen table, this time with an adding machine, and went to work punching in numbers and repeatedly hitting the long, grinding "sum" button with self-satisfied grunts. The more he pranced and pruned, the louder he punched and grunted, the madder I got—perfectly, I feared, according to his plan. Surely he was watching me out of the corner of his eye, but I wouldn't satisfy him by catching him do it out of the corner of mine.

Eliot folded first. He stood up and stretched broadly, circling round to face me as he did so and feigning surprise when he saw that I'd been sitting there all the while, just thirty feet away. Not to be outdone, I pretended that I hadn't noticed all Eliot's strutting and machining, intent as I'd been on how the courts had weighed a woman's right to her own body choices against society's interest in protecting life. Once we'd acknowledged each other, however, Eliot rested his arms across his paunch and said, "Looks like I can clear about twenty-five grand before Christmas."

The possibilities of what he might have done to prompt such bravado incapacitated me; I could only look up at him and wait. He took that as full cooperation and proceeded to answer the many questions I was apparently too impressed to utter.

"In our garage, right this very minute, are the products that are going to make us rich one day. And Kate, we've gotten in on the ground floor! Once I have a few salesmen lined up under me, all I'll have to do is sit back and count the money coming in. This first year I'll probably only make about fifty thousand, but it ought to at least double each year after that, with less and less effort required on my part." He actually paused there for my approval. When I just stared, he nudged, "So, what do you think?"

"What, exactly, is in our garage?"

Eliot lowered his voice as if our children and neighbors might be angling to take his rightful place on the "ground floor," and answered, "Homer Zuck's newest motivational business systems package, just off the presses, as they say. I'll be the first distributor in the whole Houston metropolitan area."

Now, there's a reason that no one today has ever heard of Mr. Homer Emerson Zuck. From this first mention of his name, I wished I hadn't. "How many boxes are in the garage?" I asked.

"Oh, just a few so far—maybe twenty or thirty. But we'll be getting lots more over the next week. I have to be able to outfit several salesmen with the complete product line."

"And how much has this cost us?" I pressed on to the end.

These were clearly not the giddy questions Eliot had hoped for, and this one especially resisted any peppy spin. "Asking that doesn't even make sense," he snipped. "The proper question is, 'How much will we make?' You can't freeze a balance sheet just after stocking the inventory and ask, 'How much have we lost?' Katy, surely you know that much about business!"

"OK, what inventory expenditures will we be deducting from our gross earnings to arrive at our net?"

"I think you'll make an excellent litigator if you ever learn to see the forest beyond the trees," Eliot observed. "You have the relentless interrogation skills down pat, but I'll not subject myself to anymore of it. I guess I shouldn't have expected you to support me in something that wasn't your idea. Well, soon enough you'll see just what the costs and benefits will be." Then, snatching the adding machine cord out of the wall, Eliot took his things back out to the garage where he supposedly recalculated everything and this time arrived at higher projected earnings all the way around.

I returned to my outline, more intent than ever on getting the grades that would land that lucrative law firm job. Who knew how big a paycheck I would need when all was said and done. Suffice to say, we still have about thirty moldy boxes of Homer Zuck propaganda out in our garage. Eliot has never brought himself to throw them out, sure he'll one day find a use for them that will recoup our investment and mend his reputation.

Other than this major glitch, my transition into law went much as I'd planned. I got that law firm job just in time to send Seth to college. As Eliot foretold, I went into litigation and I've done quite well at it. How else were we to dig out of the pit that his decimated ego always threatened to land us in?

That threat felt very great just now. I was certain that Eliot would erupt somehow if I brought Mother into our home to be under my care. And so I considered the other obvious option: Mother going to live with Clay and Lillian.

ℒ

Lillian Pickford made her shaky debut in the Greene family when she was twenty-seven and had very nearly resigned herself to being an old maid. Most young women by that time were married and on their second or third child. Lillian, though just as perky as Doris Day, had so far gone unclaimed. The clues I've gleaned from her over the years suggest that her downfall was her attraction to mentally superior men. By the 1960s, many women dared to display their intelligence and to yearn for more than motherhood. High-caliber men had begun to notice, and those who could stand it were choosing women whose capacities equaled and complimented their own. Poor Lillian could not stay away from them. She suffered heartbreak after heartbreak, and I think she'd lost all hope of a lifelong attachment by the time she met Clay.

He was thirty-three when she stumbled across him in the kitchen section of the department store where she clerked. He must have seemed like a lost little boy as he knocked about among the pots and pans, aiming to expand his bachelor-sized collection of those items heretofore consisting of a hand-me-down frying pan and a discolored Pyrex casserole dish. What spinster salesgirl could have resisted such a sad creature?

The skeletons in my brother's closet were those of his ex-fiancées—a string of stimulating young women who had craved more interaction than Clay could tolerate in the end. He'd been romantically sapped by these terminal commitments. All he wanted now was a pleasant girl with low expectations—someone who wouldn't mind setting the bar on the ground in some areas. So, on the fateful day when he went shopping for pots and pans, perky played quite well with him.

Lillian the salesclerk accoutered Clay with a three-tiered saucepan set, a nonstick cookie sheet, several mixing bowls, and her phone number. They were married a few months later, as soon as Clay felt comfortable that there wasn't anything below her surface that might ambush him after he said "I do." Though she couldn't really share in it, Clay presumably sated Lillian's inexplicable thirst for an intelligent, soulful man. And because she couldn't share in it, Clay has remained free to think his deep thoughts in safe isolation. When she harasses him, it's always for trivial favors that Clay can grant, or not, without significant harm to either of them.

But Mother has never seen it quite this way.

Considering the more substantial women that Clay had vowed to marry and then reneged on, Mother didn't take Lillian the slightest bit seriously right up to the day of their wedding. Even afterward, she had trouble accepting that Lillian had actually been the one who'd stuck. Soon enough, though, Mother found a way to appreciate all that she saw wrong with her daughter-in-law.

Mother's new attitude evolved during a Greene family vacation that Daddy orchestrated in the summer of 1969. I had been married for twelve years at that point; our children were seven and four. Although I'd already quit hoping to free Eliot from the narcissistic hell within him, he could occasionally straighten his back and play at being a grown-up, especially when the alternative was provoking my father to fury. Daddy's offer to treat us all to a week at the Grand Canyon thoroughly tested Eliot's mettle in this regard, but somehow he managed to go along. Fear can be a potent motivator.

It was on this trip that we fully inaugurated Lillian into our family, complete with a few rather harrowing initiation rights that all good Greenes had to endure: Daddy's unrepentant humiliation of a random majority of our waitpersons, the pun-ish banter that we began lobbing back and forth after we'd breathed the same air for more than twenty-four hours, and of course Eliot's genius at twisting people's most innocent remarks and somehow taking them personally. But Lillian's real challenge was Mother's fierce overprotection of her son. I rarely think of fierceness and my mother together in the same sentence, but they fit when it came to Clay.

Mother knew better than anyone what went on within her son. This was not because he'd ever told her, but because she'd so closely observed the trials of his life and how he had reacted to them. On many occasions throughout the promising years in which Clay fought to open himself up to a woman who could be his true companion, Mother had dared hope out loud that "this girl can satisfy him—I know she can!" But Clay couldn't bear to be satisfied in that way.

Mother recognized immediately that Lillian was Clay's white flag, and it broke her heart to see it. But she couldn't force herself to place the blame where it belonged. To Mother, Clay had always been my father's victim, never his own. Clay's ultimate surrender of himself now—after such a protracted and valiant battle against it—was not something she could ascribe to her husband and keep on living with him. And so, on this inaugural trip, somewhere along the red desert road between Pecos, Texas, and Albuquerque, New Mexico, Mother transferred all Daddy's crimes to Lillian and professed Clay to be her victim instead. Thereafter, Mother was inclined to observe privately, "Of course Clay is shut up like an armored car! Who in his right mind would open the doors with Bonnie Parker outside demanding everything from the gold bars to the petty cash?"

It was inconceivable to suggest that Mother now go and live with her nemesis. I could never have done that to Lillian.

Mother had no other feasible destinations within the family. As Samantha had already pointed out, Mother could not have handled the stairs in her condo. And Seth and Gretchen were too busy restraining their teenagers to pay attention to Mother's blood pressure. I'd have to investigate third-party alternatives.

I applied myself to this task the day after Sam stalked out of her rummy game with Eliot. It rejuvenated me to finally take some concrete action after all the energy I'd spent obsessing over which of our homes Mother would least hate to live in. Once I took the leap outside the family, the possibilities seemed relatively vast. I only had to locate the most ideal situation—the one in which Mother would be the happiest and best cared for. But one preliminary issue nagged at me as I settled down to the job at hand: What if Mother, even after I presented her with appealing options, continued to reject the whole concept, denying her need for a safer home at all? Perhaps I should first explore my legal alternatives in this regard.

Now, research is my forte. I've made a living not so much off my powerful courtroom presence but by finding and using the arcane intricacies of the law better than my adversaries. My juries rarely ever get to hear what I don't want them to, so I must seldom persuade them to disregard what hurts my case. I'm thus well positioned to note the chief complication of all research: the simplest questions have no answers.

When I asked how one would go about relocating an unwilling parent to some type of assisted living situation, I found all sorts of helpful information that waltzed right up to my question on the front side, and picked up just beyond it on the back, but never any that actually addressed it. Most of my sources seemed to presume that lots of folks face this dilemma, but none hinted at how to push on through it. "You need to sit down with your aged parent and inventory his needs," one suggested, and followed that up with a seventy-question checklist ranging from "Is it difficult for you to bathe yourself?" to "How often do you forget to lock the door at night?" Mother wouldn't even tell me if she'd been lonely since Lenny had died, so I doubted I'd get too far through a checklist with her. Another source warned me to "listen to your parent and respect their desires above all else." Well, what if my parent desired to live in peril—to worry her children into their graves ahead of her?

Finally I stumbled upon a nursing home Bill of Rights proclaiming that all competent persons are entitled to make their own decisions, including decisions about their health. Tracing this line of reasoning to its natural conclusion, I researched what must be proven in order for a person to be declared incompetent to make decisions for herself, and I found that Mother came nowhere near the legal benchmark. I thought this just as well, for it was not somewhere I wished to be tempted to go. In the state's eyes, then, a competent person could refuse to leave a home she lawfully inhabited no matter how delicate her loved ones thought her. Since we could not rely on the state to help us maneuver Mother, we'd have to steer her along by other means. Again, I saw that location was the key to our predicament. I simply had to identify the place where Mother could be convinced to live. Here my research took a decidedly creepy turn.

I began on a Web site that published nursing home statistics such as the numbers of incontinent residents, bed-bound residents, violent residents, residents who need help eating, bathing, or using the bathroom, bedsores per resident, and hours per day each resident is individually attended by nursing-home staff. Generally speaking, all of these statistics were in the double-digit percentiles for most facilities, some of them the high double digits.

Even more damning were the lists of nursing-home regulations that each facility had been cited for violating over the past six months. Most had several: "unnecessary use of catheters, restraints, and/or antipsychotic drugs"; "hiring of persons with a past history of abusing others"; "failure to store and serve food in a clean and safe manner"; "failure to protect residents from abuse, physical punishment, or separation from others"; and "failure to handle towels and bed linens in a manner that prevents the spread of infection." The daughter in me recoiled at this intelligence, wondering, *If this is only what they've been caught doing, what are they doing the rest of the time, when no one is whispering through the halls that an inspector is in the building? What if someone actually bit my mother or made her sleep on soiled sheets?* Some things just could not be.

"Still," countered my more objective self, "they say a picture is worth a thousand words. Let's just go take a look." So I selected the nursing home with the best compliance record, the most relevant "advantages over other facilities," the fewest disadvantages, and a reasonably convenient location to Clay and me, and I planned a late afternoon reconnaissance trip for the next day, February 20. I did not call ahead for an appointment.

At 4:30 the next afternoon, wearing a plain, khaki skirt and a nondescript sweater, I pulled into the parking lot of Buckhead Park Manor. The name itself—unencumbered as it was with such old-age identifiers as "nursing," "geriatric," "senior," or "convalescent"—I thought might appeal to Mother.

Though a manor, this facility sprawled wide and single-story flat across two or three Houston blocks. The home had first opened in 1967 as the Sacred Sisters Convalescent Center but had been bought by a private, for-profit corporation and remodeled in 1996. Now that it was a manor, it sported a commanding row of sculpted white columns across its upright, red-brick façade. But behind this mask it was much like any hospital, with four shiny white halls stretching out from a central nursing station like the spokes of a wheel. I entered through the double, nine-foot front doors and sat down in the lobby to form my first impressions.

I'd prepared a mental checklist gleaned in part from my Web sites and in part from friends who'd already gone down this road and knew what to watch out for. "Use all your senses," they'd said. "Just hang around and smell the smells. Listen. See what everyone is doing. Trust yourself. Is it a place you would ever want to live?"

Braced for urine and Lysol, the first thing I smelled was food, and not an unpleasant, assembly-line sort of food odor like tinny green beans or Hamburger Helper. Rather, I thought it might be real beef stroganoff. Apparently I'd arrived at the start of the dinner hour, for the lobby soon flooded with wheelchairs streaming toward a large room on the far side of the nursing station. I could thus observe both residents and attendants without being noticed amid the commotion.

Probably 90 percent of the elderly people I saw were being wheeled to dinner. I wondered if some of them might in fact be ambulatory but were simply being toted about in this fashion for the sake of the schedule. The few walkers clung to the handrails and shuffled along behind the rest. These people all seemed older than Mother—more decrepit and fearful. Had they come in that way? Perhaps so. Perhaps they'd begun shuffling and clinging the moment their children had convinced them that they belonged among the wheelchairs. Or perhaps they had arrived defiantly independent, like Mother, and the system had quickly molded them up against the handrails, biding their time until more chairs became available.

A whine accompanied the invasion of the lobby—the whine of squeaky wheels and of residents pleading for this or that from the attendants who had charge of them. Some people simply didn't want to eat dinner, as they were "not at all hungry yet," or were anxious to get to the activity center for the "dear little puppet show" apparently next on their schedule of events. Others smelled the stroganoff and whined for fish or chicken. One old woman didn't actually utter anything intelligible; she just whined generally, like an overstimulated toddler in need of a nap. All of this they directed backward to the hands that pushed them. I didn't see the residents interacting with each other. And nowhere did I hear laughter.

In the plus column, above their white Dr. Scholl's, the attendants all wore khaki slacks and golf shirts in bright, primary colors—royal blue, red, kelly green, and TCU horned-frog purple. Somebody, apparently, was shooting for noninstitutional. But I wasn't at all sure that an uppity name, a colonial façade, and nontraditional, preppy uniforms were doing the trick. Most of the attendants looked about eighteen or twenty to me. I tried to imagine them putting up with Mother's lengthy wake-up rituals and sour morning moods without getting exasperated with her. Nearby I heard a black youth in a green golf shirt chide an old man who wouldn't pick his feet up off the ground to "stop fightin' me, Mr. Mathers, or I'll have to tie your legs to your ears." Mr. Mathers snickered and made a production of lifting his huge, rubber-soled slippers off the tile and plopping them one by one onto the wheelchair footrests. "Don't know that my ears are big enough for that yet," he croaked, as he patted the black hand on his shoulder. Well, maybe it could work after all.

The residents stayed in the dining room until 5:30. At about 5:00, the central nursing station near where I sat began bustling with white uniforms dispensing pills into plastic cups and carting them off to the dining room, six cups to a tray. This procedure concluded just before the first residents emerged into the lobby, about every other one of whom was wheeled twenty feet down the hall nearest me and into a room with a big poster board taped to the window announcing: "The Fifth-Grade Puppeteers of Willow Baptist Church present the Tree of Life Puppet Show, Tuesday, February 20, 6:00 P.M. Don't dare miss it!" I had watched several women and children haul curtains, PVC pipes, and boxes into that room over the past forty-five minutes—more helpful cover for my clandestine visit. Now I slipped around the stream of wheelchairs as if I were part of the show and took a position against the back wall of the rectangular room, directly opposite the black-curtained stage that had been erected at the far end.

While the young Baptists rushed around testing their sound system and scouting for missing performers, the Manor's attendants lined their charges tightly around the stage in four awkward, robotic rows that threatened to scare the children speechless. Fortunately, the puppet script was pre-taped and they got to hide behind the curtain while they performed. Only their arms had to face the ranks of mechanical wheels crowding their tiny venue. Scarier still were the zombies that sat between the wheels, for I saw that dinner had somehow reduced the residents to lifeless drones, many of them unable to even hold their heads upright. I suspected it was the "dessert" I'd seen dispensed from the nursing station that accounted for this, but even I was shaken by it. The children looked petrified.

Finally the last child arrived and the show got underway. By now the room was stagnant—hot and still. No one could move more than an inch or two any direction, and the doped-up residents vented their displeasure with a general moan that originated from a woman sandwiched behind a two-foot post obstructing her view of the stage and that thereafter spread quickly down each row like an airborne virus. As the show progressed, the moaning only escalated. Daunted by their doleful audience, the puppets' mouths moved less and less in sync with the tape and their little bodies began to sag beneath the curtain.

The debacle ended with a fistfight. The old woman behind the post finally increased her volume to such a level that the man who was detained catty-corner began yelling at her to "shut up already!" When she answered this by grabbing a few curly gray strands of his neck hair and jerking, he quick as a rabbit flailed over his armrest and socked her in the chest. I was floored that either of them could move so fast, torpid as they'd both seemed moments before. Just as fast, a royal blue shirt somehow shimmied in between them, and several reds and purples began wheeling their neighbors out the door so the two troublemakers could be ejected. Unsure what was going on outside their curtain, the puppeteers limped along till their tape cut off. Not even the conscious were watching by then.

I couldn't bear to stay for the aftermath. I crept quickly past the eighteen wheels across the back row and ran from the stifling room. In the lobby, the combatants now sat side-by-side being dressed down by a young woman in a severe gray business suit. Though they were both semicomatose again by this time, she did not seem to consider that any reason to tone down her harangue. Perhaps she meant to make an example of them for the sake of the other residents now mutely rolling past toward their rooms. I could not help marching up to her and declaring, "If you are the one responsible for this nightmare, you should be thoroughly ashamed of yourself!" I left her agape and pushed open the grand front doors behind which my mother would never live. There was one "home" off my list.

Two or three other such outings confirmed to me that Mother was not a candidate for a nursing home. But the marketplace had anticipated such realities and reactions as mine and had already devised a hybrid sort of facility that could better cater to the legions of relatively healthy octogenarians that will only multiply as baby boomers surge into old age. "Assisted living" centers were designed to keep people out of the nursing home system with all its wheels and lifesaver attendants and its frightening regulatory rating schemes. I hoped one would not only prove acceptable to Mother but far preferable to her holing up any longer all alone on Lear Drive.

In assisted living, seniors who are still relatively independent occupy their own private living quarters but share such amenities as a cafeteria, recreation facilities, and a small medical staff on-call to assist with emergencies and advice on medications. Such facilities vary greatly in levels of assistance and in lifestyle, some resembling a boardinghouse, others a condominium, and still others a hotel. None of them are regulated by the state in the manner of a nursing home.

I did my homework and composed a list of five or six assisted living centers that I planned to canvass much as I had nursing homes the week before. At around ten o'clock that Monday morning, then, I pulled my Explorer into a visitor space at the Abbey—on paper the most promising of my handful of elite, west-Houston assisted living facilities.

Despite its distaff-sounding name, the Abbey was not a women's facility. I judged this to be essential for Mother because of her long-held prejudices in favor of men. In addition to her belief until recently that she could not survive without one living in her house, Mother was a person who wouldn't have boarded a plane if she'd seen a woman step into the cockpit in a pilot's uniform. She had never entrusted herself to a female stockbroker, surgeon, or even a gynecologist. And now that she was manless, I think she viewed Clay, more than me, as her protector. So I made sure that at least a few of Mother's neighbors at the Abbey would be men.

Like many other assisted living facilities, the Abbey was almost brand new. Constructed around 1995, it was a cross between a swanky hotel and a swanky office building. The tinted glass exterior was more the latter, but the interior was all Ritz with its burgundy carpet, navy-and-chocolate-brown paisley wallpaper, and the brass chandelier that monopolized a spacious, two-story lobby. Once I'd told the concierge on duty just inside the front doors that I had arrived quite a bit early to meet another visitor, I took cover amidst the many intimate chair pairings sprinkled throughout this large, pleasant room. From my nook, I watched people come and go for close to an hour. And none of them, I noted, rolled.

The traffic out of the Abbey on this Monday morning was much heavier than I'd expected. According to the facility's Web site, ninety-three people presently lived in its seventy apartments. This meant that approximately twenty-three were occupied by couples, or at least roommates. But from what I observed, coupling seemed the rule rather than the exception. Many left the building spruced up and holding hands, perhaps on their way out to lunch or to various appointments. Others left in tight packs of old women, duos and trios distinct mostly for their hair color. The naturals—grays and whites—mostly ran together, as did the haughty old broads like Mother who vainly maintained their anachronistic red or blonde dye jobs. What impressed me, though, was their running at all. These seniors were independent, and independence clearly kept them on their feet.

Incoming, the traffic was just as heavy. Every few minutes, another woman just about my age seemed to pop through the front door, toss a "Hi, Sylvie" to the concierge, and waltz on down the hall out of sight. Occasionally it was a younger woman—one of them about thirty with three small children in tow. I labeled these grand- and great-grandchildren and gloated over how much Mother would appreciate this aspect of her life at the Abbey. She would not have to worry about moving into a human scrap yard—forgotten except for what could one day be mined from her estate.

Smitten, I determined to see more of the Abbey though it would necessitate blowing my cover. I moseyed up to Sylvie and asked her if I could possibly speak to an administrator about the facility and also stick my head into one of the apartments for just a minute or two. Sylvie smiled, apparently accustomed to alleged visitors suddenly declaring themselves potential clients. "You'll want to talk to Robert Clarkson, our administrator. Just a moment, I'll ring him for you," she said. Thirty minutes later, Mr. Clarkson had escorted me through the Abbey's exercise room, kick pool, banquet hall, and a cafeteria where two hot selections and two cold selections were offered at every meal. We wound up our tour outside apartment 118—residence of Genevieve Lafayette Bingham for the past five years. Mr. Clarkson tapped on her door.

This Miss Bingham swung the door wide open without calling or peeping out first and smiled at us broadly. She was one of the naturals, but her careful, silver coif was anything but earthy. It set off dramatically against the fuchsia blouse that she had tucked into crisply creased black wool slacks. Her nails were painted a few shades lighter than her blouse—the same color as her tiny house slippers. This was a classy lady.

"Hello, Bobby," she drawled, taking Mr. Clarkson's arm and pulling him toward her. "You come in here right now. Who's your friend?"

Tall, middle-aged Robert Clarkson beamed down at her, then bent over and kissed Miss Bingham's cheek. When she glanced my way again, he remembered that he had a purpose for his visit besides winding round Miss Bingham's little finger. "Oh yes, this is Mrs. Ardelean. She's considering the Abbey for her mother."

"Uh-huh." Miss Bingham seemed to dissect every syllable of his simple introduction with this one word. "Is she with you, dear?" she asked me.

"Not this time," I answered her. Sensing that it would be useless to lie to this woman, I did what any good lawyer would under the circumstances—said as little as possible and then changed the subject. "Miss Bingham, would it be too great an inconvenience to let me glance through your place for just a moment so that I can give my mother an accurate description of the facility? I promise not to notice anything that's out of order."

"Why, honey, nothing's out of order. Come on in. And call me Jenny. Please."

She backed up to let us enter, and I stepped into the raspberry parlor of a Mississippi River plantation house, complete with hardwood floors draped generously with gorgeous handwoven area rugs. Where the large, high-ceilinged living area had defied such resemblance, Miss Bingham had simply painted it in, as she had the fancy French doors on the accordion shade covering the floor-length window at the far end of the room. I'd never seen *trompe l'oeil* used so effectively before. Of course, the mahogany and cherry wood antiques positioned around the room also helped quite a bit, as did the big-leafed houseplants reclining in every corner. "Mother would absolutely love this," I murmured before I remembered that Mother's apartment would not come furnished with antiques or houseplants, nor probably even the six-inch, white crown molding that Miss Bingham had likely installed on her own dime. Still, look what one could do with it!

Miss Bingham stood back and let me take it all in. "Now, I have one of the end units, you understand," she said. "Most of the others are not quite so large and don't have as many windows. Still, the high ceilings and hardwoods throughout the facility make it well worth the price, I think." Hmm. The price. I hadn't quite gotten around to asking Mr. Clarkson about the price yet. Well, that could come later.

"Does your mother like to decorate?" Miss Bingham asked, as she led me through her equally adorable kitchen and bedroom. "They are really quite good about letting us have our way with our own units, even though we're technically just renters."

"I suppose they couldn't possibly complain about any of your additions," I gushed. "You're from the South, I presume?"

"Why, of course I am, child. Louisiana. But don't believe everything you hear about old ladies from Louisiana. Not all of us are boozers and husband haters, despite what you might read in the *Ya-Ya Sisterhood.*"

"Have you been widowed long, Miss Bingham?" I asked.

"No. I'm not widowed at all, my dear. I've never been married a day in my life." With that, she batted her eyes at the silent Mr. Clarkson sprawled comfortably in a white whicker chair, and this immediately drew the blood to his cheeks. "Perhaps that's why I'm not a husband hater!"

"Perhaps." I agreed completely.

"What about your mother?" she queried, leaving room for numerous interpretations of just what she was asking me. When I had trouble selecting one, she giggled, and added, "How long has she been widowed?"

"For the second time, only about two months. But my father died almost twenty-three years ago."

Miss Bingham frowned slightly, then asked, "Is that all that's wrong with her—that she's newly widowed?"

"Well, she's recently had lung cancer too. They removed it in October."

"Sounds like she's had a very rough few months. Why do you want to ship her off to a place like this?"

"I don't want to 'ship her off.' I just want her to be safe. She's weak a lot of the time. She sometimes seems depressed. And recently she fell out of bed and couldn't get up without help from the EMS." So much for my lawyerly discretion. "I thought the whole purpose for a place like this is the security, the camaraderie. Are you saying you don't like it?"

"No, no, no, honey. I'm just saying that you and me liking it is beside the point. Why don't you bring her to see me sometime? She and I can hash it out over a pot of coffee. I import a mean chicory blend."

I pondered this. Mother might like Genevieve Lafayette Bingham very much, despite the difference in their hair-coloring philosophies. On the other hand, she might despise Jenny Bingham for no better reason than her sassy southern drawl. With Mother it was hard to say. "That's a very generous offer, Miss Bingham. I'll consider it. Thank you."

As we inched toward the door, Mr. Clarkson arose, his work here done. I suspected that Miss Bingham was his secret weapon in the recruitment department. Perhaps that's how she paid for all her extra amenities. At any rate, she'd persuaded me on several fronts. I said good-bye and reluctantly stepped back into the paisley hallway.

She stuck her head out and took my hand. "By the way, honey, what's your mother's name?"

"Josephine Greene Van Zandt."

I felt her little hand go slack as she flinched at an apparent speck of something suddenly in her eye. She must have needed to rush off and attend to it, for she sang out hastily, "All right, dear, then best of luck to you," whereupon she released my hand and shut herself away, leaving Mr. Clarkson and me staring at one another dumbly in the hall.

"Uh . . . would you like me to explain the costs now?" he asked finally.

I agreed and spent the next twenty minutes in his office getting this bad news. Mother, of course, was worth it. Better still, she could afford it. So what if our inheritances would diminish in direct proportion? What mattered was Mother's safety.

In deference to thoroughness, I visited all the places on my list over the next few days, but none of them drew me as the Abbey had. Perhaps this was because I wasn't welcomed into any other charming raspberry parlors. Or perhaps it was because I wasn't welcomed by any other charming Miss Binghams. By week's end, I was convinced that the Abbey would soon be Mother's new home. Now I had to convince my brother.

I called and made an appointment to drop by Clay and Lillian's house on Thursday night—the only evening that Clay said he would be available for the next ten days. As the owner of a small brokerage firm, Clay had been slaving to soothe distraught clients ever since the markets had begun to throw off their inflated valuations the year before. That the 1999 peak had been exponentially higher than was ever justified by most companies' financials had only made investors more indignant when everything fell back down to earth. My brother was now doing triage, and the casualties were mounting still.

I arrived on Thursday night with my arguments rehearsed and my colorful exhibits clearly labeled. That afternoon I'd driven by the Abbey and had taken a few exterior photos to supplement the interior shots adorning the facility's slick brochure—also in my folder. If I could sell Clay on the Abbey at the outset, he might never get sidetracked questioning whether Mother should move anywhere at all.

And sell him I did. He conceded that the grounds were noninstitutional and that the decor was "sufficiently uptown" for our mother. "Maybe she'd really enjoy it," he'd said. But somewhere along about the pricing portion of my Mr. Clarkson imitation, a glitch cropped up in my program. That glitch was Lillian.

Usually Lillian took so little obvious interest in our family affairs that Mother was able to rail convincingly that her daughter-in-law didn't give a hoot about most of the Greenes; all she cared about were her own progeny and the ditzy characters in her romance novels. I had long suspected that Lillian's apparent disinterest was part self-defense and part futility; we scared her, and besides that we rarely listened to a word she said. Tonight I had counted on Lillian's practiced indifference.

Instead, just when I'd gotten Clay all the way down to the fine print of the Abbey's cost sheet, she asked, "But, Katy, does your mother want to move?" I glanced at Clay and relaxed when I saw that he hadn't paid her any attention.

"I can't wait for us to show her all this," I announced more to Clay than Lillian. But I hoped that it would shut her up. "In fact, I met a resident over there who I think Mother will be great friends with. She's not your typical old lady anymore than Mother is."

Lillian was too dim to follow my lead. "I haven't gotten the impression she has any intention of leaving her house," she persisted.

This time Clay let his eyes rest on his wife. I saw her comment register in his overworked brain. "Katy, do you think we'd be jumping the gun suggesting something like this to her?" he asked. "Now that Lenny's gone, she only has herself to take care of, after all."

"You mean like she did in January when she took every medicine that every idiot doctor had ever prescribed to her without making sure they were compatible first?" I demanded.

Clay was busy nodding his agreement when Lillian piped up yet again. "But now that Josephine has had that security system installed and she's signed up for in-home visits from Dr. Gerard's nursing assistant, why does she really need to move?"

Clay and I stared at her, clueless as to what she was talking about. "Security system?" I murmured.

"Yes. Samantha arranged for it all last week, and I think they installed it on Monday." The very day I'd made a friend for Mother at her safe new home.

"And what's this about Dr. Gerard?" Clay asked her.

"Well, you know he's her primary care doctor. And she found out that since he has so many elderly patients who need his attention more than he can give it and they can afford, he's recently started this new program where he sends a nurse around to check on everyone. She'll go see your mother about twice a week, I think. Take her blood pressure, check her medications, whatever else she does. . . .You know?"

I suppose my look had begun to cow poor Lillian but not so much that it squelched one last headline. "Oh, and Samantha bought her a cell phone too."

✤

As fate would have it, Samantha did not answer her phone when I called twenty minutes later from my house. Snatching my purse, I started out the door for a much deserved drive-by, but I couldn't content myself with such iffy gratification. I came back in and rang Mother instead.

"Hello, Katy," she said first.

"How did you know it was me?"

"I got caller ID yesterday. How did you think?"

"I just want you to know that I know what you and Samantha have been up to, Mother. And I don't appreciate it one bit," I growled, incited by her haughty tone.

"You do?" Now she sounded meek enough.

"Yes, I do. Just how long did you plan to keep me in the dark?"

"I wasn't trying to keep you in the dark, Katy. I wanted Samantha to tell you."

"That sounds about right. You always want someone else to do the telling, don't you, Mother? Someone else to do the telling, someone else to do the confronting, someone else to do all the hard parts. Don't worry, Mother, I'll be talking to Sam about this plenty, but right now I'm talking to you."

"Well, I don't know why you're being so mean to me, Katy. It's not like I encouraged Samantha to hide her pregnancy from you."

And that was just the start of my Thursday night.

CHAPTER 12

Jo

March 6, 2001

Recent events have almost made me yearn for those tranquil November days when all I had to deal with was my husband's funeral and recuperating from lung surgery. At least back then Katy was on my side; now she thinks I'm the enemy. Over and over, I hear Sam's words, "Anything can be made too much of, Gammy, and Mom is the one to do it. . . . You know how she can be about things once she starts obsessing . . ." But I don't believe I really did know.

The moment it had sunk through my cloudy old head that I'd divulged Samantha's secret to the one person she'd begged me not to tell, I took what feeble steps I could to repair things. I practically hung up on Katy and called immediately to alert my granddaughter about what I had done. I confessed the whole thing to her screening machine without regard for who all might be listening in. Several times, as I rushed through my story, a click on the phone line signaled another caller bent on cutting in. The resulting clatter so discombobulated me that I abandoned my narration and let the ominous clicks tell the tale. "I'm afraid she's coming, Sam," I whispered. "I'm so sorry. But you'd better get ready." Then I hung up and started praying. True enough.

Now, my granddaughter is no coward. Though she'd over-heard the whole wretched tale I'd left on her machine, she didn't jump in her car and try to outrun the tornado heading her way.

She didn't even take cover in the broom closet under the stair-case, as I'd have done. Rather, when Katy arrived a few minutes later and demanded entry, Samantha let her in and submitted to her frothy interrogation with the grace and grit of Hester Prynne upon the scaffold. And, like Hester, Sam conceded all the particulars to her inquisitor—save one. Despite all Katy's pains to squeeze it out of her, Sam would not disclose the father's identity. She knows her mother well; she knows that the plans she has for herself and her baby would be compromised if Katy got her hands on the father. And if Katy knew who he was, she'd find a way to get her hands on him.

But Katy hasn't let this little gap in her view of the thing keep her from analyzing it all out on Samantha's behalf. Over the past five days, her bullish advice has crystallized into the fol-lowing simple formula: either marry the father, whoever he is, or abort the baby. Katy has fully considered other options and found them all grossly lacking. If Sam doesn't see it this way, it's because she refuses to accept the realities of the situation. Nothing about raising a newborn alone, without any outside financial assistance, would be glamorous or noble or fulfilling, Katy has assured her. Indeed, Sam must avoid this at any cost, including the cost of an unborn life. If Samantha feels so strongly about her baby, she should marry the father. If he isn't marriage material, she should not have the child. Now, which does she choose?

Samantha maintains there are shades of gray that Katy can't discern. She'll bow to neither of the pat solutions that her mother keeps pressing on her. And she still won't tell Katy any-thing at all about the father, even who he isn't. A fiercer stand-off I've never seen.

March 7, 2001

Yesterday afternoon Samantha called and asked if she could stop by my house on her way home from a photo shoot. I could tell she wasn't coming just to distract me from the investment news station that I've recently adopted as my companion whenever remembering and writing get to be too much for me. A visit from my granddaughter would give me something to think about besides my abysmal stock market losses, and for that I was grateful, though I suspected she might want to discuss something equally unpleasant. I made us some lemonade and then flirted with a novel until the doorbell rang.

Sam wasted no time plunging in. "Gammy, do you think Mom would have aborted me if it had been legal back then? Maybe she'd have done it anyway, knowing all she knows now."

"Why on earth would you ask that, Samantha?" I poured two glasses and made her carry them out to the back porch. Spring is already well underway in Houston, and I have very few opportunities these days to sit out in my garden with another human being.

"She seems to think single parenthood is the worst possible fate—worse than aborting your child. The way she says it, I can tell she thinks she knows what she's talking about."

"But your mother wasn't a single parent," I noted, grasping at the technicality that might deter her.

Sam scowled. Absently fingering a mature stem on my Lady Banksia rosebush, she corrected me. "Come on, Gammy. Mom thinks she was a single parent. That's how she lived our lives."

The snap I heard just before Sam said "lives" was a large section of the rosebush being emancipated from its roots. The branch still wound coquettishly up and around its trellis but now halted abruptly about a foot off the ground. Perhaps a garden talk hadn't been such a good idea. I offered no further dissent, given that deep down I, too, believed that Katy had been a single parent.

"I'll never abort my baby, Gammy. And in one more week, it won't be legal anyway."

"Hmm." Here was a variable I hadn't yet focused in on. "And does your mother realize that, Sam? Is that why she's so ruthlessly after you right now?"

"She knows," Sam said, the heft of her lemonade glass suddenly too much for her. Juice sloshed over the top as the glass plopped to her lap. Sitting there, no doubt contemplating another whole week of her mother's assaults, my little granddaughter looked ancient—as old as fear, which Adele used to say was born in Eden when men first questioned the goodness of God.

I thought this the right moment to air a few of my own concerns—things that had been bothering me since our dinner at the bistro. "Samantha," I ventured, "are you absolutely sure you don't want to marry the father of your baby? You know, in my day we would have considered it immoral to have a child out of wedlock, whether or not the woman had the means to support it. In fact, we considered sex before marriage immoral. There may even be some people today who'll disapprove of your becoming a mother if you're not married, and for no other reason than the obvious fact that you've given yourself away so cheaply. Have you thought of that?"

"Yes, I've thought of it, of course. But I just don't understand it, Gammy. I don't think what I've done is any worse than

170

what anyone else does—cheat on their taxes, turn their backs on people in need, lie to get what they want, drink too much. Who can point a finger at me?"

"Oh, I think that very few people would hesitate to wag their fingers at you, regardless of what they have or haven't done themselves. Remember that poor little gal last summer who forgot her baby in the backseat of the car when she drove up and saw her front door banging open from a burglary? Did you hear anyone on TV or the radio or even in your own circle of friends confess that they could imagine accidentally leaving their own child to suffocate in these circumstances? All I heard was 'No decent mother could do that. Period. She needs to be put away.'"

"I can't worry about those people, Gammy. I have to do what I feel is right."

"And did it feel right to have sex with a man you didn't even want to marry?" I showed her no mercy. "I remember overhearing Adele once tell your mother that all other sins are exterior to us, but that one is worse because it's against our own bodies."

"And what did Mom say to that?"

I let her sidetrack me. "Oh, she went along. You know your mother. She's never been tempted to lose control of herself—"

"By lust, you mean. . . . She's never been tempted by lust to lose control of herself."

"Yes, she's never been tempted by lust. But the point is that Adele was right, I think. I've had a bit of experience with that myself—giving my body away for reasons other than committed love. I know how it really feels."

"Well, Gammy, I can't do anything about that now. An abortion can't be the solution. Besides, I didn't know when I slept with him that I wouldn't want to marry him."

"So he's not married already?"

"No, he's widowed."

"Did you really know him . . . at all?"

"Yes, I knew him . . . I, I know him. That just doesn't matter, though."

"Why not? What's so wrong with him? Is he a bad person? Wouldn't he care that he's having a child? Is it that last fellow you dated—that dentist who your mother thinks it is? Even if you don't love him, Sam, there are worse reasons to marry than raising a child together."

"No to all your questions. If you must know, the father is someone I met researching a story I did several months ago. There's nothing wrong with him, but I just don't think I could marry him even if he wanted to. Besides, I have reasons to think he wouldn't want to marry me or be a father either one. And that's all I want to say about it. I can't take anymore questions now, Gammy. Please."

"All right, Samantha. I think you're right to have your baby, no matter what anyone says to try and shame you or change your mind. I know better than most how fruitless it is to try and live your life to please other people. But just be sure this man deserves not to know he's going to be a father."

The phone rang then, and Sam ran inside to answer it. She was gone a long time, long enough for me to amputate the severed rose branch from my trellis. I was staring at the lopsided remains when Samantha stepped back outside and approached me soberly.

"Gammy, that was Lillian. She said you might want to know that Mom has found you a new place to live." The ship had abruptly come about, and now it was me looking down the barrel of its cannon.

March 9, 2001

I woke up earlier than usual this morning, flapping my hands in the air trying to dog-paddle to the distant shoreline of Galveston Beach. I'd been alone in the choppy dream-water, a thirty-foot wave racing after me like a menacing bully. Surfing on its crest was this grand old house that Vic and I had built during the good part of our marriage. Or was it the one I grew up in on Front Street? Yes, it was these two, and the Byway house, all rolled into one.

I neither made it to shore nor was drowned by my pursuer, for dreaming minds will rarely endure the fantastic climaxes they so love to tease us to the brink of. Perhaps this comes from some sort of rupture in our imaginations—a creative stage fright in moments of supreme stress. More likely it's the law that our consciousness sets down for our subconscious before retiring: "Now, I'm leaving you alone for a short time. You can play in the yard as much as you like, but I'm watching from the window and if you start to step over that curb I'll be out here so fast your head will spin, you'll scream for mercy, and you'll probably even dog-paddle in the air. Don't make me warn you again."

In 1956, Vic declared that our home on the Byway had become too great an embarrassment to him despite the patchwork additions we'd made to it over the years. Even his underlings lived in better neighborhoods, and with clients he'd fallen into the slippery habit of grumbling vaguely about how his house was "under infernal, eternal construction" as justification for why we never invited them to dinner. Vic now issued an edict that we were to forgo new investments and unnecessary purchases for the next few years so as to put all our resources toward attaining a suitable homestead for the president of one of Houston's premier insurance companies. Powered by such commitment from the only one of us ever to make this type of expenditure, we were able to break ground on what turned out to be our retirement home in 1958. Adele, who'd been with us for sixteen years at that point and had seen both Clay and Katy out of the house, had recently mentioned "needin' to go full time with my grand-chillun," but so far I'd always managed to change the subject before anything concrete had materialized along those lines. I hoped to entice her along to wherever we moved.

Once he'd located the perfect lot, Vic tackled the new house the way he tackled everything he chose to do. I saw how it was going to be before we even left the starting gate. I remember it so well because he came home a good bit earlier than he normally did one Thursday night in September to tell me his plans.

I was standing in front of the kitchen sink at about 6:30 that evening, absently snapping the ends off some green beans. I was absorbed in a war going on outside my picture window between two huge squirrels and about five or six little songbirds. As in all wars, the sides were fighting over possession of the same territory—in this case the new birdfeeder I'd first filled with seed about three days before but that had not seen any action until today. Everyone, it seemed, had discovered its load at the same time.

For about twenty minutes, I observed the combat like a nervous Swiss—neutral as to the victor but much concerned about the future of my feeder. I soon found myself drawn into the fray, however, by what I saw as undue intimidation on the side of the squirrels. Basically, once they had figured out how to shimmy down the chain onto the birdfeeder roof, they took turns hanging by their toes over the edge until they reached the feed below with their mouths. Then they snarfed enough to fill their cavernous cheeks, somersaulted to the ground "neener-neener" fashion, and sprinted right back up the tree from which the feeder hung. One had barely dropped off before the other was sleuthing down the chain. Disheartened by these gluttonous gymnastics, the birds zoomed all around the feeder, hyper but a safe distance away, furiously watching their dinner disappear squirrel-full by greedy squirrel-full. Finally I'd had enough.

As the brasher of the two squirrels lowered himself over the edge of the roof, I snatched the biggest green bean I could find and slapped it hard against the window a few feet from his face. The result was most gratifying. He instantly catapulted into midair, his four paws splayed like he was being held up at gunpoint, and his big black eyes gazed into mine for a terrified second before he fell and then scurried double-time up a distant tree several yards away. The feeder swayed wildly from the force of his frantic dismount, and I could almost hear the birds cheering as I pulled back my arm to whack the window once more for good measure.

"Jo!" came Vic's voice from somewhere behind me. This time it was my turn to go airborne, arms flailing and green beans flying. The big one I was using as a stick grazed Vic's face on its way into the den. He was still holding his cheek when I turned on him.

"What in tarnation are you doing?" I squeaked out between pounding heartbeats. Adrenaline apparently had given my question plenty of punch, though I myself could barely hear it.

Vic understandably took up a defensive tone. "I came home to give you some news. Why are you beating on the window with our supper?" he demanded.

As I considered the account I might give of what I'd been doing, everything came into perspective, and I burst out laughing in the way Vic always found contagious. Soon he was doubled over howling at he knew not what, and, well, we never did eat those beans that night. It was the next morning before he remembered why he'd come home early the night before.

"So, Jo, Tommy recommended a good architect to me, and I met with him yesterday to talk over what we want in the new house."

"Oh? What is it we want?" I asked, the sarcasm concealed perfectly by my earnest tone.

"Well, I've thought it over quite a bit. We'll need five bed-rooms, three baths, at least a six-hundred-square-foot living room with hardwood floors for dancing, a somewhat smaller den, and a pool, gazebo, and antique wet bar in the back. We need to be able to entertain, put up plenty of company, and yet feel at home in it ourselves. I told him we'd have to have a three-car garage, minimum. He suggested a Tudor style, and I thought that sounded fitting for our purposes. He'll have a draft of the plans ready for me to look at in three weeks, and we hope to get going by the first of November. Then we'll start thinking about all new furniture. What do you think, Jo?"

How good of him to ask. Actually, it sounded like a whole lot of work to me. But that wasn't my line, I knew. "Could I add just one thing?" I asked instead.

"Sure, dawlin'," he answered, patting my hand under the covers of our modest double bed, soon to be garage-sale inventory. "What?"

"Could I have a picture window with a nice big tree outside it, and then will you give me a birdfeeder for my forty-fourth birthday?"

"I know just the tree," he said. "Would you like a side order of green beans to go with that?"

March 10, 2001

Christmas that year came and went almost unnoticed in the frenzied blur of repairmen and yard sales. While Vic was orchestrating things at our new residence going up across town, I was supposed to be getting the much maligned old house on the Byway packed up and ready to sell. Katy and Adele helped out, but twenty-five years is an awfully long time to dust off and cram into boxes, and I found a fond memory in every corner conspiring to undermine my commitment to the coming transition. I was limping along in this halfhearted fashion when it became apparent that yet another house would soon pass out of my life.

Daddy had always said he could smell the past. That's because he was so often caught a whiff of something that propelled him back to the person or place where that scent had first registered in his brain. Pungent buttermilk landed him in his father's barn fighting back vomit as the old man taunted him with their cow's milk—fresh and nonhomogenized, right out of the pail between her legs. He said his father would take a big slurp, smack his lips, and cry, "Ahhh, der's nuttin' like it, Joey. Want some?" Much later, after Daddy had retired but before his memory had betrayed him, he loved the smell of fresh-cut cedar because it could magically deposit him in his now gobbled up little shop on Main where he'd once stored thick bolts of wool in specially constructed cedar crates to keep the moths from feeding on them.

I wonder which smells would have brought our years on Front Street to life for Daddy. Would the memories they triggered have been pleasant ones? And what of she who polluted our little house with astringents, who relentlessly enslaved us to joyless, labor-intensive tasks that filled our fallow rooms with clean, stinging odors like starch and bleach and lye? What of she who grudgingly set our table mostly with sharp, mean-spirited foods like sauerkraut and pork chops hastily blackened over a too-hot fire? How would Daddy have felt about the part of his past that reeked of her?

My past is filed away under a different system—according to place. Mostly buildings. Mostly houses. And so it was that my 1959 "Saga of Three Houses" took me on a wild and bumpy trek through time, much as this diary has thus far. Leaving the Byway would sever me from my children's childhoods; I'd somewhat prepared for that. But when Daddy's old house on Front Street began to sink faster than we could buoy it, I saw that I'd soon be severed from my own childhood as well, whether I was prepared for that or not. The house would have to be sold for its property value, and my mother Irene—now legally blind and suffering from all the internal corrosion that typically attends a heart of stone—would have to be relocated to a nursing home, if one would have her.

From the moment we finally made the decision to close up the Front Street house, I lost my ability to sleep through the night. If Vic and I had already been in our burgeoning castle on Lear Drive, I'm sure he'd have moved into one of our many spare bedrooms to escape my constant night-tossing, trudging to and from the bathroom, and flipping on lights to fetch things that might possibly knock me out—milk, medicines, magazines, music—anything to get out of my mind. For several days I even tried a glass of wine just before bed, and that helped turn me off, but I inevitably turned back on again just a couple of hours later. It wouldn't do. So I determined to physically exhaust myself and sneak up on sleep that way. I packed harder and faster but to no avail. That only made me more miserable and frustrated through the endless hours of the night when normal, healthy people with only one house to think about were all busy sleeping.

One morning at around 3:30 A.M., I flopped over in the darkness and found Vic's haggard eyes glaring into mine. "Jo, we can't go on like this. I'm juggling too many things during the day to get no more than three or four hours of sleep each night! You have to get a hold of yourself. What can we do?" His voice got higher and higher as he spoke until he sounded very much like a woman. My hysteria was seeping over into him.

"I, I . . . can't sleep," I finally confirmed. That's as much insight as I could offer. Beyond that, all I could do was cry. Any solution would have to come from him.

"OK," he began, running his hands through his sloppy night hair. "We need a new plan. You trying to tire yourself out isn't doing the trick. Maybe we should switch gears on this house thing, Jo. For now, we could just keep your father's house. We

179

could hire someone to live there with your mother, at least for another year or so until our lives settle down and you can better handle the alternative."

I'd never noticed before how gray Vic had gotten. And his eyes were so wrinkled now. When had that happened?

"Jo, did you hear me? You're not sleeping now are you? Are you sleeping with your eyes open?"

"I don't think so," I mused. I was having trouble caring what Vic was chattering on about. What had he asked me just now?

"Of course it will cost us a fortune to hire enough people to do everything that needs to be done over there now—a part-time nurse, a full-time caretaker, and then someone to actually keep the house standing. That place may be only a storm or two from falling over as it is."

I nodded. I couldn't argue with anything at this point.

Then Vic cocked his head and searched me as if to mentally take my temperature. That was mildly interesting, but soon I got distracted comparing the color of his chest hair to his head hair. Then there were his eyebrows. It seemed to me that they all had different proportions of gray in them. It was very odd.

Vic grabbed and shook me gently until I returned my eyes to his face and focused long enough for him to fire an unexpected shot: "There's another option, darlin'. You know what it is. It's not the solution that either of us would prefer—Irene being so sour and all—but if it's the only one you can actually live with, then maybe we should just take her with us to Lear. At least you'd have lots of room there to hide from her."

Somehow this got through my stupor. It drove right in like a poison dart penetrating the inch-thick hide of a giant grizzly bear. I reared up. I roared, frantically, out of control. Alarmed, Vic promptly withdrew the dart. There were no other options after all.

That's when he hit upon the strategy that saved me.

"Why don't you paint the old house, Jo?"

March 12, 2001

I'm a little embarrassed to admit that Daddy's house is the only thing I've ever painted on location. All my other subjects I photographed first and then reproduced in oil. That way my scenes were already one-dimensional, and I didn't have to figure out how to eliminate the other two. But this time I knew I had to face the thing itself. It was an important part of my therapy.

Late the next morning I gathered together my supplies—a fresh canvas, my easel, my paint box and brushes, palette and palette knife, a smock, rags, mineral spirits, and a plastic jug of distilled water. I asked Adele to finish cleaning out the kitchen cabinets, and then headed over to Front Street. All morning I'd been pondering which face of the house I should paint first. I settled on a full frontal view and set up my easel in the middle of the sidewalk, adjacent to the address stenciled on the curb—"3207." I meant to work that number into my painting somehow, but of course I couldn't actually position myself in the street so as to capture its true appearance. This was going to be a stretch for me in more ways than one.

Three days into my enterprise, sleep finally came to me, and Vic began to calm down. But then I had a realization that threatened to halt my progress and reduce us once again to sluggards. It came to me as I repainted the living room windows for the fourth time. The awnings were giving me the trouble; they just wouldn't take on any depth. I was glaring at them when it occurred to me that I had always hated them. Not only were they ugly—green-and-white-striped with ragged fringes—but they also made the living room so very dark. At all hours of the day it was gloomy in that room, no matter how bright the sun. And in that interminable darkness, at the callous, calloused keys of our baby grand, I'd been defined and controlled by the notes that had ultimately driven me away. Because they hadn't wanted me, I'd finally cast them off.

The awnings mocked as I fought to treat them with objectivity and competence for the sake of the painting. I was engrossed in this little contest when my tormenters threw me an unexpected lob. "You'll have to take everything," they whispered so softly that I could barely hear them from where I sat on the sidewalk forty feet away. "Everything." Everything?

It's then that I understood. As sole heir to this house and all that lived within it, I would have to take—or otherwise dispose—of all its contents. Everything. Not just the old woman who'd darkened its windows with ugly, striped awnings.

What would I do with my other foe—the indestructible old instrument whose perpetual tour de force she had commissioned? The enmity between us, too, was deep and thick and somehow still fresh. Could I allow it, anymore than her, into my house? Even a huge new stranger of a house with plenty of rooms where I could stuff it and almost forget it was there? But I never would be able to forget. The notes would come to me. They would find me and drive me off yet again. I couldn't stand for it.

But neither could I destroy it, sell it, or give it away. We were too intertwined, this piano and me. Its past was my past;

I'd never had a life without it. And I could not now choose to live entirely apart.

So I sent it into exile—somewhere where I could visit and redeem it if I chose but far enough away that the notes couldn't reach me. I lent it to Fran. She'd always wanted a baby grand, and she graciously housed it for thirty years before Silver got sick and they moved off to Wisconsin. Now restored, it sits in my living room. I occasionally go in there and sit with it. And I listen. In twelve years I've not heard a single note. I don't know where they went.

The picture hangs there over the piano bench. The number "3207" is artlessly affixed to one of the porch posts as if I'd literally glued it on to the finished painting. The awnings look like ratty pieces of fabric lying flat against the house, strangely shrouding the living room windows. I suppose they foiled me. But my sleep came easier after that.

March 13, 2001

Unwilling to upset my delicate new equanimity, Vic handled the dissolution over on Front Street. It all happened very fast. The house went the way of Daddy's shop—sold to a commercial developer who promptly demolished it to make way for something more useful, something that wasn't "a storm or two from falling over." The empty lot was combined with several adjacent ones to support a state-of-the-art, five-story office building that itself would be a casualty of the high-rise condo boom of the early 1980s.

One Saturday morning in September, after the house was already gone, I sat in my car and watched them bulldoze what was left of Daddy's once bountiful garden. Soon it would be paved and striped for parking. A life grows stale so quickly; it makes one wonder why we're here at all. I drove from there over to our new house on Lear Drive where Vic and I had moved in the month before. I'd said good-bye to the Byway with relatively little fanfare besides a few waterworks when Adele had wistfully recalled to me how she'd watched my family grow up there, "You not least among 'em, missy!"

The next time I drove up Front Street, the office building was fully grown and strangers bustled in and out of it. I felt relieved as I watched. I'd divorced myself from those premises as cleanly as souls must throw off the corpses they inhabited in their earthly lives. Once again I had only one house—albeit a huge house—to worry about, and my sleep returned almost to normal. Only occasionally over the next few years did Vic have to scamper off to another bedroom in the middle of the night. And then, for a time, I lost interest in sleep altogether. But I'm getting ahead of myself.

Chapter 13

Katy

The April issue of *Lone Star* magazine arrived in my mailbox on March 12 boasting two meaty articles written by my daughter—the two I'd seen pieces of scattered across her den floor a month earlier. Samantha had never had two stories in one issue before, and I thought it ironic that she'd progressed to this professional zenith in the same week she was choosing to sabotage her cherished and hard-fought career.

On the cover, George and Laura Bush hovered crisply under their inaugural umbrella. Hovering outside the camera's focus just behind them was a blurry but recognizable George Bush Senior. I'd have chosen that very picture to tease Sam's story on the mysterious source of Dubya's strength and wherewithal. Was it the elder Bush or not? I read the piece and granted her semisubtle contention that the son has a far greater inspiration than an ambitious, exacting father who was also a president. Perhaps it is that higher stimulus, which Dubya maddeningly refers to in public simply as "faith," that has allowed him to overcome some of the paternal damage that all sons apparently must bear. Parents not only enrich, it seems, but they impair. Even the parents of presidents. Even parents who are presidents.

Samantha's second article fell much deeper in the magazine, I suppose to camouflage the fact that she had written practically the whole issue. Here she told the story of Bruce Canmore, a Scottish foreign exchange student whose hands and face had been seared off in a head-on collision three years before. The then twenty-year-old college junior had accepted his host family's invitation to spend spring break in their Corpus Christi beach house with a few friends, and the five of them were heading down Shoreline Boulevard on their way there one evening when a Lexus driven by a drunk teenager approached at high speed with its lights off. Bruce, in the front passenger seat at the time, was the only one in his car not fortunate enough to die instantly. He was pinned by the glove compartment mashed against his knees, and his door was crushed shut. When the engine ignited and the fire spread inside the car, good Samaritans on the scene had no choice but to watch the flames creep across the dash and consume Bruce's upper body just as rescuers showed up with fire extinguishers and the Jaws of Life. He'd been conscious throughout the horrific ordeal, begging for it to end. But somehow he'd survived.

In the three years since the accident, the young man had undergone thirty-seven surgeries to graft skin, construct eyelids, enlarge the pinholes where his ears had been, reduce exposure to his now gaping nasal passages, attempt the repair of his widely damaged nerves, and even to attach a pacemaker to his traumatized heart. At night he had to be slathered in cream and then buckled into a silicone mask to protect his taut, poreless face—already one huge scar—from tearing or further scarring. This procedure had to be conducted by someone else, as Bruce was partially blind and had no fingers left below the upper joints. His father, William, had been Bruce's fingers and eyes and ears and heart since the moment the elder Canmore had gotten the call from the University of Texas Medical Branch burn unit and had beelined for Galveston.

This past October, Bruce had submitted himself to public display in order to see the other driver punished for her crimes. She'd been spared significant injury by the deployment of a first-rate Lexus air bag. His testimony at her trial secured her conviction on four counts of vehicular manslaughter and one count of assault. Her sentencing—ten years, with no chance for parole until she'd served a large chunk of it—was not the most televised portion of the trial. It was Bruce's grisly testimony, uttered as it was from the lipless mouth of a faceless, fingerless young man once so handsome and virile, that had catapulted the court-TV ratings and dominated the evening news for a week in six Texas counties.

Samantha had told the Canmores' story with an arresting mix of frankness, admiration, and sorrow. Some of the details they had shared with her could only have been entrusted to a friend, for only a friend could retell them with honesty and respect, and without resorting to ghoulish melodrama or simplistic sentimentality. Sam had accomplished all of that and more. In her hands, Bruce and William's story was a hopeful tragedy. They planned to keep on seeking the regeneration of Bruce's sight and touch, as well as his will to live. Parents not only impair, it seems, but they enrich. And they redeem.

Samantha had written such beautiful accounts of these two father-son struggles that I fell again to brooding about the career she was jeopardizing with her obstinate refusal either to undo her mistake or to make it right. I determined to try once more to change her mind before it was too late.

〽

The fact was, I could now see only one viable alternative for Samantha. Her elusive partner in this madness was so out of focus for me, and her reluctant references to him so painful and cryptic, that I'd half convinced myself that he had raped her. She denied this, but I could not make myself think of him as a father, nor the consequence of his trespass as a child. And this helped me to advocate abortion as strongly as I did. I had little time left to bring Samantha around.

I called her at work that very afternoon. This was the one place where she generally answered the phone, as she had no secretary to take her calls. I leapt right in. "Samantha, I want to see you this evening. Before you brush me off, let me say that you are being juvenile and selfish. You're not the only one who'll be affected if you go through with this. Who do you think will have to go fetch it from day care when its nose is running but your boss needs you to finish his filing and won't let you leave? I deserve to have my say."

"Don't you think you've said enough by now, Mom?" she asked. Her tone was plenty cold, but I sensed a wound opening where my dart had struck. I pressed this small advantage.

"I don't know," I said. "Have you changed your mind about the abortion?"

"There is no abortion. You say it like it's a thing that has substance anywhere except in your head. I can't agree that I have or haven't changed my mind about something that has never entered my mind."

"Then, no, I haven't said enough. I just want an hour of your time. Let me talk to you for one hour, and then I promise not to bother you about it again."

"I can't imagine that you have anything new to say. What's the point?"

"The point is that you haven't yet listened to what I've said. You just admitted that. Samantha, I hate to resort to threats, but if you don't talk to me this evening, I swear to you I will never, ever lift a finger to help you care for this child if you have it. I think that's fair. All I'm asking for is your open mind for an hour."

Samantha said nothing for enough lengthy phone seconds to worry me that I'd overplayed my hand. "OK, Mom," she said finally. "But let's make it two hours. I have a few things to say to you too. If you'll listen with an open mind, I will."

Nothing these days seemed to go quite as I planned.

As a general rule, I didn't do heart-to-hearts in my own living room or at my own breakfast table. Eliot was just too much of a wild card to risk such a thing if it could be avoided. I hadn't even mentioned Samantha's condition to him yet because I still hoped it would cease to be an issue very shortly. Of course, he'd have to be told if he were about to become a father-in-law and grandfather, but he had no need to know that he'd only come close. So I'd suggested to Sam that we unburden ourselves at her house.

After inviting me in, she took the stiff, straight-backed chair in the far corner of her cozy den and assumed a similar posture. I took a seat opposite, in the corner closest to the door, and prepared to make my opening remarks.

Although we'd both promised to come with an open mind, I believed that Sam's was still set on self-destruction. I had to find new words, and to that end I launched into the following confession: "Samantha, you and I have never talked very much about your dad. I haven't tried to hide his depressions from you, or the fact that our relationship is strained as a result, but I've never told you how it was early on, before you and Seth came along."

"OK," she said. "Let's hear it."

"Your father probably had more natural giftedness than just about anyone I've ever known. I watched him in high school and was so drawn to his abilities that I couldn't see his fatal flaw: he didn't believe he was enough. He pursued me with such determination that I mistook it for confidence. I was flattered . . . and totally smitten. But really he was just desperate. Somehow he'd latched onto me and become convinced that his success was dependent on my adoration. He was sure I'd give him that something that he thought he lacked . . . maybe a little like Samson and his hair."

I stopped there to make sure Sam was listening, and she nodded me on.

"Well, at first, I had in fact adored him. I'd adored him because he was charming and romantic, intelligent, funny . . . Like I said, he just had more gifts than other people. I was too young to bother about his character; I just assumed that that was intact. Of course he'd be hardworking and honest and forgiving. And even if he lacked in these areas, the physical passion that juiced our relationship would somehow fix any deficiencies. I thought that Eliot was a perfect package for me.

"Your grandfather tried his best to convince me otherwise, but I didn't consider him worth listening to. I'd never seen him take Gammy's desires seriously or even inquire as to what they were. And, because she wasn't one to voice them unsolicited, it seemed that everything, always, went his way. What credible advice could he offer me on love and marriage?"

Here Samantha nodded her agreement. She was old enough to recall her Poppy's less-endearing traits.

"Legally we were old enough, so we married, both of us making huge presumptions about the other. Your father presumed that my adoration would never wane, not for a moment, and that the jolt he got from it would propel him wherever he wanted to go. On both counts, of course, I couldn't have been a bigger disappointment to him. No, really. It was a crushing disappointment. He never recovered. He still won't accept it and take responsibility for himself. I tried for several years to be what he needed, but his need seemed bottomless. Finally I quit even feeling bad about it."

I paused there and felt bad despite this boast. I still grieved it all. Oh, how I grieved it!

"You can't just let life happen to you, Sam, because it'll smash you against every rock. You have to think things out, make reasoned choices, and listen to the advice of people who love you and who are still wiser than you are. Regret should not define a life, Samantha. How can I get that across to you? Please, please don't let it define yours."

Sam raised her hand to stop me. "I have a few questions," she said, quite a bit less hospitably than I thought was warranted at that point. "First, just what is it you regret? Do you regret having had children with my father? Is that where you meant to go with this? Do you regret marrying him at all? Or maybe you regret having turned him into Jell-O?"

"Just what does that mean?" I asked, astonished.

"I mean I don't believe you when you say you didn't know from the start how he needed you. I think you saw that very clearly, and that's why you were so smitten, as you say. You were going to turn Dad into something great, weren't you? And you were the one to do it—always so sure of yourself and so ready to take charge of other people's lives. Here was a piece of clay crying out for a potter, and you couldn't wrap your hands around him fast enough. I think you chose Dad quite deliberately."

I started out of my corner, perhaps to slap her, but I stopped in the middle of the room. "What could you know about it? You weren't there. Where did you even get these opinions?"

"Do you think I couldn't see it all for myself? You say Dad was disappointed, crushed. Wasn't it you who were so disappointed when he never became the powerful, ambitious man you'd planned for him to be? Hadn't you counted on being able to draw the necessary qualities out of him, creating them out of thin air where they didn't exist? And when he didn't train up, wasn't that when you quit adoring him? How'd you think he'd ever become a man if his wife didn't respect him?"

"Could I make him respectable by respecting him? Are you saying you think it was all my fault?"

"I . . . I'm . . . I guess I'm saying I don't think it was all his fault," she stammered, abruptly throwing up her arms in a halfhearted gesture of surrender. "Oh, I don't know. What do I know about marriage? Y'all were such a mess that I've never wanted any part of it."

My anger was quickly numbing. I stalled while I dove deep for some other emotions. "Well, Seth seems to have done all right," I noted weakly.

"Thank God," she said. "I don't know how he's done it. A lot of it must be Gretchen."

"Samantha, is this why you won't consider marrying this man?"

She stood up and shook herself off much in the way a dog might after strenuous petting, then she began pacing the modest length of the room. I fell back onto the couch and braced myself as she marched past. "It is in part," she said. "It's also the reason I'm afraid to be tempted by your talk of an abortion. I can't think about that possibility, Mom, because I might just do it if I think about it. I'd often like nothing more than to run away from motherhood. It scares me to death."

"As well it should," I quickly agreed. "It is scary. But it might not be so hard if you had help." I'd reverted to plan B—"marry him"— without even thinking about it.

"Don't you understand that I can't see a husband as help? All I can see is another huge scary thing to compound the first. I can't marry him even though I think this man is a really good one. I just don't trust myself."

I finally grasped that Samantha's goblins were bigger than the mere loss of a career. So rarely had I heard her doubt herself this way that I'd just assumed she was as pragmatic and resolute as I was. Here she seemed to question even her ability to love well—a concern I'd never had about her. But how could I help? I felt as useless as when she'd asked me what it was like to be in love.

"Sam, I won't suggest an abortion anymore. When the baby comes, I'll help you as much as possible. And if you want to tell me who this man is, you can. I won't try to find him or talk him into anything."

Perhaps she was so desperate to share her burden that she couldn't stop herself. Without hesitation now, she looked right into my face and flashed a grim, longing, little smile. "His name is William Canmore."

So many things come into focus when we listen.

Two days later I got a call from Robert Clarkson at the Abbey. He said that one of his residents had just given notice that she would be moving to a nursing home at the end of April, and her apartment would become available at that time. No, it wasn't Miss Bingham, he assured me, but this woman's unit was also on the end and had the same layout as Miss Bingham's. If I was interested in it for Mother, he would need a nonrefundable $4,500 deposit by the following week. Then, before the month was out, he would have to interview with Mother to ensure that she was an appropriate and willing candidate.

Now, I've never been a person who had many friends. I've over-seen a civic project or two, orchestrated multiparty lawsuits, organized institutional functions, and I've even done my share of public speaking, but I've never felt very comfortable in a room with only one or two people I'm unrelated to. When I find myself in that situation, I often get the feeling that the other person is trying to steal something from me, seducing me into telling him things I don't want anyone to know. It's easier just to be the boss. That way no one feels entitled to your stuff.

I guess I thought that marriage would be a trusty oasis amidst the shifting sand dunes of such outside relationships. Here would be a person whose whole assignment was to walk alongside me and share my cares. Evasion would not be necessary because all my stuff would be his stuff, too, and vice versa. So I'd never be alone again, and because of that I'd always be safe out in the world. As it happened, I felt more threatened at home than I did out there. And the loneliest moments have always been those in which I've had to weigh big decisions. Try as I might, I couldn't make this particular decision tip in either direction.

The next morning I drove over to the Abbey, allegedly to get another feel for the place. Could this really be a happy home for my mother? Perhaps if I could identify a significant enough shortcoming, I could cross the Abbey off my list and avoid the confrontation I was dreading. I hadn't asked if they accepted pets, for example. But as I pulled into the drive I saw an old man follow his poodle out the front door onto the lawn. And all the other objections I could think to pose went the way of the poodle. The Abbey really was a delightful place, but was I willing to bet $4,500 that I could convince Mother of that over the next seventeen days?

Once again, I found myself standing outside apartment 118, this time with no Mr. Clarkson there to listen in and relish the benefits accruing to him as a result of Genevieve Lafayette Bingham's very stout charms. More than anything, I wanted to be sipping tea in her raspberry parlor, handing her my troubles one by one. Not since Adele had I wanted to do that with anyone. I lifted my fist to the wood and was preparing to knock when a squeamish, inner voice assaulted me. "Wait a minute! What are you doing? You don't even know her. What makes you think she wants you to unload a bunch of personal stuff on her? What makes you think she'd care or have one bit of wisdom to offer? Why, you'd just be exposing yourself and your whole family to ridicule. You're being a weakling. Just pay the cursed deposit and go tell Mother she has to move."

Of course, this was all true. I had no way of knowing anything about Miss B really. I just had a sense that she wasn't someone who needed anything from me—that she'd have no use for anything of mine, and so no motivation for trying to take it from me. Why, then, would she also care to hear all that I suddenly so wanted to tell her? She wasn't Adele; we had no quarter-century of shared history to inspire her. It was a hopeless endeavor. I withdrew my fist, grateful to have come down to earth before exposing myself, and started back up the paisley hallway toward the lobby.

I was approaching Sylvie's desk to ask for a brief interview with Mr. Clarkson when Miss B fluttered in the front door with two or three other ladies. She wore a turquoise knit dress and a wraparound belt of copper medallions strung along a leather strap. As before, her silver hair gleamed strikingly against her bright, hip outfit, which somehow suited her despite her years. I saw Miss Bingham recognize me with a brief, startled look, and then she rushed over and gave me a hug. "Katy, right? How have you been, dear?"

"Oh, just fine," I lied.

"Have you brought your mother to see me?"

"No, Miss Bingham, she's not with me this time either. But the Abbey has an opening coming up soon, and I'm here trying to decide whether to put down a deposit."

"I absolutely insist that you call me Jenny. Would you like to come to my place for some refreshment? I'd be happy to answer any questions you've got, this time off the record." She held her hand out to me in the way an old woman has the perfect freedom to do, and I couldn't bear to withhold my own. With this firm grip on me, Miss Bingham looked over her shoulder to the little knot of women she'd walked in with and said, "I'll catch up with you girls at dinner. Right now I'm going to have tea with my friend Katy here." I blushed a deep red. This old darling claimed me as a friend, even if it was just her wide, southern way.

Inside apartment 118, everything was just as it had been on my first visit—charming, warm, and perfectly kept. Miss B waltzed me over to her sofa and nestled me into its deep floral cushions before standing back, surveying me with her head cocked and hands akimbo, and asking with utmost seriousness, "Now, will it be lemon or lime?" To the Miss Bs of the world, tea is strictly something one serves over ice with a tart chaser.

"Whichever you already have cut up would be fine. Lemon, if neither," I answered. While she was gone, I got a chance to examine her things a little closer. What I hadn't noticed at all before were the many bookshelves tucked hither and yon, most of them small or makeshift—a row of novels across the top of a secretary between two ivory and mahogany magnolia blooms, a shelf dividing the decorative fireplace into upper and lower, books on the New Testament above, and books on the Old Testament below. A vertical stack of gardening books propped up the lamp on the end table next to me, and forty or fifty other such titles occupied a gorgeous, glass-fronted tiger-oak cabinet inlaid on each side with intricate *fleurs-de-lis* patterned out of cherry wood and maple slivers. The many dozens of books in the room shared one characteristic: they all looked old. Not in bad condition but none of them new. Even the novels were exclusively classics—Steinbecks, Faulkners, Whartons, and Cathers. Not a Grisham or Kingsolver in the bunch.

By the time Miss B returned hauling her tray loaded with tea and cookies, sugar and lemon, I was bursting with questions. Was she a big gardener? "Oh, goodness yes, I was at one time. I spent many joyful years rooting out weeds, anticipating the month each spring when my azaleas would blaze the hottest possible pink. That's one of the primary advantages of the South, you know; its soils favor the fairest, most fragrant bloomers—camellias, azaleas, gardenias, magnolias. And of course the southern rose garden can't be topped. What about you, Katy? Do you garden?"

"Just enough not to discredit the neighborhood," I confessed.

"I've always worked long hours, and I had two kids to raise. I guess I never had much energy left over for pleasure." I took the glass that Miss B handed me and squeezed a lemon into it. "What about all these other books, Jenny? Do you have something against contemporary authors?"

She laughed as generously as she hostessed. "Well, I probably do. But the main reason I have so many older books is that it's my business. I was a dealer in rare books until I retired a few years back. I still occasionally fix an old friend up with an old book though it's squarely against the Abbey's rules to run any sort of business out of your home. Don't you dare tell Mr. Clarkson on me." Her wink assured me that such infractions had already been blessed.

I was intrigued. Daddy had once gone through a spell of rare book collecting, but I'd never cared enough to ask him what it was all about. "So, these books are rare? Is it mostly age that makes them rare?"

"Not at all. That's just one factor—a minor one really. It has more to do with the author, the edition, the number of copies printed in the edition, illustrations, the way the book is made, how well it's been preserved, and any special markings. Look, I'll show you." She pulled a green hardback volume off the secretary and held it out to me. It was heavy, well conditioned. The data inside the cover said it was published in 1934, a first edition. On the title page, beneath the printed *Tender Is the Night*, was a penned inscription, "My darling Zelda, I would rather have you with me. Your Scott."

I looked up at Miss B, trying for all I was worth not to drop the book on the tea tray. "Zelda? *The* Zelda? This is written by Scott Fitzgerald himself to his wife?"

"It has been thoroughly authenticated," she assured me. "What makes this book so valuable is not only its very personal, unique markings but the story behind the sentiment. It's rumored that Fitzgerald essentially stole portions of *Tender Is the Night* from Zelda, sure he could put them to better use than she could. No doubt he did. But right around the time of its release, she had another breakdown and was institutionalized for the rest of her life. Many have speculated that she was driven down in part by her consistent inferior showing against her spectacular husband. Seems she viewed marriage as a competition."

"How much is this book worth if you don't mind my asking?" I couldn't resist.

"That book was appraised fifteen years ago for about forty thousand dollars, but its real value is whatever someone will pay for it. I should really have it in a vault somewhere, but I'm too self-indulgent. Why own wonderful things if you're going to hide them away from everyone?" I had the growing sense that I could spend weeks with Miss B and never begin to reach the bottom of her.

"But that's not why you're here," she said, returning the book to its modest spot on her secretary and then taking a seat next to me on the couch. "Is there any way I can help you decide about the Abbey?"

"I'm not sure. Honestly, I don't often feel this perplexed about things, Jenny."

"I can imagine that," she said, so gently that I could laugh. She joined in with me, and then patted my hand in encouragement.

"I still haven't talked to Mother about it directly. But I think she may know through the grapevine that I've been investigating options for her. A lot has been happening in my family over the past few weeks; I'm not even sure anymore that I'm right about this."

"Unsure is usually a pretty good place to be when it has to do with other people," Miss B noted, as much to herself as to me. "Go on, hon. Would you like to tell me what's been happening?"

"Well, my thirty-five-year-old daughter, Samantha, told me the other day that she's so confused about marriage, she can't make herself do it even though she's been seeing a man she seems to love and has conceived a child with. How's that for starters?"

"It certainly gets one's circulation going," she said. "Why is Samantha so confused?"

Normally this is where I'd have panicked and tried to diffuse the conversation with some misleading tripe like, "Oh, she's just a perfectionist. If she can't figure out how to do something without making any mistakes, she doesn't do it at all." It's a tribute to Jenny Bingham that no such inclination moved me this afternoon. Rather, I blurted out, "She says she was so damaged by what she saw go on between my husband Eliot and me that she can't trust herself to pick a good man or treat him right."

From all appearance, I'm sure, I'd announced this to the tea glass in my lap. When I was through, I glanced sidewise at Jenny to gauge how much I'd thereby diminished myself in her eyes. I found them square upon me. She even snatched a pair of trifocals off the coffee table and put them on so as to see me better. "Bless your heart, Katy," she said. "Don't think you can shock an old gal like me!"

Encouraged, I rushed on. "The thing she really accuses me of, Jenny, is wanting Eliot to be my puppet, wanting to shape him and direct his every step. She claims that I found the man I thought I could do that to, and before long I'd destroyed him. I can't tell you how contrary that is to what I've always thought about my marriage. I know I'm a strong-willed person. But, honestly, I think I'm strong because of my difficult marriage and not vice versa. If I hadn't taken charge of our lives at some point, we'd have been out on the streets. Oh, I know you can't understand all I'm saying. It's such a very long story." I petered out there, returned my tea glass to the tray, and stood up. "Maybe I'd better just go. You've been very gracious to listen, Jen—"

"You tried for years to boost him up and help him to like himself, didn't you?" she interrupted. "But he wouldn't have it. Nothing you did was ever enough." She pulled me back down on the couch beside her. "Samantha is a relatively young woman who hasn't yet let herself live nearly as much as you have, Katy. Don't assume that her conclusions are necessarily more right than yours. She may very well have something to teach you—some perspective that's in your blind spot—but remember that her view is far narrower and further away than your own. She was just a child observing most of it."

"Yes, but she's always been very mature in certain respects."

"Perhaps not as mature as you thought," Miss B noted. Her comments had been so incisive that it seemed she knew me already. Maybe she could help me to understand Sam as well.

"Jenny, I wonder if you would mind me asking why you never married. Were you ever afraid of it the way Samantha is?"

Miss B sat back on the couch and forced a smile. While I waited for her response, she took her trifocals off and twirled them in her hand a tad nervously. I was about to conclude that she simply didn't trust me with such information when she nodded to herself and exhaled a resigned little sigh. "I don't believe I was afraid of it, Katy," she said. "I would love to have gotten married and had children, but that's not the path I chose in the end."

"What do you mean?"

"I was a late bloomer. Certain things you've heard about Cajuns are true, particularly their earthy lifestyle that tends to indulge the appetites. I was quite a wild one in my youth, and by the time I was ready to limit myself to just one man, I found that the choicest ones were already taken. I could never make myself settle for mediocre, so I tried to find meaning through my career and travel. With age, I grew increasingly eccentric, but my family finally warmed up to my ways and I became quaint old Aunt Jenny to my many nieces and nephews."

"So you never had a love?" I pried. I couldn't bear to think that this tender, fascinating woman had never given her heart away. But she winced at the question, and I regretted having asked it. "Never mind, Jenny. You don't have to say."

"No, no. It's all right. In the late 1960s, when I was about forty-five, I met a man who I couldn't resist as I had all the others. He was a traveler, a successful businessman, a reader. He had a great wit and a sharp mind. He first contacted me to locate a book for him, and after that he called once a month or so to put me on the trail of some new title. I knew he was married, and I had no intention of getting involved with him, but that didn't stop me from falling in love."

"Where did you live at that time?" I asked, struggling to look as directly into the face of her confession as she had mine.

"I lived in Lafayette, of course. The Binghams believe they predate even the Indians and dinosaurs in Lafayette Parish. That's why nearly every Bingham, male or female, is saddled from birth with the middle name Lafayette. The presumption is so strong that the occasional newborn who's denied the name—always the result of an uncooperative outsider in the marriage—is forever after suspected of somehow or other representing a break in the bloodline."

"So how did you get to Houston?" I persisted, not altogether certain that I wanted to know.

"He moved me here in 1969 and set me up in a sweet little cottage in West University. I remember the year because that first summer we sat on my back porch together and tried to picture Neil Armstrong and Buzz Aldrin taking man's first steps on the moon. It was such a magical night—with radios on countless back porches broadcasting the astronauts' actual words across fences and borders around the world—that for a moment we believed we really could see them prancing near a crater 250,000 miles above us. I can still feel the shiver through my body as his goose bumps mingled with mine. I've never been so proud to be a part of the human race, even while I felt myself a dim representative of it.

"Anyway, I won't bore you with any excuses for what we did. He never divorced his wife, but we kept up our affair until he died many years later. By then my family back in Lafayette had deduced what I'd been up to and didn't much want me back, so I settled in Houston permanently. That was over twenty years ago. Eventually I made peace with myself for what I had done."

Miss B did not steal any glances at me, and I was glad for it. Despite myself, I felt ashamed for her, but my reaction didn't seem to figure into her well-being in the least. As she leaned back and closed her eyes briefly, I even thought I saw a smile play across her mouth.

"How?" I asked.

When she opened her eyes and cocked an eyebrow at me, I elaborated. "How did you make your peace?" The incredulous tone that I didn't try to disguise only made her smile outright.

"Oh, Katy dear, I let God forgive me. And if he could, who was I not to do likewise?"

As I was leaving a few minutes later, Miss Bingham said the strangest thing to me. "Ask your mother," she said. "She can tell you what you need to know." I assumed at first that this was just some southern platitude, but I caught an odd note of earnestness in her voice as I replayed the conversation on my way home. It's then I realized how powerfully Miss B really did remind me of Adele.

When I was eleven, Adele helped me to make a few adjustments that I thought at the time saved my life. I doubt she had any such grand ambitions, but that was the effect just the same. These adjustments had to do with my father, my mother, and me.

I guess there comes a time in every child's life when she must embrace the fact that adults are not always right or good. And this isn't just true of the lawbreakers and despots we hear reports about on the evening news, or the "obnoxious neighbors" who oppose our parents' politics. It's true of the adults who teach in our schools, who live in our houses, and who try to indoctrinate us into their world-views, however wanting.

As a little girl, I had belonged to my father. At six, seven, eight, nine, there was nothing about our relationship that I remembered being unhappy about outside of his occasional "no" when I insisted on such obscure pleasures as roller skating across our lawn or pur-chasing a stable full of horses. But as I matured, and my world expanded well beyond the two of us, I couldn't help noticing how differently Daddy had always treated Clay, Mother, and most every-one else. He wasn't mean to them exactly; he just didn't seem to cher-ish them as he so clearly cherished me. And for this I began to suffer tremendous guilt.

Eventually I came to concentrate my anxieties upon a particular evening ritual that had long united Daddy and me. After I crawled under my covers to go to bed at night, I always called for him, and he came in and sang me songs until I really did get tired and needed him to hush his hilarious croaking so I could finally go to sleep. There came a time when all I could think about while he sang was the fact that I'd never ever heard him sing to Clay, that every night he was in here with me instead of helping Clay with homework or Mother clean the kitchen. And I had to force myself to keep calling out to him. But I was terrified to stop because Daddy expected it, and I didn't want him to stop loving me the way he didn't seem to love Clay.

For a few weeks during the summer that I turned eleven, I was so agitated about this predicament that my appetite disappeared and I mostly sat around the house in a funk despite being off from school and homework-free. Adele was the only one who seemed to notice that for days on end I told friends who rang our doorbell that I couldn't come out, that I didn't feel like riding bikes or playing in the neighborhood tree house just then. She cornered me in the backyard one morning when she found me sitting alone on the woodpile along our breezeway. I was just sitting.

"Katy, child, why don't you go do somethin' productive, like ask your little friend Lucille to come over and make cookies with us?" Adele suggested. She had a big basket of freshly folded laundry under one arm and waved me off the woodpile with the other. "Come on now," she said. Like a sluggard, I slid off the logs and followed her into the house. But I made no move to go and fetch Lucille.

"What is it, girl? Why've you been mopin' round here almost the whole summer so far? This ain't a bit like you." While Adele's words were cajoling, there was real concern in her voice. I felt a warm rush of relief that another human being seemed poised to share in my worries, but I feared the chain of events that a disclosure might set off. Whatever I said would betray my father, would it not? It never dawned on me that what I now saw about Daddy for the first time had long been obvious to anyone else.

"Nothin', Adele. I just don't feel like makin' cookies," I answered. At least one firm dodge would make me feel better about letting Adele drag the truth out of me.

"Just as you didn't feel like pancakes this morning nor ice cream yesterday? Now I know somethin's wrong. What is it?" Adele, who'd been standing over me effortlessly dangling that laundry basket under her arm, now plopped the basket down on the kitchen table in a no-nonsense way that I found very comforting. Here was a capable someone who could guide me. "Go on now," she said. "Ain't nobody here but you and me. What's the trouble?"

"Well, . . . uh, . . . Mother and Daddy just treat me like I'm a little kid still, and I don't know how to get 'em to stop."

"Uh-huh," she said. "And how 'bout a samplin' of what you mean?"

"One thing is when I go to bed and Daddy wants to come in and sing to me. . . . He doesn't go in and sing to Clay." Adele cocked an eyebrow at me, and I rushed on headlong. "He didn't sing to Clay when he was ten either." In response to this last bit of intelligence, I expected an exclamation of some sort, at the very least a gasp. But Adele just nodded and ran her hand up my arm.

"And you just want to be treated as grown-up as Clay? No worse, no better." She was reading my mind.

"Uh-huh."

"Have you talked to your mother 'bout this?"

For some reason I couldn't articulate to Adele, I thought that telling Mother about my problem would just make matters worse. She was a coconspirator in my mind. After all, she'd observed our bedtime ritual for years without once seeming to notice the disparate treatment. She'd never convinced Daddy to love Clay more; I assumed she'd never tried. She didn't even seem to notice that Daddy's doting left her out. "No," I answered. I couldn't see talking to my mother about this.

"Well, honey, I think you should," Adele urged. "She can help you understand all sorts of things about it that I just can't. But as for your Daddy singin' to you at night, if you feel too old for it now, just say, 'No, thank you, Daddy.' He'll get over his letdown quick enough. Sometimes daddies are the last ones to see that their little girls is growin' up, that's all."

I could simply say, "No, thank you." How I took Adele's words to heart! From then on, I began to believe I could control my own destiny. I didn't have to be my mother, grateful to live in the farthest glow of the stronger personalities around me. I did not have to accept whatever scraps were tossed my way, disingenuously prop anyone up, or seek other cover when I couldn't take one more moment of neglect. I didn't even have to tolerate a favored status if I didn't want it. I could say, "No, thank you." I just had to trust myself a little more, that's all.

I never thought too much again about Adele's counsel for me to ask for Mother's help. I didn't understand the source of the confidence Adele seemed to have in her, and fifty years later, on the afternoon that Miss Bingham made a similar suggestion, I understood it no better. Mother wasn't interested in hard stuff. Why couldn't they see that?

CHAPTER 14

JO

March 14, 2001

Katy called this morning and asked quite nonchalantly if I was ready for her to help me move my plants from the greenhouse back out to the porch. I told her I thought I'd give it one more week, and then I shut up and waited for the mask to come off.

"Yes," she teased, "I guess there's always the off chance that this'll be the one year in five hundred when Houston freezes after March 15."

But I couldn't laugh. Why didn't she just come out with it—admit that she's scheming to send me away and tell me how she means to accomplish it? I waited, still quiet.

"Just kidding, Mother. That's fine. We'll do it next week," she said.

"That's fine," I chimed.

"We'll do it next week," she repeated.

"Next week, then," I said.

Another long silence almost did me in. "Is that all, Katy?" I demanded.

"All what?"

"All that you called for?"

"Why? Do you have some pressing need to get off the phone?"

"I have a few things to do if you have nothing else you mean to discuss." I would make her tell me or else leave me alone. "What about you, Mother? Is there anything you want to discuss? Are you still feeling weak?" But she sounded too hopeful for me to gratify her with any sort of "yes." From now on I must be careful to reveal nothing she might use.

"I feel better than I have in months," I answered. "Now I better scoot. Ginger is pawing the back door to get out."

"Well, OK, Mother. Bye."

"Good-bye, dear."

Then I set about second-guessing myself. Perhaps I should have gotten this contest over with already. As it is, I feel a little like Atlanta waiting for Sherman's Yankees—I'm so wearied by anticipation that I'm almost ready to light myself on fire. What's stopping her?

Maybe Katy's the one losing sleep now. She did seem a bit wrung out. Is she agonizing? Is she frightened? I was afraid that my mother would have to come and live with Vic and me. Is that what Katy's afraid of? Maybe if I assure her I have no intention of doing that to her, she'll give up her crusade. That's what I'll do. The next time I see her, I'll promise to check myself into a nursing home if I ever get to the point where I can't live alone. I'll swear never to need her anymore than I do right now.

Then there's my appointment this afternoon with the oncologist. I haven't let myself think about this all week, but now that it's upon me I'd better consider the possibilities. He'll do a blood test to figure out whether the cancer is back. I'm almost certain that it isn't—yet. But in case I'm wrong, I pledge here and now to stick with my decision to forgo chemotherapy. This is one matter that Katy will have no say in.

Here's what my daughter doesn't know: I'm plenty scared of being thrown away, but I'm not afraid to die. I just don't think that dying will be the hard part. Understanding it all is surely harder.

March 15, 2001

Whenever I started to like my life, or at least to feel comfortable in my own skin, it seemed that someone picked up the little snow globe in which I lived and shook it until everything that I thought to be anchored to the ground was suddenly flying off through the sky. I concluded that this was simply the human condition, which always made me a little afraid that God really exists. For if he does, what did this say about him? I couldn't bear being at the mercy of such an arbitrary God, so I tried convincing myself that all of life is random. But that didn't much work either.

In my snow globe there were few anchors really—Fran, Vic, and Adele, who had in fact come with us to the new house to help me acclimate to its big, empty opulence. Katy might have been an anchor, but she was always so used up by her own struggles that our relationship was typically very one-sided. That's OK. It's a mother's lot in life, I suppose. Still, I had these others who by and large held me in place.

I vividly recall the morning in September 1966 when I first sensed that my cozy if uninspiring life was about to undergo a major shift. I was sitting out by the pool watching my toddler grandson splash around in the baby end. Adele and I had just shared a pot of coffee while she told me all about her spinster daughter's fabulous new boyfriend—"a man after God's own heart," she assured me, "just like David." Fran and I were meeting for lunch in a couple of hours to whine about menopause and celebrate her fiftieth birthday. And Vic was still in bed, resting up from many late nights spent luring a very large account away from his chief competitor. Everything in my globe was still, everyone where they belonged—on the ground.

I glanced over at Adele sitting next to me, beaming, and I smiled back at her good fortune. It would be quite a triumph to marry off a daughter at Rachel Lorena's advanced age of thirty-seven. Perhaps this wasn't the very impulse behind Adele's joy, but it's the closest I could come to feeling it with her.

"Gammy, watch," Seth called to me from where he was now fearlessly poised on the edge of the pool, already in a crouch. The words were still drifting over to me when I knew. I knew as surely as I knew my own name that something bad was going to happen.

I sprang out of my chair at the same moment that he sprang off the edge of the pool. I could see that I needed to be on an intercept course, so I headed right into the water. He hit first, at about the four-foot-deep mark, but I was so close behind him that I had him in my arms and out of the water before he even realized he couldn't breathe. My housecoat floated up around my shoulders as I clung to the little rascal, ordering him never ever to jump again unless I was in the water to catch him first.

If that had only been all.

March 16, 2001

A week or so later, Adele and I were cutting out patterns in my sewing room when she flashed me one of those harsh, gentle looks that meant I was in for a well-meaning lecture of some sort. Over the years, I'd come to view these talks much as I viewed flu shots—I rather dreaded them, but after the sting subsided I felt utterly protected.

We had just shared a laugh about some very grown-up advice that Seth had given the filling station attendant the day before when Adele abruptly turned the tables on me. "So," she said, "Mr. Vic's been telling me you won't go over to that nursing home no more, not to save your life." The one topic I had no desire to discuss.

But I'd never been able to refuse Adele's intrusions into my personal places, and I began to let her in this time too. "There's no point, Adele. Our visits aren't good for either of us." This was the whole truth as I saw it.

Adele kept silent just long enough to expertly freehand a lining for the pastel pink linen skirt she was making for Katy. "It don't matter if you can see that it's helpin' or not. Trust me that it helps," she said, slapping her scissors down on the table decisively.

But I didn't think anything had been decided. "How?" I cried. "What good could it do for me to go over there so we can sit and stare at each other? She doesn't want me there, and I don't want to be there."

Adele sidled up to me and flashed a particularly penetrating look. "I'm only gonna say this once, missy. If you think you feel too guilty to go over there an' sit while she's a-dyin', just you wait till she passes all alone and see how the guilt burns into you. This'll seem like your proudest hour compared to that sort of shame. That's the kind that makes you smaller and smaller each and every year that goes by."

"Guilt?" I cried, pulling away from her hand on my forearm. "Me guilty? What in the world do I have to be guilty about?"

She took hold of my arm again. "Trust me," she repeated. "I can't, Adele. I just can't."

March 17, 2001

The phone rang at about 3:57 A.M. I'm that sure of the time because I heard the old grandfather clock in our cavernous hardwood entry hall chime four times while Vic was talking—or I should say listening—to someone who appeared to be telling him something unpleasant. Typically on such occasions, the mind spontaneously launches a program entitled: Inventory of People I Love and What Horrible Things Could Possibly Have Happened to Them. But that night, as I watched Vic nodding his resignation to some undisclosed act of God, the thought that consumed me was: "It's finally, finally over."

Throughout the conversation, Vic repeatedly mumbled, "OK, I see, uh-huh," and finally, "Thank you," whereupon he hung the phone up gently and looked over at me sitting on the edge of the bed, waiting for him.

He walked over, sat down right next to me, and tenderly took my hand. How sweet! He was apparently afraid I would take it as I had Daddy's death. He needn't have worried, but I went along with it as a support to him.

"Jo," he said finally, "dawlin', . . . " Then he faltered. He squeezed my hand tightly. Good heavens, was I going to have to say it for him? I tried to look reassuring, and presently he went on.

"Jo, that was Isaiah." No. No. That's not what he was supposed to say. I instinctively began to reel in my hand.

"Adele—"

"What's Adele got to do with it?" I snapped, as I got my fingers free of Vic's and stood up, lurching to the other side of the room as far as I could get from him. I didn't really want an answer, so I went on before he could offer one. "How is it she's able to interject herself into the center of every event in my life? Why, it's an outrage that they called her first. I'm sure it's against all the rules. It's probably even against the law! I might just sue. That would show them."

I had begun a filibuster. This strategy came to me as naturally as breathing. I just knew I couldn't let Vic speak. And for a few minutes he let me go on, ranting louder and louder, until there was a real danger I'd wake the neighbor across our lavish side yard and beyond the dense privacy hedge that separated us. Still he kept quiet.

"I'm sure it's all her fault," I continued. "She probably took it upon herself to go down there and weasel her way onto their call list. I can hear her now: 'You people have to call me first when she passes. Promise you'll do that. I have to be the one to tell Miss Jo 'cause she'll have all this guilt I'll need to help her with. I won't leave till you promise.' And they did it because there was this mountainous black woman standing in front of them threatening to beat them up with love and compassion if they didn't. They spared themselves at my expense. After I sue them, I swear I'm going to fire her." On and on I went along these lines.

I vaguely recall Vic coming at me and wrestling me into his arms until I couldn't move except to kick my feet if I'd wanted. I wasn't quite that far gone.

As I hung there in my spousal straitjacket, Vic was finally able to make his heartsick pronouncement: "Adele went to the convenience store last night to say hello to her cousin Bertrand, who worked there as a clerk. While she was at the counter talking to him, two men came in to rob the place. They started shooting when Bertrand tried to flip a panic switch to alert the police, and Adele was hit. She's been in emergency surgery for the past several hours, but they couldn't save her. Jo, Adele died a little while ago."

Snow swirled all around me. And I shook with my world, this way and that, in great racking spasms of confusion and pain. The ground was gone.

March 18, 2001

This morning I found Adele's obituary from the Houston Chronicle that is taped onto the blank page just before the Gospel of Matthew in our family Bible. I remember watching Vic mount it there thirty-five years ago. It reads:

On October 26, 1966, Adele Lorena Smith returned to her Lord Jesus Christ—surely the happiest moment of her life. Born January 15, 1904, in Beaumont, Texas, Adele was orphaned at the age of nine, and thereupon commenced her long career as a domestic helper. She married Isaiah Jacob Smith in Houston on May 29, 1922. Together, they had eight wonderful children, six of whom survive her: John David Smith, 43; Ruth Naomi Hopson, 42; Rachel Lorena Smith, 37; Hannah Joy Krump, 36; Sarah Anne Johnson, 35; and Moses Aaron Smith, 31. Lesha Marie Smith died as a baby, and Andrew Joshua Smith was killed six years ago in a construction accident at age 34. Adele is also survived by twenty-three grandchildren and seven great-grandchildren. Her desire was to be a light to those she knew and loved, showing them the grace of Christ in all her words and acts. The many whom she served in this way include not only her own family, but the family that employed her for the past twenty-four years—Victor and Josephine Greene. Until we meet her again, she will be greatly missed.

It was very nice of Isaiah to mention us, but I'm still over-come by what this obituary doesn't say, perhaps important only to me: that Adele, in truth, was my mother too. And besides that, she was the wisest and strongest and most vulnerable woman I ever knew. I still ache for her to somehow know these things. How I would dearly love to "meet her again," if that were possible.

A few of the yellowed though otherwise pristine pages of our Holy Bible are turned down. Vic did that too. It was a fam-ily custom he brought with him from Louisiana. Each dog-ear marks a passage that was read at some occasion important to him. I found the one with "funeral of Adele Smith, 1 Peter 3:13–18, 10/28/66" scrawled beside several lines of text. Those verses say:

Who is going to harm you if you are eager to do good? But even if you should suffer for what is right, you are blessed. "Do not fear what they fear; do not be frightened." But in your hearts set apart Christ as Lord. Always be pre-pared to give an answer to everyone who asks you to give the reason for the hope that you have. But do this with gen-tleness and respect, keeping a clear conscience, so that those who speak maliciously against your good behavior in Christ may be ashamed of their slander. It is better, if it is God's will, to suffer for doing good than for doing evil. For Christ died for sins once for all, the righteous for the unrighteous, to bring you to God.

I can only imagine how richly Adele is blessed in the heaven in which she's found herself. What I can't imagine, however much I try, are her sins for which this Christ needed to die. The friend I knew was very nearly perfect.

March 19, 2001

When a da Vinci dies with his brush upon a canvas or a Shakespeare with Act III just scribbled notes, the world at large is always prone to dwell on the masterpiece of which it's been deprived. Did he mean for that building to be gold or brown in the end? A cathedral or a courthouse? What of the water—ocean or lake, green or blue, violent or calm? Would that character have betrayed her lover, been defeated by that which she feared most, admitted the truth? We can barely tolerate the not knowing, but our every attempt to guess at what was in the creator's mind falls short. An orphaned creation cannot be completed.

In the weeks that followed Adele's death, I felt like such a frozen work-in-progress—as yet only a hint of a woman. That's not to say I was ever destined to become a masterpiece, but with Adele in my life I always had this powerful sense of expectancy. She knew something or actually was something different and wonderful, and it seemed she had promised to show me what it was. I felt that over time, almost imperceptibly, she was transferring it to me. It was to be mine. It was to be me. But she died before I could close my hand around it. And she hadn't even left a thumbnail sketch behind.

I wrote her this letter, which I found just where I tucked it thirty-five years ago inside the tarnished brass frame of a photo of Adele and her family that I keep on my dresser:

Dear Adele,

I am so angry with you. I think you couldn't wait to get there, that you preferred where you are to being here and loving us any longer.

And I am also furious with your God. Why did he have to take you away from me just when I so need you to help me find my way? Why did he want you with him anyway? What's wrong with him? Doesn't he have enough wisdom and compassion in and of himself? Was he actually lacking something without you there—the way I am lacking? I am temped to hate him.

Jo

March 20, 2001

Another obituary is taped to the inside back cover of our Bible. With an economy that I applauded, Vic authored this announcement less than a month after Adele's death:

Irene Suzanne Wilhelm—Died November 17, 1966, born May 8, 1876. Married to Joseph Clayton Wilhelm from 1915 until his death in 1955. Survived by daughter and son-in-law, Josephine and Victor Greene, grandchildren Clay Greene and Katy Ardelean, and great-grandchildren Seth and Samantha Ardelean.

Another dog-ear marks the following passage, which I recall Isaiah reluctantly reading to the fifteen or twenty of us littering his little church on November 19, 1966:

SUSAN OLIVER

Then the Lord came down in the cloud and stood there with him and proclaimed his name, the Lord. And he passed in front of Moses, proclaiming, "The Lord, the Lord, the compassionate and gracious God, slow to anger, abounding in love and faithfulness, maintaining love to thousands, and forgiving wickedness, rebellion and sin. Yet he does not leave the guilty unpunished; he punishes the children and their children for the sin of the fathers to the third and fourth generation." (Exod. 34:5–7)

This was my selection. It took many long hours to find just the right thing. In my mind I substituted "mothers" in place of "fathers" in the last line, and I resolved myself to the much-deserved reckoning that Adele had foretold on that September afternoon when we'd last sewn together. As for the means of my demise, Vic and I had by then eased into a soft, upper-class lifestyle that naturally promoted the very self-destruction that I sought.

Each year thereafter, I drank a little more and I got a little smaller.

March 21, 2001

Katy called this morning at 9:00 A.M. to say she needed to come by immediately and discuss something important. She refused to tell me what it was over the phone, and I hung up thinking, Sherman is finally on the march! What do I do? It's times like this that I most wish Adele were still here to help me figure things out.

I was so flustered by the prospect of Katy's visit that I forgot about my blind dog when I took her out to potty a few minutes

219

later, I often stand near the pool's edge just to make sure Ginger doesn't blunder in while she's sniffing her way around the yard. Her nose has always been trustworthy—better than a white cane in the hands of most blind humans. Still, since even her residual senses have been failing lately, I should have been on higher alert this morning.

Instead, I gazed a hole in the statue of hound and hunter that stands against my back fence and fretted about the multitude of things I seem powerless over these days. While I was so engaged, Ginger wandered up onto the concrete sidewalk surrounding the pool. I heard a splash and turned to see her flailing in the deep end. She'd never much been able to swim, and she was all the more frantic, I'm sure, because she'd expected her little paws to rest on the spongy comfort of the lawn when she'd stepped off the concrete on the pool side. Water filled her lungs when she opened her mouth to yelp for me. I rushed to the edge of the deep end as quickly as I could.

By now Ginger was in the middle of the pool, at least four feet from either side, and her legs were pumping so wildly that she repeatedly pushed herself under with the force of her fear. The water here was eight feet deep. I hadn't tried to swim in several years, and I felt so fragile and doddering just then that I could see no way to rescue a panicked schnauzer from water over my head. I'd surely drown myself if I tried. So I screamed her name repeatedly, hoping this would somehow draw her close enough for me to pluck her out from where I crouched along the side. But her movements were all vertical—above the water and below it, above and below. She never drew any closer.

Ginger's thrashing slowed until finally she relaxed and slipped beneath the surface one last time. I'd always kept her fit;

without any fat to buoy her, she sank leisurely to the bottom of the pool. Minutes before, she'd been strolling along from one armadillo puncture in the grass to the next, snorting like a warthog and stuffing her snout in where the armored critter's had gone before. Now she was gone. My last companion, snatched away from me. Why would God want that?

I was on my hands and knees crying her name when I heard Katy's car in my drive.

Chapter 15

Katy

On the morning I finally went over to tell Mother that I'd put down a deposit for her at the Abbey—just in case she thought she might want to move into a posh new apartment surrounded by people she'd have gobs in common with—I chanced upon a scene so pitiful that I'm still reluctant to remember it. Mother was hugging the concrete lip of her backyard swimming pool, her housecoat twisted up around her thighs and her bare knees grinding heedlessly into the mottled sidewalk. An amorphous gray object hovered on the pool floor, changing shape and size as the water sloshed slightly back and forth against the sides. When I got up-close enough, I could make out four paws and a head, and Mother's tear-streaked face came up to meet my glance accusingly.

Her look alone was like a blow. When she cried, "See what you did," and then melted back over the edge of the pool, it was all too incongruous for me to accept calmly. I grabbed her by her spindly upper arms and tugged her to her feet. Then, with one swift gesture, I twisted her to face me. I gave no credence to her quivering lip. "Mother!" I demanded. "What has happened here?"

Her commitment to an offensive posture faded instantly, and she fell sobbing into my arms. I walked her over to an iron love seat, fruitlessly scanning the water for bubbles as we passed, and sat her down. "I don't suppose there's any point in my jumping in to get her right now?" I asked, returning to the poolside. "You're sure she's gone?"

Mother vigorously nodded, so I joined her on the love seat. Presently she'd collected herself enough to tell me what had happened. It was every bit as bad as anything I might have imagined.

"I don't know why I didn't cement that useless thing in years ago," she concluded, as I wiped a mascara smudge from her creviced cheek. "Lenny couldn't even stay away from it, and he had a bigger brain than Ginger's and two good eyes."

"Yes," I said, "it was just an accident waiting to happen—until now." I'd have to fish Ginger out soon. I knew she was dead, but leaving her to drift in the bowels of her killer seemed unduly cruel. First, though, I wanted to straighten a few things out.

"Mother, why did you accuse me of having something to do with this?"

"No reason. I was just upset, Katy. I didn't know what I was saying." She tried to stand then, but she was still too shaky and ended up right back next to me on the love seat.

I didn't believe her, but I decided to circle around from another direction. "This is the kind of thing that makes it dangerous for you to live here all alone, Mother." I didn't see how she could argue with such a statement at a time like this. "Wouldn't you feel better with other people around in case you get into trouble again and need some more help?"

"That, Katy. That right there!" She yelped. Finding her balance this time, Mother stood successfully and took several insulating steps toward the house before she turned on me. "That's why I said it. Because I knew you were on your way over here to try and force me to move to some . . . some . . . nursing home. Don't deny it. Lillian told me all about it. That's why I wasn't watching Ginger when she fell in. I was preoccupied with what you were going to do to me!"

Mother's housecoat was hitched up slightly in the front, apparently glued to one of her bloody knees. She'd begun to cry again, sending more absurd mascara down her cheeks, and she was standing there glowering at me like I was Cruella De Vil come for the hundred-and-one puppies. What kind of monster did she take me for?

"Mother, I'm not going to do anything to you. Why would you say that?" I stood, too, at that point, and she edged backward a step.

"Lillian told me—"

"Did she say I was coming over here to bind and gag you so I could kidnap you off to some torture chamber? Why would you think that of me?"

"Were you, or were you not, planning to come over here this morning and try to get me to move out of my home of forty-two years and in with some strangers?" As she said this, Mother hitched her fists up to her absentee hips and squared her feet. This caused her housecoat to peel away from the gooey knee and gave her a slightly more lucid appearance.

"Not exactly," I answered, lawyerly. "But I'll agree to the spirit of your question. I was going to suggest that you move to a very exclusive assisted living center where you'd have your own apartment and complete autonomy, but where you wouldn't have to worry about being all alone when your dog is drowning or you fall and don't have enough blood pumping to get up off the ground. Now, what's so terrible about that?"

"How were you planning to make me go?" she asked, a quiver creeping back into her voice.

"I wasn't planning on making you. I was planning on giving you all the facts and hoping you'd agree that it's the best thing for you. Really, Mother, I don't see what you're so upset about. I wasn't going to do anything underhanded."

She looked pretty shaky again, so I calmly got a chair and walked it up behind her, then stepped away. After a moment or two, she relaxed into it. Her face softened, and she put her hand to her head as if to hold some ache inside of it. "You aren't going to try and force me?" she tested.

"No, Mother. But I did put a deposit down to reserve you one of the nicer apartments. It's being vacated next month, and if you want it, it's there for you. You just have to go in for an interview sometime in the next few days."

"Oh? How much was the deposit?" she asked.

"Forty-five hundred."

"Can you get it back if I don't want the apartment?"

I saw that this was a tricky juncture. Mother's questions implied a spark of guilt that I might just set aflame with an honest answer. Still, if you pushed Mother too far . . . Remembering the little dog resting at the bottom of the pool behind me, I decided I had no choice but to seize this apparent advantage. "No, it's nonrefundable," I said.

"Just as I thought!" she snapped, forgetting her headache and pumping her index finger at me. "You were going to force me. Why else would you be willing to put up $4,500 that you couldn't get back if I didn't like the idea? It's not as if you have that kind of money to waste."

"That's not true," I insisted. "I would simply have eaten the loss if you'd refused to go. Why can't you believe that I care about you and that I might have good reason to be worried? Why do you assume I'm being sinister?" I'd had just about enough of her incriminations. Was I so reprobate for wanting to protect my mother, for searching out a safe home for her, for caring when no one else seemed to?

"Because, Katy," she sputtered, "you went off on your own to find this joint and you put down the deposit before you ever mentioned any of it to me. All of that feels a whole lot more like manipulation than caring."

Well, that was certainly one way to view it, I supposed. But if she only knew how much energy I'd put into finding her just the right place. "OK, Mother, my methods were not the best, I admit that. But can't you still consider whether this is something you should do? The Abbey is not a 'joint.' I promise you, it's a wonderful place. Not cheap, but I think you'd be pleased with the facilities and the active people your age who you could befriend. This one woman I've met has decorated her place like a French drawing room. Why don't you go take a look?"

"I don't need to go look because I don't have the energy to start over again anyway. What I need now is familiarity not new friends. I'm comfortable in this house. I know it's big, but I just close off the upstairs and the southern hall downstairs, and I'm perfectly fine here. Please don't make me leave, Katy."

Glancing toward the deep end, I hardened myself to her plea. Why did she protest so much? "What do you mean, you don't have the energy to start over, Mother? Why not?"

She only pawed the ground with her metallic gold bedroom slipper in response. It's then I recalled that she'd had a doctor's appointment a few days earlier. "You never told me the results of your blood tests last week," I rushed in. "I assumed you'd call if they found something . . . Well? Did they?"

"Why?" she flared up again. "If they did, do you plan to use it as evidence that I can't take care of myself? Do you think you can just deposit me away somewhere and check me off your list: 'Took care of Mother'?"

"That . . . is . . . ridiculous," I stammered. "Mother, you can't really think that little of me."

"I don't know what to think, Katy. I just know that I can't let you run me out of my house. I'll do whatever I have to to stop you."

"What are you implying?"

She trembled visibly. After one huge sigh, she said, "I believe I'm prepared to cut you out of my will if you carry on with this."

Never had I heard my mother say anything so insulting before, not even to Lenny. The suggestion that being disinherited would stop me for one minute from protecting her if I thought she was in real danger hurt me even more than her outrageous inference that I was merely trying to subjugate her to my whims. At that moment I could make myself speak to her no further. I went into the house and changed into a swimsuit, dove down eight feet to the bottom of Mother's deep end, and scooped Ginger into a plastic trash bag. Then I emptied it of water, tied it off, and put her into my trunk before I drove away.

Mother, as far as I could tell, hadn't made another move.

I am not an introspective person. Perhaps that makes me more like my father than I'd care to admit, but I've always viewed action as braver than hiding away in one's head. And it's also, coincidentally, safer than facing whatever invisible demons may lurk up there. I believe that this commitment to act first, and ruminate later or not at all, has made me a good lawyer, a competent parent, and a stalwart survivor of a long and difficult marriage. It's been an honorable creed. But there have been a few times in my life when no reasonable avenue of action has presented itself and I've been left with a less tenable choice: to look inside, to stuff, or to act unreasonably. Following

Mother's threat to disinherit me, I tried all three of these, in reverse order of course.

Mother herself had suggested the first tack: trying to make the case that she was indeed incompetent to decide her own fate. I'd considered and discounted that possibility before, but I had reason to worry that she'd now slumped into this precarious legal category. Why else would she have leapt to the wild conclusions about my intentions that she had at the pool? It smacked of paranoia to me. I feared that her next step might be full-fledged martyrdom. If, in her self-inflicted isolation, she couldn't stop her dog from wandering into the pool and drowning, could she keep from doing so herself? If someone found her floundering there, the water sucking her down and saturating her desecrated half lungs, would she even let them save her? My imagination swelled with horrific possibilities. The worst of these had to do with cancer.

I'd never trusted Mother with major healthcare decisions, even when she was talking to me about them before her paranoia had soared into the stratosphere. Of all the arenas in which her cursed passivity ruled, this one was the most dangerous to my way of thinking. And now it seemed she'd made the terrible decision not only to navigate it alone, but to suspend radio communications back to the control tower as well. I assumed the worst—that she was experiencing serious technical difficulties—and prayed that she was keeping in touch with some more distant tower. Clay and Lillian were my best hope in this regard.

But Clay assured me that Mother had not said a word to him about the results of her checkup the week before. Lillian likewise, though I wasn't sure I trusted her. And even Samantha and Seth swore they didn't know a thing about it. Having alerted them all to the possibilities, however, they descended on her so kinetically from so many sides over the course of twenty-four hours that she finally buckled and attested that her lungs were still clear. The cancer had not returned. What, then, was all Mother's talk about having no energy to start over? More than ever, I worried about her emotional health. And when I recounted the awful episode at Mother's pool to Clay, he began to worry too.

"Pretty scary," he agreed. "But, sis, becoming flustered on one occasion surely doesn't render her incompetent to make her own decisions. After all, she didn't hurt herself; she just watched her dog drown. Are we legally required to protect our pets from accidents or else risk losing control of our lives?"

"It was not just Ginger's accident, Clay," I said. "She accused me of conspiring to force her to move and even suggested that I'd use negative doctor reports to accomplish it." His look told me he didn't quite grasp the insanity of this. "Clay, she's wildly paranoid!"

"But isn't that what we're talking about doing right now—forcing her to move, even using doctors' reports to accomplish it?" he asked in his typical bull's-eye manner.

"It's only because she's so paranoid that we have to consider this option. I certainly wasn't planning any such thing before she attacked me. Don't you understand the difference? She actually threatened to disinherit me if I 'carry on with this' imaginary conspiracy to put her away. I've never been so shocked in my life. And this after I put up forty-five hundred dollars to secure her a spot at the Abbey just in case I could sell her on it." With that, I believe I poked out my lower lip, quite naturally reverting to childish gestures with my only sibling.

"Still, it's just one incident, Katy. What does the law say about it?"

"Of course it's a big technical definition. We'd have to prove that she's an incapacitated person, which is: 'an adult individual who, because of a physical or mental condition, is substantially unable to provide food, clothing, or shelter for himself or herself, to care for the individual's own physical health, or to manage the individual's own financial affairs.' And it's true that in making this showing, the statute says that incapacitation 'must be evidenced by recurring acts or occurrences,' and not merely 'by isolated instances of negligence or bad judgment.'"

"My gosh, have you got the whole corpus of Texas Civil Statutes memorized, or only the parts you're conspiring to use against our mother?" Clay asked, trying and failing to lighten my mood. "Seriously, how can we demonstrate . . . what was it? Recurring acts or occurrences? At worst it seems to me we have one case of possible negligence and one of bad judgment."

"What about the blood pressure incident back in January? That's another one we already know about," I urged.

"But, Katy, how was that negligence or bad judgment on Mother's part? Her doctors, yes; but her?"

"That's just the point. She doesn't hold her doctors to even an idiot's standard of competence, and in that particular situation it almost killed her. I'd call that more than an incident of negligence or bad judgment on her part in that she flagrantly operates this way all the time. It's a recurring act, a pattern. Don't you see?"

"I see that you are a terrific lawyer who can convincingly argue most anything. But, Katy, we're talking about our mother here. Come on. Do you really think she's demonstrated a pattern of being unable to provide her own food, clothing, and shelter?"

"I don't know. Since I quit taking groceries over there in January, I have no clue what she eats or really even if she eats. Do you? Do you know if she's paying her exorbitant taxes? Her electricity? Her water? If she locks her doors at night? I'm just saying that if she can't keep her dog out of the pool, can't keep her doctors informed of her various medications, and doesn't recognize that I love her and wouldn't intentionally harm her, how do I know that she's able to provide her own food, clothing, and shelter? Even more than that I think she's shown herself unable to care for her own physical health, which is an alternative showing under the stature."

Still my brother seemed skeptical and a little bit afraid of me.

"Look, Clay, the one thing that would be harder for me to take than her looking me in the eye and threatening to disinherit me for doing what I think is necessary to protect her, is something actually happening to her as a result of my not doing so. Am I the only one who can see this? Why do I feel like I woke up on some other planet a month or two back?"

"So, you are really proposing that we file an application for our mother to be declared incompetent and put under the authority of a guardian? Think about actually doing that, Katy. Think of the examinations she'd be subjected to in order to prove her mental state. Think of her having to try to talk a jury into believing she can do for herself. Are you really ready to put her through that?"

"Honestly? I don't think we'd have to."

"How so?"

"I think that if Mother knew you and I had agreed to do it if it becomes absolutely necessary, she'd fold and move somewhere she'd be safe."

"Some place like the Abbey?"

"That's right. They have a cafeteria so she wouldn't have to grocery shop or cook. They have security, a doctor on call for emergencies, and other attendants who can even assist with minor medical and grooming needs. Plus, she'd have neighbors close by who would keep an eye on her. Right now her nearest neighbor is a hundred yards off on another estate."

"So, if she moves to the Abbey, you'll think she's competent?"

"Something like that."

"You sure you didn't plan this all along?" he kidded, straight-faced. "I knew you were shrewd, Katy, but I'd never have believed you could orchestrate events this complex."

"Yeah, I even sacrificed Ginger to get my way."

He smiled then, but wryly. "Look," he said, "I appreciate what I think you're trying to do, sis, but we'd only mess things up worse if we went through with it. You'll have to count me out." Clay was never waylaid by the guilt that so often induces women, and perhaps men unschooled in the ways of business, to agree to things just because other people have the gall to demand them face-to-face. Due to this, I could ask or tell him anything.

I fingered the copy of the Texas Probate Code that I'd brought along to help persuade Clay of the strength of our case. But it hadn't been necessary. Merely stating the case out loud had been enough to expose its unconscionable marrow.

"Yes, well, frankly that makes two of us," I said.

Having put my law books back up on the shelf, I was left to view the present crisis from the suppressed perspective of a daughter, nothing more. It was a role I didn't find empowering. To me, the term connotes childhood, need, and—worse—vulnerability. I much preferred the impervious role of the lawyer, buttressed and buffered as she is by arcane libraries, stalwart hierarchies of legal precedent, and judges to make all the hard decisions. Who can hurt a lawyer? It's a dusty, distant existence whose strength lies in its immunity and detachment.

So as to steer clear of those interior crevices where invisible demons might lurk, I'd generally resisted thinking of myself merely as a daughter. Predictably, then, not long after Clay relegated me to this defenseless status, I fell prey to sweaty nightmares in which my subconscious tortured me with long dormant childhood terrors. In one, I was milling through the lobby of a large theater-in-the-round that was packed with an audience completely shrouded in darkness, catcalling and throwing garish papier-mâché angels at a tiny circular stage down below. The stage was brilliantly lit but otherwise empty. Presently, I was shoved through a curtain that opened onto one of several runways connecting the lobby to the stage. I was handed a microphone and prodded forward with the clear expectation that I'd give some sort of performance when I got there. But I had nothing prepared. I always managed to wake myself up just before reaching the stage.

In another, all the members of my family had been abducted and replaced by alien look-alikes who tried to pass themselves off as my mother, father, brother. I lived among them for days without realizing—with just a vague, gnawing sense that my world suddenly felt very plastic. Had it only been the counterfeit Mother and Clay, I'm not sure I'd ever have found them out, but a trip to the grocery with my supposed father finally enlightened me. The pseudo-Daddy didn't try to get a rise out of me for the whole hour that we were together. He had nothing but kind words even for our checker and bag boy. Rather than get back into the car with this stranger parent for the ride home, I ran screaming into the parking lot crying for help.

And on it went. But during the days I fiercely, doggedly, thought about other things. Billing long hours helped. I was still working off Eliot's weekend in Lake Charles, and now Mother's Abbey deposit as well. For a full week I also indulged my wanderlust by contriving a list of the "Ten Places I'd Most Like to See before I Die," and mapping out intricate, hypothetical trips to each of those locations. I wrote them up in David Letterman fashion, from least to most, as follows:

10. The fifteenth-century painted churches of northeastern Romania—part of my children's heritage through the Eastern Orthodox Ardelean branch of the family.

9. The Himalayas in Nepal. And while I'm in the neighborhood, China's Yangtze River and Forbidden City of the emperors.

8. The Bering Strait of Alaska, the existence of which mesmerized me as a schoolgirl because, by some ancient twist of geographic fate, America was there forced to kiss her otherwise far-off and terrible archenemy—the United Soviet Socialist Republic.

7. Paris, France, my not-so-imaginative favorite city in the world.

6. The great coral reefs of Australia (before global warming has completely destroyed them).

5. Istanbul, Turkey, where humanity in all its incarnations throughout the past few millennia seems to be duly represented by some venerable relic that one can visit, or that can at least be experienced as a cultural dross still hanging about in the people and the air.

4. The Appalachian Mountains, which I regret never having hiked all 2,000 U.S. miles of, from Georgia to Maine.

3. Florence, Italy, my favorite city that I've never seen.

2. Saint Petersburg's Hermitage Museum to covet the sublime art treasures of Catherine the Great, a few of which I once saw exhibited in my own home town.

1. *Ireland's Ring of Kerry, where, as a newlywed, I spent the best week of my life before the other shoe fell.*

Practicality was obviously no part of my selection criteria. In truth, I thought I had a shot at living only one or two of these fantasies, and those only after a few more years of high billings and an unprecedented degree and duration of self-restraint on Eliot's part. In the meantime, therefore, I cast about for other distractions.

The most effective was a new approach I adopted to reading the newspaper. I'd always been a skimmer—hitting the headlines on the front page of every major section, sans sports, and then reading the first paragraph or two of the articles that interested me. Rarely did I go inside these pages, even to chase the second half of a story that started on page one, except to read the obituaries. Obituaries intrigue me because of the amazing economy and understatement with which people express their profoundest emotions when it costs them several dollars a word. I find most obituaries to be terse, raw things of beauty.

Sometime late in March, I abandoned my old newspaper reading habits and became an intransigent cover-to-cover reader. I didn't skip a word except on the classified and sports pages. I even perused the display ads, Ann Landers, the movie star gossip, the stock market tallies, and Cynthia Cranenberg, whose mean-spirited editorials syndicated from the *Dallas Times Herald* as often as not made me ashamed of being a Texan. The entire procedure consumed about three blessed hours of every weekday, three and a half hours on Saturdays, and could be stretched to almost five on Sundays.

During one of these marathons, while I sipped my fourth cup of Maxwell House and scoured the recondite "South Texas" section of the Sunday paper, I came across an item at the bottom of page J-12 that actually interested me. The single paragraph, appearing in a column headlined only "South Texas People," read as follows:

Bruce Canmore, the 23-year-old Scottish exchange student who narrowly survived a 1998 head-on collision in Corpus Christi, has re-enrolled for summer courses as a Junior at the University of Houston. Late last year Canmore shocked Corpus Christi court observers when he appeared as the prosecution's only eyewitness in the trial of Marie Victoria Lucinda Domingo. On the strength of Canmore's gripping testimony and the highly visible injuries that have left him permanently disfigured, Domingo was convicted on several counts of vehicular manslaughter. Canmore, a declared math major, said that he and William Canmore, his father and primary caretaker, will not return to Scotland for the foreseeable future. Father William is a novelist and professor of Celtic literature.

Well, I declare. How I wanted to call, explore, inquire, poke around. Had Samantha seen this little news item? Was she perchance behind it—somewhere, somehow? For once, I knew I must bide my time in order to find out.

§

A day or two later, Miss Bingham called and asked me to take her shopping. I hadn't seen or spoken to her since the afternoon three weeks earlier when I'd walked away from her little apartment worrying she was as faux as her drawstring French doors. I'd been outraged then on behalf of her victims—people I'd never known, whom she had wronged in a lifetime she'd renounced long before we ever met. In the intervening days, I'd begun to feel personally disillusioned by her lengthy affair, but I was equally mortified that I'd let myself be in a position to feel that way. Where had I gotten off presuming that Miss B was wise, virtuous, or even decent? And what right had I to hope that she would somehow lead me out of the quagmire into which I'd recently found myself slipping?

Her phone call therefore puzzled me very much. I knew that my reaction to her story hadn't been subtle. Subtlety is not part of my makeup. I received only Daddy's genes in this regard as well. And yet, when I'd fizzled out on her confession, when I'd secreted disdain and disenchantment from every pore, Jenny Bingham had not shown the slightest inclination to apologize or even hang her head. And the past three weeks had apparently enlightened her not at all; I heard no hint of shame in her lilting southern drawl this morning—a fact I found oddly infectious.

I picked her up in front of the Abbey on my third swing through the wide circular drive. As usual, she wore vivid colors and projected a style that demanded attention from every passerby. Most people, I've found, have developed highly distinctive personal dress codes by the time they're in their thirties. If you don't believe it, watch the same television station's evening news for a few nights running. Each of us settles on three or four rules that reflect what we think looks best on us—no straight skirts, only full-length sleeves, two pleats across the front, nothing tight around the middle, always tailored at the waist, sports jacket over T-shirts, golf shirts buttoned to the neck, heels at least two inches high—and we buy wardrobes that conform precisely to these facile, idiosyncratic criteria. This becomes our uniform, and having a uniform enables us to forgo many capricious shopping hours ever after. We must modify our dress codes only occasionally, usually to accommodate physical transitions into new phases of life, as when a man's stomach no longer submits to a belt directly across its middle. My own long-standing uniform was comprised of straight cotton skirts and tailored blouses, all in earth tones of black, taupe, khaki, brown, cream, and white. Miss B contrasted sensationally to my unfashionable camouflage.

Since she was someone I hadn't yet begun to figure out, I determined to let Jenny Bingham set the tone for our interactions that afternoon. Despite her past sins, I felt safe in her hands for present purposes. And so she popped into the passenger seat of my Explorer while I was busy walking around the front to help her in, and then she waited for me to clamor back into the driver's side.

"Katy, dear, it's so good to see you again," she gushed as soon as I reached my perch. I was inclined to dismiss this as a meaningless pleasantry, but Miss B had a way of making such things sound completely heartfelt. It was in the eyes, and hers twinkled at me elfishly as she said, "I've been thinking about you every single day since our last visit." Somehow I knew that those thoughts had not been shame-faced or sheepish.

"Oh?" I responded, unsure where we were going with this. "Uh, do you have some specific store in mind where you'd like to shop?"

"No, ma'am. Wherever you'd like to go is fine with me. I just needed a little field trip, and I couldn't think of anyone I'd rather take along than you. Eh, . . . I should say, anyone whom I'd rather be taken along by." Then she beamed at me and clapped her hands together in a gesture at once childlike, graceful, and disarmingly expectant. "Where will we go? What will we discover about each other this time? When, I wonder, will I begin to love you?" her look seemed to say.

I felt the leftover shards of icy pride in my veins begin to speed toward my heart, where they would either be warmed and filtered, or pumped back out to reclaim the members of my body. She couldn't have guessed my struggle, so far removed from her tender, trusting intimations. Unaware that she needed my forgiveness, Miss B simply waited for my sure affirmation of our blossoming friendship.

I didn't know what to say. A decision seemed imminently in order. If I dallied too long, her confidence in me would doubtless begin to wane. Was I willing to risk that? I suspected it was too precious a thing to lose even a sliver of. I would accept her, and accept her completely, because I wanted to know her undiminished by my judgmental reservations.

"Why don't we go to the Freemont Room at the Windsor Court Hotel?" I suggested, tapping the top of her hand. "They serve high tea with all sorts of coffees and pastries. We'll go shopping some other time."

"Just what I was thinking!" she crooned. And off we went.

Jenny, I later discovered, had known quite well the conflict that had plagued me on the afternoon that we went to the Freemont Room. Turns out it wasn't me in whom she'd had such confidence.

℘

I stopped in to see Miss B again later that week, the day before her eightieth birthday. She informed me of this important occasion after I'd already shown up on her doorstep empty-handed.

"Tut, tut," she chirped, when I whined that she should've mentioned her birthday before. "I didn't even remember it myself until this morning. I happened to be showing my driver's license at the grocery store when the date caught my eye. Eighty years on this earth is a pretty good showing; I'm satisfied with it. How old is your mother, Katy?"

"She'll be eighty-five in August," I answered. "My father died when he was just sixty-seven."

"Uh-huh," she said. "How does your mother feel about being eighty-five?"

"I don't really know. We haven't talked about it. Mother doesn't share her feelings much. I suppose she must be fairly grateful to have made it this far, considering recent events."

"And how is she doing these days, anyway? Will she be applying for Madge Fontenot's place here at the Abbey?"

At the tea room I'd carefully avoided any discussion of Mother, not yet wanting Jenny's take on our rift. I'd sensed she might urge me to do something I wouldn't feel particularly enthusiastic about. And I still sensed that. But further omissions would surely amount to lying, and so I told her the whole sorry story, from my arriving on the scene of Ginger's drowning, to the awful accusations Mother had blasted me with afterward, and concluding with a rundown of my own thin legal arguments against Mother's competence.

"And to think I missed out on having my own children," Jenny said mildly, impressing me again with how gently she could admonish. "Are those unusual things for her to say to you, Katy?"

I pondered that for a minute or two. "She's definitely gotten surlier over the last few years, but now I chalk that up to being unhappy with Lenny—her second husband. I didn't realize until she nimbly shipped him off to his sister's last October that she'd apparently been miserable with him for years. That's how closely she holds her cards to her chest, Jenny. Anyway, Mother's never said anything so hurtful to me as she did that morning by the pool. She seemed nearly hysterical. I still don't know what to make of it."

"And you can't quite forgive her?" she asked, more curious than accusing.

"She hasn't asked for my forgiveness. She hasn't even spoken to me—at all."

"Is that unusual, though? Does she typically hole up all alone when something scares her?"

"She has always holed up in some form or fashion when she's bothered about something. Usually it amounts to little more than keeping to herself, or reading a lot, or going on a painting jag," I explained. Jenny nodded knowingly, and I continued. "Sometimes it's more destructive hiding, and occasionally she's done truly reckless things like getting married or lashing out as she did at me the other day. What she does not do is discuss—neither what bothers her nor what bothers others about her. What do you think she's scared of, anyway?"

My question seemed to interrupt some other train of Jenny's thought. Refocusing, she said, "Being old, sugar. It's terrifying to get old, to feel like you're becoming a child again physically. It's far scarier than being a child, though, because mentally you're still sharp and so you know all the things that can happen to you. Yet the law holds no one else legally responsible. You fear that you'll become such a tremendous burden on the people you love that they'll get tired of it and not be there when you really need them."

I pictured Mother sitting in her big house all alone, the upstairs and southern wing closed off, and Ginger's well-worn paraphernalia piled up by the back door ready to go out in the trash. Were those the thoughts haunting her, cleaving her to the address where she'd so long been strong and safe and young?

I glanced at Jenny, again lost in her own thoughts, and wondered for a moment about her fears. Did she even have anyone to burden? This time it was she who broke in on my reflections.

"What did you mean when you said that Josephine has occasionally done reckless things like getting married?"

"Well, twice she married men she didn't know in order to evade something else in her life that she found unpleasant."

"Even your father? What has she said about marrying him?"

"Mother never talked to me about that particular impetuousness. That story somehow came to me through the backwaters of family rumor, possibly from my grandfather Wilhelm. But there was something about how stealthily Mother paddled around it that made me trust in its general accuracy. She married Daddy to escape my grandmother, whom Mother actually referred to once as 'your grandfather's wife' when she spoke about her to Clay and me."

"But she loved him, didn't she?"

"Did Mother love Daddy? Yes, I think she did. In her way, I think she loved him very much."

"Hmm. Good." Here Jenny paused long enough to signal she'd be plunging into some highly ticklish territory. Sure enough, she next declared, "But you've never been quite sure if she loved you. Why?"

"How do you know that?" I asked, suddenly defenseless.

"The way you talk about her sometimes. You seem tentative, yet—please forgive me if I'm overstepping, Katy—but at other times you seem inclined to almost manhandle her. You're quite clearly conflicted. The only thing I'm sure of is that you always feel strongly about her."

I sighed and fiddled with the hair that had untucked itself from behind my left ear. "Well, I've known her all my life," I murmured.

Miss B quickly circled back around. "So, why the conflict? Why do you question her devotion to you?"

I could see that Jenny was committed to her line of inquiry, and I gave myself over to it, secretly a little relieved to finally voice these things out loud to another person. "When I was a child, Mother orbited her family from a great emotional distance, like, like . . . Pluto. She sometimes tried harder with Clay, but not with me, and as far as I saw, not with Daddy. But I don't think grown men notice those things the way little girls do."

Miss B didn't agree or disagree, but she cocked a silver eyebrow at me ever so slightly.

"Anyway," I continued, "she was different with just one person who seemed to trust in a way she didn't trust any of the rest of us. Our—"

"Your housekeeper." Miss B finished my sentence.

"Yes. Adele. I must've told you about her already. Well, when Adele died Mother just fell back in on herself. It was a very long time before she got over it. I'm still not sure she has. But it's kind of hard to pinpoint just which things Mother has or hasn't dealt with. Generally speaking, she doesn't deal at all."

Miss B eyed me for a long time. Then she pushed my unruly hair back in its place behind the other ear. "Katy," she said, "you know what I told you about the things the elderly most fear? Well, those fears sometimes inspire them to deal with matters they've never been willing to before. I think you should talk to your Mother about all this, but not when either of you are upset, or as an inducement to get her to move out, or just after the dog drowns. Do it when the two of you are at peace, when you can be tender with her."

"What if we're never at peace?" I whined.

"It's up to you to make the overture."

"And you think that would help me somehow?" I asked, trying to imagine Mother and me having a peaceful—much less tender— discussion along these lines.

"Possibly. But even more than that, if you do it right I think it might help her somehow. That's just what my old bones tell me."

"You know, Adele once urged me to talk to Mother about just this sort of thing," I mused, letting Jenny infer that I never had. And

I still wasn't ready to take such a radical step. Though I was weary of my quarrel with Mother, not to mention my self-inflicted, strangely punitive readings of Cynthia Cranenberg, how could I "do it right" when the very thought of confronting her made me feel helpless and endangered? What if she wouldn't talk to me about these things, as I suspected would happen, or if she would talk but wouldn't acknowledge the truth of them? I didn't want to be invalidated any further. Didn't I owe it to myself to ensure that didn't happen? After all, I wasn't the one who'd spent most of my life either hiding in the shadows or fleeing. On the contrary, I'd generally adhered to a courageous, head-on philosophy of life that had helped me to sidestep all of Mother's mistakes, had I not?

"Well, Jenny, I'll take it under advisement," I finally muttered in my gentlest door-slamming fashion. She understood perfectly, I thought. After eyeing me a minute longer, she nodded and changed the subject.

"I'm having a few of the Abbey girls over for bridge and coffee in a few days—sort of a belated birthday celebration. I know we're a pretty senior bunch for you, but it would mean a lot to me if you could come, Katy."

"Oh, I'd love to, but my bridge is very, very rusty."

"Don't you think twice about that, dear. Bridge is mostly just an excuse for us to gab anyway. Instructing you will only help launch us quicker on the main event. Next Wednesday morning at ten, and don't you dare bring a gift."

"I'll be there."

CHAPTER 16

Jo

March 28, 2001

My world is now a 400-square-foot den, a bedroom, and a kitchen. I have a hallway that stretches the twenty-five feet of my bedroom wall and conducts me to the den each morning, and a utility room through which I must traverse to reach my back door, if ever I use it. The wide-planked entry hall I have abandoned, along with the nine-foot, arched front door, the oak staircase, and the oversized living room that it so auspiciously services. I have no formal guests to welcome, no lodgers, no parties to hostess. The southern bedroom that Lenny requisitioned as his "office" and converted into a four-walled filing cabinet I have not opened since his death. And these remaining rooms—a den, a bedroom, and a kitchen—are where I do my living now.

I remember and I write in the den, which still grants its place of honor to a console-style television adorned by the brass candy dish that once supplied my grandchildren with greedy, carefree handfuls of red hots and candy corn. The side wall is mostly fireplace—long cold now and bookended by book-shelves. All the novels bulging out of them I've savored before, and though my senescent memory makes that point increasingly moot, I rarely pick one up anymore. What keeps me from it is boredom. I just don't care much what other people are doing, fictitious ones especially.

Since I killed Ginger a week ago, I haven't been out of the house. Still, the day before yesterday, in a sudden fit of sympathy and stewardship toward my good-for-nothing old body, I called over to the gourmet grocery down the street and asked them to deliver some supplies. This particular grocery has been in business for over twenty-five years, and I was friendly with the owner back when I lived the sort of lifestyle that called for handpicked cuts of meat and wedges of parmesan sliced right off the wheel. He actually answered the phone, the owner did, and after some cajoling I managed to remind him who I was and convince him to send someone over. This didn't really feel like reaching out, though. It felt more like reaching back to an earlier world infinitely larger than the one I live in now.

The older we get, the more we contract.

Wisdom says it shouldn't be this way. Wisdom says we should get braver as we age since life affords us such constant opportunity to master our circumstances and relationships. So trained, we should be flying ever farther from the nest, frequenting groceries ever farther from our houses. We should always be stepping outward, embracing people and ideas beyond ourselves, until we finally reach God, yes? Like Jonathan Livingston Seagull.

But this isn't reality. In truth, if we live long enough, we all begin to shrink. Adele said that some king in the Old Testament was the wisest man who ever lived. I think she called him Solomon. He wrote a whole book of the Bible to chronicle the wisdom he'd collected in his lifetime. But he later wrote another that declared his wisdom meaningless—along with his wealth and his power and even his philanthropies. All man really gets is the chance to eat and work and love, Solomon said, and he can't enjoy these unless God grants it to him to be content with them. So even wise King Solomon shrank in the end. All of us, somewhere along in late middle-age, simply stop expanding and begin to contract—letting people fall away but not adding new ones, increasingly preferring home to travel, comfort to adventure, routine to challenge and change. The question is not where you end up, but how high you flew while you were flying.

Once the contracting begins, our world gets smaller and smaller until, at eighty-four-and-three-quarters, a den, a bedroom, and a kitchen are its contours. But are we necessarily living less at that point? Or are we simply soaring through our pasts, trying, trying to make sense of the bigger places we've seen? The way Solomon did. Yes, I suspect all this revisiting is work that must be done and that too wide a present view would distract me from it. Perhaps I'll even come to see why Ginger had to die.

March 31, 2001

The years 1966 until about '72 were easily the worst of my adult life. They were years of death and fear and menopause. As I recall, they were not good for the country either. Vietnam was consuming our youth—both those who went there and those who stayed home and committed themselves to cynicism because of it. As a people, we'd seen our confidence blow away with the back of John Kennedy's head, and we'd simmered in shame and sorrow for five long war years afterward. To demonstrate the colossal disillusionment that finally overtook us in 1968, we assassinated two more dreamers and elected Richard Nixon, who at least had the good grace not to lie to us about what we could become. Before he was through, Nixon had officially surrendered Vietnam, our remaining innocence, and the White House as well. The one national triumph of those few years took place on the moon, mercifully if momentarily lifting us off our own map.

At home I struggled and grieved much more personally. Early in 1966, right on schedule around my fiftieth birthday, I completed the Change of Life and stepped into my "post" years. In October of '66, Adele flew away from me. In November, Irene left too, but not nearly so peacefully. Adele's exit, though violent, was crisp and strangely loving. She'd lived purposefully and died that way—without hesitation. Irene meandered meanly to her death and made sure to leave hate in her wake. All of it resided in me. In December, then, I drank my first "to forget" drink.

The insidious, malignant thing about drinking is how it twists the truth at every juncture. Watch: I drink today to ease the disappointment. It's OK because it's just one drink, and it's the cocktail hour, after all. This one episode somehow initiates a rite, which I brand a "custom," and henceforth I believe I drink not for the pain, but for the ritual. Down the road, when I realize that I wake up most mornings with a fat, dry tongue and a headache, I wonder if perhaps I have a problem. Now the most subtle lie of all: I believe that my problem is drinking.

In reality, a drink is just a coward. I'm still such a coward that as often as not I put down a book or change a channel when the story I'm reading or watching takes a bad turn. I don't want to know that the husband hits the wife, that the runaway resorts to prostitution, that the hijacker shoots the pilot. I just want to believe that everyone gets along, acts right. Drinking helps a lot with that sort of pretending when the bad actors we're confronted with are real people.

At first Vic mistook my new custom for our old custom of occasionally sharing a cocktail simply to be social with each other. Or perhaps pouring me a drink was the only way he could connect with me during those years. But early on he tried many other ways. On my fiftieth birthday, he threw me a wonderful surprise party—the only one I've ever had. And after the deaths that fall, he brought me flowers every few days for several weeks. Each batch I thanked him for, dutifully put in water, and didn't glance at again until they'd rotted. I actually remember thinking things like, Oh, look at those roses with the brown petals sagging off them and the water all milky and viscous. How funny that the leaves on those stems are still erect. Don't they get it that they're dying? Yes, that's what I want all around me—dead roses with oblivious leaves. I can surely identify with those stupid, doomed leaves. But Vic got tired of the constant decomposing, and he soon quit bringing them.

By late spring of 1967, Vic was quite put out with the depth and duration of my gloom. I'm not sure he understood its inspiration, as he kept assuring me that "you'll feel better if you just start living again, Jo. Time really does heal all wounds. You even got over your father's death eventually, remember?"

I ignored the question. "Vic, I don't need any platitudes now," I said.

"That's not a platitude, dawlin'," he responded, forcing a peppy tone. "Platitudes aren't true. 'Things are really better than they seem.' Now, that might be a platitude. But what I said is clearly true. So, it may be an aphorism, an axiom, or an adage, but it's not a platitude."

I refused to play. "Fine. Then I don't need any aphorisms right now. And I also don't need my comments to be nitpicked to death. That is, I don't need to be corrected, edited, or . . . or . . . amended," I squealed.

"OK. But I know what you do need, and I've arranged to give it to you," he said, rubbing his palms together expectantly. I couldn't tell whether he was anxious or excited about his apparent surprise, but it worried me either way. I thought it best not to encourage him, and I said nothing.

"What, you might ask, do I mean?" he said. "Darlin', we are going to the one place you have always told me you'd most like to see. I've booked us on a month-long tour of Greece. We leave August first, so we'll also escape Houston at its stickiest. What do ya' think?"

What I thought was infinitely less generous than Vic's gesture. I thought, I wonder why it took all this trauma to get him to care so much about what I want to see? And why is he offering it now, when I have no interest at all in seeing it? Out loud I said only, "I'm sorry Vic, I can't go now."

"It's not now. It's in August. Why couldn't you go in August?"

This question struck me as inane. Did I have to paint him a picture? "Because I'll have some dead flowers to tend," I wanted to say. But I knew he was trying to help me, and besides he wasn't bringing me flowers anymore, so I fished around for a nicer, truer answer. Presently one presented itself. "I guess because I want to stay close by in case anyone else I love gets caught in a gunfight. I'm sure that sounds lunatic, Vic, but I just know I can't go anywhere. I can't go. Thank you for trying, but I can't."

He didn't badger me about it. He quietly canceled the trip, and we stayed home. But he soon began traveling alone. A golf tour of Scotland with his foursome from the country club, an Alaskan cruise he took clients on, a jaunt to Louisiana to track down some rare books he hoped to add to his collection. While I drank, he was developing hobbies I knew nothing about. The only trip I went along on in these dark years was to the Grand Canyon with the whole family not long after Clay and Lillian married. It was enough to convince me that I wasn't yet ready to travel again, even if the people I loved went along.

April 3, 2001

I didn't really begin to grasp the effect that my drinking was having on others until the early seventies, and then only with the help of my little grandson, Seth. He was about ten at the time, and he and Samantha had spent the week with us while Katy was overseeing some sort of law conference in Dallas for her firm. On the Saturday morning when Katy came to pick them up, she stayed for a cup of coffee and to tell me about her week. Seth listened, too, while Samantha watched cartoons in the den. After awhile, I decided that my headache needed more soothing than the coffee could provide, so I left Katy and Seth at the kitchen table while I went to the bathroom for some aspirin. They didn't see me come back into the kitchen from the dining room, and before they noticed me I heard Katy ask Seth if he'd had fun while she was gone.

"Uhhhhhh, yeeeah," Seth said with obvious hesitation.

Katy didn't respond for several seconds. I imagined her trying to read her son's face, which I couldn't see because I was now hiding in the kitchen corner.

"Did something happen?" she finally asked, rather too nonchalantly.

"Sort of. You know," Seth answered. He said "you know" as if Katy really did know.

"Anything unusual?" Katy whispered now.

"Well, . . . one night Gammy fell off my bed while she was tucking me in. Mom, she just slid right off like a noodle, and then she was so surprised to be on the floor. It scared me."

Not until Seth said "noodle" did I have any idea what he was talking about. Then I had this flash of flopping around on the floor of the guest bedroom, sputtering something about "those darn slick sheets." I shrank down in the kitchen corner and held my shameful breath.

"What did you say to her?" Katy asked.

"Nothing, Mom. I just acted like I agreed that it was the sheets' fault. But I don't know if I want to stay over here again. Do I have to?"

As I considered curling up on the floor, Vic came through the den and into the breakfast room from the other direction, which gave me a chance to slink back out through the dining room unseen. I hid in my bedroom for thirty minutes crying and torturing myself over the fact that even my grandchildren knew this about me. When Katy came knocking on my door to tell me they needed to leave, I went with her and pretended that nothing was wrong.

But at the car, saying good-bye to them, I kissed Seth and whispered in his ear, "Honey, I'm sorry I scared you."

He looked relieved but didn't say anything. And I was glad when he did come back with his sister to stay with us for a week or so the next summer. I never let myself get out of hand around any of my grandkids again.

But I didn't stop drinking either. After all, it was my custom. The trick was simply to contain it.

April 5, 2001

Still, the 1970s felt like recovery. I thought I was expanding again, and even resumed painting after about a five-year hiatus. I'd never decided to stop painting; I just hadn't picked up a brush in all that time. Now I went to work on it every afternoon, and the same odd subject matter always captivated me these days: clowns. I was drawn not to the jolly, slapstick type of clown, but to the type whose masks mock, depress, and frighten. That should have tipped me off that I was only enjoying a remission phase in my contracting, but I simply viewed it as a healthy acceptance of my limitations in the portrait painting arena. I'd finally unearthed a species of face that I could realistically recreate—those already distorted by someone else's painting.

Fran and Silver became a bigger part of our married life during this time. Vic and I had grown accustomed to Silver's pomposity and could even tease him about it with smiles on our faces. Our acceptance of him breathed new life into my longtime friendship with Fran, who'd abruptly disappeared on me while I grieved Adele much as she had after Daddy had died. I admit that I'd somewhat expected it this time, but it had hurt just exactly the same. And it would have been the end of us all over again if I'd been able to shut off Adele's voice in my head hounding me to "love through the darkness" and "love through the evil." She taught me even from the grave.

And so the four of us implemented a new tradition that we dubbed "Third Fridays." That is, on the third Friday evening of every month we had a standing double date to either play bridge or go dancing, or both. And, since Silver had already passed through his competitive bridge phase so as to make room for some new obsession, he was willing to fraternize with the rest of us plebes so long as we drank lots of martinis and let him settle all disputes.

That last part would have been very nearly impossible for Vic had he not pretty quickly found a way to capitalize on it: he turned our bridge nights into a battle of the sexes. This way Silver's refereeing usually favored Vic's position. And Fran and I were able to hold our own because Silver was somehow dealt mostly bad hands for about seven years running. I must admit this made it fun for me.

Then, every New Year's Eve, the four of us hosted a dance in our mammoth living room, just as Vic had envisioned that we would. We'd roll up all the rugs and replace them with a rented dance floor to protect the hardwoods, bring in caterers, and even hire a bartender most years. Ironically, both Vic and Silver were in their element at this party—my husband in one corner passing out cigars and shrewdly sizing up a roomful of tuxedoed business prospects, and Fran's husband in the other passing out the bull and flirting with whomever it appealed to. Fran didn't mind; she was just as whimsically sparkling in her own corner. I guess that left the final corner to me. I typically drank my way out of it to the center of the room, and then I would dance, dance, dance.

How fondly I remember those nights—until our guest list began to dwindle. By the mid-seventies it got to be depressing to sit down each December and address the invitations. Many of our friends were older than us, and it seemed that every year another couple or two lost a half. We knew our tradition had run its course on New Year's Eve 1977, when we could only come up with seven other whole couples to invite who weren't our own children, and the rest of our guests we ruefully dubbed the Wall of Widows.

April 7, 2001

A month or two after we called New Year's quits, something happened to Vic that gave me a foretaste of life along that wall. Up till then, things had gotten better and better between Vic and me as the decades had progressed. Finally I felt comfortable with him. After almost fifty years, I actually thought I'd begun to know him a little bit. It had never been a verbal, hidden-treasure sort of knowledge like women can have of each other, where you can gab blissfully for endless hours exploring your many areas of shared interests and like-mindedness. Rather, with Vic it was a roaming, experiential sort of knowledge gained by living so many seasons at his side.

I think we first realized this about each other one morning in 1976, not too long after Vic had supposedly retired from actively managing the insurance company. It was a Friday, and Vic had a ten o'clock tee-off time. Usually when he played golf in the mornings, he'd have a cup of coffee with me, and then go to the country club around eight or eight-thirty to have the buf-fet breakfast with his foursome. But this morning he just prowled around the house, hovering nervously in my way, ask-ing annoying questions and doing everything he could to push my buttons. He didn't even get dressed until nine-thirty.

I knew just what he was up to, but I shooed him around for an hour or so as if I didn't just in case he was disappointed in the end. There was to be an important meeting at Dawson Insurance at eleven o'clock—the first under J. D. Giles, the able new president that Vic himself had handpicked and groomed.

By 9:45, Vic had to leave or else miss his tee-off. I'd just given him a relatively passionate kiss and closed the door behind him when the phone rang. It was J. D. needing badly to talk to Vic. "Not half as badly as Vic needs J. D. to need to talk to him," I mumbled to myself as I somehow got my sixty-year-old body to running down the driveway and then the street chasing Vic's Cadillac as it picked up speed with an air of resignation.

Thankfully, he saw me pretty quickly. I suspect he was looking exclusively in his rear-view mirror as he drove off and not at all at the street. He hit the brakes and started to back up almost before I could get out of the way, but paused next to me with a hopeful look. I nodded and smiled, too winded to speak. No need. He was inside and on the phone gleefully barking instructions by the time I hauled myself up to the back door and could listen in.

When he hung up, he just came over and hugged me. He was grateful, I think as much for my knowing and caring about his plight as for the call itself. We could finally play off the same page. Maybe we'd been doing it for a long time, but I never saw it before now.

And so it was that I felt betrayed by the stroke Vic suffered in early 1978 because it seemed to erase much of our mutual knowledge and the trust that had been so long in coming. After that, Vic's churlish tendencies took on a life of their own. During Christmas dinner that year, when Vic said something particularly biting to Samantha in front of the whole family, it struck me that "disagreeable" and "snide" were the default settings for Vic's personality. When the personality that had grown up during the forty-five years of our marriage suddenly got zapped by a wayward brainwave, Vic's default personality was the one left calling the shots. He became almost intolerable.

I sometimes fear that this is the only Vic our grandchildren remember.

April 10, 2001

This morning I glanced out my den window and saw a mama cat ripe with kittens lumber across my yard and slink into the hedge along the back wall. Short-haired and pure black except for a white nose and front paw, she was a stranger to me. And from where I stood at the window, I saw no collar on her either. She must have come in under the side gate where Lenny rammed it with the lawn mower several years ago and broke off the bottom six inches of three or four boards. I actually went out and tried to run her off, but by then she was gone.

April 12, 2001

It seems that the carnal aspects of life are destined to intrude on the contemplative hideaway I've created here for myself. That mama cat I saw two days ago has resurfaced, much depleted and scavenging my backyard for sustenance. Already her tits are beginning to sag sacrificially. When I saw her, I sneaked out, followed her from a distance that I hoped she'd feel comfortable with, and ultimately discovered her lair under the azalea bush in the farthest corner of the yard. She'd made a tall, sturdy nest out of pine needles and had deposited three perfect kitties in it. I could have tucked each one into my palm if I'd been so inclined. But it's best not to put feral mothers to the test, even if their territory is only alongside a stoplight or a shopping mall. I let her be.

Still, she preoccupied me all afternoon. I kept seeing those three babes and how hungry she looked. How would she have anything to pass along to them? So awhile ago I slid a bowl of milk and a plate full of Ginger's dog food under the azalea bush and stood back watching until I was sure she'd go for them. I suppose I'm now overseer of a cat family, at least until the kittens are weaned. And all I wanted to do was think and write.

Since I was already out and about in the exterior world, I called Fran in Milwaukee and begged her to come for another visit next week. I believe it may be our last, but I didn't tell her that. I just said that I need her to help me remember some things, and she seemed to understand. She comes in on the eighteenth.

Chapter 17 ❧

Katy

I said earlier that Eliot would only have to be told about his prospective grandchild if we first determined that one was actually going to come along. Well, for weeks now I'd known that Samantha meant to have her baby. At four months pregnant, it was safest to assume that she'd succeed in giving birth. And Eliot would have to be told before her condition became apparent to him.

Lately Eliot had been spending his time in a backyard storage shed that he'd made into a woodshop over thirty-five years ago. This hobby represented the one perseverance of Eliot's life; to it he had returned after every dark spell. Maybe it was proof that at some level Eliot had always aspired to be truly alive. Whenever I started finding him out there, I was inclined to let my guard down a bit. Things might be all right, for a little while anyway.

But whatever it was that periodically drew Eliot out of himself and into the woodshop just as strongly set me off imagining the multitude of ways he might get himself, and me, into trouble. When he was curled up in his room, I knew where he was and basically what to expect from him. But when he came out, I could almost hear the bolts on the base of the cannon pulling free of the ship deck.

Eliot had been frequenting his woodshop since the week that Mother had threatened to disinherit me. I was cynical enough to suspect that my distress had somehow lifted his spirits, and he was celebrating by building us a new dining table out of a heavy, golden

259

oak into which he was busy carving an intricate pineapple pattern on each leg.

This was the task to which Eliot was applying himself on the rainy Saturday morning along about mid-April when Samantha called and asked if she could bring over some sandwiches for the two of us to have for lunch. She sounded like she had something on her mind, and since it seemed that our relationship had recently degenerated to little more than that of acquaintances, I thought it best to welcome all overtures on her part. I told her to come on, knowing this meant that I'd have to face Eliot with the pregnancy story first. When I'd last seen Sam two weeks before, she'd already begun to thicken around the middle. An observant father would have noticed it already.

Despite the rain, Eliot didn't reward my tap on his woodshop door with an audible invitation to come in. I entered anyway and found him swaying red-faced under a thick sheet of glass that he was trying to fit onto the little ledge that he'd constructed along the inner edge of his tabletop. I rushed forward, scolding as I grabbed one end of the glass. "Why in the world didn't you come get me to help you with this? You could have knocked yourself out or destroyed the whole dang table trying to put it together all by yourself," I huffed. But he ignored me, and as we lowered the glass carefully into the groove that Eliot had fashioned, I saw that it fit perfectly. The rounded top edge of the oak frame was exactly flush with the glass, and the glass kissed the rim of the frame along every side. The table's sculpted legs—each one a whole piece of fruit with a dramatic, leafy hat on it—were visible even from above. It was a breathtaking piece of furniture.

Together, we stood back to appreciate it, and for the briefest moment we shared the same vantage point, the way you might with a stranger you find standing next to you when you first glimpse the

Grand Canyon or the ceiling of the Sistine Chapel. At such moments you're tempted to touch that person's sleeve and whisper, "Can you believe we're really standing here?" But of course you don't, because you don't know them. At most, you exchange a glance of mutual reverence and wonder; and then you peel off into your separate worlds forever after.

And so, without blessing Eliot or his table with a spoken compliment, I focused on the hard news I'd come to share. "Eliot, I have to tell you something that'll probably shock you. Before I do, I want you to promise that you won't overreact. Just listen to the whole story first. And try to remember, this is not about you."

My opening drew the grunt that I'd come to expect from him, and I went on. "It's about Samantha. She's coming over here this afternoon, and you need to know something before she gets here."

"OK," he said, pulling up a stool. He sat down and faced me with an unnatural calm, thereby succeeding in throwing me entirely off rhythm. I was prepared for some paranoid retort like, "If it's so all-fire important, why isn't Samantha telling me herself?" or, "Why is it I'm always the last one to find out about everything?" or even, "I don't like the tone of your voice, Katy. Why can't you ever be polite?" And so his cooperation—conspicuous and suspect whenever he extended it—very nearly deterred me. But I told myself it was just elation over his artistic accomplishment that made Eliot so agreeable now, and I continued.

"Well, Eliot, there aren't many ways to say it. Samantha has made a mistake that she's chosen to live with. I think we can feel proud of her for that, even if we're disappointed in her for making the mistake to begin with." I paused there to let him flare up, but he just sat and waited for me to go on. Miles away, it seemed, I heard the steady strum of raindrops bouncing off the tin roof of the shed.

Soon Eliot began to slide his fingers over the beveled edge of his tabletop. "Eliot," I barked, "she's pregnant!"

"Pregnant," he echoed, now caressing the oak frame. As I waited for him to say more, his fingers backed up over the wood and he furrowed his brow, obviously registering a careless bubble or two in the varnish. He didn't ask how long. He didn't even ask who.

"Yes, pregnant," I snapped. "For four months now. And she means to have the baby and raise it herself, without getting married." I'd get that rise if I had to slander Sam to do it.

Finally Eliot squirmed a little on his stool. He let one foot drop to the floor and shifted his weight to it. Then he crossed his arms and gaslight me while I was making this rare gesture to treat him like an equal. The man simply couldn't stand to be respected; he'd go to any lengths to head it off.

Did I think she wouldn't tell him? I was so sure of it that I didn't believe what he was saying now. That would be just like him to try and sputtered, "Er . . . well . . . Katy, Samantha told me about all this a few weeks ago. Did you think she wouldn't tell me?"

"I won't dignify that with a response," I said. "Eliot, just this once why can't you let me talk to you grown-up to grown-up? There is no way that Samantha would have told you without warning me that she was doing it. I don't want to hurt your feelings, but you can't be trusted with the truth because you always take it personally. See, you can't even listen to it gracefully."

Again, I won a grunt from him, and then he fell silent. So I continued on. "It seems that Samantha got involved with someone she met writing one of her articles, but she doesn't think she can marry him and doesn't even plan to tell him about the baby from what I understand. Not that it matters, necessarily, but this man's name is—"

"William Canmore," Eliot interrupted. "Yes, I know. I've met him."

"Met him," I repeated dumbly. "I haven't even met him. When . . . did you?"

"Oh. Well, Samantha brought him by a few days ago while you were at the Abbey visiting your new friend. She pretended to be dropping off a present, but I saw later that there was nothing but tissue paper in the bag. I thought Canmore was a good guy, and I told her so when she asked me later. I'm also betting that he knows she's pregnant. Anyone could see it."

Never, ever, had I felt so discounted or betrayed.

❧

Even a strong person has a breaking point. I reached mine somewhere between slamming the door of Eliot's woodshop behind me and Samantha's arrival a few hours later with our lunch.

One alarming truth blared repeatedly through my head: no one in my world was acting the way he or she was supposed to, and nothing I did was changing that fact. My mother seemed intent on dying, if not from cancer then from some more pedestrian danger to which she insisted on subjecting herself. My brother was putting up no fight to stop her, apparently resigned to her noxious desires. My daughter had made a ruinous mistake, blamed me for her own unwillingness to mitigate the bad consequences, and had since taken to treating me the way she might treat the greeters down at Wal-Mart. Now she'd gone behind my back to share her plight with the man I'd subjected myself to for decades mostly just to spare her and her brother the damage of divorce. And Eliot. Eliot! The unspeakable nerve he had to insinuate himself between my daughter and me. How dare he pretend to be a father now, when Sam's terror of winding up with someone like him threatened to triumph as the dominant motivation of her life.

I'd not been seduced by Eliot's attempt to chase after me—running out into the rain before I could escape to the house, and yelling, "Katy, I'm sorry to have told you that way. We weren't trying to hide it; I thought you knew him already. I know how bad it feels to be left out. Please calm down."

I spun around in the mud and disdained everything about him, from the gray swipe of his comb-over now slicked straight up on his head, to the insulting words that had come out of his mouth. Most especially those words. I held up a hand to stop them. "Don't," I ordered. "Don't ever compare me to yourself. And you needn't worry about Samantha and me, either. It doesn't concern you or have a thing to do with you, so you can just go back in there and build your furniture. You're good at that. The table is exquisite." I aimed by that belated compliment to demote him from father and husband back down to mere craftsman servant.

In response to this diatribe, I saw Eliot struggle inwardly, the old self-hatred longing to obey me. But some other impulse battled against it. What was this? Again the eerie calmness, and then he dared to step up to me and touch my arm, pressing me toward the house. I held out until the rain soaked through to my skin. Then, crimped and defeated, I let him lead me inside to my room, where I sobbed on the floor for almost an hour before I got up and stripped off my sopping clothes.

❧

I've long gone without such frills as elegant clothes, flashy, nonessential jewelry, provocative lingerie, or a lover for whom to wear them all. These are the bounty of women insightful enough to choose husbands who contribute more to the family's subsistence than an occasional superfluous dining table, however gorgeous. I've made do with a minimal, utilitarian wardrobe, floor-length night-gowns that I replace only when they begin to yellow around the neck, and strictly serviceable jewelry—a reliable Timex that I've worn for twenty-five years, a pair of gold loops that keep my earlobes from growing over my piercings, and my wedding rings, which I wear to ward off flights of fancy. Every morning I wake up in a lonely, queen-sized bed that I've inexplicably drifted to one side of. When I need to feel special, I reach for my briefcase or I recall the great sacrifice that I've made by staying so long with Eliot. Whatever else they may say about me, no one can say that I walk away from my mistakes.

Tears were another extravagance to which I'd long felt unenti-tled. And I could not remember the last time that they had crept up on me, clubbed me over the head, and thoroughly had their way with me as they had that morning. Afterward, I couldn't resist feeling that I'd been purged or somehow restored, like a flu victim after a long, unavoidable sleep. Utterly unpremeditated—something done to me rather than by me—this mourning was a gift. And its license extended beyond tears.

Tranquil now in a distant, absentee sort of way, I floated from the closet where I'd dressed over to the single-drawer, brown leather jewelry box on my nightstand, and I emptied its contents onto the bed. Out plopped a tangled glob of costume jewelry rep-resenting years of birthday and Christmas gifts from my children and unemployed husband, but not the item I was fishing for. Even the momentary prospect of having misplaced this torturous treasure didn't shake my strange new equanimity. My fingers simply reached into the unexposed back portion of the drawer and meandered around till they felt a chain anchored by something hanging over into the shallow depths of the box. I tilted the drawer until the chain's pendant cleared the back, and lifted it out.

It was a large, oval cameo of a woman's bust, the raised face in onyx and the background in ivory. You would not realize, unless you were looking for it, that this cameo was also a locket. I felt for the tiny clasp that barely protruded beneath about a quarter-inch of the ivory, and pressed on it. Nothing happened. I tried moving it to one or the other side, but the old hinges still didn't spring. Finally, while pressing the lever with one hand, I pried the locket open with a fingernail on the other. There, pasted into the right-hand side, was a picture of Mother, Adele, and me taken on the porch of our house on the Byway not long before I graduated from high school.

On the afternoon that the picture was taken, we had treated Adele to a matinee Christmas concert at the Houston Music Hall, so she wasn't in the white uniform that she always wore when she was "a-hunkerin' down on her cleanin' and her cookin'." To Mother's right in the photo, Adele was buttoned up to her neck in a smock-type dress that blazed a royal purple in the encroaching afternoon sun. Her smile dominated the scene; I could even see the toothless hole that had been put there by a childhood employer who claimed that she'd let some apples go bad in his pantry.

On Mother's left, I beamed less brightly, but I seemed content enough to be pictured with the women in my life. Adele had reached behind my mother's scrawny shoulders and rested her fingers lightly on my arm. Always her touch was light, but deliberate and reinforcing, like the ubiquitous "dark matter" that astronomers say keeps our universe from blowing apart.

On the whole, I thought it a fond, comforting moment to memorialize in a photograph and also in a locket. And so I had prepared it and given it to my mother for a Christmas gift in 1966—the year that robbed us of Adele. I meant it to say, "I know how you feel. Look here, I feel it too. You're not alone." But Mother was deaf to any such sentiment. She opened the box, glanced at the picture when I showed her the secret clasp, and set the locket aside with barely a murmur. After a few years had passed without seeing her wear it, I rummaged through her drawers one day and found it still in the gift box. I took it home with me and tossed it in with my guilty little stash of neglected costume jewelry. And then I'd reached for my briefcase.

But on this Saturday thirty years later, I let myself cry over it—a thoroughly premeditated but shameless jag of tears that fell within my new license. "And this is the woman I'm supposed to bear my heart to," I blubbered to the empty room. "How can that be?"

When Samantha arrived, I was sitting in my reading chair, still pondering how I would confront Mother with any of the things that Adele and Jenny Bingham thought I should. I heard the bell ring and Sam's father answer the door. They stood in the foyer and exchanged words that I couldn't discern from behind my closed door down the hallway. I didn't even try.

Samantha knocked on my bedroom a few minutes later. I believe I looked at her when she came in, but I didn't get up. "Hey," I said. "Hey, yourself," she replied, squinting at me and trying to smile. I might have been holding a hand grenade for the wary way it came off.

"Samantha, I hope you didn't go to too much trouble with those sandwiches. I'm not very hungry, but your father might be." My tone was earnest, but my daughter wasn't buying it.

"Are you upset?" she asked.

"Yes. And no," I said, not trying to be coy. "It's nothing you can do anything about, or that you should even try to. Let's just let it go."

"Mom, I'm sorry I didn't tell you that I'd told Dad I was pregnant. It never occurred to me that you'd think it was your responsibility to do it, for one thing. But I guess the real reason I didn't tell you I'd done it is because you might think he shouldn't know."

"That's probably true," I conceded. "I would probably have insisted that he not be told yet. I only tried to tell him today because I thought he might flip if he figured it out on his own."

"So you understand why I didn't tell you?"

"Yes."

"And you understand why I told him when I thought the time was right?"

"Sure. I guess."

"Well? Is there anything else you need to say about it then?" Sam pressed.

"Nothing else. I really didn't need to say this much, dear."

She nodded her head and cast one last fretful glance my way before turning to leave. "OK, then. I guess I'll try you another time."

Before the door clicked shut, however, I remembered something and called after her. "Samantha?"

She swung it back open and looked in. "Yes?"

"Why did you want to talk to me today?"

"Oh, I just wanted to ask you some questions about being pregnant," she said, averting her eyes but stepping back into the room. It's then I noticed that the tail of Sam's oversized work shirt hung out over a baggy new pair of jeans. I suspected they had an elastic tummy on them. My baby was going to have a baby, and she didn't know how to do it.

I wanted to run over and prop her up, but first I asked, "Why now, after so many weeks have gone by when you could have called but didn't?"

"Because I felt like the pressure was off," she answered.

"Pressure?"

"Yeah. Ever since that night when I explained to you why I couldn't abort this baby or marry Bill, you've given me plenty of space to do this thing the way I need to. So I guess I finally felt like I could ask a few questions without you viewing it as leave to take over my whole pregnancy. I'm sorry if that hurts your feelings, Mom."

I was so stunned by this revelation that I didn't respond for several seconds. Here seemed to be an important puzzle piece, if I could just figure out where to put it. The very "space" that I'd viewed as a snubbing, Samantha had viewed as freedom in which to seek me out.

"Mom?" she said, interrupting these meditative baby steps.

"Hmm? Oh. No, no, you didn't hurt my feelings. In fact, that really helps me. I tell you what—maybe I'll have that sandwich after all. Let's go talk about being pregnant."

❧

Miss Bingham had instructed me to arrive at her place at 10:00 A.M. on the eighteenth. In my typical fashion, I was standing outside her door on the appointed day at twenty till, and I noticed that she'd installed a shiny brass knocker in the shape of a magnolia bloom since I'd been there last. This seemed to be some sort of trademark of hers, like her drawl and her flashy, sophisticated dress. Perhaps Mr. Clarkson had given it to her as a gift for her eightieth birthday. I could hear him selling it to Abbey prospects even now: "You see, Mrs. Cravitz, we encourage all of our residents to transform their flats into homes unique to their own personal tastes and interests. Take lovely Miss Bingham over here in 118 . . ."

I withdrew from her door and self-consciously fingered the gift under my arm while the twenty minutes began to tick past. My mother had taught me never, ever to knock before party time, no matter how early you actually arrive. So I was busy examining the other doors along that hall when a clot of old ladies rounded the corner nearest me and headed straight for Miss B's new knocker. Straightaway I decided to let them go in ahead of me. But the gift wrap had given me away.

A short old girl in a muumuu with her hair dyed a red seen nowhere in nature spied me first and waved her companions over. As she approached, I noticed that the top of her thin, purplish curls barely cleared my chin. Hasty streaks of rouge stained each of her cheeks, and she'd slathered her full, O-shaped lips with a high-gloss, alarmingly fuchsia lip product. I thought her gorgeous in a fleshy, generous way that seemed to promise endless laughter.

"I bet you're Katy," she said. "Am I right?" Then, without waiting for my "yes," she launched off on a roll call, tapping the others' forearms as she went along. "I'm Iris. This is Natalie, who we call Nat for short. This doll here is Mary Faye. And last but by no means least, meet Bunny." Then a smile flickered ever so briefly across her round face, and she deadpanned, "which of course is short for Jackrabbit."

Iris held her breath and waited for me to get her offbeat improv, but the snickering and eye-rolling of the other three soon relieved me of the burden. When I hesitated to join in with them, Iris shrugged her shoulders and reassured me with a wave of both hands. "I take some getting used to," she sang.

"Yes, don't mind Iris," seconded the tall, handsome woman whom Iris had identified as Nat. With commanding familiarity, Nat stepped forward then and took my elbow. "Now, shall we all go see

Jenny? Maybe there's something we can do to help her get ready for us," she said, nudging me along. Nat's gray hair was unsparingly cropped in the ultrashort, rather spiky style common to much younger women. This left her ears entirely exposed and highlighted the rhinestones that glistened from her fake-gold clip-ons. I was sure I'd once given my granddaughter several similar pair when she'd gone through a dress-up phase at the age of five. But Nat's rhinestones apparently made her feel elegant, as she tilted her head slightly to show them off when she noticed me looking.

"Yes, let's get going. I'm starving!" Iris said, stroking her stomach and smacking those lips. "Of course, there's no real danger of that, but I've been fantasizing about Mary Faye's eggplant quiche ever since I got up this morning. You're in for a real treat, Katy." To taunt me further with this alleged delicacy, Iris thumped on the large, square Tupperware that was tucked under the arm of her white-haired friend. She and Bunny carried similar containers, and Nat had brought along a bulky foil pouch. "Brownies," she reported when I glanced down at it. "Somebody had to do it."

Of the four of them, Mary Faye appeared far and away the most decrepit. Stooped and hunchbacked, she bore the obvious ravages of osteoporosis and leaned heavily on a wooden cane. The lenses of her ancient glasses were so heartbreakingly thick and clunky that I wondered if they didn't help to tip her forward. Because of them, Mary Faye's watery gray eyes looked like they'd better fit a horse's face, but behind the tired horse eyes her smile was quick and gracious. There was nothing decrepit in Mary Faye's smile.

As we neared Jenny's knocker, I fretted that I was the only one without any edible contribution to make to Jenny's party. Bunny saw me biting my lip and noted that I alone had brought a present. But this only served to remind me of the risky nature of my gift.

Fidgeting, I answered her, "It's just a small thing, but very personal. I hope she likes it."

"I'm sure she will, dear. We'll let you give it to her after we leave," she said, again reading my mind. Aside from her springy name, everything about Bunny was light brown and careful, from the thick, uniform layers of beige foundation and powder that drew attention to the crisscrossing weave of her wrinkles, to the tailored tan dress she wore, to the tight way she carried herself—her elbows pinned to her waist and her shoulders pulled slightly forward. Even her words seemed brown and careful. "Maybe we should give Jenny a few more minutes before we descend on her," she suggested, checking her watch. "Let's wait out here awhile longer."

"Nonsense," Nat said. "Jenny can handle it if we show up a wee bit early." With that, she reached forward and slapped the shiny magnolia against its brass back. The party had begun.

§

For their ages, Miss B and her friends demonstrated quite robust appetites as they consumed the varied goodies that we helped Jenny set out for us. Not a sliver of Mary Faye's splendid eggplant quiche survived the first hour or so of our visit. Though I'd been doubtful when Iris had first singled it out for praise, I matched the others square for square in the eating, and I was busy jotting down the recipe when Nat called out "bridge time" in a manner that left no uncertainty as to what we were doing next. I felt my stomach do a little back flip and was just about to declare my incompetence when Jenny took control.

"OK, ladies," she said, clapping her hands together like a school-teacher. "Here's how we're going to do this to start out with. Since Katy tells me she hasn't played much bridge, why don't you four play a few hands while I try to explain to her what you're doing and why. Of course, feel free to jump in and explain it yourself if you like. Once she gets the hang of it, she can rotate in and the one who rotates out and I will coach her."

"If it comes to that," I angled. "I'd be as happy just watching and learning this time around."

"We'll see," she said, directing me to a chair slightly removed from a round game table already set with four coasters, two decks of large-print cards with riverboats on the backs, and a scorecard. I obediently slid into the chair, and the other four took their respective places around the table, Iris and Mary Faye squaring off against Nat and Bunny. While Bunny shuffled and dealt the first hand, Jenny began my instruction.

"First and foremost, bridge is a game of communication. If you communicate well in real life, chances are you'll be good at bridge, at least the bidding portion." Had Jenny given us white rather than avocado-green napkins that morning, I'd have gone ahead and thrown mine onto the table without further delay.

"The key is subtlety," she continued. "The thing you're not allowed to do is say anything outright. You must try and tell your partner what you have in your hand—points, high cards, long suits, weaknesses—without coming right out and telling your partner what you have in your hand. Think of it like any other conversation in which you must be mindful of the other person's feelings, point of view, biases, and level of comprehension. When do we ever get to tell people exactly what we're thinking? Would we really want to? More to the point, would we want anyone else to tell us exactly what they're thinking?"

"Doubtful!" Bunny volunteered. But this little outburst embarrassed her, drawing a pretty crimson flush up through the caked-on beige of her cheeks. "Um, at least, I wouldn't," she murmured.

"Certainly, you have to be diplomatic with people," Mary Faye said. "I always try to tell the truth just as gently as possible."

"Relating to others is like a dance," Iris philosophized. "The dance is what I think makes life enjoyable. Everyone's dignity must be preserved even while each of us strives to be more authentic. Neither dignity nor authenticity can be sacrificed for the other, right Jenny, Mary Faye?"

"Precisely," the latter agreed. "Knowing where that line is requires significant wisdom and—"

"And love," Iris finished for her. "It's easier to avoid trampling someone else's dignity if you care about people, particularly that person. You have to get into their shoes, walk around in them."

"Thank you, Atticus Finch," Nat cut in. "But I think we digress far too much. The dealer opens the bidding, Katy. Go Bunny."

Squirming under Nat's imperial stare, Bunny took a nervous little sip of her iced tea and opened with a defense of her forthcoming bid. "In my opinion, it's best to be conservative. Say as little as possible. That way the other team doesn't know what you've got," she said. "I pass."

"Pass," Iris echoed.

"But, of course, when you take Bunny's tack," Nat gusted back across the table, "the opposing team isn't all alone in the dark. Your partner doesn't know what you've got either, and this roundly defeats the main purpose of bidding. Here, let me show you. I'll open this hand with three hearts. That's called a preemptive bid, meaning it cuts off any communication between the opposing team at the cheap one and two levels. If they want to share information now, they'll have to pay dearly for it. I've hereby told my own partner that I have low points—ten or fewer—but I have at least seven hearts, which only leaves six hearts unaccounted for. If she has heart support and decent points, she should take us to game at the four level."

"Pass," Mary Faye cooed, a sage smile playing on her lips.

The bidding thereby returned to Bunny, who had pouted up mightily toward the barbed beginning of Nat's speech. She took the opportunity to be equally contrary. "Of course, if your partner doesn't have heart support and decent points, you've most likely stranded your team at the three level without enough points between you to win that many tricks. If the other team elects to let you hang yourselves, you'll win the bid and probably get set. I'm afraid I, too, must pass." She'd said it without sounding the teensiest bit sorry. Closing her fanned hand with a single brisk tap on the table, she looked prepared to lay down already.

Iris brought it home with a wink my way. "And, of course, I pass as well."

"There," Bunny gloated. "Do you see how valuable it was for Iris and Mary Faye to say nothing? I reiterate, it's generally best to say as little as possible."

"Hey, I'm not set yet, am I?" Nat demanded. "I'll pull this off if I have to cheat to do it." But no one thought she could, and sure enough she went down by three tricks. So much for seven small trumps when the ace, king, queen, and jack are lurking in the hands of the opposing team.

"Dignity," Jenny whispered in my ear as Bunny galloped to trade seats with Iris for the next hand. "Above all, you must preserve each other's dignity. Say what you must, but do it with humility. And always keep in mind the possibility that you might be wrong."

"Thank you, Jenny," I whispered back. "I'll try to remember when I talk to Mother." Who could resent being set up so sweetly?

After the other ladies had gone home for what Iris labeled their "octogenarian siesta," I helped Miss B put away her teacups and serving pieces. When we'd finished, I walked over to where I'd stowed my purse and the gift I'd brought, and flirted with simply slipping the latter into the former and skating out the door. But my purse was not big enough, and besides, something about that strategy seemed too Bunny-like. So I bucked up and handed her the box. "Happy birthday, Jenny."

She didn't bother scolding me for disobeying her earlier "no gifts" command. Accepting it with a barely perceptible squeal of delight, she sat down, looked me in the eye, and said, "Katy, it means very much to me that you came today. Thank you. And thank you for this too." The nervous little shrug with which I met Jenny's smile did not escape her. "But why do you seem so shy about it?" she asked.

"Oh, you'll know when you see it. Giving you this particular thing is a bit like inviting the chef at K-Paul's to be a guest at your Cajun dinner party. It's something you might be able to appreciate more than I do, but then again, it might not be anything at all," I croaked lamely.

With that mysterious introduction, what could Jenny do but say, "I'm sure I'll appreciate it, whatever it is, dear," and then set upon the package? When she got down to the naked box, she lifted the top off and began to fold the gold tissue papers back one by one. Hearing her gasp even before she'd completely stripped the last sheet away and exposed the little book to my anxious view, I exhaled conspicuously.

There was Daddy's thin, worn volume of favorite poetry, bound in a soft-sided, cinnamon-colored leather that appeared almost suede in this its seventieth year. No title or markings of any kind were visible on the cover or its slender, woven spine. Still, Jenny placed her palm on it, let her eyelids flutter shut, and thereby coaxed the contents up through the blank front flap. "Prufrock," she whispered. "I . . . we . . . I remember . . . my . . . favorite stanzas:

Let us go then, you and I,

When the evening is spread out against the sky

Like a patient etherized upon a table;

Let us go, through certain half-deserted streets,

The muttering retreats

Of restless nights in one-night cheap hotels

And sawdust restaurants with oyster-shells:

Streets that follow like a tedious argument

Of insidious intent

To lead you to an overwhelming question . . . .

Oh, do not ask, "What is it?"

Let us go and make our visit. . . .

And would it have been worth it, after all,

After the cups, the marmalade, the tea,

Among the porcelain, among some talk of you and me,

Would it have been worth while,

To have bitten off the matter with a smile,

To have squeezed the universe into a ball

To roll it toward some overwhelming question,

To say: "I am Lazarus, come from the dead,

Come back to tell you all, I shall tell you all"—

If one, settling a pillow by her head,

Should say: "That is not what I meant at all.

That is not it, at all."

Here she reluctantly halted her rushing, sing-song recital and returned to me, opening her eyes. "It goes on," she said, "but the ending disappoints. I choose to imagine that the moment was forced, and it proved worthwhile indeed. I won't lie to you, Katy. The answer to your brave question is yes. I have seen this book before."

It's then I saw how I had tested her. Without once allowing the startling hunch to infiltrate my conscious mind, I'd settled on this gift and laughed off all my jitters as the natural hesitations of a novice daring to present a specimen to a collector. Had I in fact been squeezing the universe into a ball and rolling it toward some overwhelming question that I didn't even know I had?

Or had Jenny done most of the squeezing and the rolling? I could not say for sure.

CHAPTER 18

Jo

April 17, 2001

Living in the year 2001 increasingly eludes me. It has become the trivial, bothersome part of my existence, like personal hygiene or taking the car in for an oil change—things that have to be done just so you can get to where you're going and your teeth don't fall out when you get there. I sometimes can't see that I have even that much reason to reside in the present. And so, as the past and future demand more and more of me, I resolve less and less to live in today.

But I can't float away completely just yet. For in a moment of creaturely weakness I set something here in motion, and now I must see it through. So I change sheets, lay out a second set of towels, and try to pry myself far enough open to let Fran in for the next few days. I wonder what another person might like to eat—surely not the persistent slabs of boneless baked chicken breast and the canned sauerkraut that have become my daily fare. It seems like years since I've had to recall other options. What else is there to drink besides water, skim milk? What other meats besides chicken? Do normal old ladies still eat fruits and vegetables? I must unfold quickly now; tomorrow she comes.

I know that my real aversion to sharing this space with Fran is the sure return to isolation afterward—infinitely worse than never leaving it in the first place. When I was a child, before I could escape to school and during the summers ever after that,

I'd yearn unbearably for Daddy to come home until the very moment each afternoon when I saw him materialize in the distance, his German clip hurrying him toward me, shoulders forward and fedora pulled snugly over his forehead as if he were one of our Wilhelm ancestors shielding himself from a harsh Frankfurt wind. During the intolerable hours that I waited for him, I tortured myself wondering what I would do if I didn't have this Daddy to come home to me, if all I had were the crimped shoulders of my mother turning ever away; I must have been thirteen before it occurred to me that without Daddy, I wouldn't have had to endure all that yearning. I would never have known to yearn for him.

I suspect that whatever we can think to hunger for is somewhere real, though our actual exposure to such things may barely hint at their existence. Perhaps all we have is a rumor that we've read about in books or heard snippets of in grocery aisles: "There is a father you'll want to rush out and meet." Or it may be just a glimpse of a far-off image, hazy and shifting along the horizon until the moment you divert your eyes, when a scruffy fedora and forward-leaning shoulders quicken in your periphery and take your breath away. A waft of his cologne, whiskers on your cheek, tales of buttermilk tauntings. These are enough to awaken the longing.

April 18, 2001

Samantha surprised me this morning, showing up out of nowhere to transport me across town to fetch Fran. Then she sweetly insisted on escorting us to lunch at Rafael's, where I chose the tortilla soup and a decadent slice of caramel cheese-cake over their famous, kraut-bloated Reuben sandwich.

Though a tiny victory, I know, I puffed up at this wide departure from the lazy, atavistic menu I've tortured myself with lately. I was in high spirits.

Throughout the main course, Fran updated us on her horde of brilliant and talented grandchildren—not a dud, according to grandma, in the whole bunch. I was just sinking my fork into the crusty, two-inch-thick tip of my dessert when my own dear grandchild pulled a sneaky, uncharacteristic maneuver that might have come right out of her mother's playbook.

"So, Gammy," she said, "when is the last time you talked to Mom?"

I squinted hard across the table, and Samantha gazed back at me with a fixed, premeditated smile. "Good lands," I said, laying the fork aside. "How should I know, Samantha? I can't keep tabs on when I talk to everybody."

Sam took a slow, fruity bite of her cobbler, studying me while she swallowed. "That's odd," she said, exaggerating each word, "Mom was just as ornery about it when I asked her."

Flustered, I let Sam's seditious comment hover too long in the air about Fran's head. An instant later I heard her coffee cup slam onto the table next to me. "Blast it, Josey. What is up with you two now?"

"I don't want to talk about it," I spat. And to emphasize the point, I snatched up my fork, still loaded with cream cheese and caramel, and shoved it into my mouth.

"Mom finally admitted to me that y'all haven't spoken directly to each other in nearly a month," Samantha tattled on.

"Well," I said, "there's the answer to your question then. Can we talk about something else?"

"But she wouldn't tell me why. All she'd say is that she didn't want to prejudice me against you. What's she talking about, Gammy?"

"Honey, it's way too complicated for me to explain. I don't understand it myself." I paused to see if this might by chance suffice, but both of my inquisitors were still pursing their lips at me, so I tried again. "It had something to do with Ginger drowning, OK?"

Not OK. Fran finally leaned against me and whispered, "Spill it, Jo."

An hour later they knew everything about the situation that I did. I even told them that I'd threatened to cut Katy out of my will if she didn't quit talking about that darn nursing home. "Of course, to hear her tell it," I said, "this Abbey place is better than a chateau on the Riviera. But I don't care even if it is. I don't want to leave my house, and there's no reason why I should. Isn't that right, Samantha?"

"Absolutely none," Fran cut in. "You're far too belligerent to get hurt or robbed now that someone has challenged your ability to take care of yourself! Katy couldn't have come up with a better strategy for protecting you."

"Very funny," I sneered. "The truth is, Fran, that Katy seems to be against me these days. It feels like she's angry with me, but I don't know what it is I've done to her . . . unless it's just being sick."

"That may be enough," Fran mused soberly. I suspect she was remembering her last bittersweet year or two with Silver. But, ever the survivor, one last big bite of chocolate brownie wiped the gloom off Fran's face, and she swooped back down on me. "So tell us how you're going to deal with it," she ordered.

"Huh?"

"Well, you say all this happened nearly a month ago, and you've been holed up in your house ever since. So by now you've surely come up with some plan for fixing things with Katy. What is it?"

"Well, Miss Sassy Pants," I said, "let's just say that I've had a few other things on my mind."

"Gammy, listen. I can tell you that Mom hasn't been doing at all well with this. Please, please end it."

"But, Samantha, she's the one pushing me away."

"Josey, at our age we flat don't have time to waste on rifts with our kids. You have to find out what's bothering her—now." Fran then grabbed up the neglected lunch tab and began rummaging through her purse as if the matter were now officially resolved. I went along, content enough to have been delivered from battle that I didn't let anyone's specious assumptions trouble me.

The valet brought my 1976 Mercedes sedan around to Rafael's portico, and Samantha delicately eased her stomach behind the wheel. While we'd eaten and argued, a spring rain had rinsed the city, but the sun was breaking through the clouds as we coasted away.

About fifteen minutes later, we were traveling east in the HOV lane on Interstate 10. Fran and I were busy educating Samantha on the pre-war childbirth philosophies about which we are experts. For one thing, we assured her, a free flow of painkillers in the delivery room is a good thing, not the crime against nature that many young women these days make it out to be.

"How is it different from killing any other pain?" Fran asked Samantha. "According to the naturalists' reasoning, couldn't one argue that God means for us to experience the undiluted pain not only of childbirth, but of broken limbs, cancer, death? That there must be something wholesome and honest about that too? And pretty soon you reject every modern medicine entirely, and then you have to reject every modern advancement, and you find yourself taking the position that God put man on earth with a brain that he didn't mean for us to use at all!"

Now, I felt that Fran had ridiculously overstated our case, and so I was just about to reach over the passenger seat and yank a strand of her gray hair, when our car began spinning. With no warning. At sixty miles an hour. With no warning, at sixty miles an hour, we spun round and round just exactly like a glass Coke bottle used in that kissing game. I felt my stomach soar and my shoulder slam into the back door; but nothing so alert as fear arose in my conscious mind. Mentally, I was still pulling Fran's hair.

When we came to a halt, my Mercedes was horizontal across the right lane of traffic and the shoulder of the freeway. The front bumper rested a few inches from the guardrail overlooking an intersection about twenty feet below, and a pickup truck had screeched to within a foot or so of my nose, now pasted to the side window. We had not touched or been touched by another car, and neither had anyone else. The police, coincidentally in the flow of traffic just behind us, pulled up before anyone could even get out of his car, and they took statements after clearing several of us off to the side. No one could identify any obvious traffic condition or driver error that had caused the incident;

Samantha could only tell us that she'd felt the gas pedal pump of its own accord, and then we'd gone spinning.

In the taxi on the way home, I counted three times in the past seven months that I've been within striking distance of my own death, and yet somehow walked away. That isn't even including my decision to let Ginger drown rather than risk drowning myself. Why all these near misses? Was Adele's God demanding my attention?

"If so," I whispered aloud, "you've got it."

Fran, now over her shock and repossessed of her salty, prophetic self, overheard my little prayer and appraised me from the far side of Sam's stomach. "Remember what I said, Josey?" she asked. "You of all people have no time to waste on rifts with your kids."

I gulped but couldn't bring myself to nod.

April 19, 2001

I should never underestimate my Franny. This morning, after I showed her the three kittens being suckled under my azalea bushes, she asked to look at my photo albums, and for three long hours she patiently endured the most mundane minutia of my life. There were bright, flash-lit pictures of Daddy displaying each new innovation that he'd ever had installed in his little tailor shop; faded snapshots of Vic's mama and younger siblings splattered to their knees and elbows in swamp mud from the fresh new vegetable garden just behind them; and multiple rolls featuring our brown Ford station wagon posed in front of national monuments from the Petrified Forest to Niagara Falls.

Ultimately, we reached Fran's destination: an eight-by-ten wedding picture of Katy and Eliot grinning and rushing down the front steps of the church with their hands clasped tight. When she saw it, Fran let loose a sailor's whistle and tapped her finger over Katy's likeness. "She sure was a looker!"

Suspecting nothing, I agreed.

"And she had the brains and personality to match, didn't she?"

"Before Eliot messed her up," I clarified, unable to resist.

Fran looked pleased.

"Yeah, that may have been the problem," she said.

Having thus laid the bait, Fran coolly made the switch.

"Why do you figure you're so wary about talking to her any-way?"

She had me where she wanted me. I might as well go along.

"Oh, heck Fran. I guess it's because I don't know what she might say. She's trying to put me away. Why would she do that? What could I have done to her to make her hate me? I don't think I want to know."

Fran thought a minute, or pretended to, then said, "Even if you're right, could knowing really be worse than never speaking to her again? What do you gain by not knowing?"

"Peace. Time. I've been working through a lot of things these past few months—things about the way I've lived my life . . . and about what comes next. But I'm not finished, and Katy's just too worried about today."

This disclosure actually stumped Fran for half a second.

"Good for you," she said finally. "But don't you think there's a chance that this problem with Katy may be part of what you're trying to figure out? Are you ignoring the obvious?"

"Maybe so," I conceded, more than ready to discuss something else. "Hey, since we're facing up to things, Fran, I have a question I want to ask you."

"Well? Should I be worried?"

"I don't think so. I doubt the truth could be worse than what I've imagined."

"Hmm. There's a scary teaser. OK, what is it?"

I took a big nervous breath and exhaled when I was grieving someone's death? did you always disappear on me when I was grieving someone's death?"

Fran's attentive smile didn't falter for a good while. Then she shook her head a time or two, and let it fade away. "Well, well. I guess we're all destined to learn a few things this week," she said. "I've always wondered what those crises looked like to you. Jo, each time someone you loved died on you, you cut everyone else off. It's barely metaphorical to say that you'd curl up into an impenetrable little ball, and there was no getting in. I thought it best to be gracious about it and give you the space you'd take anyway. And eventually you always signaled when you could bear to be close again, though this last time—with Vic—it took you several years. Honestly, it's been really hard for me to accept this about you."

I felt blindsided, and something told me that this was only one of several blows that I still had to weather before I got wherever I was going. At some level, what Fran had said was surely true. I knew this because it made so many other things finally fit. I looked at her and waited, trying not to run away.

At length, she smiled at me.

"But somehow you did?" I made myself ask.

"Yep."

"OK. Thanks."

"Look at it this way, Jo. For the first time, you've been willing to ask me the truth. That's progress."

"Only because I don't want to die quite so dumb."

"Well then, talk to Katy."

April 23, 2001

Yesterday Fran and I said good-bye. Her plane was already loading, and she was in the stream of passengers flowing toward the ticket taker, when I grabbed her arm and pulled her back. I wanted to say that I'm not feeling so well, that we may not ever get another visit, that I can't imagine my life without her having been in it. But when she turned to me, I couldn't get any of those things out.

Fran reached over and kissed my cheek. "What was it Betty Davis said about getting old?" she asked.

"Old age ain't for sissies."

"Yeah, that's it. She knew what she was talking about, didn't she, Josey?"

"I love you, Fran."

"I know it, honey. I love you too."

April 24, 2001

At 3:18 A.M., the mama cat living under my hedge let loose a scream like only a frantic mother can. I heard one long, chilling warning, and then the mindless, mutual screeches of a death fight. Used up by her duties, Mama Cat lasted less than five minutes, and then fell to moaning through the rest of the night. When I checked her this morning, only two kittens nestled against her bloodied chest.

A day earlier, I'd seen a tough-looking tomcat prowling the brick wall behind the hedge.

April 25, 2001

I've been asking myself what Adele might say about these last few months of my life. What would she make of all these chances I've had to die, and of my dogged survival despite them? What would she say about Katy's misbehavior and Fran's loud advice?

Looking back, it seems to me that Adele's answer to the big questions was always the same: Jesus. I could never fully appreciate this view of things. What does Jesus have to do with changing your eighty-year-old father's dirty diapers? With a son-in-law whose chief accomplishment has been the hardening of your daughter's heart? With convenience store robbers who kill whatever moves?

"It's why we're here," Adele would say. "God gave us life so'd we get a chance to know him and give him his due. Only there's major problems a-thwartin' us, such as our selfishness and fear, to say nothin' of the everyday evil that's in the world 'cause o' the fall."

"Yes, what about that, Adele? If God is so good and powerful, why does he allow all this 'everyday evil' in his world?"

"Would you rather he'd have plopped our first parents down in Eden and made 'em so's they had no choice whether to love him or not? He could a-done that, and we'd all still live there, born with just the one thought in our heads—'I adore him.'"

"I guess that doesn't really sound much like love," I conceded.

"There you go," she said. "God knows best. He knew he had to let us mess it all up so's the end result would be what he wanted—that some of us, from the depths of the sin and darkness that he let us choose, would see how gorgeous and wonderful he really is. Then we can love him truly."

"I guess that makes some sense, Adele. But how is it that we have any advantage over Adam and Eve when it comes to recognizing all this about God? I mean, if they lived in a paradise surrounded by his goodness, but they didn't choose him, what chance have we got living in a world that you so mildly call 'fallen'?"

"It ain't up to chance," she said. "Before time got started, God aimed to send one who'd reveal him to sinful, cloudy-headed creatures like us. Why do you think he'd risk the fall in the first place?"

"This is where Jesus comes in?" I asked. Here we were again. I wanted to get it this time, and I think Adele sensed that. She plunged further in.

"In the Son, we get to see everything we need to see about God so as to fall in love with him. His comin' at all shows God's tender mercy for us. His sinless life is a display of God's righteousness. The fact that he had to die for us leaves no doubt how fixed God is on his own holiness—that he can't let no sinful creatures near him till they been atoned for and washed clean. But his actually a-doin' it, now, that shows how much God loves us in spite of our disbelievin' ways. And then there's Jesus' resurrection, where we see God's amazin' power and get a peek at what he's got planned for us too."

"If it's all so obvious, Adele, why doesn't everyone see the God in Jesus?"

"'Cause most people keep their eyes shut tight!" she cried. "They don't try to find out if there even is a God, and if so, who he really is and why he'd bother creatin' us. If they'd look, he'd show hisself, but they never look. I mean, when you factor in the thrust of that matter for each and every person ever born, how do you explain such willful, willful blindness?"

Though I knew this question was rhetorical, and Adele's present pause merely a dramatic effect, I had to break her off here. "Now, why is that such a critical matter to each and every person ever born?" I questioned.

"For one thing, missy, 'cause every single one of us lives in eternity after we leave this world with its time all laid flat. Don't you sense that inside you? Don't you know this body ain't all you are?

"Yes, I, . . . I guess I've sensed that sort of thing. At least I've wanted it to be true," I conceded. "But I've always worried it was just wishful thinking."

"Where do you think wishin' comes from?" she asked. "You think you're creative enough to make up eternity out of your own head? Try imaginin' somethin' that you know don't exist. Anything. Take the five senses. Now, try imaginin' a sixth one— a sixth way of beholdin' the physical world."

She waited while I attempted the futile assignment. "Now," she ordered, "describe it to me."

I shook my head.

"Couldn't do it, could you? Have you ever even wished for another sense? Course not. No one can wish for what don't exist. So you can count on eternity, Miss Jo. The question is whether you'll spend it with your blessed maker, who created you for hisself, or whether you'll be a-trapped inside yourself from here on out. Make no mistake—hell lasts forever."

She was finally beginning to scare me a little. "How would one avoid that second fate, Adele?" I asked.

"Like I was a-sayin'"—Jesus. When we look at him and eat up his words and when we reckon on all his actions, we know God hisself. His is words spoke out loud from a human throat, so we can really hear 'em. And his acts was in front of hundreds and thousands of people who really saw him do those things. He touched them. He ate with them. He wept over 'em. It's in him—nowhere else—that we see how deep God loves both his own holiness and his fallen creatures. Believe who he is and what he did for you. Then live for him."

She ended as passionately as she'd begun, always most alive when she talked about the savior she adored. I really hated to disappoint her, but I had to do it.

"Adele, I'm sorry, but I just can't see him yet."

"Well, I'm a-gonna' pray that you will. And soon. The wise man warns:

Remember your Creator
   in the days of your youth,
before the days of trouble come
   and the years approach when you will say,
   "I find no pleasure in them"—...

Remember him—before the silver cord is severed,
   or the golden bowl is broken;
before the pitcher is shattered at the spring,
   or the wheel is broken at the well,
and the dust returns to the ground it came from,
   and the spirit returns to God who gave it.

"Scripture?" I asked, by this time accustomed to using the word for "Bible" that I knew Adele liked best.

SUSAN OLIVER

"Twelfth chapter of Ecclesiastes," she answered, "right after
Proverbs."

I never told her, but I memorized those seven words and
later wrote them down. The drugstore receipt that I scrawled
them on has been in my underwear drawer all these years.
Today I pulled it out, translated my "Eklezeasteaze" into something I found listed on the contents page of our Bible, and
finally hunted down the passage—a belated dispatch from Adele
that frightens me all over again. For the first time, I read it
myself, especially noting a part in the middle that she left out:

when the keepers of the house tremble,
     and the strong men stoop,
when the grinders cease because they are few,
     and those looking through the windows grow dim;
when the doors to the street are closed
     and the sound of grinding fades;
when men rise up at the sound of birds,
     but all their songs grow faint;
when men are afraid of heights
     and of dangers in the streets;
when the almond tree blossoms
     and the grasshopper drags himself along
     and desire no longer is stirred.
Then man goes to his eternal home
     and mourners go about the streets.

My God, it's me there in the window growing dim.

Chapter 19

Katy

Mother started it. That was my first surprise.

I'd assumed—and would probably have bet some serious money—that I'd get to choose the venue, the time, and the circumstances of our big encounter. I would do it in a way that would make Miss Bingham proud, once I'd really figured out how. But when Mother arrived on my curb in a taxi the morning of April 26, I was not ready; I especially wasn't ready for her frail appearance—a great deal frailer than just one month before. My guilty heart raced.

"Mother, what are you doing here?" I asked the woman propping herself up on an ugly metal cane at my doorstep. I hadn't seen that apparatus since late December, when Mother had finally gained back enough strength after her surgery to steady herself on her own two feet. I wanted to ask what the heck she'd brought it for, but somehow I held back.

"Can I come in?" she asked, breathy and pale.

I moved aside and instinctively grabbed her free arm as she stepped over the threshold and scooted into my entryway. "Are you all right?" I asked, glowering at the cane once more.

"I'm just especially tired today," she said. "I don't usually carry this thing, but I've got a wildlife situation in my backyard that's been keeping me up at night."

Without bothering to find out what she meant by that, I made some awkward joke about the last "wildlife situation" she'd had in her backyard—a cruel, crude reference to Ginger's death. Mother picked right up on it.

"I don't want to fight with you, Katy," she said. "Not about Ginger. Can I sit down?"

"Certainly. Here." I cleared a spot on the sofa and she plopped down, barely denting the cushion.

"What did you come to fight about?" I asked, taking the other end of the couch. I still wasn't in control here, and humor seemed to offer a hope of seizing it.

Mother pulled the cane across her spare little lap and clutched it with trembling hands. "I came to tell you something," she announced, slow and deliberate. "I didn't want to say it this way, Katy, but your attitude leaves me little choice. I'm going to die."

I flew to her side. "Oh my God," I said, "they've found more cancer?"

"No, no. That's not it. Calm down, dear. I don't mean that I'm dying in the next five minutes, or even the next six months—necessarily. I mean that sooner or later I'm going to die. And there won't be anything you can do about it. Do you understand?"

I stood abruptly, afraid I might strangle her if I stayed so close. "That is absolutely ridiculous, Mother. You scared me half to death! Why would you come over here and say such a thing to me?"

"Because it's true and I don't think you're accepting it; it's the only reason I can imagine that you're being so mean to me." By now she was sniffling, and that made me madder still.

"Stop it. You're wrong. I haven't been mean to you. I'm the only one who's tried to help you. And, if you recall, the last time we spoke you implied that my primary concern is getting my hands on your money. Now, who's been mean to whom?"

"I'm sorry. That wasn't kind and I don't really think that. But I had to fend you off. It's the first thing I could think of to accomplish it." Then she swallowed, tightened her grip on the cane, and hurried on while her nerve was up. "You weren't listening to me. As is so often the case, you unilaterally decided how things needed to be, and then you set about railroading me."

I knew that had cost her a lot, and despite myself I admired it.

The second surprise.

"Well, Mother, you weren't thinking very well for yourself. Why wouldn't you want to take obvious steps to protect and prolong your own life? It's as if you wanted to die. Is that it? Do you want to die?"

"Not yet. That's exactly why I don't want to go off to some nursing home. People die there; they don't come back. And I'm not quite ready to die."

Now I could touch her. I sat down at her side and pried a hand off the cane. "The Abbey isn't like that," I assured her. "It's not a nursing home. The people there aren't dying. I just want you to be safe."

"I know, Katy. But you don't get to decide that. And when it is time for me to die, you won't get to decide that either."

"I still think you're making a terrible mistake living alone," I persisted. "Look at yourself. You're just a wisp of a person. Whatever wildlife you've got in your backyard could probably swallow you whole."

Mother extracted her hand from mine and fumbled around with the cane's rubber tip. "That's the other thing I want to talk to you about," she said, her eyes fixed on the tip as she rotated it back to its starting position. "Why do you treat me like I'm incompetent? It isn't new; you've been at it for years, maybe your whole adult life. And I want to know why."

This was the biggest surprise of all. My mother was facing me down, demanding information that it would pain her to have. She was asking me to say the very things I most needed to. Even so, it would crush her. "Are you sure?" I asked. "Do you really want to know?" She couldn't have missed the caution in my voice.

I thought that she might bolt for her taxi, still idling out front, but presently she mumbled something about sitting in a window, and then, squaring her shoulders, she said, "I'm sure."

Dignity, a soft, southern voice drawled in my mind. *You must leave her with dignity.*

"Well, um, I guess it's because you've always been so prone to avoid hard things, Mother, to hide from them. What you're doing right now, though . . . asking me this . . . it's brave. But it's also quite unusual." I waited to see how she'd taken that much.

Mother nodded thoughtfully for a long time. "OK," she said, "so you don't trust me with myself, and that has probably made you lack respect for me. Is that why you're so often hostile?"

I could hardly believe who I was talking to. She actually wanted the truth. Did this mean that she had it in her to understand, to be sorry? And if she did—here was the tricky part—why hadn't she understood fifty years ago, when it might have done me some good? My thin, new commitment to Mother's dignity died away as a white-hot fury arose to take its place.

"Oh, sure, Mother. I just feel sorry for you and that's why I want to browbeat you so much of the time. Do you really suppose that it's only yourself I don't trust you with, that your fear and self-preservation never damaged the rest of us?"

She flinched visibly, but made no other move. "Go on," she said.

"It wasn't just the hard things you hid from, Mother. It was also the things that should have been happy, comforting. 'Aloof,' my friends used to call you. 'Why doesn't your mother like me? She seems sort of aloof.' I was too hurt to tell them that you were ten times friendlier to them than you often were to me. Or to Daddy. I was grown before I figured out that's why he needed me too much. You'll probably say you don't know what I'm talking about, and the reason for that is because you were off protecting yourself. Sometimes . . . sometimes I thought you hated me."

Finally I'd drawn blood. She wept, but after several minutes she recovered enough to respond. "Katy, the truth is I was dazzled by you. You were always so vibrant and confident—like your father was most of the time. I didn't want to hold you back, either one of you. My own mother bore down so hard on me, and I felt so unloved by it, that I equated love with a light touch. I just wanted to let you be your own person."

"But it came across as lack of interest, Mother."

"And . . . you think your father felt the same?"

"I'm pretty sure of it," I said.

Then, showing more mettle than I'd have ever thought her capable, Mother twisted her fists around the cane a few times and pushed on through. "How? How do you know that?"

Of course, she didn't know what she was asking. I was so sure that she'd never survive this truth, that I couldn't make myself say it. "You don't want the answer to that question," I promised. And that should have been enough.

"Katy, it seems I no longer have the luxury of hiding from hard things, as you say. I want you to tell me."

Could I reward her nascent courage with a lie?

"Because, Mother, I've met his mistress."

CHAPTER 20

Jo

April 26, 2001

I despair of my simpering, self-serving memory, so prone to reinvent what I'm too weak to face up to. Is the truth about anything as I believe it to be? Did my mother somehow love me, and I missed it or forgot? Was Daddy not really a saint? Was Vic an easy man on whom I've projected the ragged edges of my own personality? If I can't remember rightly, what good is this endeavor? Perhaps I've grown too dim already.

God, help me.

My father spent his professional life outfitting other men in fine clothes; Vic back-slapped them down fairways, beguiling them with his roguish humor and seducing them to trust him with their money. Daddy's sanctuary was a greenhouse, where he retreated to cast his magic over soil and air and to imbue his blooms with ever deeper hues. Vic's retreat was a clubhouse, where the deepest hue was the rust of the Bloody Marys and "magic" was a euphemism for cheating at cards. Daddy slept in his own room out of deference to my mother's frigidity, but Vic never quit our bed, even when he took up another.

Less than a year after Vic and I married, Daddy invited me to lunch and asked me how I was feeling about things.

"About what things, Daddy?"

"Well, about marriage, . . . about Victor."

"I guess I'm getting used to it," I hedged.

"I'm glad," he said, but still something seemed to trouble him. "Umm . . . Victor's a different sort of person, isn't he?"

"Different from what?"

"Oh, from me, from you. He's . . . he's . . ."

"Fearless? Assertive? Full of life?" I offered.

"Yes, something along those lines. How is that to live with?"

"I suppose Vic sort of scares me sometimes."

"Has he hurt or threatened you, child?"

"No, nothing like that, Daddy. Maybe 'intimidate' is the right word for it. Is it horrible to say that I'm intimidated by my husband?"

"Josephine," he said, "You must never, ever think you're not good enough for him. He robbed the jewelry store when he got you. He knows it, and now I'm telling you. Don't be fooled by his swagger. If you do, things will not go well."

"All right, Daddy," I said. "I won't forget."

But I very often did.

<hr>

April 27, 2001

Now the truth about my children, else I grow dimmer still.

Vic ruled the boardroom, our bedroom, and my household budget, but only I could bear another life within my body. From my first taste of it, I welcomed this power as some great cosmic equalizer between us. And when they laid baby Clay in my arms, I suppose I wasn't ready to give the power up. Perhaps, in the unexplored side streets of my subconscious, I contrived to remain his whole world. The overtures I thought I made to let Vic in were so well timed to deter him that it's hard to assign him all of the blame.

But he double-crossed me with Katy. He found a way to dictate everything—her moment of conception, her gender, even the color of her hair. He concerned himself with her care and soon became her best friend. But his crowning achievement—infusing her with his own personality—surfaced slowly as the years passed by. Equally fearless and full of life, Katy soon intimidated me just as Vic had. How could I be her role model when she was beyond me in so many ways? I felt I had little to draw on in this regard. My most constructive models of womanhood had been the legendary Wilhelm Frauen whose stories I'd heard on walks with my father and the idyllic English heroines of Jane Austen and the Brontë sisters. What could they tell me about raising a daughter in twentieth-century Houston? I'd simply had no living go-bys.

Here, too, Adele seemed a godsend. While I could not stand before Katy and expect her to emulate me, I could stand aside and let her observe a woman whom I'd like to have been. In my own mind, I spun this as the ultimate maternal sacrifice. How better could I love a daughter who deserved more than I could personally deliver? I never considered any negative consequences, except to myself. For Katy, all I saw was gain. It didn't occur to me until this very minute that I might have been put there to save her from Vic's extremes, to teach her that we sometimes get more when we demand less.

Was I uninterested? Did I write her off as Vic's? Did I ruin our Katy—our little lantern?

April 28, 2001

I now write from bed because I'm too intent on this to dally around changing locations. Across the room, Vic's pine armoire looks deceivingly current with one door slightly ajar. Above my own dresser, pastel-shaded line drawings of Clay and Katy smile to me. I remember the afternoon in New Orleans' Jackson Square when Vic commissioned those portraits.

He was high on hurricanes, and the kids and I were stuffed full of beignets. I'd spent the past several minutes cleaning the two of them off with powdered napkins and spit so that they could be properly memorialized on canvas.

"That's enough of that, dawlin'," Vic boomed loudly enough to make a good many wives in our vicinity stop what they were doing. "This fella knows enough to leave the powder off 'em. Don'tcha, Bud?"

The "fella" Vic thus addressed was probably ten years Vic's elder, but since his bedroll and other worldly possessions were propped against the fence behind his easel, Vic clearly felt free to condescend.

"All right," I said, sparing the poor artist a response. "Vic, honey, why don't you go get me a hurricane while Katy and I watch this gentleman draw Clay."

"That I can do," he sang out, strolling away.

Twenty minutes later, Vic returned with a souvenir Pat O'Brien's to-go glass filled with the red, candy-flavored liquor. We sat on an iron bench and took turns slurping it while six-year-old Katy danced around trying to make her brother laugh. She was so tickled by the time she herself sat to pose that we had to go back to the hotel with just the one portrait. Vic tipped "Bud" handsomely and had him draw her fresh the next morning.

As age mellowed Vic, I began to cozy up to him. I even fell in love with him from time to time.

302

April 29, 2001

By 1966, this fond seed had matured into a deep trust and affection. But the events of that year came on like a relentless draught, choking the trust from me month by month until the ground around me cracked open and my roots shriveled up. I've never told anyone—or admitted to myself—what drained my last tiny reservoir of hope.

On a morning not long after Adele died, I went one more time to the nursing home where we'd left Irene. She was snoring when I arrived, and I sat in the corner of her private room and tortured myself with her wretched wheezing and gasping until she sputtered awake an hour or two later. Presently, she noticed me.

"Who is it?" she demanded, grabbing at the bed railing to try and pull herself upright. Failing that, she flopped back down and spat defensively in my general direction. "Don't come near me with any of your needles or I'll kick you," she clucked. "Waste your drugs on someone who cares!"

Had this been a television show, I might have been amused at this ancient, sickly old woman hurling such a big threat. But Irene had never amused me, and she didn't now.

"It's me," I said, standing. "Josephine."

She settled back slightly but kept a tight grip on the railing with one of her old paws, jigsawed with age spots. "What do you want?"

"I came to see you."

I should probably have tried to nail down the problem with her medications, as she was clearly upset about that. But I stood by silently. And she did no more than smack her gums a few times as if to say, "harrumph." I sat back down.

Several minutes later, Irene remembered I was there and asked me, "Why did you come?"

"Adele told me to. She said it would help." Though I was loath to admit such a thing, Irene wouldn't have believed any nicer excuse.

Irene let go of the railing and laid her hand across her heart as if she were about to say a pledge. "Adele, Adele, Adele," she mimicked. "Don't you ever tire of talking 'bout that darkie?"

I could have slapped her and no one would have noticed. If they had noticed, they wouldn't have minded. Instead, I broke down sobbing. "Don't . . . you . . . ever say her name again," I stammered through the tears. "She cared what happened to you, and . . . and now . . . she's dead!"

That must have struck Irene with the force of a slap, for she retaliated superbly. Her next words have haunted me ever since: "You probably put her in her grave with all your needing. Adele told me how you burdened her, wanting her to be this to you, be that, do this, do that. When in the world did you think she'd tend to her own litter?"

I flew to the bedside and bent over Irene savagely. "I told you not to say her name," I snarled, shaking a fist that she couldn't see.

Those were the last words I ever spoke to my mother. As I stumbled down the hall moments later, she bawled after me like a mad woman, "Adele, Adele, Adele," with all the volume her depraved old lungs could muster. And I went home to scratch and claw inside myself for the truth.

April 30, 2001

Irene had cursed me, and it was up to me to accept or reject it. At first I tormented myself with a dozen peripheral obsessions that hurt but didn't kill me: whether Adele had visited Irene on the sly to make up for my neglect; whether her children had really suffered because of our demands upon her; whether we'd paid her enough for how well she'd maintained us. I labored to evade the one aspect of Irene's curse that promised to undo me: whether Adele had really thought me a burden.

After Irene died and we'd hastily buried her, I celebrated alone one night while Vic met with clients over dinner. I really meant it to be shaming—a one-time atonement for what I'd surely done to my friend, whether she'd noticed or not. I expected drunkenness to sink me to the bottom of the murky pit Irene had left to me, and then I'd be done with it. I would go that far to appease Adele's God.

But the unexpected happened. The drunker I got, the higher and purer my pain became. Just before I blacked out, it achieved a sterling quality that made me feel altogether honorable and excellent. I'd been tragically misunderstood, cruelly handicapped from birth by a parent who'd overwhelmed me with curses. I was a martyr really. Even Adele hadn't understood. I must never again believe that anyone could.

All of Vic's efforts to pull me out of the gunk only entrenched me further. To my soggy brain, they were simply part of another grand seduction—a pretty rug that he was taunting me onto while someone else crept up behind me to jerk. I couldn't allow this to happen again. So I fended him off, retreated repeatedly to my wine and highballs, and listened for the liquid chatter I found so soothing: "Here he is, trying to make sport of you again. Don't believe him. Don't believe him. He's no trustworthier than she was. You are cursed. Cursed! Accept it and be free of the deceptions. Yours is a high calling—to live such a difficult truth with integrity, to be honest and authentic all alone. But here's your consolation: if you resist the lies, you won't get hurt again. It's what God has given you. Nothing more."

Irene had won; I hadn't disbelieved her. I'd forgotten the father who had always come home to me. I'd lost faith in the past twenty years of my marriage. And I'd let the bitter, dying rantings of a veteran hater muddle what I knew to be true: that Adele had loved me. It seemed that all my lanterns were going out.

May 1, 2001

Late in 1967, Vic began to stay away from home in the evenings. I never challenged or questioned him about this. And he never offered me any excuse. But he did grow thinner and sort of shadowy. Katy took to asking me if I didn't think he looked "gaunt."

"I don't know what you're talking about, Katy," I'd say. "I suppose it's just aging. Your father's closing in on sixty, you know."

"Aren't men supposed to be expanding at that point? Why is Daddy shrinking?"

"Have you asked him?"

"Yes. He said it must be stress. What has he got to feel so much more stressed about than usual?"

This felt like an accusation. "I don't know. Did you ask him?"

"Yes. He said not to worry about it, that he'll be fine."

"Well, then, don't worry about it," I parried vaguely. "I'm quite sure your father can handle whatever it is."

We all made concessions that we never thought we would.

May 2, 2001

And so I shared Vic for the rest of his life. He never treated me any differently than he always had, apart from this one thing. And I finally stopped wondering whether he loved me or not. If he'd loved me before, I decided, he loved me still. If he'd been pretending before, he was pretending still. I managed to trust him again, not because he loved me; I managed to trust him again because I knew that he loved her, yet remained at my side.

And it was my arms in which he died.

One morning Vic was here—in my bed, at my table—and by that afternoon he was dead of massive heart failure. Looking back, the only warning I had was the fact that he'd dropped his new golf glove on the driveway while loading his clubs. When I left to run errands a short time later, I saw the yellow dollop in my rearview mirror and stopped to pick it up. Hmm. He won't want to play without this, I thought. Wonder if something's wrong?

That was my whole heads up. Four hours later, I was called to the hospital by a colleague of Vic's at the insurance company. Vic usually stopped in there a few hours each week to field questions and advise his successors on the fine points of selling.

It was there, in the plush corner office he'd never relinquished, that his heart had clinched up and refused to cooperate one minute longer. They found a cheap cigar still burning in an ashtray on his desk, and several more in a brown paper sack at the back of a desk drawer. So much for the cardiologist's unequivocal, long-standing order for Vic not to get within twenty feet of tobacco ever again.

When I arrived at the hospital, I was ushered into a trauma room where they'd cut Vic's royal blue golf shirt up the middle and were already shocking his chest with a high-voltage defibrillator. I saw his body lurch, and then the heart monitor attached to him began to "blip" anemically and far apart. A doctor told me that an emergency bypass would give Vic about a 30 percent chance of survival. They handed me a form to sign; then they wheeled him off to surgery.

I fell in beside the gurney and reached for Vic's rough, tanned hand. "Vic," I called to him. "Vic, it's Jo. Honey, can you hear me?"

His eyelids fluttered and I felt a squeeze on my hand. Then his blipping grew erratic and finally stretched out into a continuous, flat tone signaling that his heart had faltered again. The doctor escorting us shocked Vic once, twice, then what seemed like scores of times, at ever-higher voltages. While he lurched, I could think of Vic as alive. But when they quit several paralyzing minutes later, Vic's body lay still and I knew that he had gone.

It was just as I'd have expected him to go about dying— abrupt, defiant, and ostentatious. He'd have been altogether uninterested in some listless, phlegmatic decay. Still, the suddenness of his passing was hard for me to make sense of. Why today, and not a year from now or a year ago? Would it have happened if I'd fed him Special K for breakfast that day instead of buttered toast? If he'd gotten better sleep the night before? What if he'd carried a calendar to remind him he was only sixty-seven?

May 3 2001

The business world doesn't grieve long, and Vic's stalled business dealings would not be put off indefinitely while I figured out why it was he'd had to die. As Vic's sole heir, I was hunted down and assailed on all manner of things I knew nothing about—assets, payrolls, policies, partnerships, memberships, liabilities, dissolutions, and subscriptions. And for a few months I became a grateful though doltish student in all these "ships" and "tions" because this kept me from having to understand harder things.

Daily, it seemed, an accountant, attorney, or other associate of Vic's would call and ask me to instruct them on this $50,000 asset or that $75,000 "opportunity" that Vic had been considering. Neophyte that I was, rearranging such large sums at first felt like playing with Monopoly money. But I quickly came to see it differently. In my anxious, grief-stunted mind, each such decision came to represent a year or two of my remaining life, which I'd hoped would be long and comfortable but now feared might be a constant worry. Without Vic there to orchestrate my old age, the only one who could prevent my destitution was me. So I hid my jewelry away in a safety deposit box where neither the burglars nor I could get to it, toted pockets full of "dollar-off" coupons to the grocery each week, and fired Vic's lifelong personal attorney because I feared he would bankrupt me with his nonstop, hundred-dollar phone calls. The truth was that Vic had left me with nearly a million dollars and a lovely home that was fully paid for. But I couldn't tell if that was enough.

It was about eight months into this bewilderment that I first met Leonard Van Zandt—a man with a big, aristocratic name and a small, common outlook on life. But he was a warm body. He was a warm-bodied widower in fact. And so I let myself be blinded by the name, by the tall, athletic build, and by his eagerness to put me up on a pedestal.

Aching with loneliness after months of widowhood, I finally accepted one of the pity invitations that had recently started trickling in to me. This one was to a huge country club soiree thrown by one of Vic's best clients. I was apprehensive about going alone, and so I was happy to be adopted in the lobby by Hank and Dora Youngblood, who gushed on and on about how much they'd hoped I'd come, and, oh, by the way, wouldn't I like to meet a friend of theirs? Something about the way they persisted along these lines clued me in to their intentions despite the fact that, at 64, I'd never before been the target of such an ambush. Enticed, I consented.

Out of the corner of my eye I caught Hank nod ever so slightly toward one of the hors d'oeuvre tables, and the next instant a tall, handsome stranger was standing in front of me, reaching for my hand and telling me how good it was to finally meet me. I was taken off guard by the guileless way he revealed the fact that he'd been in on this whole arrangement. And then he went so far as to apologize for it.

"Mrs. Greene, I hope you'll forgive us for surprising you this way. I'm afraid I must take full responsibility for it. Ever since Hank and Dora mentioned to me a few weeks ago that they had a charming, attractive female friend who was going through the same thing that I have for the past few years, I've been pestering them to introduce us. I hope you don't mind too much. I thought perhaps I could be of service to you." And with that he gave me the most gallant little bow. I saw that he was balding in a sexy, David Niven sort of way that I found most appealing.

"I don't mind in the least, though I'm not sure what you mean by being of service to me. My husband's death is not something I like to dwell on." I wanted to see how this Leonard Van Zandt would respond to that.

"Yes, of course. I understand entirely. But you might appreciate an escort now and then, on evenings such as this for example. By the way, could I get you a drink?"

Now he was talking. "Thank you very much, Mr. Van Zandt. I'll have whatever you get for yourself," I answered, floating another little test.

"Please call me Leonard, or better yet, Lenny. Would a gin and tonic do?"

Hmmm. Not exactly what I was hoping for. "Yes, of course," I said, whereupon he rushed off with Hank to get drinks for the four of us.

"Well, Jo, what do you think?" Dora asked as soon as the crowd closed behind them. She crooned her question in a breathy, junior high way that drew me further into the intrigue. "Doesn't he have nice manners? And isn't he attractive? You know, he's being chased after right now by about three or four old widows. He told us they're driving him crazy. We told him that you are not like that, that you would have to be pursued."

Presumptuous as it was for the three of them to be discussing me in this way at all, I rather liked the perception that Dora apparently had of me. She must think I'm confident, sophisticated, I thought. "You're darn right I want to be pursued," I said. And when Lenny sidled up next to me a few minutes later and put a drink into my hand that tasted of scotch instead of gin, I saw that he was just the one who I wanted to do the pursuing. This man was attuned to me.

"How long were you married, Mr. Van Zandt?" I asked.

He launched then into a touching narration of the forty-three years he'd spent with Vera, his childhood sweetheart. He did not skimp in his accounts of the tough war years during which he was stationed overseas, or of Vera's inexplicable, life-long barrenness that had quite literally wounded her heart, or even of how accursed he'd been in his hardware business, ever trying to expand it just when the economy was about to plummet. How refreshing to find a man who would talk and even tell vulnerable things.

I spent the next five months letting Lenny pursue me. Throughout that time, he feigned a consuming interest in every-thing I enjoyed—art, theater, travel, reading, socializing. He was a talker who didn't make me talk, and for that I was grateful at a time when I thought I had little besides him that was pleasant to talk about. I found him attentive, interested in things. I found him chivalrous and protective. Most of all, I found him terribly alluring; that was the really big surprise.

One evening, overcome with passion from our petting, Lenny somberly declared his willingness to make whatever moral sacrifices were necessary in order to be with me. Flattered though I was, I could not bring myself to do anything I'd spent forty years warning children and grandchildren not to do, and I told him so.

"Then we have no choice but to resolve our predicament in the traditional manner," he announced, and demanded that I marry him. I agreed, mostly, I think, because I didn't want him to go away.

So I told myself that Lenny was my recompense for the difficulties of my first marriage. But in truth, I felt myself a fragment without Vic—an orphaned planet, a woman drinking alone. Too diminished by the curse to stand on my own, I wanted desperately out of widowhood.

Those who loved me best were scandalized. Fran promised not to hang around to witness the debacle, and she made good on that promise when I disregarded her threat. Katy and Clay begged me to reconsider, at least to get to know Lenny better before I stampeded with him to the altar. But I'd already written myself a fairy-tale ending, and I would not jeopardize it with an overabundance of information or analysis.

One year and sixty-eight days after Vic died, I became Mrs. Leonard Van Zandt. Thus began the longest nineteen years of my life.

May 4, 2001

For the past ten days I've been tethered to my bed—roosting here from the moment I awake like Edith Wharton at her satire—compelled to remember though my memories undo me. And every evening, together with the dimmet cries of the cicada nymphs, the mama cat living under my hedge strikes up a soulful feline dirge with which she comforts herself until daybreak. Never before have I heard such persistent misery.

Today I went out back and checked on her. The two remaining kittens are as big as po' boys now, but thin and still entirely dependent on their mother's milk. She lay apart from them, flat along her stomach such that they could not have reached her nipples had they tried.

I left them all that I could think of to leave—milk, water, more of Ginger's dog food. But I fear that the mama cat will not soon recover from her broken heart.

Chapter 21

Katy

When had I become someone who would crush the person I love most in the world with the harshest truths I know? Contrary to my grand plan, Jenny wouldn't have been at all proud of how I'd handled Mother's daring confrontation; but then, I would never be able to tell Jenny since I'd betrayed her in the very process of destroying my mother. I could barely live with myself. Even Eliot noticed that something was wrong.

"Katy, you're starting to act more and more like me every day," he said one afternoon while I brooded over the obituaries more intensely than usual. Recently Eliot had been showing a latent talent for making fun of himself, but I didn't much trust it.

"What do you mean?" I queried.

"I mean you've been downright grim lately, dragging around like some sort of dejected little kid. What's going on with you?"

"Just trying to cheer you up, dear," I deflected him cruelly.

"That's not fair," he blasted back.

"I know, you're right. I'm sorry. I'm just acting the way I feel about myself—mean and hateful. You know?"

"I know all about acting the way I feel about myself," he conceded.

"Yes, I guess you do."

"So . . ." he entreated me to continue on.

"So, . . . well, . . . I'd like to talk to you about it, but . . . Oh, gosh, Eliot, please don't take offense, but I'm afraid to tell you because of how you might respond, . . . that you'll . . . make me pay. I really need you to be a grown-up man for me here."

"You need to talk to me about it?" he asked, somehow picking up the one positive thread in what I'd said.

"Yes, I guess I do."

"Talk," he commanded. Had the whole world turned upside down?

"Really?" When he nodded, I managed to advance a little further. "Several days ago Mother took a cab over here to tell me she's going to die. Not that she's gotten any such prognosis from a doctor, but she just wanted me to know that she's going to die eventually and I won't be able to stop her. Well, it made me so mad that I said some very hurtful things that I shouldn't have said."

"Why do you suppose she thought it necessary to come over here and tell you that?" Eliot asked. This was not really the part I wanted to talk about, but I'd invited him into this tangle and I could hardly shut down on him now.

"I guess she thinks I'm having trouble dealing with the fact that she's going to die one day," I tossed off, ready to go on.

"Yeah, I think so too," he said softly.

I sighed in disgust and took a long, loud time folding the newspaper while I considered my response. I did not want to get anchored on this point, but if I was going to ask Eliot to be a grown-up for me, I guess I'd have to be one too. "Why would you say that?" I asked.

"Well, you've seemed almost frantic about her ever since you found out she had lung cancer last fall. I know that you were even considering committing her."

"And do you know why?"

"I'm sure it was because at the time you thought that it would be best for her. I also think you were faced head-on with the precari-

316

ousness of her existence, and you were determined to take some action to ensure that she won't up and . . . die."

"Eliot, she's acting so cavalier about it, . . . like . . . like . . ."

"Like her life is hers?"

"Like it's only hers." I felt close to losing control.

"Katy, come on. You have to give her that much. Surely her life is hers. I mean, it's not like she's a young parent who's threatening suicide or something," he said, meeting my sharp glance with a confessional little bow. "I just think that after eighty-four years, Josephine's life must belong only to her now."

"She just can't wait to . . ." Here I got stuck on a sob but managed to fend it back. " . . . to leave me again, this time forever!"

Then the dam broke, and Eliot actually came over and hugged on me while I bawled. As I quaked in his arms, I fleetingly wondered if he'd gone off and gotten some marriage counseling on the sly.

When I'd calmed down some, Eliot stood back and looked at me rather tenderly. "You know, Katy," he said, "her leaving this time isn't about you."

"Right," I said. "It never was."

CHAPTER 22

JO

May 4, 2001

Now I knew what I had to do.

This morning I actually got out of the bed and didn't crawl back in a minute later to jot down some new recollection. Instead, I surveyed myself with a critical eye in the bathroom mirror. Neglect had left me a ruin. First off, I hadn't had my hair set in quite some time, and after being so consistently mashed forward against my writing pillow for the past two weeks, it rather resembled a stiff, upright Elizabethan collar. Worse, my gray roots were showing. This was a lapse in grooming that I hadn't allowed since the terrible months just after Vic's death back in 1979. My eyes looked sunken and purplish, my skin tone was decidedly bilious, and my ankles were once again puffing up like grapefruit. A sane woman would have rushed herself to the emergency room. I called my beautician, Coco, and talked her into an emergency dye, set, and facial. She seemed relieved to hear from me and had me spruced up by one o'clock.

Thereafter, I pointed my Mercedes—fresh from a thorough checkup that had disclosed no cause for its recent convulsion—toward the Abbey. I trembled all the way there, certain I wasn't ready to take this big a step. But my car drove on, meandering past the backside of the facility (which I mistook for an office building), then rounding the block and approaching the front via a grand circular drive.

After a time, my Mercedes spit me out, and I had no choice but to go inside.

The lobby was welcoming, though a tad overdone, and the people I saw milling about it were far less encumbered than I'd convinced myself—despite all Katy's assurances to the contrary—that they would be. I spied no wheelchairs, no white-uniformed nurses or attendants, and only one or two people dependent even on canes. Frankly, I wondered if I myself could satisfy the Abbey's self-sufficiency criteria.

Ready now to complete my mission, I approached the concierge—a businesslike young woman whose engraved name-plate read "Sylvie Placentia." She wore a tailored blue uniform like the ones stewardesses used to wear, and asked pleasantly how she could help me.

"I need a room number," I answered, "for Genevieve Bingham."

"Certainly, ma'am," Sylvie said. "Is she expecting you?"

"Not at this very moment, no. But we're old . . . old . . . . Let's just say we have mutual acquaintances very dear to us both."

"Well, Mrs.—"

"Van Zandt."

"Mrs. Van Zandt, I'd be happy to ring Miss Bingham for you." Not much got past Sylvie, I could tell.

"I was hoping to surprise her, dear. Surely you're not worried that I'm a thief or a solicitor or something?" I asked, discreetly adjusting the sleeve of my jacket to make sure Sylvie had a satisfactory view of my ruby-studded bracelet.

"Oh, no, Mrs. Van Zandt. It's just that I'm not allowed to give out apartment numbers. We sign a privacy policy with all our residents stating that they alone have that prerogative. Again, though, I could ring her for you."

What else could I do?

"All right, then. Please tell her that Josephine Greene Van Zandt is here to see her," I ordered, putting special emphasis on the "Greene."

I stood by as Sylvie dialed the numbers too fast for me to tell what they were. After a moment, she said, "Hi, Jenny. Listen, I have someone in the lobby who says she'd like to come down and see you. Her name is Josephine Greene Van Zandt."

A year passed for me during the pause that followed. Sylvie, waiting with me, was beginning to frown over the apparent silence on the other end of the line when Genevieve Bingham finally gave some sort of reply.

Sylvie hung up. "She said she's been expecting you, Mrs. Van Zandt. It's apartment 118."

I suppose I'd rather hoped that Genevieve Bingham would be frumpy and bland, but that wouldn't have been much in keeping with this woman's appeal to both my husband and my daughter. The woman who answered her door took me completely aback.

At 1:45 in the afternoon—presumably expecting no real visitors—silver-haired Genevieve Bingham was all dolled up in a smart black business suit, a silk, jewel-necked blouse the exact shade of her striking green eyes, and an exquisite pair of jade and diamond earrings. My surprise must have been apparent on my face.

"I just got home from an appointment with my attorney," she explained. "I try to look like an old lady to be reckoned with when I go see him."

I could only nod at that and proceed with my prepared spiel. "Miss Bingham, I'm Josephine Greene. It's good of you to receive me without any prior notice. I know this must be a shock to you, but I have a few things I feel that we need to discuss."

"Certainly. Come right in," she said, standing aside and pulling me in with her reassuring smile. "You may call me Jenny if you wish, or Genevieve, either one. How would you like me to address you? I feel that I know you too well to call you Mrs.., but I'll do that if you'd feel more comfortable."

Hmm. In all my rehearsals of the present scene, this question had not once been asked. Faced with it now, "Mrs. Van Zandt" seemed oddly out of context. I could force her to repeat "Mrs. Greene" over and over, but that seemed a bit vindictive in light of her graciousness thus far. Still, I would not give her "Jo."

"You may call me Josephine," I declared at length.

"Thank you. Now, Josephine, why don't you take a seat and I'll run and get us some tea. I'll be right back." Off she flitted to the kitchen, giving us both a chance to weigh impressions and collect our thoughts.

Genevieve Bingham's furnishings would have given away her heritage even if her accent had not. Perhaps this explained Vic's dewy appreciation for his home state late in his life. Up to then, the only spot on the Louisiana map that he'd had any use for was the lively crescent in the far southeast corner.

Too soon, Genevieve came back toting a tray with two tea glasses, sans any condiments. "You take yours straight up?" she asked, more an assessment than a question.

"Straight up," I confirmed. Then, glass in hand, I noted, "You have some very impressive books. Would you call it a collection?"

"At one time, it was an inventory. I was a rare book dealer." With that, another puzzle piece slotted into place: while I'd been off nursing my hurts with highballs, Vic was developing hobbies I knew nothing about.

"Yes, of course," I responded stiffly. I could get mired here if I wasn't careful. So, with tremendous effort, I turned that corner and came at Genevieve from a different direction. "You told Sylvie at the front desk that you'd been expecting me. Were you serious about that?"

"Completely," she said. "I've actually been expecting you for years."

"And what made you think that I knew about you?"

"You're a woman."

"But how would I have found you?"

"I had no idea. I've tried to prepare myself, but I'm not sure I succeeded."

"Katy told me who you were a couple of weeks ago."

"I'm not at all surprised. I was sorry that she had to find out, but she put it together on her own. Perhaps I was too transparent with her, I don't know."

"I'm beginning to wonder if there's any such thing as too much transparency," I confessed, caught up in her candor and my recent discoveries. "As a person whose life has been decidedly opaque, I'm about to conclude that a lack of transparency only multiplies pain."

"Yes, I can vouch for that from my own experience." She said this with a look of such sorrow and remorse that it felt like a plea for forgiveness. Emboldened by our frankness thus far, I dared to test this.

"Are you apologizing to me?"

"Most definitely, I am. Josephine, I wasn't going to hunt you down and force you to acknowledge something this horrible just to appease my own conscience. But I have longed, and prayed, for you to come to me so that I could tell you how very, very sorry I am for my appalling self-indulgence, for so belittling you and Vic and even myself. I can't tell you how much I wish I could take it back."

I sat down on her wicker couch with a thud and tried to process all she'd just said. One question seared my brain. "Why now?" I demanded. "Why not during all those years that you took up with him? Why didn't you feel sorry then?"

"The truth is that I was only sorry for it at the very first. I'd waited forty-five years to meet someone like Vic, and though I tried to resist him because he was married, I just didn't try hard enough. After I learned more about you, I was better able to justify what I was doing. I concluded that you'd had your turn with Vic and had all but discarded him. But he never saw it that way, and it grieved me that he never thought to leave you."

I couldn't respond. I could not even allow an expression to arise on my face that she might see. I'd never felt so exposed, so shredded. All my pitiful rememberings were nothing in the presence of one who really knew the damage I'd done, who knew just how tiny a person I'd let myself become. I thought I might scream or run down and beg Sylvie for her blue uniform to cover my nakedness with something thick and institutional. I was teetering there on the brink of such internal perversions when Jenny braved another observation.

"The thing was, Vic loved you."

The thing was, he loved me.

"How? How could that be?" I demanded. Despite the sound of it, I questioned neither her veracity nor her perception. I really wanted to understand.

"I don't know, Josephine. I can only suppose that it's part of what you were granted. God allows us pain and heartache, but he also gives us good gifts. One of your gifts was the love of a good man."

"And you think God gave you the very same gift?" I flared.

"No. That I tried to steal."

"And how, then, do you dare to bare your soul to me on this issue, and moreover, to befriend my daughter?" Finally I'd arrived at the purpose for my visit.

Genevieve Bingham winced only slightly. Then she closed her eyes for a moment the way I often saw Adele do when she was figuring a response to some particularly thorny question. When she opened them, her bright green eyes were awash in tears.

"I have no right," she said, "none at all. The only thing that gives me the gall to speak to you is God's forgiveness. After Vic died, God led me through hell and back convincing me what a loathsome thing I had done—what a loathsome creature I was. The first bit of hell was seeing you so devastated at Vic's funeral."

"I wondered if you were there."

"At that point, I still thought I had a right to be. But when I saw you, I started to question."

"I'm glad I didn't see you."

"So am I. I was never sure if you had or not. Anyway, that was only the start. I fell much, much farther after that. While I'd been here in Houston, believing I could put a presentable face on my adultery, I'd become a persona non grata to my family back in Lafayette. I tried to return there at fifty-eight and take up where I'd left off, running a rare bookstore that specialized in southern fiction. But my Lafayette siblings and cousins, aunts and uncles, nieces and nephews, could not accept the level of 'eccentricity' that I'd embraced by running off to be with a married man. I left there, indignant at their judging, with no place to go.

"Of course, all this time I was also grieving Vic's death. Not only was I missing him, not only did I have no one to go to, but I had no one even to care that I was grieving. People don't reach out to console the mistress. She gets no title by which she's revered and pitied. Josephine, there were times when I despised you because you got to be Vic's widow."

That presented an ironic picture. While I was rushing blindly to shackle myself with Lenny, Genevieve was envying me. Perhaps it was this reminder of my own stupid choices that helped me to see her point and even feel a little compassion for it. The worst pain that God makes us endure is surely the pain that he watches us chase down and dive headlong into.

"Finally I grasped what the whole world knew already: that I deserved no comfort. I was grieving the loss of what had never been mine to start out with. I'd always been alone in reality; that's what I chose. And I'd also chosen to make several other people's lives lonelier—yours at the top of the list, Josephine."

I couldn't let her take it all, not when she was so remorseful, not when we both knew the truth. "On that score you had plenty of help," I said. "I helped, Vic helped, a murderer who's now down in Huntsville prison helped quite a bit, and even my mother did her part."

Genevieve nodded gratefully. "Well, by the time I was sixty years old, I was struggling for a reason to keep living. I was seriously toying with taking my life."

"What kept you from it?"

"There are two things that I could never trust were true: that there is no God, and that our souls die with our bodies. If I turned out to be wrong about those two things—which I strongly suspected—I couldn't imagine how much I might regret hurling myself into eternity with a God who I'd utterly disregarded. It wasn't a chance I could make myself take."

By now I was captivated by Jenny's story. These were my issues. I'd been glued to my bed trying to resolve them. Perhaps it's why I'd come. "What happened?" I asked her. "How did you dig out of your hole?"

"First I tried what most everyone has tried from the beginning of time: to live a better life so that God wouldn't turn his back on me when the time came. I set out to be kinder, humbler, self-controlled—all that sort of thing."

Since I am sure that I don't have time to attempt such an overhaul of myself, I was grateful that this didn't appear to be the ending of her story. "And?" I said.

"And I couldn't do it. I swear, Josephine, no matter how much I resolved not to let myself be the focal point of my every decision, action, reaction, and thought, I couldn't accomplish it for more than five minutes running. I even despaired that perhaps God had made me just to be a deserving recipient of his wrath, like Judas or something."

"My goodness, Jenny. That's not what you decided, is it?"

"Well, I was on the verge of that, I assure you. But I had a last hope. One day it occurred to me—very belatedly I thought—that if I could somehow get to know this God better, I might figure out another way to appease him, though I couldn't imagine what it might be. Thus far, I reasoned, I'd been like a new employee trying to satisfy a boss I'd never even met."

"Did you do it? How'd you find him?"

"Well, I searched high and low before I stumbled over him in the most obvious place possible. Initially, though, I was determined to throw a wide net, and let me tell you it dragged in all manner of refuse. But I picked through it, bit by bit. What incredible tripe is most religion! I'd say that about 95 percent of what the world holds as sacred is nothing more than man worshipping himself when you get right down to it. I found only one thing that was big enough, pure enough, perfect enough, and beautiful enough for me to believe it is truly God."

"What is it?" I asked, a little breathy.

"Jesus Christ, the Son of God," Genevieve answered, saying the words like they were priceless artworks. Adele used to say them much the same way, except her manner was a little earthier. In her mouth they sounded more like a pan of hot fudge. I wondered what they really saw when they said that name.

"Why, Jenny?" I asked. "Why is he the only thing you could believe is truly God?"

"Because everything that I can conceive of as God is reflected in him. Is God truly holy, as the Bible claims? Yes. So holy that he'll not tolerate our sins—our destructive, gluttonous extramarital affairs, our faithless, drunken despair, our failure to even wonder much about him for our sixty or seventy or eighty-four years. He's so holy that an unfathomable atonement had to be made for those sins—a human life that was perfectly lived because it was lived by God's very Son.

"So you see, Josephine, he hasn't left our fate up to us and to our futile attempts to be good! What's more loving than that? He's both of these things—holy and loving—not one or the other as most religions teach. Everything I see in Christ is what a real God must surely be. He's the wonderful light we have."

I thought I caught a glimmer of her meaning. "You found more than you went looking for, didn't you?" I said.

"I went looking for some useful knowledge to appease an angry boss. But in Christ I found knowledge of a father—a holy, loving God who I can enjoy forever. He's given me so much more than just a pass on hell."

"Are you saying we can't find God without Christ?" I asked her.

"Christ is what we know about God. He is God. How can one reject him but find God? Don't you see that that's nonsensical? It would be somewhat like declaring William Shakespeare the greatest writer who ever lived, but dismissing his entire oeuvre of plays as worthless fakes."

"Jenny, what if Jesus isn't God?" There, I'd asked the question.

"If he isn't God, then I've based my last twenty years on a blissful lie, as have innumerable others throughout the past two millennia. Josephine, I could tell you about all those who've so fiercely believed Jesus' deity that they refused to deny it even under torture. I could show you all the places that the Bible declares Jesus to be God. I could even tell you that I've never been so sure about anything all my life, including loving Vic. But the most useful encouragement I can give you is this: when you believe, God will give you assurance that it's true. It's an incredible, mysterious gift that he gives those who obey him in this."

"What if I can't?" I asked.

"The fact is, you have no other choice. Where else can you find the deliverance from yourself that you're so desperate for? How else do you hope to be reconciled to your maker, whom you may be about to meet at any moment? Ask him to help you."

I nodded and determined to revisit this issue in the days ahead. "Thank you for being forthright with me about everything, Jenny," I said. "I can see why Katy thinks you're so special. She's really what I need to talk to you about, if you can give me another minute or two."

Jenny relaxed against the back of her chair, probably as exhausted as I was, and nodded her assent.

"I want to ask you whether you're willing to watch out for her, to keep caring for her. I know that sounds a little strange—"

"What are you saying, Josephine?"

"I'm saying that I'm dying—sooner, I think, rather than later. I don't need to burden you with why I believe that. Just trust me that it's true."

"Fair enough," Jenny said.

"I'm afraid Katy will have a very hard time with it, that she already is, actually. This is no tribute to my great mothering, I assure you. In fact, lately I've come to accept that I wasn't a very good mother in many ways. And largely because of my shortcomings in that area, I think that Katy views my looming death as some final betrayal of her."

"Yes, I see that," Jenny said. I have no doubt that she'd merely intended by that to spare me some explaining, but here

again I cringed at her intimacy with my most shameful inadequacies. It meant that I'm right about how Katy feels, that she's
so hurt by my failings that she's told Jenny all about them.
Apparently sensing my mortification, Jenny rushed to add,
"Katy's another who loves you very much, Josephine—another
of your gifts."

"Hmm. Perhaps she does love me, but right now she hates
me more. And I'm not sure that she'll be able to forgive me anytime soon. I've tried talking to her, but it didn't go well."

"So, how can I help?"

"She's drawn to you. It seems I'm destined to share my loves
with you, Jenny Bingham, though I'm not sure that I'll mind as
much after today. At any rate, I guess I'd like to hold you
accountable this time."

"Accountable?"

"Yes. That is, I'd like some sort of pledge from you that
you'll . . . you'll take up where I've left off. I want you to promise to be a faithful friend to her, and to try to do better by her
than I did."

"Josephine, are you just saying this out of guilt? You know,
we all make mistakes. And at some point everyone must take
responsibility for herself—even Katy. You're not to blame for
her life."

"I see that, to a point. But I still feel tremendous angst
about leaving her this way, at this particular time." I stood then
and started pacing Jenny's little drawing room, wondering if this
too was a mistake.

Jenny cleared her throat while I waited for a response.
"Well," she said, "I've never been a mother myself, of course,
but what time do you think would be better for Katy? What if

your leaving her at just this time and in just this way is the very stimulus she needs to change the lousy things about her life? When does transformation ever come easily? It didn't for me, and it doesn't seem to be for you either."

How much this woman had given me to think about!

"Josephine," she continued. "I won't promise to become Katy's new mother. That will always be your place in her life. But I do care about her very much, and I'll do all I can to help her see things clearly."

Jenny stood then and took both my hands in hers. I sensed that they were strong, safe hands, neither too gentle, nor too rough. It would be OK.

"I guess I can live with that," I said, "so to speak." And we giggled together like a couple of schoolgirls.

Chapter 23

Katy

After talking with Eliot, I knew I needed to go check on Mother. So, a few days later, I ventured over to her house loaded with two big bags of groceries and a stunning bouquet of tulips and roses. I'd rung the back bell several times and was just about to insert my own key, when I heard movement inside and then the door cracked open.

The sliver of Mother that I could see in the opening did not cheer me. She looked all too at home in the ochre brown robe I'd given her for Christmas a few years back. It now wrapped nearly double round her dwindling frame, and out of the bottom stuck two thick pillars that only vaguely resembled Mother's ankles. I'd come, it seemed, in the nick of time.

"Katy?" she said, as if she didn't recognize me.

"Of course it's me, Mother. Who do you think it is?"

"Well, I just wasn't expecting you."

"That is to say that you were expecting me to be a stranger, and yet you just opened the door right up to me?" So much for bearing gifts to smooth things over. Nothing she did could please me.

"Did you just come over here to chastise me some more?" she asked in a small, rather timorous voice that would have been strong and deflective a year before.

"I came to see how you are and to bring you some groceries," I said. "Can I come in before I drop all this?"

"Umm, I suppose so." But she hesitated to move out of my way, and I soon discovered why. The house was a wreck, and Mother didn't look any too healthy.

I pushed aside the mess on the kitchen counter with my bags, and I turned to face her. "Mother, have you been taking your medications? Have you been getting dressed? Have you eaten anything at all in the past three weeks?"

"I know this place is a bit cluttered, Katy, but I've been tied up with more important things than cleaning house," she said, showing off her penchant for nonresponsive answers.

"What are you talking about?" I demanded, as I plopped a pound of fresh salmon into her barren refrigerator. "Why isn't cleaning the kitchen and feeding yourself important anymore?"

"I've been remembering, Katy. All the things we talked about last week—I've been thinking about them and trying to understand why."

I finished unloading the second bag of groceries and started on the dishes. "That's fine, but can't you do it dressed?"

"There's no reason to get dressed," she declared. "There's nowhere else here that I want to go."

"What does that mean—'here'? As opposed to where, Mother? You aren't making sense."

She snatched a dirty saucepan out of my hand. "Stop cleaning, for goodness sakes! I'm trying to tell you, I've been figuring things out about the past. Important things."

"OK," I cried, "but how do you expect to enjoy the benefits of all these discoveries if you let yourself deteriorate physically? It's inexcusable. Have you been taking your pills or going to your doctor appointments?"

She herded me out of the kitchen then, pushed me down into a chair at her breakfast table, and took a chair opposite me. "Look," she said. "You don't need to feel guilty about anything you've seen here today, or anything I'm either doing or not doing. I'm making all my choices consciously, and I understand them. You are not responsible for me. OK?"

"And just who is?"

"I am. And you're responsible for you. Perhaps that should keep you busier."

I didn't know if I felt guilty or not, but I knew I was angry. "So, is this your fair warning that you're now going to starve yourself to death, or let your ankles swell till they pop, or just hang out here wasting away until you can't move fast enough to save yourself from peril?"

"There is no peril, Katy. Now who's talking nonsense?" she exclaimed. "Besides, if you must know, I'm getting a housemate."

"What?"

"A housemate. Samantha is moving in here next week. So, you see, you don't have to worry about me anymore."

Mother had really lost it now. "How could Sam be moving in here? What's she going to do with her condo?" I demanded.

"She's selling it. Didn't you know? She got a full, asking-price offer the day she put it on the market. I think that was last Saturday."

This was awfully specific information for Mother to be mistaken about. "Are you saying she's actually selling her condo so she can move in here and keep you company?" I queried.

"No, she was just trying to get a good price while the market was still hot. She asked if I'd let her live here for the two or three months until, well, . . . " She left off there, suddenly reticent with her vast wealth of information.

"Until what, Mother?"

"Until she gets married."

I couldn't move for the longest time. It seemed that I was being excluded from every loop that I cared about being in—loops that I'd once have been central to if not fully in charge of. First Mother, now Samantha. As soon as I was able, I stood up. Mother watched warily as I walked back into the kitchen and pulled a vase off the top shelf of her pantry, opened the flower box that I'd set at the back of the counter as a surprise, and carelessly crammed the tulips and roses into the vase. I grabbed up my purse and smacked the vase down on the kitchen table in front of her.

"Happy Mother's Day," I said. Then, "I have to leave. I'm sure you and Samantha will both be in very good hands now. Good-bye."

❧

When had I become a person who couldn't be glad for my family's comforts and joys unless I myself had orchestrated them?

CHAPTER 24

Jo

May 13, 2001

Mother's Day. Whoop-de-do. By my calculation, this is my sixty-seventh Mother's Day, and I'm no better at playing the part than I was back in 1935. Perhaps motherhood is just another word for sorrow. I doubt that God lets any motherhood into heaven.

This morning Clay and Lillian took me to brunch at the Hopscotch Grill, where Lillian treated me just as carefully as she has since first warning me in March that there might be an Abbey in my future. Go figure. They chatted me up till I couldn't chat anymore, and we had a nice time. But as my "special day" wore on, nothing could distract me from the angry, accusing hush that settled over my phone after each of my grand- and great-grandkids called to log in.

I've really done it now.

May 15, 2001

Mama Cat was still crying at 9:00 A.M. this morning. When I heard her ratchet it up to a full-blown wail at around 9:15, I went out to see what else could possibly be the matter.

Her lair was a terrible mess, its contours destroyed by the insouciant play of its youngest occupants, the milk and water bowls I'd left the day before now upended, lying off to the side. The kittens—one a calico, mostly white, the other mostly black like his mother—were facing off in the scattered pine needles, baiting each other as five-week-olds are want to do, and they ignored entirely the hysterical discontent that their antics caused their grieving mother. When they finally pounced, Mama Cat stopped her carping just long enough to intercept the calico with a splayed paw, its claws brandished. The kitty thudded against the turned-up water bowl, and bright red streaks of blood quickly stained the white side of her face.

I moved without thinking. Stripping off my robe, I threw it over Mama Cat—still hissing—and had her bound and dragging along behind me a moment later. I was able to deposit her into Ginger's carrying box and slap the door shut before she even began to put up much fight. Then I changed my clothes and went and got the kittens for a trip to the vet. On the way there, I stopped and dumped Mama Cat into some weeds next to the bayou about a mile from the house.

A mother has no right to be the enemy. Just ask my daughter.

May 24, 2001

Samantha is now settled in one of my upstairs bedrooms. All her boxes are in another, and my Mercedes is parked on the driveway because her furniture has squeezed it out of the garage. But it's nice to have someone around again, and I really like her fella. The other day I asked what had changed her mind about him.

"Well," she said, "he kept asking me to marry him even before he knew about the baby. He said he's been looking for me ever since his wife died of breast cancer several years ago.

Then, when he found out I was pregnant—"

She teared up here and couldn't go on—not at all Samantha-like. But I well remember how the baby hormones took me hostage when I was pregnant with Clay and Katy. When they're acting up, you must simply let them have their way.

Sniffling, she continued. "When he found out I was pregnant, he was so pleased, Gammy. I'd never dreamt he'd want our baby that badly. But this wasn't even it, really."

"Yes?" I cajoled her.

"It's how he is with his son, Bruce. You wouldn't believe Bill's unflagging devotion to him. He gets so exhausted sometimes, but he never complains. He's always there at Bruce's side, hoping. I just can't let a man like that pass out of my life, Gammy, no matter how scared I am. Somehow, he brings the best out in me too."

I hugged her, overjoyed. That sounded like a fine basis for a marriage. Even Katy would probably agree, if she were speaking to us.

<hr/>

June 5, 2001

We've been told that a fledgling tropical storm whipped itself together in the Gulf overnight and will make landfall near Galveston within the next few hours. Since she's the first storm of this five-day-old hurricane season, they've named her Allison. The weathermen warn us that Allison is weak but tricky. The coastline has had no chance to brace for her.

I haven't written lately, but I've still been thinking. I've been thinking that Katy has finally written me off, and I fear that that's just what I'm due. Don't our sins deserve consequences, punishment? I know that isn't a popular notion these days, but we all recognize at some level that it's true—usually at exactly that level which expects justice when someone else wrongs us. It's then that we know that each of us is responsible for his own choices, despite whatever regressive ripple of excuses one offers in defense. And so our justice systems ask only, "Did he do it?" Not, "Was his crime understandable, given his advantages and disadvantages, the experiences and philosophies to which he was exposed, the quality of his parents' love?" No, we're responsible for our own choices.

I've long thought so when it came to Irene. She was surely responsible for marrying a man that she may not even have loved, and for bearing a child that she clearly didn't want. And she was responsible each and every time she chose not to begin loving me. But early on, I didn't know that Irene was the guilty one.

When I was just eight years old, the sickly little boy who lived next door to us came down with a case of polio that went undiagnosed until the disease had already affected his lungs. Because Jack's immune system had been so severely compromised in the flu epidemic of 1918, he was unable to put up any effective defense to the polio, and it finally became apparent to the grown-ups that he was actually going to die. Daddy wouldn't let me go over there, hoping to shield me for awhile longer from this particular type of evil. But tragedy can't be easily hushed, and word of Jack's terrifying doom soon reached me less directly. I couldn't sleep at night for fretting about it. I was afraid to eat, to drink our water, and most of all to breathe the air. What would stop that invisible child-killer from crossing our yards and seeping into me?

Since I knew that Daddy didn't want me to know about Jack, I decided to probe Irene regarding my concerns. I found her, as always at that time of the day, applying herself to Daddy's unfinished suits, giving them the hand-sewn slits that would enable their buttoning.

"I'm done practicing, Mama," I announced, and waited.

"A full ninety minutes?" she demanded, her diligent back still bent to its task.

"Uh-huh."

"Yes, ma'am' will do from you, young lady," she said.

"Well then?" Having crossed that shaky hurdle, I was permitted to proceed, and so I asked her the sidewise question that I'd prepared so carefully.

"Does polio get little girls, ma'am?"

Irene finally looked up, peered at me briefly, and then went back to her sewing. "Certainly," she said, pausing to pull a gray thread up from her lap, expertly knot it, and bite off the excess.

"What did you think?"

"I was just asking. Does it float around in the air, do you s'pose?"

With unflinching resignation, Irene said, "Very likely." It sounded to me as if this was her hope, her wish. "I hope polio floats right into my own little girl," her answer implied. Suddenly, the disease itself was a far-off worry.

Children see straighter lines between things than adults give them credit for. And sometimes those lines are really there, more or less, though no adult ever acknowledges them. "Was my playing very bad today, Mama?" I asked her.

Irene had started a new buttonhole and was losing patience.

"I don't know," she murmured. "I wasn't listening."

"I can try harder, Mama. I can do better."

"Well, go on then," she said. "You know how much work I have."

So I returned to the giant keyboard and practiced another "full ninety minutes." But I was crying and made many mistakes. I doubted such a sorry performance could make Mama not want me to die. And for months after that, I thought it only a matter of time before polio or some other fitting ailment struck me down and took me to the bad place where Jack had gone.

Daddy called it "heaven."

June 6, 2001

Did I make up her hatred for me, choosing to see something that wasn't there? Did I take responsibility for what was there but wasn't mine? Even so, does Irene have excuses that exonerate her? It's powerfully confusing to me now. But a few things I know were true, most especially regarding the piano.

Daddy and Irene bought the shiny, black Steinway immediately after they married in 1915. First they bought the house; then they bought the piano. Though neither of my parents was particularly musical, they put a small fortune into the fantastic instrument. I came along fifteen months later and was given four short years to reach the pedals before my lessons began. I didn't know how lucky I was to have such a privilege. That's what I was regularly told.

For the first fourteen years that we coexisted in that house, I never thought to ask anyone where the piano had come from—— why it was there at all as the torment of my life. From the way we'd both been treated, I simply assumed that it had as much standing as I had, and that it might just as reasonably ask why I was there ever making it sound bad—banging the wrong keys and pumping its delicate pedals like an organ-grinding monkey. But at fourteen I got curious, and I got angry, and I asked my father, "Why?"

"Your mother wanted it and paid for the whole thing with her own money," he told me.

"Where did she get the money?" I asked, aware that I was treading boldly in Mother's private, pre-Wilhelm waters that Daddy usually patrolled the parameters of with great care.

But he went this distance with me. "She'd inherited it a few years before. Had never spent a penny till we married, and then insisted that we use the whole $5,000 on the best piano we could buy."

"I don't understand," I said. "She doesn't even play."

"Yes, but she once knew someone who did. I think she considers it sort of a memorial to them."

"Then why didn't she just take lessons herself?"

"You don't need to know that, Josephine. Simply appreciate that it's something she's given you."

"Like a punishment," I murmured.

"Like a heritage," he said. "It's a heritage from your mother to you."

That it is.

The next year I took up smoking on the sly. It made me feel like the tragic leading ladies of my favorite Hollywood films—Joan Crawford, Greta Garbo, Marlene Dietrich. I'm sure I didn't mind that it might also aggravate Irene. After all, cigarette smoke wasn't the sort of smell she tolerated in her *presence, and I was pleased to smuggle it in on my clothes without thereby committing any overt house crimes.*

June 7, 2001

Tropical storm Allison drifted off yesterday, permitting us just enough sunshine to behold the destruction that up to eleven inches of rain can cause in twenty-four hours. And today she's back over, bullishly inflicting more of the same. But this is the sort of risk that Houstonians are accustomed to, much as Californians risk earthquakes and Israelis, car bombings. My rain gauge has registered four inches since midnight.

Katy was fifteen when she came to me confused and a bit distraught because it had occurred to her that she didn't know why she was here. That is, "What is life for?" I reared up defensively at the question—perhaps the only really important question that Katy had ever asked me, or would ask me again. "What are you talking about?" I demanded, hoping to deflect her.

"I mean, what is it we're supposed to accomplish? What's important, and why?"

"Can you not see anything that's important to do, Katy?"

"I'm not sure."

"Well, how about having children, for starters? Being productive in a profession; contributing something to society instead of just being a freeloader; helping people?"

"Yes, but why do all those things?" she persisted. "What's the goal? What are we doing them for?"

Since I had no real answer, I chose to be obtuse. "What else would you have us do, Katy? Just whatever we want, without any concern for anyone else, for what's right? Or, maybe we should all just lay down and die."

"I'm not saying that we shouldn't do the things you said. I'm just saying it would help me to do them—to know what's really important to do—if I knew why."

"You do them because you can, because you've been given a life and this is the right way to live it."

"Says who?"

"Says society. Basically, we've all agreed on it. There. There's a reason."

She shook her head emphatically. "There has to be more, Mother. I know there's more than that. I sense it. Don't you?"

Not much; not anymore. But I remembered that I, too, had once felt a terrible longing for something I couldn't name or describe. That longing had attended me throughout my lonely childhood, throughout all the years of somber obedience that had made not one dent in my mother's mantle. I'd eventually pushed the longing away, leaving it under the bleachers, and I'd thereafter fought hard to keep it at bay. I could not even recall what it had once whispered to me about.

"There is nothing more, Katy," I lied. "You just have to learn to be content with what is."

Am I guilty for thus failing my daughter? Did I not choose to nurse my own disappointments rather than tell her the truth? Have I any excuse that absolves me from cursing her in her turn?

<u>June 8, 2001</u>

Six more inches of rain fell at my house yesterday. It's raining again this morning, and we're told that "thunderstorms will intensify throughout the evening." One wonders what that could mean, given our present saturation and nonstop precipitation. On television they've shown some frightening footage of my usually mild-mannered old neighbor, Brays Bayou, now bloated and threatening in a manner I've rarely seen before. It was along her banks that I dropped off Mama Cat three weeks ago.

Maybe it's all this rain, but I just did something that I haven't done in a very long time. I sat down at the Steinway and tried to recall a piece of music. My old fingers are so slanted now that I could barely keep any one of them from sounding two notes when I aimed at a single key. Still, Mozart might have recognized his Rondo Alla Turca.

When I reached the last measure, I banged the notes, angry that I should feel so guilty for shunning my compatriot these forty-some-odd years. For decades now, I've touched her keys only to dust them. But what do I owe her? Why did she ever have anything to do with me?

Irene left one small box of what the nursing home called her "effects" behind her when she died. I threw away the few bleak old dresses that she'd worn till she was confined to her bed. Her wedding ring I had melted down to use the gold in a pair of earrings. And the last item—a small packet of letters, all postmarked before 1915—is in a box of other family documents stowed at the back of my closet. I have never read them.

But it occurs to me now that they might offer some clues. Perhaps they'd tell me who Irene meant to "memorialize" with her misspent fortune, her vindictive parenting, and her conscription of the two of us—the Steinway and me—to battle each other these many decades in accordance with her secret little war.

Then again, why should I look? Irene's crimes can't be dismissed. There are no tolerable defenses for them. Whatever evil inspired her, she chose to perpetuate. And so, long ago I tried and sentenced her to seven stinking years in a nursing home though she begged me at the time to take her in. She begged me at the time to take her in. But I would have my justice, as it appears Katy is intent on having hers. Who curses whom? Where does it end? And how does God bear with any of us, I'd like to know?

Later, June 8

It's almost midnight, and I'm afraid the weathermen got it right for once. Thunderstorms have indeed "intensified throughout the evening"—so much so that I'm a little worried about Samantha and William out on their date. But the two of them together can surely manage to avoid the dangerous low spots.

In the meantime, I sit here with Irene's letters in my lap. There are six yellowed envelopes—four addressed to her, one addressed to Daddy, and one to someone named Calvin Stockton, care of Southside Hospital. Three of those to Irene are postmarked before 1904 and were written by the same hand. The envelope addressed to Daddy, and the final one to her, are both postmarked 1914. They bear each other's handwriting. Irene also addressed the envelope to Stockton, postmarked 1911.

So, who was this Calvin Stockton? And what might she have written to him that she thought worth keeping for fifty-five years? I notice that his envelope bulges slightly in its lower left-

346

hand corner. Without disturbing the letter itself, I open the flap and reach in to investigate the bulge. But I worry that I'll unwittingly extract a petrified bug, so I pull my hand back. Then I turn the envelope upside down and shake a thin gold wedding band into my lap. In my less arthritic days, I believe it would have fit my ring finger.

Again, I worry that these letters might somehow exonerate Irene. But I can't allow for that possibility, despite what they may say. A mother never has a right to be the enemy. Besides, I've already convicted her and carried out her sentence. She begged me at the time to take her in, and I can't forgive her now. If I do, then that too will fall upon my shoulders—more guilt than I think I can even bear for a moment.

Perhaps my old foe will help buoy my outrage, help me safe-guard the stout, unimpeachable grievances in which I've so long gloried. I sit again at her keys and play. I play Bach and Beethoven, Schubert and Schumann, Haydn and Handel and Chopin. I play horribly. I play beautifully. And every note I play condemns me. Was it so awful that she made me play?

What is in the letters?

If I can't forgive Irene, how can I hope that Katy will ever forgive me? If I do forgive Irene, how will I forgive myself for all that I did in the name of my grievance? How can God for-give either one of these?

If there were only some way it all could be forgotten. But what did Jenny say? Sins can't go unpunished; God's holiness won't stand for that. If the letters exonerate Irene, what defense will I offer if I soon stand before God to answer for my life? On the other hand, what defense do I have right now? I can't expect leniency for: "I drank because my mother hated me. I hid from my husband and daughter because she hated me. I hoarded my son because she hated me. And when she begged me at the time to take her in, I showed her no mercy." I'm damned either way.

Water seeps under my front door for the first time I can remember. The street out front is gone, as are the bottom thirds of all the cars parked along it. Brays Bayou has more than broken her banks. Perhaps God finally comes for his vengeance. And then? I fear that hell is neither fiery nor full. It is dark and cold and me alone. Forever.

God, help me. Please, please help me.

Isn't this just what Jenny and Adele said that Jesus did for me—what I can't do for myself? I think I've always bristled at Jesus because I didn't want to give up on myself; I wanted eternity to be mine to accomplish, or not, but always up to me. Now its being up to me is my greatest fear. Still, I wonder if Jesus' sacrifice—"atonement" they called it—covered even my mean little grievance against Irene. Did it cover Irene's grudge against whomever she really hated? Katy's fury at me, and all I did to earn it? Did he take the punishment for all that crud, all the ways and reasons that we curse the people we're given the chance to love?

Ten more inches, and the water in my living room will reach the curvy, sleek torso of the Steinway. I have this compulsion to try and save her, but of course she outweighs me by many hundreds of pounds. The best I can do is stay by her side.

If Jesus is God, then I think he could have done all that. If he is infinite God, how could his act have accomplished less? The question is, was Jesus God? If he wasn't, then I can't see that any of God's creatures have a way out of hell. But then, how could that be? What about the longing?

I sit atop the Steinway now, my feet dangling over her side just above the murky waters that have engulfed her sturdy black legs. With my flashlight I can see fire ants from my infested front yard floating along the surface; their frantic bites are what drove me to the higher ground. I would be busy fearing for my life, but these last few months have taught me that that's not in my hands. The questions are what consume me now.

I open the envelope that the wedding band fell out of, and remove its letter, dated February 17, 1911. The letter reads:

Cal, my darling,

I write this to you because it would be far too sad for me to tell you these things when I am with you. I doubt I could get through it. I'm not sure that I can even here.

Knowing you has been the joy of my life. I never expected to find such a thing—joy. And so you know how long it took me to trust that you were real, that you truly wanted to be my husband, that you weren't going away. Our son was like a seal on our love; once he came along, nothing could break it. I let myself believe that.

And I allowed you to make us a family. I let you sweep Jamie and me up in your winsome melodies and even your ominous, low-noted harmonies that I now see foreshadowed things to come. It was a fantastic ride, and we went on it with you because you were our life. You were our life.

When Jamie left us, I sensed that all was lost. Still, it felt like you took my life when you tried to take your own. I wasn't quite ready. I hope you can forgive me for getting in

your way. I know it was only a postponement; your existence here has always been precarious. How twisted God
must be to combine glory and desperate melancholy
together in the same psyche. I'm so sorry that this has been
your lot.

I wish I were brave enough to follow you, darling, but I
can't promise that. Just know that I'm not sorry. I don't
regret the love. I don't regret our son. And I do not even
regret the music, though I never expect to hear it again.

Ever yours,

Irene

*God, you even wooed her! If she refused to be wooed in the
end, can I blame that on you? I want to believe you. I want to
hear the music, to see your Son.*

Do you come for me in these floodwaters?

Chapter 25

Katy

That evening—the evening of the 2001 Houston flood—I'd been watching the news coverage pretty closely. Eliot and I lived miles from any bayous, but I knew that Mother and Samantha were within the one-hundred-year floodplain of the Brays. So I was relieved when Channel 12's Norm O'Donahue announced on the ten o'clock news that the worst of the thunderstorms seemed to be moving out of the area. The flooding that had occurred had generally all been in the southeast portion of the city, well away from anyone I knew. I went to bed before the sports, believing all was well.

When the phone rang at about 1:15 A.M., I was deep into some tense melodrama that suddenly involved a phone booth standing in the center of a crowded train station. Someone was calling it, but I was the only one who seemed to hear. And I was afraid to answer, certain that the caller was a Mafioso or another dangerous character who was out to ensnare me in some felonious scheme. It took awhile before I realized that a real phone was ringing on my nightstand.

"Ye-us?" I grogged thickly.

"Mom, it's Sam. Are you asleep?"

"Ye-us," I confessed, sensing even then that this was the wrong answer.

"You haven't been watching the news?" she demanded.

"Uh, I watched at ten. Why?"

"Well, it's after one now. I've been out with Bill, and we had to abandon our car several blocks from Gammy's house on the way home. Brays has flooded, and Gammy's street is almost certainly under water. But she isn't answering her phone. Maybe the phone lines are out, or just jammed with callers. I don't know, but I'm really worried."

This was a lot for me to take in. I tried to imagine all the possibilities, but I kept getting distracted by my own irregular breathing and the hot fist that repeatedly squeezed my lungs and sent convulsive little panic spasms up into my throat. "There are no perils," I remembered Mother assuring me. Yet she might be drowning in one right now. I wasn't ready.

"Mom, are you still there? Are you OK?"

"Have you called 911?" I croaked finally.

"Tried, but it's busy. The situation is bad all over town."

"OK, keep trying. I'm getting dressed and going over there. You call my cell phone if you hear anything, and I'll call yours. Oh, and let Clay know what's going on."

"OK, but I don't think you'll get any further than we did. We had to drive into someone's yard to escape the water in the street that had risen up over our car doors. And it's only getting worse."

"I have no choice, Sam. I'll call you."

☙

When I'd dressed, I found Eliot waiting in the den with two ponchos and a pair of fishing waders. "I heard," he said. "You're not going alone."

"Eliot, we have to get to her."

"We'll do all we can."

Outside, the rain pounded in a manner that made the downpours of the past few days seem like child's play. The roads that we could actually see, we took as safe enough to brave in our Explorer, but high waters repeatedly barred the way and we'd have to turn back. After forty-five minutes, we hadn't accomplished what would usually have taken us only ten. Neither had Eliot yet gotten through to 911. "All we can," it seemed, would be very little.

We had to accept defeat about two miles from Mother's house. This was the closest we'd gotten from any direction, and wading in on foot from this distance would have taken us hours if we'd survived it at all. That's when I remembered that the fire station servicing Mother's neighborhood was just a block west of us. If we couldn't get through by phone, just let 'em try and turn us away in person.

That road was clear, and we soon pulled up to a full-fledged disaster scene. Everywhere, flashing lights and sirens. One fire truck was swinging out of the driveway just as another was sidling up to the curb to drop off a cabful of civilians in soaked pajamas and bathrobes. Several white SUVs with governmental emblems on them were also coming and going, many toting thoroughly wet but otherwise well people in all stages of dress and undress. The yard in front of the station house was crowded with such deposits. Perhaps Mother was among them.

Forgetting my poncho, I sprang from the Explorer and began stalking the evacuees. I hollered for "Josephine," but her name just collided with the chaos and was muted out. So I searched for an ochre robe, a child-sized adult, a woman standing alone. Just as I was about to give up, a fireman came into the yard carrying a megaphone.

"May I have your attention please? Red Cross has opened an emergency shelter at the junior high school on the corner of Hamlet and Marlowe. We need you all to go there so that we can do our work without endangering you. At the shelter they'll have blankets, coffee, cots, and maybe even some dry clothes. It's a two-block walk from here—presently clear of floodwater. Or you can wait for a ride."

Amidst the buzz that this created, I made a dash for the announcer and managed to catch him by the rim of his horn. "Excuse me," I bellowed through the rain. "I need a rescue."

All business, he turned to me and said, "Address?"

"5520 Lear Drive. It's an eighty-four-year-old woman who's alone and ill."

"Relationship?"

"My mother."

"Lear's under about three feet of water, lady. What's her status?"

"I'm not sure what you mean, but I haven't been able to talk to her. Her phone is out."

"Great," he said, indulging in one incredulous sigh. "OK, we'll get to it as soon as one of our motorboats is available. That'll be the only way we can pick her up till the waters fall back."

"Yes, please do it now," I said. "But I want to come along."

"Nope. Regulations don't allow it."

He started back inside then, but I stopped him again. The hot fist was squeezing me inside out. "Please, officer," I said. "Her name is Josephine. We haven't spoken in a month. I've been too angry with her." That's all I could say.

Towering over me, with water running off the lip of his fire hat like a gutter drain, he nodded slowly and then patted my forearm. "Got it," he said. "Now, you go to the shelter. That's where we'll bring her. Oh, and take some of these other folks with you."

We arrived at the school at 2:45 A.M., our car loaded with a dripping family of five. On the way over, they described the horrors of their last few hours in far more detail than I wanted to hear given that Mother, we hoped, was still living it. The children were especially wired, and told us all about the bugs that had bitten them on the way out to the fire truck and inky black water that had gotten as high as the mattresses that they were crouched on trying to stay dry.

"It might be all the way to the ceiling by now," one little boy of about nine assured me, "'cause it was going up really fast!"

I tried to imagine how Mother might escape fast rising waters once they'd topped her mattress. Would she get up on a countertop or dresser? Could she make it to her stairs from wherever she was waiting? Surely she wouldn't try to leave her house; she'd never make it. Then again, I wasn't sure she'd do anything at all to help herself. Would she even think to unplug things? We might be as likely to find her electrocuted as drowned. At best, she'd be cowering on the kitchen counter in the dark, with no phone and no clue how high the water would rise. Squeeze, squeeze, squeeze.

Preoccupied with such thoughts, the fleeting hour from three to four was almost my undoing. I willed for time to stand still, but it galloped along, bringing a steady parade of soggy newcomers that never included Mother. Every minute that passed without her materializing, in my mind, made it more likely that Mother's status would turn out to be "missing" or "injured" or even "deceased." And I needed desperately to talk to her first.

At about 3:50, I heard a woman call out "Katy!" Wheeling around, I braced for my first sight of her. But it was Lillian who ran up to me, Clay right behind her. They'd ended up at the same fire station, and had been similarly ordered over here to await word. At least the rain had let up, according to Clay. Moreover, their fireman had told them that the floodwaters might finally have peaked—the first encouraging report I'd heard since the ten o'clock news. Eliot procured us some coffee, and the four of us huddled in a corner seeking comfort in others' misery.

"The far southeast and northwest sides of town are supposedly hardest hit," Clay offered. Our present location, due south of downtown, fell conveniently outside of those descriptors. But it was no use. I couldn't imagine anything worse than what I'd seen right here.

"You know, the flooding they had in Pearland yesterday receded just about as fast as it rose up," Eliot noted. "Plenty of people rode it out in their homes." That was a helpful comment. I felt a little better.

But that glimmer of optimism had thoroughly faded twenty minutes later, and we sat silent and solemn listening to the Red Cross weather radio with the rest of the grieving, bedraggled crowd. By then, new arrivals had tapered off noticeably.

Then I saw my megaphone man slip through the gymnasium door—all alone. He looked around, I feared for me. When I stood, the others stood with me, and the fireman noticed us. He headed our way, squishing as he clomped across the wood floor in his regulation waders. I'd never seen anyone look so wet and exhausted.

"Did you find her?" I blurted when he was still twenty feet off.

"Yep," he said. "A doctor's lookin' her over in a classroom down the hall. She was kinda' bunged up, but seems to be OK overall. You can go on down there—room twelve. Can't miss it with a big red cross on the door."

She was only "bunged up"! What a sweet, sweet proclamation. I bear-hugged Mother's scruffy guardian angel and then turned to my family. "Will y'all give me a few minutes alone with her first?"

"OK, Katy," Clay said. "But be nice."

I'd deserved that, so I nodded and went off to find room twelve. Looking in through the window, I saw Mother sitting on one of several makeshift beds that probably served as school-day worktables. They'd wrapped her in a blanket, and she was sipping coffee. With the other hand, she clutched some sort of book, and her feet rested on an animal carrier. A youngish man was stitching up an apparent cut on the back of Mother's head. When he finished, I went in.

She straightened up a bit when she saw me—put down her coffee and took a few swipes at her hair. But dirty water and week-old hair spray are no submissive mixture, and all her thin red curls drooped just as rigidly as they had before.

"Mother, don't." I said. "Please don't worry about your hair."

"I'm not as bad as I look, Katy. I'm fine, really. I just crawled up on the piano till they came for me."

"Were you afraid?"

"Oddly, no. I think I'm finally ready for it."

"It?"

"Death. I know that makes you furious, Katy, but I can't help it. You'll just have to be mad at me."

"Mother, I'm not mad at you."

"I didn't set out to have anything like this happen. I didn't go looking for it."

"I'm not mad at you."

"Then what is it? What is it you want to say?"

The moment had come; finally I could say what I'd been so scared I'd never get another chance to. Instead, I broke down. The dread and anxiety of the past few hours leaked out of me like a ripped air mattress. I couldn't speak for crying. The doctor even came over to see if I might need medical attention. Mother finally folded me up in the blanket with her and simply let me sob on her breast while she rocked me gently. "It's all right, Katy," she whispered. "It's all right."

When I could, I pulled away just a bit and looked at her. "I was afraid you'd die," I sputtered, "without . . . knowing . . . that I love you."

"You're my little girl."

I'll not soon forget how that statement rallied her. First I saw the "aha." Then an unguarded joy kindled and spread across her weary old face. She hugged me hard. "I love you too, sweetheart," she said.

Water and fire ants had filled the chassis of Mother's Steinway, rendering its strings about as musical as fishing line. The keys had warped and the finish was mostly gone. Repairing her would have amounted to a "reconstruction," so we let the insurance company total her and accepted $37,000 in her stead. Not a bad investment, all things considered.

So too went Mother's house, which was eventually demolished and the property sold to a tenacious homebuilder who had plans for a thick foundation and a palatial new entrance involving lots of stairs.

Eliot and I took Mother home with us on that Saturday morning, June 10, and she lived relatively peaceably with us until the doctors acknowledged that the cancer had returned and taken charge of her whole body. This was not news to her; nor was it to me. Not really.

After Mother died, as I said, I found this journal of hers, and it's still revealing her to me. I've even shown parts of it to Jenny, just to get her take. She seems to understand things about Mother's journey that I haven't yet been able to grasp.

Susan Oliver

I only wish that Mother had lived to see the birth of her newest great-granddaughter—Joanne Irene Canmore. At the hospital, while the families came and went in the waiting room, I met her half brother, Bruce. That incredibly scarred young man will have a great deal to teach his sister about fortitude and overcoming. Little Joanne, on the other hand, was born "perfect in every way, without a blemish on her." So her hopeful daddy assured us when he came out to the waiting room to announce her birth.

Well, perhaps that's how she looked to him.

But I, for one, know better.

Acknowledgments

I'd like to thank Reg Grant, my professor at Dallas Theological Seminary, for encouraging my writing and for his guidance on this project in particular. I also appreciate the many friends who read early versions of the manuscript and provided a more objective perspective on its strengths and deficiencies: Selah Helms, Susan Strohschein, Julie Thompson, Karen Olson, Carol Weiser, Lynda Meyer, Kathy Csoltko, Mary Ragna Evans, and Maria Stewart. Finally, I thank my editor, Gary Terashita, who saw value in my work and whose interest helped to shape the final product.

I can't go without mentioning one last person—my grandmother, Maxine Culbertson Ozmun—who we lost to lung cancer in 1997. Her death inspired this work of fiction, and I dare to hope that certain aspects of it also reflect her life.